TREASURED MEMORIES

OF

Inspirational Stories

By Marie Schoendorf

Order this book online at www.trafford.com
or email orders@trafford.com

Most Trafford titles are also available at major online book retailers.

Printed in Victoria, BC, Canada.

ISBN: 978-1-4269-1844-5

Our mission is to efficiently provide the world's finest, most comprehensive book publishing service, enabling every author to experience success. To find out how to publish your book, your way, and have it available worldwide, visit us online at www.trafford.com

Trafford rev. 1/19/2010

Trafford PUBLISHING www.trafford.com

North America & international
toll-free: 1 888 232 4444 (USA & Canada)
phone: 250 383 6864 ♦ fax: 812 355 4082

Contents

DEDICATION

I would like to dedicate this book to anyone who reads it and enjoys the inspiration from Jesus, or maybe just a chuckle for the day or even just a bit of pondering on my part!

I send letters to old folks that may be otherwise forgotten, in Nursing Homes, the lonely ones in Prisons and others who are just shut in, or those who seem to have no one who cares. These are copies of the letters sent to my "Treasured Friends".

But, I want to give glory to God, because He called me into this ministry and He gives me the stories to share with you. Some are farm stories, some are things that friends have shared with me, but most are truly inspirations from God. I thank God that He gave me the opportunity to share the first book with you, "Precious Treasures", and now has provided this one, "Treasured Memories". May you find the touch of Jesus in each one of these stories. They were blessed when I wrote them, and I think they are blessed when they are read!

"I have not yet reached my goal, and I am not
perfect, but Christ has taken hold of me. So I
keep on running and struggling to take hold of
the prize. My friends, I don't feel that I have
already arrived. But I forget what is behind
and I struggle for what is ahead. I run toward
the goal... so that I can win the prize of
being called to Heaven. This is the prize
that God offers because of what
Christ Jesus has done! "

Philippians 3: 12- 14

In memory of my Mother and Father:
Floye E. Souderes 1912-2008
Earl O. Souderes 1914-1984

TICKET TO HEAVEN

Heaven sometimes seems to be a far away place....then at other times it seems so close. To travel anyplace else, you can go to a travel agency and they will set you up with a ticket, reservations, motels to stay in, road maps, and even try to accommodate you with how you want to travel; plane, boat, train, bus, car, etc.

Well, I have a travel agent who will take care of my trip to Heaven! His name is Jesus. He's already paid for the ticket...He died on Calvary for me. To redeem my ticket, I only have to give Him my heart.

Throughout time man has imagined how we will travel to Glory. They have said we'll just fly away, or we'll cross over Jordan. Then there's the King's Highway, Life's Railway to Heaven, Golden Stairs, Jacob's Ladder, that old Ship of Zion, or the Old Gospel Ship. Some say we will be escorted and serenaded by Angels, catch a Chariot of Fire or just leave with the Rapture.

Personally I don't care what mode of transportation God sees fit to use to transport me to Heaven, I just want to go! I gave Him my heart so I have my ticket in my hand. We won't need roadmaps because it will seem as we know the path by heart, even though we have never been there before. We have a reservation confirmed in our own mansion. We have a place at the banquet table for the Marriage Supper of the Lamb, and none of us will have to worry about dinner reservations because our name is in the Book of Life. He has our trip all planned out for us. We won't have to be apprehensive about knowing someone by name up in Heaven, because He said we would know them as they were known...even the Saints who have been there for thousands of years.

We'll talk to John about what he saw when the New Jerusalem came down. Moses will tell, with excitement, how magnificent it was when God opened up the Red Sea and the children of Israel walked through on dry land. Adam and Eve will tell us how sorry they were that they took this perfect world that God had created and was the first to sin, but how glad they were that Jesus forgave them. Peter, with a smile on his face and a twinkle in his eye, will tell of the thrill he had when he walked on water. Elijah will tell us how it felt to ride the chariot of fire straight up to Heaven. Mary will talk about Jesus, her son, and what He was like as a child, and Noah will tell us about the flood. Joshua will relate to us the sight of the wall of Jericho just falling down when they marched around it seven times. Jonah will explain to us how horrible it was to be in the belly of the whale for three days. Old Daniel will smile and recall the lion's den and maybe David will dance and play his harp for us. The list goes on and on.

But even if we don't see or know anyone else there, if we don't have a mansion, we will still be able to look on the face of our Jesus. We can touch the nail-scarred hands and hear Him say, "Welcome, my good and faithful servant."

Regardless of how glorious and easy it may seem, we don't deserve to go to Heaven. We are sinners and we deserve to go to Hell. By Jesus dying on the cross, He gave us oceans of mercy and rivers of grace to be forgiven of our sins and spend eternity in Heaven with Him. He died for our sins! Isn't all of this worth giving our heart to Jesus and living our life for Him? After all, He paid for our ticket. The rest is up to us. How bad do we want to join Him in Heaven.......?

Luke 13:24-25
Make every effort to enter through the narrow door, because many, I tell you, will try to enter and will not be able to. Once the owner of the house gets up and closes the door, you will stand outside knocking and pleading, "Sir, open the door for us." But he will answer, "I don't know you or where you come from."

****

HE HEARS OUR PRAYERS

Have you ever heard a child calling for "Momma?" When he is hurt, no one can comfort him but "Momma." Maybe the child has gotten lost from her sight in the grocery store and he calls out, "Momma! Momma!" Momma is just out of hearing range, and she doesn't hear him. The child then panics and starts to cry out, calling, "MOMMA! MOMMA!"

When we call out to Jesus, He is always close enough to hear us. He hears the prayers from the hospital beds, the lonely rooms of a nursing home, the prisoner on death row, the scared, the crippled, and the abused. He hears the silent cries from the minds and hearts of the ones who can't speak. Jesus hears the prayers from the eloquent speakers as well as the ones who stutters and stumbles through words. He doesn't care where we are when we pray, as long as we pray with our heart. He always listens, patiently and lovingly. We could be in a mansion or a hovel, a ship, a plane or a car, or just on our knees in the back yard... He listens! We may be on the top of the mountain or deep in the valley, but He is always there! Jesus never turns away from a prayer from the heart. If we ask in prayer, believing, He will always answer.

The answer may not come immediately, and when it does come it may not be exactly what we had prayed for, but He answers in His own way and in His own time. After all, He knows what is best for us. No sincere prayer ever goes up that doesn't come back down abundantly blessed. Sometimes we don't think He hears us and we think God is not going to answer us. Then, at a time when the answer is needed, we see the answer and know He is there.

God doesn't turn away from His children. He listens to each and every prayer. It doesn't matter to Him what color you are, how much money you have, or what you look like...but He wants you to talk to Him. "Ask and ye shall receive." Talk to Jesus today my friend! He is waiting.

Romans 4:7
Blessed are they
whose transgressions are forgiven, whose sins are covered.

****

GOD ON THE MOUNTAIN

Sometimes in our walk of life on the mountaintops, we forget how it feels to be in the valley. We arrogantly look down on those in the valley, like for some reason we are better than they are. But we are not! God made us all and He made us equal. Oh, but for the grace of God it could be us in that valley. There in the valley are the sick, the lonely, the confused, the heartbroken, the poor. But you know what? The same God that walks with you on the mountain top, walks with them in the valley.

It is not a shame or disgrace to be walking in the valley. God is there! This is a time of learning and adjusting to life itself. It is a time to learn to walk closer to God. One day God will give you the foothold to climb out of the valley, and you will start up the mountain. Most mountain climbers will tell you that coming up the mountainside is rough, but, oh the victory you feel when you reach the top.

It is not always something we do that plunges us into the valley. Sometimes it is circumstances of life itself and sometimes I think it is God's way of getting our attention. We are often too hardheaded to listen in any other way. But the healing and the learning occur in the valley.

No matter why we may find ourselves here, God is still walking there with us, just waiting for us to ask for His help. When He thinks we are strong enough to scale the mountain, He holds out His nail-scarred hand and leads us right up to the top. Jesus Himself will raise our hand in victory.

After a trip through the valley ourselves, we should have a better outlook on our life and the problems of others. We will feel more compassion for the broken and hurting, and we will sincerely pray for them. Soon, you will see Jesus reach out His hand and help them up the mountainside just like He helped you.

If we stayed on the mountain top all of the time, we would forget to humble ourselves, faith would be pushed aside; compassion would be snuffed out and we would forget how much we need Jesus! You see my friend, we see where we are, but Jesus sees where we need to be! May you never be too proud to ask Jesus for the help of His hand. God bless you.

Isaiah 41:13
For I am the Lord, your God,
who takes hold of your right hand
and says to you, Do not fear;
I will help you.

****

THE GOOD OLE DAYS

Let's jog a few memories. I don't know how many of you are as old as I am, but if you are, I am sure you can relate to this. If you are just a young whipper-snapper, then just enjoy it as a good old fireside story.

People often refer to their younger years as the "good ole days." Well, there are different ideas about the "good ole days." Lets go back and just look at them.

I imagine that most of the house heat back then was from a fireplace and a wood stove. That meant that a lot of wood had to be cut and kept on hand all year long. I have cut a bunch of wood in my time. I have spent the day in the woods when I was young, holding the end of a probably dull, cross-cut saw. There was not anything even close to a chain saw then. Now that it was cut, the wood had to be hauled home from the back of the pasture, arm-full by arm-full. We didn't have the option to just turn on a knob for the stove or adjust the thermostat for the heat.

Kindling for the fire was pine splinters that had to be chopped into small pieces, or pine knots. Pine knots were little remains of pine stumps that were left in the pasture when trees were pushed up or blasted up for clearing new ground. The best way to gather these was to get a grass sack, pull it around the pasture for an hour or two, throwing these knots into it. This took up the time that the kids spend at a video arcade, in front of a computer or watching TV. It also kept us out of trouble. When we got the chores done, well, we were just too tired to think up trouble.

Have you ever eaten a biscuit baked in a wood stove? WOW! Just the thought makes me drool! I can remember Momma mixing up the biscuits with her hands, rolling them out into little balls, flattening them out with a knuckle tap on the top. She would put them in a big iron skillet and bake them in that old wood stove. (No one had invented biscuits in a can yet.) M-m-m-m-m, I can almost smell them cooking! When they would get done we would open them up and put a glob of home-churned butter on them. Then we would sop them in some homemade syrup with real country cream on top of that.... There weren't many skinny kids back then.

I can remember Momma spending hours over the old wood stove preparing dinner. Most everything we ate came out of the garden and not convenient little cans or boxes. We got the meat for dinner out of the old smoke house out back. That smoke house was one of the best smells you could find. Now, if you have never smelled meat curing over a simmering hickory fire, you have really missed something.

In the "good ole days" there was the fun of building the fire in the fireplace about daylight on a cold winter morning. The embers from the fire last night had usually smoldered out by morning, so you would have to start a fire from scratch. Mornings would find you dreading to put one foot or hand out from under the pile of quilts you were sleeping under. You knew the house would be cold, and you had worked all night just to keep that spot in the bed warm! Your bed didn't come with warm blankets to sleep between, but sheets... often called sheets of ice. Well, finally, you push yourself out of bed and hit your bare feet on that cold floor...nope...no carpets either. This instantly starts a cold shiver from the tips of your toes to the top of your head. Your gown or pj's seemed very thin and cold. Not many of us owned housecoats, robes or slippers. You walk out on the porch, gulp in a breath of fresh air, pick up an armload of wood and a few splinters. Now, you are shivering uncontrollably. You kneel by the fireplace, slowly starting the fire. It seems to take forever. Air from the cracks in the floor and the broken window panes sweep up around you, and your thin gown or pajamas seem almost invisible to the cold, and it would make you shake so bad that you can hardly connect the match to the kindling.

Finally, there is a fire going. You stand close, backed up to it, warming your back side while you freeze on the front side. After you feel life in the back of your body from the heat, you turn to thaw the front. It seems to take forever to get the house warm. Now we can just set a thermostat and for months we never have to be concerned with the temperature. The beds are warm and the floors are most of the time carpeted. Bathrooms are indoors and not a quarter of a mile from the house, and the lights are electric, not lamps or candles.

When it was washday, a big iron pot was filled with water and a fire was set under it. You would put your clothes in it to boil them. It usually took all day to wash clothes. The dirtier work clothes were laid on a rock or something and you literally beat the dirt out of them. Buttons would break and buckles would bend. Then they were hung on a barbed wire fence. The clothes pins were the barbs on the fence. Wind would blow and wrap the clothes around the wire and when you brought them in, there was usually a three-corner plug torn in them marking the spot of each barb. Think of how easy it is to wash clothes now.

A few other fun things in the "good ole days" were dishes were always washed by hand after heating your water on the stove. Baths were taken in #3 washtubs on the back porch, cows were milked by hand, floors were mopped with corn shucks and the water had to be drawn from a well. Transportation was crude. You either walked, rode a horse or in a buggy. Nothing was weatherproof, and the toilet was a quarter of a mile from the house...two miles if it was cold or raining.!

We refer to these as the "good ole days" but they were hard. As for me they definitely were not the "good ole days." Not only was the work hard, but my soul was not right with God. Now, these are the "good ole days" because the work is much easier and my soul belongs to God.

Where would you be friend, if like the song goes, "If the rapture was yesterday would you still be here today?" I think the rapture is coming soon. Are you ready or will you be like the two standing in the field, one will be taken and one will

be left? Will you be the one left? Ask for forgiveness! Pray for salvation! I want to see all of my treasured friends in Heaven. That will truly be the "GOOD OLE DAYS!"

2 Peter 3:9
The Lord is not slow in keeping his promise, as some understand slowness. He is patient with you, not wanting anyone to perish, but everyone to come to repentance.

****

JESUS LOVES YOU

Sometimes we feel alone and we feel like we don't matter to anyone. Our self-esteem is low and we think no one cares. But, my friend, you matter to a King ... King Jesus. You've probably crossed His mind a thousand times, just today. He doesn't care what your circumstances may be ... He loves you!

Mankind has pulled you down with words of hurt and anger. People have forsaken you... the world may have made fun of you, but you are very important to Jesus. He would have died on the cross for you if you had been the only one. He will make you a child of the King and clothe you with a robe of white. He only wants your heart full of love for Him. It doesn't matter what the world thinks of you...He loves you.

I have been teased and made fun of all of my life. I have always had trouble coping with the world. When I was a child I was very poor. People sometimes can be very cruel. They seemed to think that God made them better. They judged friends only in terms of money or position in life. God judges us for who we are living for. I have always had a weight problem and the mirror I look into tells me that I am no beauty. Throughout my life, I have taken a lot of teasing and some even laughed at me. I stayed in my own little corner of the world having my private pity party.

Later in life I found Jesus. What a difference that made. He pulled my self-esteem up and I feel good about myself now. I am important to Jesus. There is a richness in my life now. I feel like no matter what Jesus tells me to do, I can do it because He will give me the knowledge and the strength to do His work. Jesus doesn't care if my face is wrinkled, or my hair is gray. He doesn't care if I am pretty or not, nor does he care that I am still overweight. He looks into my heart and he finds love there. He lives there. He made me to look like I do and He doesn't make mistakes. I am proud to be who I am, and to know my soul is saved.

I feel so very blessed that He has allowed me to do this letter ministry. I was telling a friend the other day that when Jesus gives me these letters to write, it is almost like He is reading me a bedtime story. I can sit back and close my eyes and He tells me what to say. I feel so special in the sight of Jesus. Just like an earthly father reads his child a bedtime story, my Father in Heaven reads to me. Then He permits me to share them with others.

We can look back in our past and find all of the good things we have done in our life and weigh them against all the bad things. Some people think if the good things out-weigh the bad, we will go to Heaven. But, my friend, it doesn't work that way. There is nothing we can do to EARN our way to Heaven. We are only

able to enter there by the Grace of God Himself. When we ask Him into our heart, He forgives all of the sin in our past, and He forgets all of it. He will never bring it up again. But if we don't turn from our evil ways, all of our sins will be held against us. If the beauty and love of Jesus is not in your heart, Heaven won't be your home. Fill your heart with Jesus my friend. You are always in His heart.

Philippines 4:11
I am not saying this because I am in need, for I have learned to be content whatever the circumstances.

****

HOSPITAL STAY

I find that even in a hospital room, God gives us blessings. It seems He never leaves us, never forgets that we do need Him, even though we often forget we need Him.

Let me tell you a little story. In this particular room, there were two gentlemen. Joe had the bed by the window. He seemed to be OK, never complaining, but always wanting to make his room-mate feel better. Bob had been in a bad accident about five months ago and was burned really bad. He was covered with bandages, even over his face and eyes. Bob would lie on his bed and to get his mind off of his pain, he would ask Joe what he saw out the window. Joe would tell him of beautiful sunrises, the breath-taking sunsets, the rain clouds and the storms and how the sunshine was streaming through the window. Each day he told Bob of the gorgeous beauty just outside the window. He described children playing in the yards beyond the parking lot, the flowers blooming in the yards and fields, gentle summer breezes blowing the tree-tops, beautiful cars pulling in or out of the parking lot. He would tell Bob of a couple walking hand in hand to the car, two little boys playing ball in the backyard of one of the nearby houses, or the lady sitting on the bench outside crying.

On and on the days would go. Joe would always lift Bob's spirits and somehow lessen the pain. Anytime Bob would ask, "What do you see Joe?" Joe would respond untiringly. This always made Bob forget about how bad he was hurting. But no matter the time of day or night Bob asked, Joe was always there to tell Bob once again about the beauty just outside the window.

One day, as Bob awakened, he heard doctors and nurses quietly comforting each other. God had taken Joe home through the night. He had died of a heart complication and was now looking at the beauties of Heaven.

Lonely weeks progressed and Bob was healing. He was getting better, but he sure missed Joe telling him about the things outside the window. It was now time to remove the bandages on Bob's face.

"Wait," said Bob, "before you remove the bandage, move me to Joe's bed over by the window. Joe saw so many beautiful things, and now I want to see them for myself."

They moved Bob to the bed by the window, sat him up facing the window. They then proceeded to unwrap the bandages. He sat in silence for just a minute with his eyes closed. You see, it had been close to six months since he had been able to see anything. Slowly, he opened his eyes, only to see a brick wall out of his window. He gasped and asked the nurse where was all of the beautiful scenery Joe had so delicately described to him during his recovery.

A nurse laid her hand on Bob's shoulder and said, "Joe was completely blind. God had painted those beautiful scenes in his mind so he could keep you seeing the beauty in God's creation. This kept you enthusiastic and wanting to get better. God even changed the scenery in Joe's eyes so you in your own blinded eyes could see it just as clear as he saw it with his completely blind eyes."

God always takes care of our needs. He sends us angels and we think they are just ordinary people. Always, look for the beauty in everything.

Philippians 4:19
My God will meet all your needs according to His glorious riches in Christ Jesus.

****

EARTHLY TREASURES

Down here on earth we usually work hard to amass treasures of some sort or the other. Some cannot live in anything that is not considered a mansion. Others want the biggest and best car money can buy. Some will actually go berserk if they don't have that full-length fur coat in the window, even though the weather never gets below fifty degrees.

There are those who strive for the large bank account with enough money to buy or do anything that their heart desires. For some there is the privilege of owning a yacht, belonging to country clubs, owning motorcycles, fine clothes or even a thriving business. They never realize that the greatest treasure of all is Salvation.

If you have Salvation, you can be content with a cabin on the hill, the old beat up Chevy truck, a simple denim jacket, or even hand-me-down clothes. You see, my friend, we'll leave all of our earthly possessions behind when we cross over that beautiful threshold.

That mansion on earth will crumble and decay just like the little cabin on the hill. The big fine automobile will rust just as fast as the old Chevy pickup truck. Moths and rats will eat the fur coat as well as the hand-me-down clothes. For when Jesus takes His children home, He gives us a brand new white robe, a golden crown and a fluffy white cloud to travel on. We have a beautiful mansion in Heaven that will never rot or decay. Termites will never be a threat, and we will never have to leave anything in Heaven behind. We will not need any kind of vehicle because now we can fly.

Jesus tells us that if we have Salvation, we are millionaires...We are a child of the King! We will never again have to worry about having enough money to pay the bills or buy the food. We will have no insurance payments, house payments, or car payments. There will be no sickness, no sorrow, no death, nursing homes, broken families, jails and no one will want what the other one has. The streets won't be filled with potholes or water puddles or covered with gravel or pavement...they will be covered with pure gold. The Crystal River will not be polluted with garbage or poison chemicals... It will be pure. The walls of the city will not be of brick or wood or plaster, but will be made of the finest of jewels. They will glow in the light of the Savior. This city will be more beautiful than we have ever imagined. There will be contentment, peace, beauty and love.

Wouldn't it be worth leaving the pleasures of Satan alone while we are here on earth and turn our lives over to Jesus? After all, I have told you what Jesus is offering His children...what does the Devil have to offer you? Fire and Brimstone

.... Torture! Give your heart and life to Jesus! Don't delay. Tomorrow may be too late! Follow Jesus my treasured friend, and one day Heaven will be yours.

Psalm 19:1
The Heavens tell of the glory of God. The skies display His marvelous craftsmanship.

****

BELLENGRATH GARDENS

I would like to tell you about a trip that two of my sisters and I went on a few years back. We decided to take a weekend getaway to Mobile, Alabama, and visit the Bellengrath Gardens. I had never been there before. As we parked the car and got out, all you could see was blooming flowers. Azaleas were the prominent flower, but others joined in the beauty. Every nook in between rocks, every available space around the walkways, around the little ponds and semi-lakes, there were azaleas and other flowers.

Each view seemed more beautiful than the other. We had cameras but we ran out of film early because we were trying to get every inch of this beauty to take home with us. The landscapers must have got the design from the Garden of Eden. Nowhere could you see a dead flower hanging on the bush, or a wilted flower that needed water, nor did you see a weed, or anything else that would distract from the flowerbeds. Each bush that needed trimming was trimmed like a fresh haircut, every leaf in place. Every thing just seemed perfect. There was a bridge crossing over the water and hanging baskets landscaped the rails so thick that you couldn't tell the flowers were in hanging baskets. They just looked like they were growing there in a flowerbed of some sort. We are usually quite a noisy bunch when we get together, but today, we could only look in wonder and awe. In one pond I saw an alligator about four feet long swimming side by side with a fish the same size.

Then we toured the mansion there at Bellengrath. This was almost as pretty as the outside. You could stand on a balcony and look down at little goldfish ponds, and again, every lily or any other flower or plant was landscaped to the nth of a degree of being perfect. If the place hadn't been so full of people I would have sworn it was the Garden of Eden.

Well, they had a tour boat, or something like an old river boat, that you could ride around the waterway and view the property from there. My sisters suggested that we take a ride. Well, I didn't want to spoil their vacation, so I said OK. Now me and water are not friends. I cannot swim, and I don't like to push my luck with it. I usually just stay away from boats and ponds and lakes, etc. But, I clenched my teeth and agreed. I didn't say anything to them about my fear, but I think they knew anyhow.

We boarded the thing and as you stepped on it, it rocked just a bit... I wanted OFF! But, no, I managed to go on. On the lower deck there was a dining room, all glassed in. Well, that looked safe enough, but it was on the bottom and if the thing sank, this would be the first to go, and I surely wouldn't be able to get out. So, we ventured up to the top deck.

They had little white plastic chairs sitting there on the deck. They were not bolted down or nothing ... just sitting there. I looked around real good, like this might be my last time and I sat down. Just as I sat down on the chair, it scooted just a bit, and my heart stopped. Then, they cranked the motor and the whole boat rocked. By this time there was no more blood in my body.... I think it had all drained out into the water. As if that wasn't bad enough, the Captain showed us where the life vest were, how to wear them and what they would do. Did he think we were gonna SINK or something? OH NO!

Well, the cruise lasted for about thirty minutes and we headed back for the shore. My knees were so weak I could hardly stand when this monster stopped. I struggled to take one step and then another, and finally my feet were on the ground. OK, I made it through that, but it is not something I want to do again! I looked at my feet and there were no webs between my toes, so that told me that I needed to stay on dry ground. We all laughed about this later, but it wasn't one bit funny then. Bellengrath Gardens are beautiful, but that boat will just have to entertain some one else next time.

When Peter saw Jesus walking on the water, he asked to walk on the water too. As long as he kept his eyes on Jesus, he walked. Personally, I didn't want to walk on the water, but I was doing some serious talking to the Master...like, "Please Lord, just let my feet stand on dry ground again." He heard my prayer, and everything was OK...but if it is OK with Him, I had just as soon not get in a boat again. Relax friend...God is watching over you.

Jeremiah 32:27
"I am the Lord, the God of all mankind. Is anything too hard for me?

****

GROWING OLD

When you were young, did you ever think about becoming old, or did you always imagine that you would be forever young? Did you think that age was somehow something that you could control? Well, we can't! Sometimes people age faster, as far as their looks, than others. Some of the richer people manage to get face lifts each time a new wrinkle appears... why, some have had so many face lifts, each time they blink an eye, their socks fall down ... but inside that body, no matter how much youth is displayed on the outside, you still get old.

Growing old is actually a blessing because each day we live, we learn. Just think of all of the wisdom that some of us have accumulated...all of the time you have had to share your knowledge... and all of the fun you have had getting "old"!

It shouldn't be a surprise. We should expect it. Some of us age gracefully, and others age with complaints, moans and groans. Our disposition sometimes consists of a continuous pity-party. When someone is asked how they feel, it takes a day and a half to listen to the complaints. Some just gracefully smile and say, "God let me wake up again this morning and I am so thankful."

When we were young we often done things without thinking. It may be a little harder to think now, but we usually weigh the pros and cons a little better. Think of all of the advise you have been able to give to all of your family and friends... all of the time you were able to share with them.

You have to look on age as preparing you for the memories your children will cherish. Maybe this final test in your life will be the one most remembered. It will be the sweetest for our family to recall.

So, the next time you look in the mirror, and it seems like there is a new wrinkle or gray hair, just thank God that He let you earn one more. You have been blessed to live to an old age. Some people die very young. They never see their children grow up and their grand-children born and grown. They never had the pleasure of waking up and looking in the mirror at a new wrinkle caused by years of smiles or another gray hair that announces one more precious memory of age has progressed.

God made us exactly like we are. The only thing that is really important is WHO lives in our heart. I sometimes don't think God looks at the outside beauty. He judges us from the beauty of our works and our love for Him in our hearts.

Love God. Thank Him for letting you grow old and learn and love all of those years. God bless.

Isaiah 46:4
Even when you are old I will be the same. Even when your hair has turned gray, I will take care of you.

****

KEEP AMERICA FREE

There is no doubt in my mind that there is a God… a precious loving God. God has carpeted the grounds with grass, green and lush. He has placed a bouquet of flowers on every corner. For the birds He spreads out leaves on the trees to make a nest for them and protect them from the elements.

He places the sun high in the sky to light up the world and lets its warmth thaw a land of cold and ice. He gives us birds in the air to serenade us with beautiful songs. He gives us the fresh air to awaken our inner thoughts and ideas. There is a smell of fresh dirt being prepared for vegetable gardens and flower-beds, a gentle spring shower to make the planted garden grow. Now the old concrete bench in the garden is occupied. Momma sits there in the shade taking a break from her chores.

Little worms emerge to the top of the ground, enticing amateur fishermen to go to the pond and give it a try. Colors are changing, and the leaves are soft and pastel.

But, even with this awesome beauty and newness, there is a dark cloud that spreads over America. Our Navy, Army, Marines and Air Force have moved into a foreign and hostile land of Iraq. This land is ruled by a Prince of Satan. It is evil and they don't like Americans, especially Christian Americans. This is just one more effort to keep America free. The military forces should be especially commended and our prayers for them should never cease. God Himself said, "Greater love has no man than to lay down his life for a friend." They are laying their lives on the line for us, my friend, to keep America free.

I know many will lose their lives, and will never see another spring day. Some will be taken prisoner and God only knows the torture they might endure. Some may even have to become a martyr for Jesus. Others will come home, broken and confused, but probably walking a lot closer to God.

God has told us that in the end times there will be wars and rumors of wars, parents against children, children against parents. This is happening right now my friend. Could it be that Jesus is about ready to come and take His children home? We just need to be ready, my friend, for I feel that the time is getting very close. I can see signs of Satan fighting harder than ever to win people to his army. He knows he is losing the battle and he wants to take as many soldiers with him as possible.

Let's turn our eyes to Heaven and get ready to face God's eternal spring. There will then be no wars, no evil, no murders, no worries….just peace and love. Think about that, my friend, PEACE AND LOVE.

Hebrews 4:16
So whenever we are in need, we should come bravely before the throne of our merciful God. There we will be treated with undeserved kindness and we will find help.

****

MILKING COWS

Let me take you back a few years. When I was about thirteen years old, Momma and Daddy had a little dairy. We only had a few cows because all of the milking was done by hand. I loved the outside and the animals, so I volunteered to do the milking.

In the summer months we went barefoot most of the time. Now, in a dairy barn, that has its advantages and its disadvantages. The advantage was that you didn't ruin a good pair of shoes and you could wash your feet off with the hose..... when you stepped in a cow patty.

The disadvantage was a cow has a sort of built in radar as to where your feet are placed. Without looking she can manage to step on your foot with one move. She then puts all of her weight on that leg. You know how someone puts out a cigarette with the toe of the shoe? They take the toe and twist a few times to make sure the cigarette is out. Well, I think they learned this from the cow. This old cow now has her hoof on your foot, all of her weight on that leg and then twists her hoof into your foot. You don't move her until she is ready to get the hoof off of your foot. Then she looks back at you as if to say, "Oops, did that hurt?"

Dairy cows seem to love good country music or gospel music. So, as you enter the barn, you turn on that worn out old radio, using a clothes hanger for the antenna, set the dial on a good country music station and turn it up loud! Then you proceed to take your position to milk the cow. You sit on a milk stool about ten to twelve inches high and maybe a ten-inch square seat. Needless to say, your seat never fits that seat. You plop down! From behind you probably resemble a gigantic Texas grass-hopper... nothing but knees and elbows, and an overhang on the seat of the stool. I think I have been five feet eight since I was six years old, so the grasshopper look was definitely there. You place the milk bucket between your knees and hold the bucket firmly. Now we are ready! Some kind of a boogie-woogie song by Jerry Lee Lewis would be playing on the old radio and you take a teat in each hand and milk with the beat of the music. SWISH, swish, SWISH, swish, ... As soon as you have finished those two, you grab the other two and continue with the beat. Before ole Jerry Lee Lewis could finish his song, you were through milking the cow... unless this was a bad day for Bossie.

Sometimes you have a cow that likes to kick every now and then, so you bend forward, bucket still firmly held between your knees, and place your head in the cow's flank. (This is just below the hipbone and in front of the back leg.) Pressure with your head here keeps her from kicking a lot. Now, have you ever watched someone playing the game "Twister?" Well, in this position you feel you must be the champion of this game. Just as you are about through, the bucket is getting

heavy, the music is good, and you are a bit off guard.... Bossie punts the bucket ten feet up in the air, and you take a milk bath.

In the summer there are little burrs called cocklebburs. They are about one half-inch long and covered with needlelike protrusions. As the cow walks through the woods grazing, these cockleburs tangle in the brush of her tail, mixed with mud.... and worse. This is summertime, so there are flies. She swats at a fly and the burrs hit her back and hurts. For some reason, she thinks you are the cause of the pain. While you are sitting on the stool in this very "dignified" position, you look up and she slaps you right across the face with that mass of burrs, mud...and worse. YUK! OUCH! If you don't look up, she swats the back of your head and instantly you and the cow are bonded. The burrs, the mud ... and worse are now stuck in your hair, along with the cow's tail. There are two ways to get untangled ... pull them out (along with a glob of hair) or cut them out, (along with a glob of hair.) If you listen closely, you can almost hear the cow laughing.

All of this good stuff was before hairdryers and if these accidents happened before school, you had to work real hard at washing and drying your hair. Sometimes you probably went to school with wet hair.

If you had to walk between two cows, they both took a step toward you and literally tried to squash you. They would press tight together and just before you completely lost circulation in your lower body, they would quickly move and you'd almost fall to the floor.

This was just an example of one milking of one cow. Just think of the fun you had with ten or fifteen cows each day, twice a day, seven days a week, three hundred sixty five days a year. Don't that just make you want to go out and buy a few cows and milk them?

The funny thing about it, I really liked it.....most of the time anyhow. The dirt and the grime washed off and on you would go. When I was grown, we had a dairy and milked ninety to one hundred cows... but the modern way with milking machines.

The devil works sometimes just like an aggravating cow. He will take your Christianity and your dreams and punt it ten feet in the air, making you wonder if following Jesus is worth it all. When things are going good, Satan steps on your toes and makes you stumble and fall. He will slap you in the face with situations that are almost impossible to free yourself from. But, my friend, when you feel the work of the devil, call out to Jesus and watch Him work. Jesus is in charge. May you always walk with Jesus, my friend.

1 John 5:4

For everyone born of God overcomes the world. This is the victory that has overcome the world, even our faith.

****

I AM A SOLDIER

Did you ever consider yourself as a soldier? Well, I am a soldier in the "Army of the Lord." Jesus Christ is my Commanding Officer and the Bible is my handbook and my book of conduct. My weapons are prayer, faith, and the word of God. This is warfare! The devil is my biggest enemy. I have been trained by the school of experience and taught the right way by God Himself. I have been tried by Satan's best leaders and have been tested by the fire of the Holy Spirit.

I volunteered for this Army and my enlistment is for eternity. I have two choices; I will either retire from this great Army of God at the Rapture or I will die an earthly death to live again in a glorified body. There is no way I will want to get out. You can't talk me out of it and Satan can't push me out. I will remain dependable to do my Master's work, capable of anything He asks me to do, reliable and a faithful soldier for Jesus. If God needs me I am ready. No matter what He needs me for, I will do the work of my Lord. It may be preaching, or teaching, or just learning how to live my life better for Him. It might even be sending these letters to my Treasured Friends. If He calls me I will go!

I am a soldier in this great Army...not a baby. I don't need to be begged, bribed, beaten, bought, buckled up, or backed up. I will take the responsibility of being a soldier. Sometimes I am scared, but I will go on. I know Jesus is with me. I am dressed in my full dress armor and I stand ready, saluting my King.

Ephesians 6:14-17

"Stand firm then, with the belt of truth buckled around your waist, with the breastplate of righteousness in place, and with your feet fitted with the readiness that comes from the gospel of peace. In addition to all this, take up the shield of faith, with which you can extinguish all the flaming arrows of the evil one. Take the helmet of salvation and the sword of the Spirit, which is the word of God."

To serve in this army, no one has to remind me of the purpose, write me, visit me, pay me or send me any kind of gifts or food. I will just obey any order He gives me. I will praise Him forever and hold His banner high. There is no need to feel I have to be catered to, crutched, or coddled. Jesus is all I need. His strength is what I rest on. I am committed to be the best soldier I can be. No matter how sick I may become, or how much I may ache in pain, I will not turn around. Satan can't discourage me enough to make me turn aside and I will not quit!

When Jesus called me and I joined His Army, I had nothing. Even though I may not have anything in the end, I will have the love of Jesus and I will be ahead. We will win.

I don't have to wait for a government to supply my needs; Jesus will supply all of my needs, continually. I am not just a warrior, but with Jesus I will never lose the war! There is nothing I can't do with the helping hand of Jesus.

The devil is not strong enough to defeat me. No demon is strong enough to hinder me, weather will not slow me down and sickness will not stop me. I can't be bought with money, a government cannot control me, and with Jesus at my side, Hell cannot have me! I won't even give in to death, for I will live again.

You see, when my Commander Jesus Christ calls me from this earthly battlefield, I will be promoted and He will allow me to rule with Him in Heaven. He will change my uniform to a fluffy white robe and a crown of gold. I am a soldier! I am marching to the beat of Amazing Grace and I will march to victory on my knees. I am Heaven bound ... I will win!

Matthew 4:19
"Come, follow me," Jesus said, "and I will make you fishers of men."

****

WHO LIVES ON THE STREETS

Have you ever wondered why there are so many people living on the streets in cardboard boxes or less? Who are these people that society seems to ignore? Has God forgotten them too?

A wino sits on the street corner begging for money…not for food, but more wine. He now feels that the only nourishment that his body needs is wine. Where did he fall from? Oh, he could have been a businessman that fate tossed a losing coin or a family man who lost his family by death or separation and he just couldn't handle the pain. If only he would have turned to Jesus instead of the bottle. It still may not be too late.

There are the teenagers who thought things were bad at home. They are here wandering the lonely streets in the night looking for drugs or ways to get money to buy drugs. They are scared and confused. Were the rules at home really that bad? Was the Bible ever read there? Did the family pray together? Jesus would have been there if He was only asked.

There is an elderly woman, bent under her burdens, pushing a grocery cart, which holds everything she owns. She was probably somebody's wife, maybe someone's mother. Did her family turn her away when she got old and in their way? Wasn't there anyone to love her? Didn't anyone care?

There is an old man riding a worn out bicycle, his cherished possessions draped over the handlebars. Did the world make him feel worthless because of his problems, so he just quit trying? No matter what happened, if his heart is right with God, there will be a special mansion waiting for him in Heaven.

There is also the family; Momma, Daddy, and three children, begging on the street for food and sleeping in an abandoned car at night. Momma lies awake and cries for the things she can't give her children. Daddy's heart breaks when he hears his children or his wife crying because of hunger or fear. The cold and the heat has to be dealt with, and it is hard. There is no warmth of a home or food on the table. How did they get here? Maybe they had a run of bad luck or bad health and Daddy lost his job. Maybe an uncaring landlord, greedy for money, turned them out into the streets. How do you sit and watch these children and good people live in situations like that? Pray for them. Love them. If you possibly can, find shelter for them and some kind of a job. Talk to them about Jesus.

Then there are those who are just plain lazy, living on the streets. They had rather live here than do a day's work. They think the world owes them food or things of comfort, without them working for it! But Jesus said, "Go to the ant thy sluggard, and consider her ways as wise."

I have often wondered where the families of these misplaced persons are. Aren't there sisters or brothers, aunts or uncles, or even Moms and Dads of these people, that if they knew they were on the streets would offer shelter, food and help? Is America getting that cold that we just don't care? Where is love...where is compassion? Why do we avoid these cast-a-ways? Jesus loves them. Do they know that Jesus loves them?

So many times we get into situations where we are ashamed and know we should have handled it better. I think they call this pride. We won't call on God because we think we are too low or too bad for Him to care. We can get out by ourselves. We'll try to clean up our act some before we ask Jesus to help. But my friend, Jesus will take us just as we are; dirty, sinful and lost, if we'll repent of our ways and reach out to Him, He will help us out of these bad situations. He'll pull us out of the dirt and sin of the street. We have to ask Him with our hearts and believe in Him. The shelter you find might be a hovel and you may only find a very low paying job, but that's a start. If you walk and talk with Jesus, whether you are in a mansion, a hovel or a cardboard box on the street, He will hear you... He will help you. He will send Angels to rescue you.

If you know people who live on the street, or if you see people that live on the street, pray for them. Buy them dinner if you can or a hot cup of coffee. Smile at them. Speak to them when you pass. Think of all of the things that these people miss out on that most of us take for granted...a warm bath, a hot meal, a hot cup of coffee, a cold glass of tea, a hug from a family member, a home, a job, warmth in the winter, coolness in the summer, friends, a future, a family, memories in the making.

Jesus loves these homeless people, but sometimes He doesn't like what they are doing. But, there is no sin so bad that God won't forgive someone for, if only they ask and repent. May Jesus always bless you..

Isaiah 6:8
Then I heard the voice of the Lord saying, "Whom shall I send? And who will go for us?"
And I said, "Here am I. Send me!"

****

HEAVEN OR HELL

If you had died just a second before you read this letter, where would you be? Would you look down and see a beautiful robe of white, soft and flowing around you and a beautiful Angel beside you taking you to Heaven to see your Savior? Or, would you be dressed in coarse, scratchy material like a grass sack ... or less, and you would be alone, panic stricken in darkness?

As you get to Heaven, the gates of pearl glitter in the light of Jesus. Gabriel welcomes you. You hear people praising Jesus, heavenly music of harps and other instruments and beautiful singing from Heaven's choir. You see beauty like the Garden of Eden. Flowers are everywhere. The grass is green and trees line the pathways and everything is just perfect and beautiful ... Or, would you smell the putrid scent of burning flesh and rotted matter. The smell would be so awful you would vomit until you couldn't stand up. You only see darkness around you and there in the distance you see flames ... a pit of burning fire. You want to stop but you feel like a force is pulling you on. You hear millions of people cursing, blaspheming, crying, screaming, and feeble prayers for God to save them, but never reaching the Master. You hear begging for just one drop of water for scorching tongues. You panic... because you know where you are and there is no way of getting out.

In Heaven, you see the streets of gold, the Crystal River, mansions, city walls of every jewel you can think of. Light from Jesus is reflecting off of them making them glitter and sparkle in an iridescent light everywhere. ... In Hell there is only darkness, fear and fire. It is a land where the worms never die and you will burn forever. (Now friend, you may think that you are now dead and you won't feel this. WRONG! You will feel the flames, the torture and the worms for eternity and you will never be able to permanently die.) It will cross your mind a million times the opportunities you had to serve Jesus and walked away. Now it is too late. This is your eternal fate.

In Heaven you look around and Jesus Himself welcomes you home with outstretched arms of love. You see family members who have gone on before. They are not sick or crippled or blind anymore. They greet you with joy and love. There is happiness everywhere and will never be any more night. There is not even a bad thought here. You will never be sad or worry about tomorrow. God invites you into His beautiful mansion and there in this huge dining room, the table is set for the "Marriage Supper of the Lamb." Your place is reserved there. I don't know what kind of food will be served, but I am sure living water will be on the menu.

In Hell, the devil will grin with victory as you walk through the dark portal. Demons will dance with glee because they won! You lost! You will see family members here, too. They are still sick and lame and blind. They were not healed. They are crying ... they are screaming ... they are begging for you to help them get out, but you know it is impossible. You see the devil and the demons torment and abuse your children, your spouse, your brother or your sister ... your mother or you dad... friends and other relatives. They ask why you didn't talk to them about Jesus while here on the earth. They scream in bitter agony from torture that the mind cannot imagine. There is no God to help you here, and the Devil and the demons can abuse and torture you anyway they want to, and you can't do a thing about it. I don't even want to imagine the ways the devil and the demons will torture and abuse these lost souls. You watch and cry and know you will live eternity here in Hell. You will beg to die a permanent death, but you can't. You feel the flames lap up around you and you scream in agony. This is not a nightmare.. you have waited to late. Can you even start to imagine life for eternity here?

Well, my friend, this was just a warning. You are still alive and you can make the difference in where you spend eternity. If you don't know Jesus .. fall on your knees and pray until you get the answer. If you wait, the next time you live this nightmare in Hell, it may be the real thing. Jesus is waiting for you my friend. He wants you to give your life to Him and spend eternity in Heaven. Please don't wait until it is too late!

Rev. 3:20
Here I am! I stand at the door and knock. If anyone hears my voice and opens the door, I will come in and eat with him, and he with me.

****

A WAY OUT

If you are ever backed against the wall, my friend... pray! God will make a way out. All through the Bible it tells us that. Moses was facing the Red Sea. Pharaoh was behind him. God made a way out. He opened up the Red Sea and they walked across on dry land. When Elijah thought he just wanted to die, God sent a chariot of fire to take him straight up to Heaven. This was his way out. Noah found the way out of the flood with the ark. Daniel found the way out when God closed the lion's mouth. Samson found his way out when God renewed his strength.

God is always there if you need a way out. Is drugs and alcohol taking control of your life? Pray! God will show you the way out. If you have lost a spouse or a loved one and the pain won't go away, well, have you talked to God and asked for a way out? He'll put His arms around you and He'll take the pain away and let you heal. Has finances backed you in a corner? Pray! When the doctor comes in and tells you that you have cancer and you will soon die, and your very soul seems to crumble in agony, pray! Your life on earth may be ending and it may be your turn to cross old Jordan, but God will take you in His loving arms and hold you close to His breast and He will comfort you and give you the strength to carry on. He will show you your way out.

What happens when sin has drug you through every gutter and Satan tells you that you don't have a chance for Heaven? He tells you there is no way out ... no one to listen to you. Pray! God is still on the throne and He'll reach out His mighty hand and pull you out of any situation. After all, over two thousand years ago, God made a way for you to go to Heaven. He died on the cross for your sins. He sent mercy and grace to carry you through.

The Devil always tries to convince us that we've lost the battle... no one cares and there is no one who will hear your prayers. There is no situation you find yourself in, praying and believing, that God won't make you a way out .

Jesus loves us all, and it really breaks His heart for us to turn away from Him. Jesus is always listening ... Always waiting for you to call on Him!

"Jesus, Precious Jesus,
Make a way for me. I want to follow You, Jesus. I want to live in
Heaven with You for eternity. Forgive me Jesus for my sins ...
Jesus, Precious Jesus ..."

Matthew 17: 20-21

Jesus replied, "It is because you don't have enough faith. But I can promise you this. If you had faith no larger than a mustard seed, you could tell this mountain to move from here to there. And it would. Everything would be possible for you.

****

PRISONS

We live in a free country, yet so many times we find ourselves imprisoned by Satan's plans. He works very hard to take away the happiness and freedom we find when we get salvation. He has learned every trick in the book to make us stumble or fear something that will take away the happiness and contentment that a Christian feels.

Some of us are engulfed in a prison of fear...fear of succeeding, fear of failing, fear of who they are, fear of who they want to be. The walls are dark and they sit huddled in a corner fearing what lies outside.

Then there is the prison of work. Some people are slaves to work. They don't have time for the family or church or even enough rest. All they can seem to function with is work. They always worry about getting a larger house, a finer car, or making a bigger impression on others.

The prison of society makes us think that if we don't attend all of the social gatherings, mix with the elite crowd, dress like the others in society, give parties, drink or try other immoral things, we just won't fit in the "click." The sad thing is that most of the time they don't even like the people they socialize with and they are tired of the parties...tired of the entertaining, but, for the sake of society, they carry on. Satan smiles and passes you another round of drinks, or some other temptation of sin.

Some have been abused in their lifetime and there are prison walls of hurt and degradation surrounding them. They have been used, abused, and refused. They tend to stay in their own little cell, afraid to seek friendship or love.

Satan welds the bars on the prisons of debts. Credit cards are so easy to get. They are used for frivolous things that we don't even need. It is "such a fun thing to do!" ... Just whip the card out and charge it! They show off for their friends and pay for their goods, too. This is trying to buy a friendship, I guess. These prisoners forget there will come a day to repay these debts and money gets even shorter. Then they start to pay the credit card bills with other credit cards. Before long, they realize that they will never get out of debt and now they can't even pay the interest on the cards. .... so, Satan sends them another one!

There are prisons of hate, where people just won't let go of something said or done years ago. The walls of these prisons are scribbled with reminders of who done what or who said what. This way they know they won't forget. Sometimes Satan lets the hate get so deeply imbedded in their hearts and minds, they can't even think of why they hate that person...they just hate! Satan padlocks the doors to the prisons hoping to always have control. We ask God for forgiveness, but Satan keeps reminding us of it, and he keeps trying to make us believe that

is a part of our punishment to remember our sins and relive them over and over with guilt. God tells us that when He forgives us, our sins will be remembered no more.

But, my friend, no matter what prison Satan has locked you in, there is a King who can set you free. He can loose the chains, open the doors and give you freedom from Satan. What does it take to set the prisoners free? One prayer from the heart...one prayer asking for forgiveness, direction and strength. It doesn't matter if the prayer is bellowed from the highest roof top or whispered from the lowest prison cell, God listens. There are no bars, no walls, no chains, no locks of any prison that God can't tear down. He can take the threats of Satan and silence them. When we are forgiven, our sins are thrown into the sea of forgetfulness, never to be remembered anymore. Jesus tells us that our sins are forgiven, forgotten and we are covered with blood. Satan can't penetrate the shield of love that God places around us. Keep praying my friend.

Psalm 103:12
As far as the east is from the west, so far has He
removed our transgressions from us.

****

MEMORIES

Often we look back in time and discover memories...memories that for some reason or the other have been pushed aside, buried deep under other memories, whether they be good or bad, are just too much to deal with and our mind seems to conveniently lock them away. The dust and the cobwebs camouflage them into being just a part of the surroundings. Some of these are not really painful, they are just old memories replaced by something else. The attic of our mind is full of treasures, waiting to be uncovered.

Remember your childhood, your scraped knees and your momma's kiss...the strength of your daddy and his big hands. Then there were the special smells of the family kitchen. The first day of school and new friends imprinted our minds in fear as well as fun.

There were ghost stories around a campfire and the goose bumps on the back of your neck. Remember your first dog or your first cat, and how you cried when they died. Memories include your first love and your first heartbreak, and then, that is replaced by someone else and you don't think about it much. Do you remember your first car and your first day on your own in this big old world? Well, that too was probably replaced by a job and career...and the old clonker didn't seem that important. It was just life.

There are memories of marriage, birth of children, sometimes divorces or the death of your spouse or child, or other family members. Each time we think we have tasted life at its best or its worst, something else comes along to challenge our memories.

Sometimes we pick up an old picture album and reminisce about times and family of long, long ago. We chuckle to see the funny way everyone dressed or fixed their hair. We look at pictures of our parents and see our faces. As we gaze on a picture, we relive in our mind, the time this picture was taken. We are amazed how beautiful grandma was at eighteen, and how handsome grandpa was. Sometimes, we were just amazed to realize that they were once young. Our grandchildren will one day look at our old albums and wonder the same thing. We brush off the cobwebs and find life of long ago. Along with the memories come smiles and tears.

We sometimes forgive people for something they said or done, but in a moment of anger or in our own little pity party, we toss this back, not caring how it hurts. We forgave, but we never forgot it. But Jesus is not like that, my friend. He forgives us of our sins and He tosses them into the deepest sea, never to be remembered again. All we have to do is ask for forgiveness from our heart. We

can mess up time after time, but he will never toss the past back at us. He just forgives us again and forgets it.

You know, you can meet me or someone else and be friends for a while, and you can go on your way and forget us. You have lost nothing. But if you meet Jesus and forget Him, you have lost every thing. When you ask Jesus to forgive you of your sins, and ask sincerely, they are forgiven, forgotten and covered with blood. God bless you my treasured friend.

Psalm 32:1
Blessed is he
whose transgressions are forgiven,
whose sins are covered.

****

YOU ARE ON HIS MIND

It seems like in our wildest pity-parties we think that there is no one who cares. But that is not so. While Jesus was hanging on the cross on Calvary, He was thinking of you. He could see the time span you would be born, and how you would live your life, and just how long you would live. He knew the exact time you would be born and the exact time you would die. He knew then, just what work He wanted you to do for him.... You see, you were on His mind way back then, and you have been on His mind constantly ever since.

He smiles when you smile, and He is sad when you are sad, and He wants so much for you to be able to join Him and His Father in Heaven. The plan of Salvation was given to you on that cross.

No matter what the world says about you, or does to you... they can't take the love of Jesus away from you. He loved you even before you were born and He will always love you. No matter where you are, He can always hear your prayer. You may be there in your workplace or in the comfort of your home. No matter where how deep in sin we get, or how bad we break His heart, He is always there ... waiting and hoping for us to come back to Him. All it takes for forgiveness is a whisper of a prayer from our heart, asking for forgiveness and He hears us and forgives us. With prayer, He will give us the wisdom and the strength to stay away from the pitfalls of life, and that way we can live a better life for Him. Keep Jesus in your heart friend, you are always on His mind.

Romans 8:38-39
For I am convinced that neither death nor life, neither angels nor demons, neither the present nor the future, nor any powers, neither height nor depth, nor anything else in all creation, will be able to separate us from the love of God that is in Christ Jesus our Lord.

****

CALLIE, SASSY AND THE RAT

I have introduced some of you to my dog, Callie. To those whom I haven't, well, she is a beautiful red-mearle, Australian Shepherd. I've raised her from a baby and she is over sixteen years old. She can't have babies, so she adopts and loves any other baby.

About six months ago, a friend gave me a six-week old black and white kitten named Sassy. Now Callie loved her right off. She would snuggle up to Sassy when they slept, making sure she was safe and warm. Callie tried to protect Sassy from getting hurt and made her feel loved. I don't think Sassy ever missed her real Momma. Callie has real long hair and sometimes I would come home to find the cat almost buried in Callie's fur. Callie would seem to sense the time that Sassy was getting on my nerves with her hyper-ness. Callie would come and get Sassy, picking her up by the nape of her neck, (just like a momma cat would do,) and take her to the other side of the room. Here she would play with Sassy until she wouldn't be hyper anymore. She would wrestle with Sassy, roll with her, chase her, and then when the cat was all tuckered out, they would snuggle up together and take a nap.

Callie would tolerate anything from Sassy. Sassy would jump on Callie, bite Callie, slap Callie, take Callie's bowl of milk and simply just aggravate her. But, Callie always loved the cat and would never hurt her. When someone accidentally hurt Sassy, she would meow real loud, Callie would rush to her side to make sure she was OK. No matter where they were, Callie was always watching over her "Baby."

The cat was raised really not knowing she was a cat...she thinks she is a dog! Instead of rolling a ball around on the floor, she fetches, (picks it up and brings it back to you to toss again!) When a cat gets mad at someone, usually the first thing they do is scratch...Not Sassy! She bites and bites hard. She will shred paper in a minute...chew up a pair of shoes, gnaw on a purse or destroy a roll of toilet tissue. I am just waiting for Callie to teach her how to bark. Ha Ha. Callie truly has her hands full raising this "Baby!"

The two of them stay indoors most of the time, especially at night. They live in contentment with a goldfish and a parakeet. Sassy is so much a dog, she doesn't even worry about the bird and the fish. After the lights are off, you never hear a peep out of either of them. Callie will bark if someone comes up, but otherwise it is good and quiet. The other night Callie woke me up barking. I had been asleep for a while. I sat up in the bed listening... She would bark loud and I would hear a couple of thuds and then the cat would bellow out a loud meow. I wondered what in the world was going on.

I got up and turned on the lights and watched the two of them. I couldn't help but laugh. Callie, as I said, always respected a "baby" (which always included anything small,) and didn't want to hurt it and didn't want anyone else to hurt one. Well, the cat had found a little mouse and was trying to catch it. Each time she'd try, Callie would protect the baby mouse. The cat was so confused. (Well, it was real hard for Callie to visualize Sassy actually acting like a cat!) Sassy would chase the mouse and time her paw hit the mouse, Callie would knock the cat over and hold Sassy down with her paw. Finally I called Callie off and let the cat have the trophy. I guess, in her way of thinking, the mouse was the "baby" and she wasn't gonna let it get hurt.

We are God's children and God protects us. When others are hurting us physically or otherwise, He steps in and protects His Children. I am so glad Jesus loves us. I am so glad I am a child of God!

Psalm 91:4
He will cover you with his feathers,
and under his wings you will find refuge;
his faithfulness will be your shield and rampart.

****

THE SHEPHERD

This is a story you need to use your imagination while reading it. You can see a Shepherd on the hillside. He's standing there with the sheep all around. It is so peaceful. The sheep trust him for their safety, food and their lives. They know his voice and when he speaks they follow him. Then the shepherd's attention seems to be on something in the distance. Oh, No! It's a wolf! He quickly counts the sheep...One is missing and he knows he must find it before the wolf does. He commands his faithful sheep dog to take care of the sheep. He leaves the flock and ventures out in the edge of the woods...always looking back at the flock and checking on the wolf.

The wolf is slowly stalking closer. The sheepdog is alert and waiting to defend the sheep if he needs to. Then the Shepherd hears the cry of the lamb. He gently picks it up and returns to the flock. The shepherd and his faithful dog stand in defiance against the wolf. The message is conveyed to the wolf, "You will have to overpower us to get to my sheep." The wolf tucks his tail and slinks away. He'll go hunt a flock of sheep where the Shepherd is not as strong.

Now friend, Jesus is our Shepherd and we are His flock. The wolf is the devil and the sheepdog is the Angels God puts in charge of His sheep. Jesus loves all of His sheep. He knows each of them by name. Some of the sheep stray away and He leaves the flock in care of Angels, and seeks the lost one.

In Matthew 18:12-13, it says, "Let me ask you this. What would you do if you had a hundred sheep and one of them wandered off. Wouldn't you leave the ninety-nine on the hillside and go look for the one that had wondered away? I am sure that finding it would make you happier than having the ninety-nine that never wandered off." Jesus told Peter three times to "Feed My sheep!" He was speaking to him to spread the gospel. Give His sheep food for the soul.

Jesus will protect His children against the forces of Satan. He hears our prayers for help and mercy, like the lost lamb in the bushes. He'll save our soul from Satan's evil plans. He loves you. You are special to Him. He lay down His life for you there on another hillside called Golgotha. Our Shepherd hung there on that old rugged cross in agony for His sheep. He defeated Satan and death and by His mercy and grace, He made a way for us to live eternally with Him in Heaven. He still watches over His sheep from Heaven above, and always hears even the softest prayer sent up to Him.

One day, our Shepherd is coming back for His sheep. We'll go to a land where we will never have to worry about wolves, or what Satan can do to us. We won't have to worry about falling from Jesus' grace because everything there in Heaven will be perfect and good and sin cannot abide there. Death will never again be

known. There will only be singing and praising and peace and happiness…. For ever and ever!

Psalm 23:1-2
The Lord is my shepherd, I shall not be in want.
He makes me lie down in green pastures,
He leads me beside quiet waters,

****

REAP WHAT YOU SOW

When I was younger, Momma and Daddy always had a nice vegetable garden. We had almost any kind of vegetable that you could think of. We might not have had the meat as often as we would have liked to, but we could eat all of the vegetables that we wanted.

At planting time, Momma and Daddy would prepare the garden for planting. When us kids were old enough, we had to help plant the seeds. Momma would tell us, "This row needs to be planted with butterbeans, this one with black eye peas, and this one with corn." Another was fixed for Okra, squash, tomatoes or any other vegetable known to man. She would hand us a sack with some seed in it and tell us to put so many seed, (maybe 2 or 3), in each little hollow that she had cornered out with a hoe. Then she would come back behind us and cover the little seeds. Sometimes I think she might have said a little prayer over each hill of seed because they seemed to always come up. But there was always one thing we could count on....If we planted beans on a row, you could count on it being beans when it came up. It didn't come up like a peach tree or a grape vine. We planted beans and had bean sprouts, then, we harvested beans when it was ready.

This often reminds me that we reap what we sow. We sow the seeds in the garden and most of us expect that kind of a plant to emerge from the fertile ground.

When you sow seeds of dishonesty, gossip, crimes, injustice, prejudice, moral disrespect or any other seeds, do you think your life will prosper with plants of contentment, peace, joy, appreciation, love or happiness? NO! You reap the same kind of plants from the seeds sown. So I think we need to plant our gardens with rows of contentment, peace, joy, appreciation, love, and happiness and pull out the weeds of dishonesty, gossip, crimes, injustice, prejudice and moral disrespect.

If you plant seeds in the garden real close together, your plants will come up thick and your vegetables will be abundant. But if you plant them sparsely, that is how they will come up. Food will be scarce. If you do only a few good deeds along life's way with a lot of bad things, your field comes up with a few good plants and a lot of weeds. The good plants, (good deeds) will be choked out by the weeds. On the other hand, though, if you strive to do good and you walk with Jesus in your daily life, most of the plants will flourish with only a few weeds, which God Himself will pull out.

Isn't it great that God loves us so much that He wants nothing but the best for us. He patiently waits for our harvest to ripen and He takes us by the hand as we stroll through the field, and He plucks out each weed of sin and forgives us. Our harvest of rewards in Heaven will be bountiful.

All that this great harvest takes is for us to trust and believe in Him and obey Him. Have you got a bountiful harvest, my friend?

Isaiah 58:11
The Lord will guide you always;
he will satisfy your needs in a sun-scorched land
and will strengthen your frame.
You will be like a well-watered garden,
like a spring whose waters never fail.

****

PORTRAIT OF JESUS

I got to thinking about something the other day. I was looking at a painted picture of Jesus. For some reason, even though I have seen this picture time after time during my lifetime, I didn't get the same picture in my mind.

In the paintings he was light skinned, with brown, well kept hair, perfect skin, lighter colored eyes ... sort of a mixture of green and blue, and a well-trimmed beard. He always looked at peace and rested. His hands were smooth and almost delicate looking. His feet were always clean and His sandals looked almost new. It seems like He always wore a garment of white in the pictures. But He had no home on this earth as He preached. He had no place to keep His clothes or other possessions. There was no bed for Him to sleep on, no table to serve His food on. There was nothing to call His own while He was here on earth. In Matthew 8:20 it says, "And Jesus saith unto him. The foxes have holes and the birds have nests, but the Son of Man hath no where to lay His head."

In 2 Corinthians 8:9 it said, "For ye know the grace of our Lord Jesus Christ that though He was rich, yet for your sakes, He became poor, that through His poverty ye might be rich."

He came as a baby, meek and mild. He was abused, mistreated, avoided, and pushed aside. (That is still happening today!) Some people though, loved Him, walked with Him, had faith in Him to just touch His garment and they would be healed. (There are still good Christians today.) We can walk with Him and with faith we can touch Him, and talk with Him. He listens and He will always answer our prayers.

Well, I looked at this painting of Jesus, and then closed my eyes and this is how the picture in my mind looked. He was from the area of Israel. The people here are dark skinned and have dark hair and dark eyes like the Arabians. So, I see Him with the dark skin and His face is weathered. His hair was cut unevenly in places and sometimes shaggy looking. His beard was not trimmed nice and neat. His eyes are dark, but through them one could see eternity. His smile showed teeth straight and white, and with this smile you could feel peace and comfort even in your worst storm. He looked much older than His thirty-three years. His statue is close to six feet, and He is muscular. After all, He grew up as a carpenter. I see His hands held out to me, large and calloused, but gentle to the touch, yet strong enough to carry your burdens. His sandals are worn and dusty and His feet are also calloused from all of the miles of walking. Probably most of the time He was covered with dust from traveling around on the dirt roads. I don't see Him wearing white all of the time, because He didn't even have a home to freshen up His appearance when He needed to. Colored garments didn't show

the marks of hands reaching out and touching Him, or stains from kneeling while talking to the Father. The garment that the Roman Soldiers were gambling over was mentioned to be purple. The only place He had to take a bath was places like the muddy old Jordan or the Sea of Galilee.

Oh, I'm sure He wore a glorious white garment when He arose from the grave because that stands for purity. When He rose to Heaven on the cloud, He glowed like a bright light, and the robe He was wearing was surely spotless white. Maybe the only garments worn in Heaven will be of purest white and we will all glow with the purity of the soul because of the mercy and the grace of Jesus.

This is only a thought on what He might look like. Right now on earth, the only thing that matters to me is that my name is written in the Lamb's Book of Life. When I get to Heaven and look on His glorious face, whether it be fair or dark, I will love Him still and praise His Holy name forever. Keep on praying. I am praying for you, please pray for me too.

Rev. 2:7
He who has an ear, let him hear what the Spirit says to the churches. To him who overcomes, I will give the right to eat from the tree of life, which is in the paradise of God.

****

SEPTEMBER 11

Here we are on the anniversary date of the horrible attack on the Twin Towers and the Pentagon on that fateful September 11th day.

Can you imagine standing for a moment, admiring the site of the Twin Towers, marking their place in the landscape of New York City? They are landmarks that can never be replaced. You watch as a plane hits one of the towers sending it up in flames and smoke, and your heart breaks because your friends are working there. You think it was a horrible accident...then you see another plane swerve and take a direct hit on the other tower and your heart stops!

Can you imagine being in the towering inferno, thinking about the work you needed to do, or your family at home, your child that was sick or the Anniversary party tonight? Did you have time to think of the angry words spoken to your mate before you left home... or did you tell them you loved them? Would you have had time in that confusion and death to call out to God? Had you waited too long? You probably never knew an evil enemy had done this mass murder. Thousands never made it out!

Then you could have been the ones scampering, stumbling, down the dark, debris strewn stairwell...gasping for air as the thick billowing smoke made it almost impossible to breathe, and completely impossible to see. Were you grasping the hand or arm of anyone who could help you, or holding on to others to help them? People were carrying the disabled, waiting for the older ones or the ones who were on the verge of passing out or dying. Some were burned, some were pregnant, some were having heart attacks, some were suffocating...but they all tried to help their neighbor. Firemen and Policemen worked desperately with the rescue with no rest or relief. Priest and Preachers stood by praying, helping as much as they could. Some lay down their lives to save others.

Were you one of the fortunate ones that for some reason or the other was late for work? A small list came out of why some had not got to work on time....One put on a new pair of shoes and had to walk slower. One developed a blister on his foot and stopped in a drug store to buy a Band-Aid...One stopped to answer the phone; one stopped to buy donuts; one forgot her purse and had to go back home, one over- slept; one hunted coins for a toll; one was in a traffic jam, one had morning sickness; one was delayed as she was starting her youngster in kindergarten; one took time to call her mother.

Suppose you were in the plane that made that fatal crash? Did you have time to pray? Did you even know of the fate that was about to happen? Was your soul saved?

Were you the one at home when the news ran the awesome pictures and your phone rang? Was it your loved one, or was it the bad news? How long did you have to wait and pray that maybe....maybe your love one was one who made it out?

Were you a child at school who saw this awful sight on TV and were too young to realize that your Mom or your Dad, your Grandma or your Grandpa, was one of the thousands that would not ever be coming home again?

Were you just an American...stunned, shocked, speechless and crying? Did you fall on your knees and pray for the ones who lost their lives, the ones who lost their loved ones... or the President or America? .....Or, Heaven forbid... were you one of the demon controlled enemies who caused this?

My friend, the rubble of the towers have been cleaned up, and only pictures before this tell us of the majesty and beauty of the Twin Towers. The hearts of the ones who lost loved ones still hurt and break. Children still cry for parents. Policemen and Firemen will never forget! New York City will never completely heal...and we can't ever forget how easy we made it for the enemy. We can't be caught off guard again! Wake up America! The enemy is within! Pray! Live each day in the way that if you had been on those planes or in the towers on that fatal day, you would be walking with Jesus now. This could happen again in a twinkling of an eye, and in so many other ways. Pray for America. Pray for the President. Pray for your neighbors. God be with you.

Psalm 34:17
The righteous cry out, and the Lord hears them;
he delivers them from all their troubles.

****

IF

My friend, the little word IF is a mighty powerful word. So many times in our lives, we ask the question, "What if....?" Here is a little food for the soul, based on that mighty word "IF."

What if God refused to bless us today, no matter how hard we prayed, because we didn't think it was important yesterday to thank Him?

What if God left us today because we refused to follow Him yesterday?

What if God let all of the flowers and trees die because we complained about the rain?

What if God found other things to do today because we found other thing to do on His day beside worship Him?

What if God took away the freedom to worship Him and read the Bible today because we refused our children the right to worship Him in schools yesterday?

What if God took away preachers and teachers and His word would no longer be heard because we would not listen to them yesterday?

What if God had not loved us enough to send His Son to die on the cross for our sins because He thought we should pay the price for our sin?

What if God took away our breath today because yesterday we puffed on cigarettes, killing the lungs He had created?

What if there would be no more clean water because we polluted what He had given us?

What if He decided to send no more babies to us because we abused and aborted them yesterday?

What if God let America fall because we have taken prayer out of schools and God out of our living standards?

What if God gave us no more miracles today because we didn't believe in them yesterday?

What if the doors to the churches were closed and locked, refusing to let us in today, because yesterday He stood at our Heart's door and knocked and we would not let Him in?

What if God cared for us only as we cared for others?

What if God would not listen to our prayers today because we would not listen to His pleading voice yesterday?

What if God was as slow to answer our prayers, as we are deaf and distant to answer His call for our service for Him?

What if God only met our needs today based on the extent we gave Him of our lives yesterday?

What if God didn't love us today because we turned our back on Him yesterday?

But Thank God! He didn't give up on us or stop loving us, or stop sending preachers and teachers. He told us in the Bible that He loved us enough to send His own Son to die for us. He tells us that He will never leave us. God promises us that if we pray, believing, He will answer. He forgives us time and time again. Friend, isn't it about time to heed God's call. He wants to give you eternal life. God wants to give you blessings untold, and a country that is free. Don't turn your back on the Savior. He loves you and if you will let Him, He will protect you under His wings. God bless you my treasured friend. If God loves you so much then why can't you love Him so that He will never give up on you?

Ephesians 1:18

I pray also that the eyes of your heart may be enlightened in order that you may know the hope to which he has called you, the riches of his glorious inheritance in the saints,

****

HEAVENLY GROCERY STORE

Suppose that you were walking through a beautiful park. There were big trees along the path and flowers were in full bloom. The grass was green and inviting for a picnic. But you didn't have a picnic basket. You look around and just a little piece off you saw the flashing neon sign of a grocery store..."Heaven's Grocery Store." Wow! I wonder what we could find in there...

Well, you walk to the big glass doors and they open automatically for you to come in. Instead of being regular people minding the store, they were all Angels, dressed in flowing white robes. Some were standing in an aisle and singing hymns. One handed me a shopping cart and a sign on the cart caught my eye. It said, "My child, shop with care." One Angel told me that there was no limit to anything in the store and what the basket couldn't hold, I could come back later for, if I needed anything else. I looked around and I think everything a human could use, was on display in that store.

PATIENCE was the first item and I took a lot of it....boy! Could I ever use that. I had been awfully short with the kids and my spouse and the people at work. LOVE was stacked high on the shelf. I reached and held LOVE close to my heart. I could feel the LOVE of my Savior calming my fears.

A little further down, was something called UNDERSTANDING. I picked up a box and read on the label, "This is for knowing that God always knows best. We won't always know the reasoning, but we have to have UNDERSTANDING that God does know best." I thought I had better get a couple of boxes of this.

FAITH was next. I gathered up a few bags. I was sure running low on this. God had tried to show me over and over, but I seemed to spill the FAITH I had.

Then there was a shelf stacked neatly with CHARITY. Again I read the label. It said, "To get the most out of this, give it all away." OK, I had better get a case of this. I had a lot of people in my midst who could surely use this.

There was a special on the HOLY GHOST. They were giving it away to everyone. I made sure I got a good helping of that.

A sign on the next aisle was "YOUR OWN SPECIAL GIFT!" It was displayed on the shelf and it came in little gift boxes, wrapped with sparkling paper and beautiful ribbons. Each was marked with the gift God has given each of us.... speaking, healing, preaching, teaching, prophesy, singing, writing, hospitality, leadership, craftsmanship, speaking in tongues....and on and on the assortment went. I got several of these.

STRENGTH was offered to live your life for Jesus, and if you got enough you could resist the temptations of the Devil.

COURAGE was offered with a rebate. "If you grow in COURAGE you will reap the benefits of peace. You will have run your race and won!" I grabbed a couple of cans of this.

I then stopped and remembered that I needed GRACE. For it is GRACE that will forgive my sins. To go with GRACE, I found MERCY. This will get me to Heaven even though I don't deserve to go.

On the last shelf I found SALVATION. SALVATION was the most important item of all. My heart fluttered and I felt the very presence of Jesus. I picked up a PRAYER off the top shelf and used it immediately. Sin wouldn't stand a chance when I stepped outside.

In a special place close to the checkout counter, I found PEACE and JOY, SONGS and PRAISE, which I piled abundantly into my cart.

Then as I pulled up to the checkout counter, my cart loaded with Heavenly groceries, I asked the Angel, "How much do I owe?" He smiled and said, "Nothing. Just take them everywhere you go. Jesus paid the price a long, long time ago." I walked outside, and in the glow of the sunshine, I saw Jesus smile at me. "Thank you my child. Enjoy your groceries." Enjoy your Heavenly grocery shopping my friend.

Galatians 6:16

If you follow this rule, you will belong to God's true people. God will treat you with undeserved kindness and will bless you with peace.

****

GRANDMA'S ROCKING CHAIR

There's a rocking chair that is empty in the home. This chair was probably given to Grandma as her first child was born. She rocked the babies at night through fevers, fears, teething and colic attacks. It rocked a child with skinned knees and a broken heart. Then it went on to serve the same purpose for the grand-children... each one special to her.

The old rockers on the chair are worn and chipped. It has rocked a many a mile through this lifetime. The paint is dull and worn and the finish is scratched and nicked.... But it still rocks. Many a song has been sung here...anything from a lullaby to a hymn, and even some that were just made up.

Grandma sits there now rocking in silence. There is no one here for her to hold or rock. There's no one to hold and comfort her. Where are the children? Oh, they are all grown now and have lives of their own. They have forgotten about Grandma, or just don't have the time. She now spends most of her time alone, and rocking in that old rocking chair. She rocks in the dusk of the setting sun. The shadows in her white hair seems to glow like a crown of glory. There are wrinkles on her brow and her hands are weathered and worn. Doesn't anyone care? She sits there and rocks on, her eyes closed in memories, the family Bible in her lap, and tears fall softly down her cheeks.

She sees each of them as a child again, and she rocks them and holds them close to her heart...but only in memories. She prays for each of them, one by one. Oh, how she'd love to hold them just once more. Where's all of the hugs and the laughter or even the tears they shared.

Then, there's a knock on her heart's door. Jesus is standing there. He tells her she doesn't have to be lonely anymore. It just breaks His heart to see her cry and to feel her loneliness. Time has come for her to go home. There in Heaven, Jesus Himself sits in a big old rocking chair, and holds her close to His bosom, and He Himself takes His nail-scarred hand and wipes the tears away ... and the Angels sing.......!

If you have an aging Mother or Father or Grandmother or Grandfather, don't neglect them. Visit them, call them, or write them. Let them know that the love they gave you was not in vain. If you are the Grandma or the Grandpa, then I hope you are blessed in a special way. I hope these little devotionals have brightened your day somewhere along the way.

James 3: 17
The wisdom that comes from God is first of all pure,
then peaceful, gentle, and easy to please.

****

CHRISTMAS CHARIOT

Christmas brings to mind the birth of Jesus. It also reminds us of gifts and a jolly old man in a red suit, riding in a sleigh pulled by reindeer. The thing is he only rides around at Christmas time, or so it is told. I can imagine a picture of a real Christmas rider, in my mind.

I see Jesus riding in a white chariot pulled by white horses, and ten thousand Angels sing His songs. He is clothed in the purest white and glows for everyone to see. He holds the reigns with His nail-scarred hands. He doesn't need any light, because He is the light of the world. This chariot is piled high with gifts.. but he gives them all year long, not just on Christmas Eve. His father gave Jesus as a gift to the world, but He is the gift that keeps on giving.

He pulls out a big red box, tied with a big red bow and hands it to a man with cancer. A promise inside tells him that his cancer is cured. A box wrapped in white, tied with a lacy white bow is given to a Momma whose baby had just died. As her shaking hands open it up, she sees a picture of her baby as an Angel. It has earned its wings. A smaller box inside is full of courage to go on, and faith that they will meet again.

There is a dear old Grandma, tired and homesick. For her, he pulls out a small blue box, wrapped so neat. It opens like a jewelry box to display a one-way ticket to her Heavenly home.

To the parents of a soldier goes a green box...lavished with green ribbons. A note inside says, Momma, Daddy.... I have gone on to Heaven and I'm walking in God's garden. Extra hugs and strength accompanied it.

There was a special gift of love for a mother, a new sermon for the preacher, understanding for a father, light for the blind, healing for the lame and health for the sickly.

Some of the other boxes hold gifts of blessings, peace, joy, strength and many more gifts from God. There are gifts of blessings to the faithful, and to the preachers and the teachers; courage and safety to the policemen and firemen and soldiers. Golden boxes hold golden crowns for the prayer warriors and for those who give to the less fortunate. To the church singer is given the gift of an Angelic voice...for the one who is lost is a gift box so delicately wrapped ... It's a roadmap to Salvation. To the lonely He gives a friend ... to the brokenhearted it is a promise of a better tomorrow. There are so many more gifts given ... the list is unending.

The best thing is you don't have to wait for Christmas Eve to get them...all you have to do is ask for them. We don't have to write letters or pay the postage. He just gives them to us. Sometimes He gives them before we even ask. We don't

even have to pay for them, because even before we were born, God looked in the future and saw us, and JESUS paid the price for these gifts as He hung on that old rugged cross. They are always given to us at the exact time we need them and it is always what we want and need, so we never have to exchange them.

Just think of what Christmas would be like without Jesus. For one thing, there would be no Christmas. His Holy Birth made this day CHRISTMAS! Some people don't know Jesus and their life is empty and void. If you know someone who needs Jesus, give them a Christmas present, anytime of the year, that they will never forget ... give them Jesus! Tell them about your Jesus.

Matthew 5:16
In the same way, let your light shine before men, that they may see your good deeds and praise your Father in heaven.

****

LIGHTNING BUGS

I sit on the porch tonight and watch the millions of lightning bugs light up the night. As I sit here and watch them, it brings back memories of my childhood. When we were kids, we lived in the country. We didn't have TV, computer games or much radio, or any other forms of electronic entertainment...so we created our own games.

In May, the lightning bugs would come out. After supper we would go outside into the balmy summer darkness. Lightning bugs seemed to be everywhere. In the night they twinkled like a gigantic Christmas tree. We would catch them and sometimes we'd squash the neon-like light and rub on our arms and faces. (Sounds like fun huh? Don't that just really turn you on?) The light would shine like a neon sign and would stay on us for a long time. Sometimes we would write our names on our foreheads with the light from these bugs. We would play for hours with this magic light glowing. Often we wondered how it worked and why humans didn't have any of this magic light.

Momma would give us a jar. She would punch holes in the lid so the bugs wouldn't die from lack of air. We would chase these beautiful bugs and see how many we could catch and cram in our jar. We would put the lid on it and go show Momma and Daddy our trophy. At bedtime we would set the jar on the dresser and the lightning bugs would light up the dark room like a lantern light. They would really put on a light show for us, sparkling like a beautiful Christmas ornament, continually moving and blinking on and off. It would gently put us to sleep at night just watching them twinkle in the jar.

At times we would bring our jar of lightening bugs inside at night and open the top. They would get out and would span the room from corner to corner. They would shine their little light for everyone to see. There would be so many lights flashing in the room that we would just lay there in bed quietly and awe at the sight. It was such a beautiful sight to see. The little bugs were proud of their lights and would flash them on and off. They didn't try to hide. They were bright enough that they couldn't have hid if they had tried. They seemed to want you to see them and admire them!

When we were saved, God placed a light in our heart. It is the light of Salvation. He wanted us to let it shine and for us to tell everyone we see about the Salvation we have. We were to tell them how they could become saved and get this light in their soul. If the light from the soul of each Christian would shine like these little lightning bugs, earth would be a place of beauty like nothing we have known ... a giant Christmas display, decorated and twinkling. God didn't want us to hide our light under a bushel, but to be proud that you are a Christian and let that little

magic light shine, let it shine, let it shine. May people around you always be able to see the light of Jesus in your soul!

Luke 11:33

"No one lights a lamp and puts it in a place where it will be hidden, or under a bowl. Instead he puts it on its stand, so that those who come in may see the light.

****

TAPS

How many times have you seen a military burial, and heard the haunting sound of the bugle playing "Taps". Have you ever heard the story behind taps? Well, legend has that it began in 1862, sometimes during the Civil War. The place was near Harrison's Landing in Virginia. There was a Union officer by the name of Captain Robert Ellicombe. They seemed to be fighting on a narrow strip of land...his Union Army on one side and the Confederate Army on the other side. It is said that during the night, Captain Ellicombe heard the moans of a soldier. He looked out and saw a soldier lying on the field. The soldier seemed to be severely wounded.

The Captain didn't know if the man was a Union soldier or a Confederate soldier, but he crawled on his stomach, risking his own life to get help for the soldier. When the Captain got to safe territory on his side, he realized that the soldier had died. He lit a lantern, and in the dim light of the lantern, looked at the soldier and gasped....this was his son. It seems the son had enlisted in the Confederate Army without telling his father. This young man was studying music when the war broke out and his father signed up for the Union Army. The Captain was heartbroken and asked for a full military funeral for his son. The Union Army only granted part of his request. He wanted the Army band to play for the son, but the request was denied. The Union Army told Captain Ellicombe, that out of respect for him, they would let him use one musician. The Captain chose the bugler.

The father asked the bugler to play a series of musical notes that the Captain had found in his son's pocket. This wish was granted from the Union Army. This is where the haunting bugle melody, "Taps," was born. This young man had penned the notes on a crumpled old piece of paper and included in the find was the words to the song........

Day is done...Gone the sun...From the lakes...
From the hills...From the sky....All is well...
Safely rest...God is nigh.
Fading light...Dims the sight...And a star...
Gems the sky...From afar...Drawing nigh...
Falls the night.
Thanks and praise...For our days...Neath the sun..
Neath the stars...Neath the sky...As we go...
This we know...God is nigh.....

When I hear the bugle blow "Taps", I have always felt chill bumps because of it's extremely haunting, sad sound. But until recently, I had never heard the story behind it. It is such a simple tune, yet so powerful. Each time I have ever heard that bugle play "Taps", I found a tear in my eyes. I hope that when I hear my last sound of "Taps" here on earth, I will then hear Gabriel blowing his trumpet with "When the Saints Go Marching In!"

God be with you.

Luke 10:20
However, do not rejoice that the spirits submit to you, but rejoice that your names are written in heaven."

****

HALLOWED-EVE

Let's change the meaning of "Halloween!" Let's change it from a holiday for Satan to a celebration of Jesus. Fall itself is a work of art from Jesus. The leaves on the trees are turning from green to rich fall colors...regal and royal. They are a gift from God himself. We will call it "Hallowed-Eve" instead of "Halloween."

The last fruit and vegetable harvest is in the fall. It's just another reason to thank Jesus for the bountiful harvest. The pumpkin could still symbolize the abundant harvest. On the faces of the pumpkin you could carve happy faces, which represent the happiness of a Christian. Or maybe you would carve "I love Jesus" on some of them. The light inside the pumpkin would represent the light of Jesus shinning in our heart and soul. Teach the children to say "God bless you!" instead of "Trick or Treat!" Do away with the eerie graveyard scenes and spooks and monsters. Do displays with Angel choirs singing His praises for a bountiful harvest. Invite a less fortunate family to share your Hallowed-Eve by preparing a meal for them. Or, you could fix up a nice food basket and take it to a needy family. For the centerpiece, use fruits and vegetables and colored leaves in a brilliant display.

Start the tradition of raking leaves in the yard and having a bonfire as the cool night sets in. Gather round the fire and roast marshmallows and wieners. Visit with your neighbor and family and treasure this new "Hallowed-Eve." Have a sort of prayer meeting. Pray for the country, for your family, for the church...for your friends. Sing hymns around the fire. Peal sugar cane for the children. I bet most of the kids now days don't even know what sugar cane is. Make popcorn balls. Turn off the TV, radio, computers, etc. Talk about Jesus. Thank him for the many blessings He has given you...and has given to your friends. Have a costume party, but do away with the gory demons, spooks and monsters. Dress as shepherds, Bible characters, Angels, princesses, doctors, famous people in history. Give prizes for the best. Have fun, but praise Jesus. After all, this is the day which the Lord has made. Let us celebrate Jesus on this day, and not the world of Satan.

Tell your children about this new tradition we are starting...tell your children's children. Hopefully this will change the views of the children of the future. I hope one day, long after I am gone even, I can look down and find that HALLOWEEN has fizzled out, and people now are celebrating HALLOWED-EVE. Maybe someone sitting around the bon-fire will be saying, "Legend has it that this Hallowed-Eve started back in 2003........."

Don't you think it is time we give our hearts and our time back to Jesus? He took time to die on the cross for us so that we could live eternity with him. Let's give Him the praises while we are here on earth!

Psalm 95:6
Come, let us bow down in worship,
let us kneel before the Lord our Maker;

****

UNDER HIS WINGS

There are a few Bible verses that I would like for you to read before I start this story. They are:

Psalm 36:7
How priceless is your unfailing love!
Both high and low among men
find refuge in the shadow of your wings.

Psalm 63:7
Because you are my help,
I sing in the shadow of your wings.

Psalm 91:4
He will cover you with his feathers,
and under his wings you will find refuge;
his faithfulness will be your shield and rampart.

Matthew 23:37
"O Jerusalem, Jerusalem, you who kill the prophets and stone those sent to you, how often I have longed to gather your children together, as a hen gathers her chicks under her wings, but you were not willing.

A while back, Reader's Digest ran an article just after one of the big forest fires out west. It seems as though a fireman was walking through the woods checking for hot spots. He wanted to make sure that fire would not break out again from ashes restarting. He had an old stick in his hand and as he walked, he shuffled the stick in the ashes. Miles and miles he walked, checking each place in his path.

As he came upon a big old tree, completely burned, he noticed something odd at the bottom of the tree. It was a bird, singed and charred. It was just standing there, dead and lifeless. The fireman loved animals, so in his thoughts he whispered "What a shame!" And touched the charred figure with his stick. Out from under the burned carcass, three baby birds came scampering out. This "momma" bird, regardless of the pain at the time of the fire, huddled her babies under her wings, and she withstood torture to protect them. She gave her life for them.

God does the same thing for us, my friend. He died on Calvary, with us under the protection of His wings. When we are troubled or hurting, He gathers us under

those precious wings, and He comforts us. When enemies confront us, we can run under His wings and be safe. Sometimes, we stupidly refuse to let His wings cover us, and that is so sad. There is no pain or heart ache we can go through that He won't be there for us, if we would just let Him...He would gather us under His wings like a momma hen gathers her chicks,...safe and secure. Think about it, my friend. It just doesn't get any better than that! What a God!

****

RAINBOWS

Do you think anything could have looked more beautiful to Noah and his family than the beautiful rainbow that God placed in the sky? This was a promise after the flood of forty days and forty nights. This promise was made to Noah, that never again would God punish the world in this way.

This was the very first rainbow...as a matter of fact, this was the first time that rain fell from the sky. Before this, streams would come up from the ground to water the vegetation and fill the rivers and all. Man had never before felt rain falling from the sky...something that we just take for granted now. I would think that Noah's family was in awe as they looked out of the Ark, across the darkened sky, to see this beautiful arc of colors appear. God gives us our own personal rainbow at times when we feel we are at the end of our "flood." Sometimes we don't even realize that God is giving us our rainbow promise of better things to come....The flood of tears will pass, and we will find comfort.

The clouds represent troubles in our lives... When a family loses a loved one and the tears fall like rain in a storm, and we feel like the night will never end... then an Angel passes over and allows peace in their heart, comfort in their soul, or, God gives us a Rainbow for a promise of a better tomorrow.

The storm surrounds the family of a soldier as he goes off to war, but there is a beautiful Rainbow when he comes home again.

During a serious illness, the storms of worry and pain gather around us. We feel like we just can't stand the pain any longer. We feel we are drowning in the pain. Then, sometimes when we least expect it, God sends us the Rainbow of healing.

Many storms rage around us causing depression and hopelessness. They take our lives and souls and beat them against the rocks on the shore. There is a flood of sorrow and feelings that we don't matter to anyone. The storm seems endless... and just as you think you'll be lost beneath it all, the clouds break and you see that beautiful Rainbow in your heart, and you know everything will be OK.

God wants us to have peace in our heart and in our soul, but we must encounter storms in this life as well as the sunshine. This makes our faith stronger and makes our lives much more meaningful. We appreciate the good things more. If we never had storms in our life, we never would have seen a Rainbow, and just think of how much you would have missed.

Genesis 9:13
I have set my rainbow in the clouds, and it will be the sign of the covenant between me and the earth.

****

HE AROSE ON EASTER

It is getting close to Easter. Easter should be a time of great rejoicing for the Christian. On a cold Christmas day in Bethlehem, Jesus was born. A short thirty-three and a half years later, He died on the cross, was buried in that cold dark tomb.... But on the third day He rolled the stone away and arose to live forever more.

As He awoke from death, He took a trip down to Hell. Can't you just see Satan and his demons, rejoicing...having a party. They thought that they had gotten rid of this Jesus forever. Satan was dancing around with the keys to death and Hell in his hand, shouting the victory. Satan thought he was now in charge, and there would be no one to save souls...because Jesus was surely dead!

As they were celebrating in Hell, they heard a sound behind them, and when they turned, there stood Jesus....glowing in the purest white robe they had ever seen. Satan's mouth dropped open, and he was probably speechless for a minute. The demons backed up, trying to appear invisible... they were all scared. Can't you just imagine Jesus stepping over to the devil and grabbing the keys to death out of his hand? I bet you could have knocked the devil over with a straw!

Jesus told Satan, "You are defeated Satan, and no matter what kind of battle you may fight with the Christians, no matter what torture you may put them through, the war has been won! You lost! You no longer can have the final say with death, for my children will rise again to live with me for eternity. Graves cannot hold them!" And with this, Jesus rises up to Heaven to be with His heavenly father, the keys of death and hell held firmly in His hand.

He did, however, come back to earth to let the disciples and other believers know that He did indeed arise from the clasp of death's hands. Then, He arose to Heaven on a cloud of glory. The Angels that were with Him told the onlookers that one day in the like manner that He was going up, He would come again for His children. Jesus told them that He was going to prepare a place for them, and He would be back.

I think that all of Heaven could hear the wailing cry of Satan as He kept hearing the echo of Jesus telling him...."You have lost the war!" I am sure that the devil had big plans for the world, and he had even bigger plans to destroy the Christians. But, even though he knows he lost, he will never give up. He will always place all kinds of temptation in front of the Christians, hoping that the Christian is not strong enough to fight. A lot of times he wins, but much more he loses. The harder you work for Jesus, the harder Satan works to defeat you. If you are not battling with the devil, then you must not be working too hard for Jesus. I feel blessed that the devil is always trying to trip me up, because this

makes me know that I am doing something right for Jesus. You know friend, the devil can't take your soul, but you can give it to him!

I love Jesus and I will not listen to the coaching of the devil to go with him. I will follow my Jesus and someday, He will come down on that cloud, reach out His nail-scarred hand and welcome me home. How about you?

Romans 8:31
What, then, shall we say in response to this? If God is for us, who can be against us?

****

THE BEAUTITUDES

This letter is taken from Matthew 5:3-10 and is from the NIV Bible. I hope you enjoy it!

<u>God blesses those who depend only on Him. They belong to the Kingdom of Heaven.</u>

God wants us to have faith when we have needs...or depend on Him to lead us in the right paths. He wants us to know that we have no power to do anything on our own. We need to strengthen our faith in Him.

<u>God blesses those people who grieve for they will find comfort.</u>

God is the great comforter and He will wipe away all of our tears and mend our broken hearts and dreams. He is always there for us and He will never leave us!

<u>God blesses those people who are humble. The earth will belong to them.</u>

Jesus was humble. He was not born rich and famous, but in an old stable, and lay on a trough of hay. He came here to serve us and to die for us. He was brought down from royalty to the humble environment of man. We must not let prideful ways stand in our way of Salvation.

<u>God blesses those people who obey Him. More than to eat or drink, they will be given what they want.</u>

God says if we have faith He will give us our needs, but He also knows that we desire things that would make our life better. If we obey His teachings, and give our heart to Him, He will not only give us our basic needs, but He will bless us with gifts of things we want.

<u>God blesses those people who are merciful. They will be treated with mercy.</u>

Jesus is so good and so fair and just. If we are good and forgiving to our fellowman, and we love him and be there for him, regardless of his problem, God will show even greater mercy on us. How can He forgive us though, if we refuse to forgive our fellowman?

God blesses those people whose hearts are pure. They will see Him!

If we have been washed in His precious blood and have asked for forgiveness, then our sins are forgiven, never to be remembered again. They are thrown into a sea of forgetfulness... Then Jesus only sees what is good in us and He will let us live in Heaven with Him and His Father for eternity.

God blesses those who make peace. They will be called His children.

God is love. When we love God, we naturally will love our neighbor. We cannot hate our neighbor, but we must pray for him. Pray that he will turn to God. Live your life so that he can see Jesus in you. We must not gossip about others, or cause stumbling blocks for them on purpose. We must love them as we love ourselves. That way, God will love us and will call us His children.

God blesses those people who are treated badly for doing right, they belong to the Kingdom of Heaven.

If we are persecuted as Christians, and even die for the cause, God prepares a place in Heaven for us. If we stand up for what is right, regardless of the ridicule or punishment, God will reward us in Heaven. When we stand up for Jesus, our reward is even greater. Jesus came to earth and showed us how to live...now it is up to us to do what is right.

Blessed are you my Treasured Friend! May God always find favor with you and may you always make Him proud.

****

ANGER

Do you have a temper? Do you ever lose control and say or do things that hurt others? There are so many kinds of anger.... There is the one who gets angry and keeps it all bottled up inside, never even asking why? It festers and causes health problems. Then there is the anger between husbands and wives... stupid things go wrong.... Supper is late....You're fifteen minutes late... A shirt is not ironed... The grass is not cut. Anger flares up and words of hurt and humiliation are spoken. They make accusations that cut to the core, and can never be taken back.

Then there is the kind of anger between parents, angry at each other, but the child receives the blunt end of it. The children are punished too severely, beaten, or shut up in a room, and sometimes the child has done nothing to be punished for. It is just the anger needing a place to land. The child is confused and hurt, and sometimes this damages them some way for the rest of their lives.

There is the anger that causes one to throw objects, not caring where they land or whom they hurt. Carpenters throw hammers, masons throw bricks, some throw cups, vases, dishes, wine bottles, or just anything handy at the time. Sometimes these objects hit people and hurt them seriously, but at that moment, the angered person could care less.

Anger is aired when someone can't get their way, or always wants to be in charge and others do different things, or sometimes this is just their way of being noticed.

There is the kind of anger that arises when an animal does something wrong or doesn't mind a certain command. The animal is kicked, yelled at or even hit with the fist. I saw a fit of anger once that literally made me sick! I worked on a dairy farm when I was younger. A cow, for some reason, didn't go where she was supposed to go, and the owner actually beat her to death with a two by four as I stood by begging him to stop. (Needless to say, my job at the dairy was soon over!)

Road rage anger can come when a car stops too quickly, turns suddenly, passes you or maybe follows you too closely. The angry driver sees red and shakes his fist at them and yells obscenities. Some people have even pulled out a gun and shot the other driver.

At times a gang member has been so angry that someone was on their "turf" that they shot the trespasser. This was the case for a family of three not many years ago. A mother, a father and a small baby were in a strange town, took a wrong turn and ended up (innocently) on a gang's "turf" and all three were shot and killed.

A child, who cannot get their own way, sometimes gets angry with the parents. They run away from home and find a life of misery. Sometimes they plot and kill the parents. Sometimes the problem is so small, but anger has no reasoning.

The list could go on and on. There is so much anger in the world today. Anger is a gift from the devil. Some people say, "I inherited this temper from my dad." Or "I just can't control it!" or other lame excuses. Some anger is justified, like America was angry when the twin towers were bombed, you are angry with laws that make it legal to have abortions, or angry for the government taking prayer out of the schools. I would classify this as "controlled anger!" If you get your life right with Jesus...He will show you how to control your temper. He will give you the power to do this. He can defeat the devil at any of his tricks, anytime, anyplace....and He can give you a whole new outlook on life.

There is a story about a little girl; we'll call her Courtney. Courtney had a terrible temper. He mother, trying hard to control the tantrums, gave Courtney a hammer and some large nails. She told Courtney, "Every time you lose your temper, take a nail and drive it into this board on the fence."

Day after day, the girl drove the nails...but each day fewer nails were used. One day Courtney came to her mother and said, "I think I can control my temper now."

The mother said, "OK, each time a situation arises that you would have lost your temper, but you controlled it, pull out one of the nails out of the board."

After a while all of the nails were out of the board, but there were a bunch of big, ugly holes left there in the board where the nails were. The mother explained to Courtney, "Each time you lose your temper and say or do something hurtful to someone, it leaves a big, ugly hole in their heart and it hurts. Even after forgiveness, it still hurts."

Courtney then prayed to God not to let her lose her temper again and hurt someone with words.

God is there my friend. If you find yourself in a heated argument, remember this story. Pray about it. If this problem is showing up in a friend or a family member, pray for them. If it is an enemy, pray for him too. God loves you, but not your anger.

Proverb 15:1
A gentle answer turns away wrath,
But a harsh word stirs up anger.

****

THE PLEDGE OF ALLEGIANCE

How many times have you repeated the "Pledge of Allegiance?" Did you ever think about what it was really saying? You know, America was started with a firm belief in God. The government was organized and functioned with God's laws in mind. Families held God in high regard and believed deeply in the Bible. They raised their families in accord with His teachings. Church was declared essential for the family. Children were taught to obey their parents and be kind to one another and respect one another in the church as well as the school. Prayer was never questioned as a part of the school day. Oh, there were, I am sure, those who rebelled, but the majority ruled for God to be over all!

"I pledge allegiance to the flag of the United States of America......" This means you respected the flag and what it stood for. You were proud of your country and your flag. ".....and to the republic for which it stands, one nation, UNDER GOD, indivisible, with liberty and justice for all." Well, there it is. God was so important to this nation that they included Him in their pledge... one nation under God... "...indivisible.." which means it could not be divided. "....with liberty and justice for all..." It offered freedom for all, and justice for everyone. You were given freedom of speech to speak your views about your country or leaders, or your opinion about laws, or problems as you see them... freedom to pray any place without punishment or penalty. We could pray in schools, at ball games or even on a street corner. You were given freedom to express your feelings, attend the church of your choice, freedom to protest things that you deem wrong, and freedom to raise your children as you see fit, according to the Bible. If they needed punishment, you punished them. In the Bible it says, "Spare the rod, spoil the child." We knew that a baby was a living, breathing thing and it was wrong to abort it. That was murder. We had the freedom to teach our children wrong from right and enforce it.

Now...well, the story is a lot different. People no longer seem to respect their flag or their country, nor even their neighbor. Moral indecency is flaunted in front of our children until they don't think it is wrong. To some, freedom of speech means to see how many curse words they can cram into one sentence. They don't care if they offend you or who is standing close. The words to the pop songs would be even more of an embarrassment to the United States if more people could understand the lyrics. But, too many do understand the drug promoting, violence in their songs. I think that freedom should be restated. Freedom of speech is OK as long as it doesn't offend anyone because it is clean and decent. I know we will never think alike, but we must think God-like.

We are not even allowed the freedom to raise our children according to the word of God. They call it child abuse. It is classified child labor if we demand the children to do their chores. This younger generation knows very little about discipline. The next generation will know even less and by the time the third generation gets here, well, may God help them. The devil will have complete control unless we take matters into our own hands, and live by God's rules. Put God back into schools, respect back for one's flag and country. Put the Bible back in the homes...and read it. Read it to the children, and teach them about Jesus. Pray. Take your freedom back...take charge of your children. Teach them to pray and to trust in Jesus. Teach them the love of God and have them in church each Sunday...do not send them to church...take them. You must set the example.

Put the love of God back in your life and back in your home, and you will find more freedom than you ever thought was possible!

Micah 6:8
He has showed you, O man, what is good.
And what does the Lord require of you?
To act justly and to love mercy
and to walk humbly with your God.

****

GIVE...IT WILL COME BACK TO YOU

I know you have all heard the Scripture:

Luke 6:38
Give, and it will be given to you. A good measure, pressed down, shaken together and running over, will be poured into your lap. For with the measure you use, it will be measured to you."

When you give and give freely, it will come back to you. Sometimes you see someone who is really down on his luck and you look in your wallet. There is a five-dollar bill. Well, should you give or not...after all, that money was put back for gas for the car. From a still small voice in your heart you hear God say, "Give."

You obediently give. You may wonder where the money will come from to put gas in the car. When you get home there is a check in the mail. It seems you have overpaid something and they are sending back $10. Wow! You don't always get more money back than you gave, but you do get a lot of extra blessings, and you never really miss the money. It will come back abundantly blessed!

I remember once, I was witnessing to a friend about this. She was poor, but thought this theory was....well, just a theory. I ran a small office out of my home. She was in my home one day and she needed a dollar for the kids at school. I gave her a dollar. Before she left, a lady came in and had five copies made. That was $1.25. She was impressed, but thought, "What a coincidence!"

A week or so later, she came over and said there was a bill that had to be paid and she was short $10. Again I gave. We fixed a cup of coffee and before she left, a man came in and needed to have two documents notarized...that was $10. I always told her, "You see, God always gives it back!"

A few weeks passed and she had to take the baby to the doctor and she had no money. She said, "I know you have given before...and it seems God has always given it back, but this is $100 that I need. I will pay it back later. It would just be a miracle to get this back." And she laughed in spite of her tears.

Well, for some unknown reason, I was able to give her $100. Again we sat down and had coffee and chatted for a while. About five minutes later, there was a knock on the door. As I opened the door, a lady handed me a check for $100. She had owed this to me for doing some bookkeeping for her. It was long overdue, and I really thought I would not collect it.

As I looked around at my guest, she was sitting there holding the coffee cup, while tears streamed down her face. We prayed together and God touched her heart. God is so good! Always give....it may be your last dollar but God will take care of you!

****

THE AWARDS

The other day I sat at my desk pondering. The Emmy Awards were being announced on TV. With pen in hand, I came up with a few awards myself. See what you think about the selections!

The deadliest weapon...
The tongue
The greatest deed....
When Jesus died on the cross for us
The greatest help you can give...
Encouragement
The greatest gift...
When God gave His son for our sins
The greatest insurance policy...
Salvation
The greatest joy...
Giving
The greatest loss...
Your soul
The greatest miracle...
When Jesus arose from the grave
The greatest problem to overcome...
Fear
The greatest resource for a person...
The elderly
The longest day...
Our first day in Heaven
The most beautiful asset...
A smile
The most beautiful thought...
Living with Jesus in Heaven for Eternity.
The most contagious personality trait...
Enthusiasm
The most dangerous person...
A person who gossips
The most destructive habit...
Worry

The most effective sleeping pill…
Peace of mind
The most endangered…
Dedicated preachers and teachers
The most important thing in life…
God
The most powerful book…
The Bible
The most powerful form of communication…
Prayer
The most powerful thing in life…
Love
The most prized possession…
A good name
The most satisfying work…
Helping others
The three most beautiful words…
I love you
The two most power filled words…
I can
The ugliest personality trait…
Selfishness
The world's first & best computer…
The brain
The worst disease…
Excuses
The worst thing to be without…
Hope

Psalm 136:26
Give thanks to the God of heaven.
His love endures forever.

****

GOD LOVES ANIMALS

How great is the power of Jesus? The sun travels from the east to the west each day and the moon the same at night. The stars each have their own place in the sky. They are not anchored there by anything, but, the word God spoke to them. Trees blossom and bloom in the spring, produce fruit and shade in the summer, change to magnificent colors in the fall and are bare in the winter. The animals of the forest are fed even through the winter from the fruits of the various trees and plants. They always seem to find places for shelter. ...squirrels and birds in trees, bears in caves, ground hogs and other animals in holes in the ground. Other animals are tempered to adjust to the outside temperatures and elements such as deer, antelope, cattle and horses. Bees and hornets have hives that confuse the best contractors... beavers make dams under water, yet their homes stay dry.

God seems to have thought of every animal when He made the universe. Every small detail of everything was put into perfect place. The animal instinctively knows just what kind of home he needs to make and just how to make it. He knows if he needs to hibernate through the winter, gather nuts for winter food, and birds know to fly south to a warmer climate for the winter. For animals with fur, God lets their fur get thicker for the winter, and it thins out for the summer. Without reading any books on the matter, they know how to teach their young to hunt, what to eat, where to find the foods, and how to mature into a life of their own.

I really think God loves animals. Look at all the different kinds that He made...the uniqueness of each and every one. He provided many different ways of protection of the animals. Some have horns; some have strong legs and hooves, some bite, yet others like the porcupine can stick the enemy with a quill. The skunk dispenses an awful odor. Some have powerful jaws and teeth, and some have powerful claws.

God tells us in the Bible that He owns the cattle on a thousand hills. He even refers to His children as His "sheep." He said in the end of time that the beast of the wild will be led by a child...and the lamb will lay down with the lion. He said that the beast that ate meat would graze on pastures as an ox. For anyone who is an animal lover, this is a thrill to hear. No animal will be afraid of the other, nor a threat to another. God even tells us that He will come back on a white horse at the end of time. Others in those days will be riding on horses. Death will ride a pale white horse.

Maybe pets that we have loved so much will be in this number of animals. Wouldn't that be great? Well, I guess that is just one more thing we'll have to

wait and see. God has so many beautiful things in store for us; maybe this is just one more beautiful reward....just to see all of our pets one more time.

Maybe we won't even remember our pets and we won't miss them...maybe everything else will be so beautiful and breath taking, we will even forget to ask about them. I just want to walk through those pearly gates, right past Gabriel blowing his trumpet, into Heaven and kneel at the feet of Jesus

Isaiah 11:6
The wolf will live with the lamb,
the leopard will lie down with the goat,
the calf and the lion and the yearling together;
and a little child will lead them.

CALLIE

As most of you know, Callie is my buddy. She is a beautiful red mearle, Australian Shepherd. She is very well behaved and real smart. When we had the dairy, she worked very hard, and was one of the best working cattle dogs around here. When I was widowed in 1995, we sold the dairy, and we both retired.

When we had the dairy, we used to raise sheep, too. The sheep would sometimes get into the calf pens and eat the calf feed. Callie, without being told, would get all of the sheep out of the calf pens, put them back in their pen, and never disturb the calves. It was like she could think the problem out.

When Callie was young, she was struck by lightening...not directly, but it ran underground and burnt her some and scared her to death. She has always since been afraid of lightening and thunder. When there is bad weather, she tries to get as close to me as possible until the storm passes by. But, even though she was terrified, if we had to round up the cows during bad weather, she would faithfully go with me. She would cringe each time lightening would strike or thunder would rumble, but she always stayed with me until the job was done.

Callie could always sense my feelings. If I was depressed, or the world just overwhelmed me, she would crawl up on the couch with me and put her head in my lap. This would give me peace. I have had bad days, and would be crying, and Callie would lick the tears off my face, and snuggle up close to me. She can sense my mood, and whether I am sad or happy, she is there for me. If I have a problem and need someone to talk to, she is always there. Maybe she doesn't know what I am talking about, and maybe she does, but she is always there.

Callie always watched my back when we had the dairy. We usually always had a bull running with the cows on the farm, and sometimes they would get kinda mean. I remember one day I heard a noise behind me. I turned around to see the bull starting to charge me. About that time, Callie grabbed the bull by the nostrils and turned him around while she was in mid air. The bull lost the thrill for the situation after that and he left the scene.

I can remember when Callie was born, fourteen years ago. Her mother was named Cow-li-co. She was also a red mearle shepherd, but she was more hyper than Callie. People really respected her. She got a big charge out of "treeing" them. I don't remember her ever really biting anyone, just a nip or two, but she sure acted mean. Cow-li-co had 2 puppies on that last litter...a male that was almost all white and Callie who was almost all red. I had the puppies up for sale, as Cow-li-co was a young dog and a good worker. But when the puppies were only six weeks old, the mother got out into the road, chasing a stray dog, and got killed. Callie then became my baby.

Callie started working cattle when she was too small to walk the quarter of a mile down to the creek and the quarter of a mile back...so I would carry her down there, and she would help drive them back. Sometimes we would take the ATV and Callie would ride proudly. When she got older and worked better, the cows would just see her and they could come on home. She wouldn't even have to get off of the ATV. When she was grown and she worked cattle, she put her whole heart into it. She wanted to do it right. The cows soon learned that she was not going to tolerate a stubborn cow. A couple of nips on the heel confirmed this. But with all of the impressive nipping, there was passion too. Often a cow gets a sore foot, or she may be heavy with calf, and can't walk as fast as the others. Callie would always walk slowly and just ease these along. It seemed like she knew they had problems, and they weren't just being stubborn. In the summertime, I always had to wait for her to take a quick dip in the creek. She loved water and would take advantage of the cool water.

Callie had only one puppy born alive. (She had several miscarriages before this.) Callie had a very hard time during labor and delivery. The puppy was born completely blind and deaf. I then had her spayed because her health was more important than the money puppies would bring.

Her mothering instinct was always there. She wanted to mother anything little. Sometimes the neighborhood dogs would kill a momma cat. Callie would gather up all of the kittens, one by one and bring them home to me. We would raise them. If the kittens would get out of the box or get hungry through the night, Callie would wake me up. If the kitten would get out, Callie would snuggle it up in her paws and sleep with it. She is a great mother. She has never hurt any "baby." We even had baby turkeys and chickens at one time, and she would watch after them. I am sure it made momma turkey or momma hen nervous at first, but they got used to her always laying around where the biddies were playing. She was a real good baby sitter.

We always fed Callie bones, chicken breast bones, pork chop bones, steak bones, etc. We would always ask her "Do you want a bone?" Then we would tell her she would have to sit. Well one day, I was eating a chicken breast. I heard something behind me, which sounded like "bone." I knew Callie was back there, but I wasn't thinking about her. Again I heard "bone!" I turned around and Callie was sitting by my chair and again she said "bone!" I fed her the whole chicken breast, and for each bite she would say "bone." She still asks for her bones, and sometimes she will say, "I'm hungry". (Not real plain, but audible.) If she says bone real soft, I'll say, "I can't hear you!" and she will speak louder. She is a very smart dog. We taught her to eat at the table with us. Her paws were not allowed on the table, and she had to sit in her chair. She had a certain place at the table to eat, and if someone was in her chair, she would whine and yelp...until the chair was vacated. Her table manners were impeccable. She would eat her dinner, and never bother any one else's. If her bowl would slide back on the table to far, she would just sit and wait for us to pull it back. (No paws on the table!) We could get up from the table and walk away, totally ignoring our plate. She has never

got anything off of our plate. She doesn't even get close to it. She would just sit in her chair and look dignified.

There have been times when the house would be full of children at Christmas. We would put out towels on the kitchen floor and circle the children around, picnic style. Callie would find her a place in the midst of the children to eat her dinner. When the children got up to get more drink or another piece of chicken, Callie would never bother their plate. My husband often said she was people in dog's clothing.

The children learned real quickly that we didn't allow fighting around here! When a couple of children would start fussing or shoving, Callie would charge in and stand between them and bark. At times, when one child would scream, Callie would nip the other one, thinking they had hurt the screaming child.

I went to Albuquerque one time to see my daughter for a week. I left Callie with my son and his family. She loves all of them, but she grieved my leaving so bad, she would not eat but just enough to keep her alive. When I got home, she was like a bottomless pit. For a couple of days, all she wanted to do was eat.

I refer to Callie as my diet pill. When I get a sandwich, usually Callie gets half of it. This is the same for a cookie, candy, popcorn or even a cone of ice cream. (I will eat about half of the cone of ice cream, and then I let her eat the other half. She sure likes that cone.) When I get a glass of milk, she will sit patiently and wait. She knows that I will pour some in her bowl for her.

Callie has long hair and she sheds a lot. When I vacuum the floor each day, I get enough hair to make another dog. Bath time takes a good hour. I put her in the shower and use the blow dryer on her to dry her off. I usually brush her real good while she is drying. She will just lie there and sometimes it seems as she is about to go to sleep. But she is worth all of the effort it takes to maintain her.

Callie is a great watchdog. I live alone but I feel very safe with Callie guarding the doors. She is very protective of me, and I firmly believe that she would lay down her life for my safety, if it came to that. My children left home after seventeen or eighteen years to find a life of their own. I have had Callie for fourteen years. In that length of time, I have doctored her, fed her, worried about her, and protected her the same as I have done for my children. She is very precious to me.

Now, Callie is getting old and her health is failing her. Today I sat on the floor with Callie for hours. She was having a bad day. She has three prominent tumors that swell up, one on each kidney and one on the side. When this happens, Callie can hardly move, and she hurts a lot. I think Callie knows she is losing the battle for life, and like humans, she is scared. I look into her eyes and I see fear, and sometimes I think I see pain. She isn't a whiner, so it is hard sometimes to know she is in pain. This morning she came up to me while I was in the kitchen, and she lay down right in front of my feet. She wrapped both front paws around my ankle and licked my foot. It was almost like she was telling me goodbye. She doesn't want to leave, and I surely don't want to lose her, but animals like people, all must journey down that dark lonely road of death. I pray that God will just let her just slip away when it comes her time. I ask that he will just let her take a nice easy breath and then go…not hurting.

I talked to my pastor today about my broken heart. I told him of Callie's condition and her age and how it was not an option for surgery. He called all of the children of the church together and they all held hands. He explained to them the problem with Callie and how it was breaking my heart to see her so sick and that if she didn't get better, I would have to have her put to sleep. He asked them to pray for her, and pray for me. These little children prayed, and I felt their prayers reach Heaven. Then, my pastor told the children to pray for Callie each night in their prayers.

When I came home from church, Callie was running around and playing. She seemed to be so much better. I could rub her back and it didn't seem to hurt on the tumors. The next day, Callie was like a different dog. She felt good! Within one week, all three of the tumors, that had been so obvious, disappeared.. This was in June of 2004, and so far, she has not had a reoccurrence of them.. I told the children what had happened, but told them not to stop praying for her. I know the prayers of those children saved Callie's life. Jesus truly preformed a miracle, once again for her!

I covet your prayers for Callie. I just want God to take her when it is time, peacefully. I don't want to have to put her to sleep. I don't think I could handle that. God knows when her time is up, and I know He loves her. He has shown me that over and over again.

Matthew 7:8

For everyone who asks receives; he who seeks finds; and to him who knocks, the door will be opened.

****

A ROSE ON MOTHER'S DAY

When we moved to the dairy in 1981, there was a red rose bush growing in the front yard. Oh, it wasn't a beautiful, prize-winning rose. It was fairly common. It would bloom around Mother's Day each year, but that was all of the beauty it would share all year long. It wouldn't have many blooms on it then, maybe four or five.

I would always go to the barn before my husband. (He was feasting on this last cup of coffee and two pieces of toast, which I served to him in bed just before I left out of the house each morning.) On our first Mother's day at the dairy, money was almost non-existent. My husband didn't get me anything for Mother's Day, so, when he came to the barn he gave me a rose off of that scraggly little bush. To me it was beautiful. He would say, "I didn't have any money to get you anything, but here is a rose. This is all I could afford!"

I would pin it in my hair, which I kept long, and would wear it all day. Each year I would look forward to my rose on Mother's day. Then one year, the blooming season was off. When Mother's Day arrived, all of the blossoms had fallen off...not even a bud remained. So, when my husband came to the barn on this Mother's Day, he gave me a stem, missing the rose. It was clear that the stem had once held a rose, but it was only a stem now. I smiled, pinned it in my hair and I wore it all day long. We got a lot of laughs out of it, but no matter if the rose was on the stem or not, it was in my heart. This was only about a week before my husband died. Mother's Day is the second Sunday in May, and he died May 22. The rose bush died that year, and never produced another rose blossom.

God's love, my friend, is sort of like that stem. He is always with us in our heart, even though we cannot see Him. We can see where He has touched....the leaves, the flowers, the sun, the rain, the animals and the humans...as well as everything else, because He created everything! We know in our heart that He is real and that He created the Universe. The amazing thing is that we can keep the "Rose of Sharon", (Jesus) in our heart forever. We can always remember the beauty, the love and the happiness He has brought into our lives.

1 Peter 1:8

Though you have not seen him, you love him; and even though you do not see him now, you believe in him and are filled with an inexpressible and glorious joy,

****

A MILE IN HIS SHOES

As we walk through life, we can't seem to understand the problems of others. We wonder why they can't come to grips with situations in their lives. But, we've never walked a mile in that person's shoes. How would we react in that same situation?

I've never had to walk in the shoes of a mother clinging desperately to a child, and all hope is gone...nor sat in a chair in the doctor's office, only to hear him say, "You have cancer and your time is short." I've never went through a Chemotherapy treatment, scared, depressed and sick, thinking the cure is a lot worse than the disease. I've never had to listen to the jeering because I had a deformity...I have never felt the agony of losing a child or a parent in the war.

I have never had to walk in the lonely shoes of a person who walks the streets and sleeps in the shadows....deprived of a home, food, family or even hugs. I have never had to make the decision of a diabetic who is facing the amputation of a leg. I've never trod in the heart of a mother who watches her child starve to death, and there is no way to get food. I have never had to walk in the footsteps of the man who can't see, the one who can't hear, the one who can't speak, or the one who has no motor skills for his entire body.

I've never marched in stride with a soldier, fighting in a foreign land, cold and scared ...wondering if the next bullet will be his. I have never had to watch as they pulled my son or daughter from a wreck, or walked with the teen who ran away from an abusive, unloving home, and is on the streets, cold and hungry and scared, but no place to go. Nor have I been in the mind of the one who lost all hope to live and took his own life.

I have never been locked inside of a prison, or ever been deserted by family and friends.

I have never had to follow the footsteps of Jesus up Calvary's Hill, even though he done it for me. All I have to do for Jesus for taking that long, lonely walk to Calvary, is to love Him, give Him my heart and ask for forgiveness, as I follow the footprints of love that He laid out before me.

I sometimes find myself grumbling and complaining about my small problems and then I see so many with such heavy burdens that would buckle me, physically and mentally...yet they hang on. They find the strength to go on. Jesus is that strength! Pray for these souls who know only agony and pain. Pray that they may reach for the hand of Jesus and hold on! Pray that you might not ever have to walk a mile in their shoes.

2 Thessalonians 2:16
May our Lord Jesus Christ himself and God our Father, who loved us and by his grace gave us eternal encouragement and good hope,

****

WORDS OF WISDOM

In the world today, there are laws... and there are people to enforce the laws. If you are a child and Momma tells you to clean your room, and you don't, then she will punish you. If you skip school, Daddy will probably be the one to handle that situation. If you speed down the highway, a Highway Patrolman will pull you over and give you a ticket. If you steal, murder, assault, rape, or anything that breaks the law, a Policeman will arrest you and a judge will place you in jail. God has placed the laws of good and evil in our heart so we would know the difference. If you break one of God's laws, He will be your judge. Solomon was a very wise man. In the book of Proverbs he gave us a lot of laws of wisdom. They are not punishable by law, but just good rules to live by. Let me give you a few.

Proverbs 2:6
"All wisdom comes from the Lord, and so do
common sense and understanding."

Proverbs 2:11
"Sound judgment and good sense will watch over you."

Proverbs 3:5-6
"With all your heart you must trust the Lord and not your own judgment.
Always let Him lead you and He will clear the road for you to follow."

Proverbs 3:14
"Wisdom is worth more than silver, It makes you much richer than gold."

Proverbs 11:30
"Live right, and you will eat from the life-giving tree.
And if you act wisely, others will follow."

Proverbs 15:13
"Happiness makes you smile, Sorrow can crush you."

Proverbs 16:31
"Gray hair is a glorious crown worn by those who have lived right."

Proverbs 19:17
"Caring for the poor is lending to the Lord and you will be well repaid."

Proverbs 20:4
"If you are too lazy to plow, don't expect a harvest."

Proverbs 20:29
"Young people take pride in their strength, but the gray hairs of wisdom are even more beautiful."

Proverbs 25:11
"The right word at the right time is like precious gold set in silver."

Proverbs 30:33
"If you churn milk, you get butter. If you pound on your nose, you get blood. And if you stay angry, you will get in trouble."

Ponder these wise sayings in your mind. They are good rules of wisdom to live by. If you need more thoughts of wisdom, read Proverbs. It is full of wisdom for each situation in life. God bless you.

****

10 WONDERS OF HEAVEN

As we travel around the world we see natural wonders that make us stand in awe. These wonders are not man made, but are made by nature, or God Himself. We see "Old Faithful Geyser", "The Grand Canyon", "Chimney Rock", "Carlsbad Caverns", "The melting snow and ice cliffs of Alaska", "Pike's Peak", "Royal Gorge", "Ruby Falls", "Niagara Falls", and so many others. I have been fortunate enough to travel some, and I have found myself in front of some of these wonders, while almost holding my breath for the beauty and magnificence of it all. But regardless of how beautiful some of these may be, the sights of Heaven are even more beautiful. God tells us that we can't even start to imagine the beauty there. Let's let our imagination run wild. What would the 10 most wonderful Heavenly wonders be?

1. The Birth, the Crucifixion, and the Resurrection of Jesus, God's only Son

2. The glory and majesty of Jesus sitting on the throne at the right side of His Father, God

3. The very privilege of worshiping at the feet of Jesus and looking on Jesus' precious face

4. Having Salvation, and by God's mercy and grace, being able to spend eternity in Heaven

5. The sight of the pearly gates of Heaven with St. Peter welcoming us in as Gabriel blows his trumpet in triumph

6. The voices of the magnificent Angel Choir and the rhythm of the Angel Band

7. Seeing the New Jerusalem with our mansion, streets of Gold, the Crystal River and walls of Jasper

8. Walking and talking with the great Saints of old and with our loved ones who have traveled on before us

9. Sitting at the huge table with all of the saved with Jesus Himself, at the Marriage Supper of the Lamb

10. Complete peace, happiness, love and absolutely no threat or scheme of the devil.

I think that this will out-do these earthly wonders to the point that we won't even remember what the earthly wonders looked like. Give your heart to Jesus, my friend. I want to meet you in Heaven. My bags are packed and ready to go!

Ephesians 3:19
And to know this love that surpasses knowledge—that you
may be filled to the measure of all the fullness of God.

****

SOMEBODY SOMEWHERE

How many times have you sat and wondered if anyone cares...if anyone thinks of you? Well, why didn't they ever tell you? Maybe, they just thought you already knew how they felt!

Did you know that somebody, somewhere admires your strength, treasures your spirit, or is thinking of you and it brings a smile to their lips? Someone thinks the world of you and wants to protect you or would do anything for you! Somebody remembers you and wishes you were there to laugh together again.

Someone, somewhere may be alive because of you...or someone hears a song that reminds them of you. Someone thanks God for you because their soul is saved. Someone loves you....someone is praising God for you...someone may have stayed up all night thinking about you and missing you.

Someone is praying that you are well and that you are happy. Someone loves you for who you are and they hope they can always be there for you. Somebody picked a flower today and a tear fell because it reminded them of you and they miss you.

Somebody saw a face in the crowd and they stopped...they thought it was you. Someone is very proud of you and they want to be just like you. Someone loved you when you were young and they love you still. There are those we went to school with, worked with, and grew up with. You think you never cross their mind, but you do....just as sometimes you think of them.

If you don't know of anyone else who thinks of you, well, you're always on my mind and in my prayers. But, greater than this... is the fact that you are always on the mind of Jesus. Before you were ever born, He looked ahead in time and thought of you. He loved you then and He loves you still. When you are lonely and all your "friends" are someplace else, talk to Jesus! Tell Him your troubles, ask Him for advice...tell Him you love Him! Jesus is a true friend. He doesn't gossip, or make fun of what you ask of Him, ignore you, walk away from you, and you never have to wait for Him to have time to talk to you! He is never too busy to listen, or too exhausted to help. Somebody, somewhere truly loves you, my friend....His name is Jesus.

Psalm 116:1
I love the Lord, for He heard my voice;
He heard my cry for mercy.

****

GOOD ADVICE

Here is a bit of advice to help you along your way. I hope you enjoy them!

Love starts with a smile, grows with a kiss,
And ends with a tear!

Good friends are hard to find, harder to leave
And impossible to forget!

Don't let the past hold you back...
You're missing the good stuff!

A good friend is like a four-leaf clover...
Hard to find and lucky to have!

Good friends are siblings God forgot to give you!

When it hurts to look back, and you're scared to look
ahead, you can feel Jesus beside you!

Most people walk in and out of your life...
Only friends leave footprints on your heart!

Some people make the world special just
by being in it!

Every minute spent angry is sixty seconds
of happiness wasted!

The best advice is to let Jesus be your guide. If you listen to Him, you will walk on paths of gold! He will never cause you to stray. He loves you too much to hurt you, for He is your Father and He will never leave or forsake you! God bless you.

Romans 5:3-5

Not only so, but we also rejoice in our sufferings, because we know that suffering produces perseverance; perseverance, character; and character, hope. And hope does not disappoint us, because God has poured out his love into our hearts by the Holy Spirit, whom he has given us.

****

I DIDN'T HEAR NOBODY PRAY

I know most of you older friends have heard the song that goes, "I heard the wreck on the highway, someone's life is now over. Whiskey and blood mixed together, but I didn't hear nobody pray." How often does that line fit as circumstances happen in our own lives?

One woman protested prayer in schools and "I didn't hear nobody pray!" There are nurses who hold the hand of the dying, and "I don't hear nobody pray." (It's against the rules!) A doctor prepares for a life or death operation, but "I didn't hear nobody pray." (Again, it is against the rules!)

The welfare department works with a child, beaten and abused, but "I didn't hear nobody pray!" (She would have lost her job!) A worker in mental health talks to a man. He is angry and hears voices telling him to do evil things...but "I didn't hear nobody pray!" (Their job would be on the line.)

A broken, hurting, football player lies moaning on the field. As he's lifted to a stretcher, no...not one in that crowd knelt and prayed. There's a child with a handicap, trying to find her way in school, bouncing between rude "normal" kids. Hurtful remarks start the tears to flow and her head bows low...but "I didn't hear nobody pray."

The pictures on the TV show the horrors of war and some mother's son won't come home...but "I didn't hear nobody pray." There are children dying of hunger in the United States as well as in other countries, but it seems no one kneels and prays. It's someone else's child, and you aren't very concerned.

There's a sweet old mother in a nursing home. Age has taken most of her memory. The children and spouse stay away. "Oh, she won't know me anyway..." but, she didn't hear nobody pray." An old man sits on the pew on the back row, in a stately rich church. His tears flow for his soul unsaved.... But "I didn't hear nobody pray."

There's an accident on the highway and you look at the crumbled car. "Oh, it don't seem to be anyone I know," so you travel on down the road.... But I didn't hear you pray.

There's an unwed mother...did you pray with her? Did you pray for her? The grief stricken family who just lost their dear loved one...did you pray for them? The sick could surely use your prayers.

But on September 11, a couple years ago, I saw the twin towers destroyed by the enemy. Thousands were killed. I saw the president of the United States, George Bush, stand on the White House steps and pray, with tears on his face. I saw people gather in parks with perfect strangers, neighbors, friends and relatives, join hands and pray! I saw people pray in many other public places. But, soon,

they learned to live with the disasters and they seemed to forget to pray. Anything you pray for, believing, that shall ye receive.

What does it take for you to see that no matter what "people of this world" say, God tells us to pray? We need to pray just as hard and just as sincere when the situation is not ours as when it is. Follow the example of Jesus. Pray unashamed. Pray for your family, for your friends, for the stranger and even for your enemy. Talk to Jesus, my friend. He is waiting for your prayer!

Hebrews 12 :1

Let us run the race that is before us and never give up.

****

GOD SENT AN ANGEL

When my Mother was 92, she lived alone. She is right next door to me but is very independent. She done her own cooking and cleaning and has flowers that would make an ordinary young person turn green with envy, but Arthritis prevented her from walking a lot. During the last year or so, she has had a few falls ... some severe; some she was just shook up, but not hurt! These episodes have put a fear into her days of living alone. One day she fell and required 10 stitches in her face ... another required 16 in her leg.

One morning about 5:00, (way before time for me to get up) I felt restless. I got up, paced up and down through the house, feeling a burden, but not knowing what it was. Finally, I looked up and asked, "Lord, what am I doing up?" He simply said, "Go to your Mother's!" I grabbed the keys to her house and ran over there. As I entered the house, I started calling her and turning on lights because I didn't want to startle her, if she was still sleeping. She answered me from the bedroom. When I got to the bedroom, she was sitting on the floor, phone in hand, with a puzzled look on her face. She had fell...she wasn't hurt, but couldn't get up. She couldn't remember my phone number and she couldn't reach the light. So, she said she prayed. She said, "I was trying to remember your number so I could call. How did you know to come over here!" I said, "God sent an Angel to wake me up, and He told me you needed help!" She tells everyone she experienced a miracle, and God sent an Angel to rescue her! She said she knew that miracles happen all of the time, but she never thought she would experience a miracle like this. God made her feel so important and special, by sending the Angel to wake me up.

God assures us He is no further away than a prayer. Isn't it good to know that if we are one of His children, and we need help ... God sends us an Angel! How loved we must be to have a God so great He formed the universe and everything in it ... yet so personal He hears our every prayer!

Isaiah 41:13
For I am the Lord, your God,
who takes hold of your right hand
and says to you, Do not fear;
I will help you.

****

THE HARVEST IS READY

How many times have you looked out across a field of strawberries, seeing the little red berries hidden in the green leaves? You see vegetable gardens with the vegetables ripe and ready to harvest! Fruit trees, and berry bushes are just waiting for the reapers to harvest them. Grape vines hang heavy with fruit, waiting for the winegrower to harvest them. Cotton fields are white, wheat glistens in the noonday sun, and even maple trees wait for the harvest. When harvest time comes, the owner will seek laborers to get the product harvested at the peak of its season. When there aren't enough laborers on the farm, he may go out and seek others to help him. If there aren't enough laborers, the crop will ruin!

There is a greater harvest ready, my friend. It is a harvest of souls for Jesus. Jesus will soon come for His children, and we need to be ready. You must testify to others, read the scriptures to others, sing to them, pray with them, and get their soul ready for the "great harvest"!

There are not enough laborers, (Christians) working to get the lost ones to Christ. We sit back and wait for someone else to do it ... and they do. Sometimes it is the devil that works with the soul, and he wins it! Did you try, did you pray? Are they forever lost because you didn't care? You need to start bringing the lost to Jesus. You don't have long friend, the harvest is ripe!

Matthew 9:37-38
Then he said to his disciples, "The harvest is plentiful but
the workers are few. Ask the Lord of the harvest, therefore,
to send out workers into his harvest field."

Matthew 13:30
Let both grow together until the harvest. At that time I will tell the
harvesters: First collect the weeds and tie them in bundles to be
burned; then gather the wheat and bring it into my barn.' "

Matthew 13:39
And the enemy who sows them is the devil. The harvest is
the end of the age, and the harvesters are Angels.

We have a Father who is filled with compassion, a Father who hurts when His children hurt. We serve a God who says that even when we stumble, even when we disobey, He is waiting to embrace us and forgive us. God bless you!

****

THE DEPARTMENT STORE

Everyone has a department store story! There are fifty people ready to check out and three registers open! How many times have you waited in line, wondering if you would ever get waited on or not? I think God invented the department store check out lines to improve our patience!

Doesn't it always seem like your cashier is the slowest ... has to get more price checks ... or talks too much? All in all, most of the cashiers are very good at what they do. The problem is not usually caused by them, but those who snail to the register, practicing patience!

Your buggy is laden with merchandise. The little old lady behind you has only a few. Why not let her go ahead of you. While I'm waiting in line and watching people, I listen to them! There is a teen talking ninety miles an hour to her friend on the cell phone. I only hear her side of the conversation..."Yes, Jeannie, I found a real cool blouse and it was only $29.95 ...No I didn't have the money, but I put it on Mom's charge card! ... Oh, it will take her a while to figure out she didn't spend it! ... I can't wait to show it to you!"

Or there's the Mother with three little ones ...one in the buggy, two hanging on to the sides. You can look at Momma's face and see the exhaustion of her entire body. She has a distant gaze, wondering what she will fix for dinner ... maybe she spent too much today .... Did she pay all the bills... run all the errands? .... She checks and makes sure the kids are still there... and hunts her checkbook...! Then the one in the buggy starts to cry. It's past his naptime and he's getting irritable. One of the other children has darted over to the next aisle. She gently holds his hand and brings him back to the buggy. I'm sure she was wishing the line was shorter, or moved faster, but she never complained.

There's the old man who leans on his wife's wheel chair. "Did we get everything on your list?" he asks. As she nods yes, she looks into the old gentleman's eyes and conveys a love that most would envy. Patience and love are waiting there, not worried that the line is slow, or long.

There's the old woman who is ahead of you, bent and frail from old age. She has had her groceries checked. As she is slowly counting her money, she finds she is a quarter short. Frantically and nervously she searches her purse ... and you pull out a dollar and give her. Her smile lights up the area around you, and I am sure that Heaven smiles, too.

Then there is the couple that seem to be in such a hurry. 'They tap their feet in order to get attention and maybe speed up the cashier. They look at the cashier and mumble something about her capability ... mumbles something about this little old lady ..."Just ought not buy what she can't afford...then she wouldn't

hold up the line!" ... But, when their turn finally comes, you glance back and they are at the checkout register. They needed a price check, or the item was more than they thought it was, and they wait.... mumbling and grumbling. They look around and there in line, another impatient couple stands tapping their feet, mumbling about people who are holding up the line....WHOOPS! (People who live in glass houses shouldn't throw stones!)

Don't be so quick to put people down. If the line's long, just get to know the person next to you. If the cashier looks worried that she's not going fast enough, smile and tell her it's OK, you're not in a hurry. Life is not worth the rudeness and impatience of us humans. When you go through the checkout line, think of how well the cashier is handling problems...how tired she must be, how hurtful some people have been with comments, but still when she finishes the order, she thanks you for shopping there, and smiles!

God puts up with all of our stupid impatience and mumblings of discontent, our put downs on others, yet he loves us still... He may not like what we do, but he loves us! He smiles down on us and blesses us, hears our pleas for forgiveness and holds us in His arms as His love surrounds us!

1 Peter 2:20

If you suffer for doing good, and you are patient, then God is pleased.

****

ONE WAY

Have you ever been to a big city that is set up with mostly one-way streets? Have you ever gotten on the one-way street going the wrong way? Well, I lived in Natchez, Mississippi for a year or so, and I really don't like one-way streets!

When I just moved there, I needed to check in at the Employment Office to seek work. The whole family was so helpful ... they gave me elaborate instructions to get there. No detail was missed... the number of traffic lights, landmarks, railroad tracks and everything. I got to the Employment Office without one problem. My dear family, who so carefully directed me up there, had also forgot to map me back home. I encountered the one-way streets, got turned around and lost! I used a half tank of gas... searching for familiar roads, streets or highways to take me home! Finally, after spending a couple of hours "touring Natchez" I found the way home.

Another incident in this city happened when I had to take the kids to the dentist. I was still new in the city and not familiar with the streets. A relative, who lived there in Natchez, volunteered to ride with me to show me the way... so off we went! Right in the heart of Natchez we ran into a street where there were train track runs down the center of the street! We had traveled several blocks, straddling the tracks. Feeling confident this person knew her way around Natchez, I commented, "It's sure good the trains don't use these tracks anymore!" The reply was..."They still do!" I PANICED! "GET ME OFF OF THIS STREET! KIDS, WATCH FOR THE TRAIN! LET ME KNOW IMMEDIATELY IF YOU SEE ONE!"

By now, I had probably turned pale, and I really wanted to just stop the car, bail out, grab the kids and call a "taxi"! After what seemed hours, my guide finally said, "This is the street you get off on..."WHEW!!" We made it without seeing a train. I was so excited to get off the street with the railroad tracks, I failed to see this was a one-way street, and I was going the wrong way! I was already a half block down the busy street, when I noticed that all of the rest of these stupid people were going the wrong way. Then someone from the side yelled, "Hey, Lady, you're going the wrong way! Didn't you see that arrow?" ARROW? I didn't even see the Indian!!! But here I was. I expected each car to be a Police car and I'd get a ticket. I finally found an exit street and took a deep, long breath and thanked God that we made it! Needless to say, my "travel guide" was fired!

As we wander down life's highway, are we traveling down the wrong street? Even though we are not living the way we ought to, do we look at friends and neighbors and comment on how they're going the wrong way? What you need to do is make a U-turn, right there in the middle of Life's Highway and take the

narrow, one-way street to Heaven. Oh there are potholes on this straight and narrow road, because Satan never gives up. But, if you hold out, live right, and love Jesus, you can hold out your hand to Jesus and He will get you through. At the end of the street, the Pearly Gates will open wide and you will be "HOME"!

1 John 4:8
Whoever does not love does not know
God, because God is love!

****

THE DESIRES OF YOUR HEART

Psalm 37:3-4
Trust in the Lord and do well;
dwell in the land and enjoy safe pasture.
Delight yourself in the Lord
and he will give you the desires of your heart.

When we serve God with all of our heart, I know he takes care of our basic needs. He provides food, shelter, and clothing for His children! Even the poorest... (when we believe), has the basic needs. The children of Israel escaped Pharaoh's hand in Egypt. They wandered in the desert for forty years, but their shoes did not wear out, their clothes never wore out or got too small. By this great miracle, their clothes and their shoes seemed to grow with them. Water flowed from rocks and manna was sent from Heaven.

He even provides these necessities for animals, fowl, and fish. The birds have trees to make nest in and eat berries that grow wild, planted by the Master's hand! Worms emerge the soil to entice the birds for a meal. Then there are antelope, deer, moose, elk, cows, horses, etc. The Lord adjusts their fur for the seasons, thinner in the summer, thicker in the winter for warmth and coolness! They are provided trees for shade and shelter, and plants grass and weeds for their munching. Bears feast on berries and fish, provided by God Himself. He even provides the cave and the plan for the bear to hibernate all winter. The squirrels have nuts to eat and a hole in a tree to live in, moles live in the ground and the list goes on and on.

God provides food and shelter for <u>all</u> of the animals, foul and fish. If He goes through this process to feed and shelter animals, shouldn't His children feel assured that He will do the same or even more for us? He has given us a brain to choose to live for Him or the world. Oh, how it must break His heart when we choose the world! But, I believe he loves His faithful children so much...He gives us extra. The little things that we want, but don't especially need! Whatsoever you ask, believing, that shall ye be given! Oh, I don't mean we can just ask for a million dollars and we'll get it, or perfect health, or a brand new car. Sometimes if He would give us these gifts, we wouldn't appreciate them enough and we might think that these things are more important than God is! He knows ahead of time how we would react! All our gifts He gives are based on His sound judgment. Sometimes we lose our health, our property, our money, because we need to be humbled. Sometimes we are given money that will take us through many years, but then some of us are provided with just enough to go from day to day. But, He

still provides. He has a reason for everything. He still gives us the desires of our heart, but He knows just when and why to allow some perfect health, and some are sickly. God always has these things under control.

So don't gripe and whine about what you don't have, just thank Him for what you do have! When you pray for the desires of your heart, remember not to pray selfishly. I once ran a dairy. Economy was bad and we were struggling to pay bills. As I was waiting for the milking machine sanitizer to finish, I sat down on the grass. It was a bed of clover. I found 17 four-leaf clovers. Stupidly, childishly, and selfishly, I wished our money situation would improve! ...(Not our health, our faith, our happiness.... But the money!) It did! About three weeks later my husband died instantly and unexpectedly of a massive coronary. The life insurance kicked in, paid off all the bills and the house was paid off.... I got the money! But I wasn't happy. For my wish, or my prayer, the ultimate price was paid! Be careful what you ask for.

THINGS TO REMEMBER

I was looking over some papers the other day, and discovered something very interesting. I had written down 26 very important things to remember each and every day. If we could remember these things, it probably would be no need for "Paxil" or "Lexapro" or any of the other mood enhancing drugs that so many of us depend on each day to keep our moods in balance. Think about them!

1. **Always allow yourself a sense of humor... after all, laughter is the best medicine!**

2. **Always do your best. Even though someone may do it better, and some will do it worse, but you at least tried.**

3. **Courage and faith will keep you strong.**

4. **Don't count the things that are wrong in your life, count your blessings.**

5. **Don't leave all of the decision making to someone else, that's half the challenge.**

6. **Don't put limits on what you think you can do. You may be missing something great. Try, it may be easier than you think.**

7. **Do even the simplest of things with pride and conviction.**

8. **Inside of your mind and heart are answers to many of life's questions.**

9. **If you dare to dream, dare to live out your dreams.**

10. **It's never too late, as long as there is breath, there is hope.**

11. **Live your life for Jesus. It will be a rich life, not one full of regrets.**

12. **One of life's biggest treasures is people being able to work together.**

13. **One of the best investments here on earth is friendship.**

14. **Pray each day... talk to God and tell Him your troubles...thank Him for**

the blessings.

15. Reach for the stars...aim for your peak, your goal, and your prize!

16. Remember how very special you are to at least one person, and probably lots more.

17. Remember that love goes a long way and heals a lot of wounds.

18. Remember the song, "One day at a time" and live your life, one day at a time!

19. Share your problems. The longer you carry them, the heavier they get.

20. Strive to keep health, hope and happiness alive in your life.

21. Take time to enjoy your family and friends, to smell the roses, and to wish upon a star.

22. Why worry about something that hasn't happened. That's wasted energy.

23. With the love of God, you'll make it through no matter what the devil throws at you.

24. You can make your life what you want it to be.

25. All you need is determination.

26. Your very presence here on earth is really a present to the world. You are a gift from God!

27. You're one of a kind, and no one looks, acts, talks or thinks just like you.

I hope that some of these little quotations will help you solve some of life's problems. If all of these fail, just continue to read your Bible and God will give you the answers to any of your problems. God bless you my friend!

1 Peter 2:11
Dear friends, I urge you, as aliens and strangers in the world, to abstain from sinful desires, which war against your soul.

****

HYMNS FOR OLD FOLKS

As we get a bit older, things take on a different meaning for us. A set of stairs that we used to be able to bounce up in a jiffy, seem steep and takes forever to get to the top. Work that used to be so easy for us is next to impossible now. We used to drive a car with pride and expertise, but now, coordination has left and when our mind says turn left, the car turns right. We used to be so organized, but now we lose everything. It seems to me that even the hymns of old, have taken on a whole new meaning. I have listed some of the songs that have impressed me a lot different now in my older years... I hope you get a chuckle out of them, and if they touch base at your home, you will see where I'm coming from!

1. **SWING LOW, SWEET CHARIOT...**
   (I can't pick my feet up very far!)

2. **AMAZING GRACE.....**
   (That I'm still here!)

3. **WHEN THE SAINTS GO MARCHING IN...**
   (I'll be sitting there watching 'til someone helps me up!)

4. **FARTHER ALONG....**
   (I forget more and more!)

5. **HE AROSE.....**
   (After three tries, I can too!)

6. **PRECIOUS MEMORIES....**
   (I wish I could remember more!)

7. **LEANING ON THE EVERLASTING ARMS........**
   (I left my walker at home!)

8. **I SAW THE LIGHT......**
   (I had the cataracts removed!)

9. **PASS ME NOT O' GENTLE SAVIOUR...**
   (I'm coming as fast as I can!)

10. I'LL MEET YOU IN THE MORNING...
(It will take me that long to catch up with you!)

11. SILENT NIGHT......
(I forgot to put my hearing aids in!)

12. I LOVE TO TELL THE STORY....
(Over and over again!)

Share this with some of your friends that need cheering up. I might not have any control over getting old, but I can surely have a good time getting there!

1 Timothy 2:1
I urge, then, first of all, that requests, prayers, intercession and thanksgiving be made for everyone—

****

TOMORROW

How many times do we put off until tomorrow things we need to do now? When will we learn that tomorrow never comes, yesterday is gone and we only have today? How many times have we passed up the opportunity to tell someone "I'm sorry" or "I love you" or "I forgive you", or even do that special thing for a special person? Once the person is gone, you can no longer tell them face to face. Oh, a lot of times after a loved one is gone, we say these things, but we don't know if the words are heard!

How many times have you told your son, "I'll go to your game tomorrow."? Then you look around and he is a grown man with children of his own. You have missed all of the thrills of a special time in a child's life.

How many trips have you planned to go back home to see Momma and Daddy.... tomorrow. But, before you find the right tomorrow, the phone rings and Momma went to be with Jesus. How many times has she cried because you couldn't find the right tomorrow?

How many times has a spouse gone to work angry with their mate, defiant... too proud to say "I'm sorry"? Then they come up with the lame thought, "I'll make up tomorrow. I'll let them stew a bit." But when he comes home, the argument was their last. The mate is gone and he is left alone and lonely. If only they had not put off until tomorrow, the marriage might have been saved, but, tomorrow never came.

Then there is the one who really loves his wife, but he just doesn't ever tell her... Why, she should know he loves her. He passes a flower shop on the way home and says; "I think I am going to get my wife a bouquet of flowers tomorrow, just to say I love you." But a crash on the highway claims her life and the bouquet now lies on her coffin with a note, "I love you!"

How many times do we live a life of sin saying, "Oh I have plenty of time."? You party, you drink, you do what your heart desires. "One day," you think, "I'll get right with Jesus, but not now. My life is so full of fun and adventure. I just don't have time now." Then you have a Massive Coronary and you're gone before you hit the floor. There was no tomorrow. As your eyes close in death, the only thing you see is the smirk on the face of the devil. "Welcome to Hell. It's party time!"

My friend, nowhere in the Bible did God promise us that He would give us tomorrow. Our time on earth will end as a thief coming in the night. No one knows exactly when. Just be prepared and live your life as you expect this to be your last breath. If you are faithful to Jesus on earth, He will be there for you

when death snatches you away and you can live in Heaven for eternity with Jesus. Oh, pity the soul that waited for the tomorrow that never came!

1 Chronicles 29:15
We are aliens and strangers in your sight, as were all our forefathers.
Our days on earth are like a shadow, without hope.

****

ANSWERS

As we travel through life, we are always hunting teachers. We are always seeking help with life itself. We hunt answers to life's situations..... sometimes never finding answers to the questions. Has it ever occurred to you that maybe we are looking in the wrong place. We are looking in the wisdom of man! The real wisdom is the wisdom of God ... the words of the Bible. No matter what problem we need an answer for, the Bible will show us the answer. Doubtful? Well, let's just take a few of life's problems and prove that their answer is in the Bible!

1. **When we start thinking about all of our problems and get depressed, just think of all the blessings we get. Other people don't need to be burdened down with your troubles, they have enough of their own.**
   (Malachi 3:10 "Bring the whole tithe into the storehouse, that there may be food in my house. Test me in this," says the Lord Almighty," and see if I will not throw open the floodgates of heaven and pour out so much blessing that you will not have room for it.")

2. **Just live one day at a time. This way you can control and conquer sin. You cannot worry about what has been forgiven or what you might do tomorrow. Just live one day at a time.**
   (James 4:14-15 Why, you do not even know what will happen tomorrow. What is your life? You are a mist that appears for a little while and then vanishes. Instead, you ought to say, "If it is the Lord's will, we will live and do this or that.")

3. **Learn to be a giver instead of a getter. Sometimes we expect more out of life than we give. *(Luke 6:38 "Give, and it will be given to you. A good measure, pressed down, shaken together and running over, will be poured into your lap. For with the measure you use, it will be measured to you!")***

4. **Pray every day. Make a special time in your day to be alone with God and thank Him for His blessings. *(Luke 18:1 Then Jesus told His disciples a parable to show them that they should always pray and not give up.)***

5. **Learn to laugh and to cry. Over 70% of all physical problems could be eliminated if we could learn this! When someone cries with you, you are half as sad, but when someone laughs with you, then you are twice as happy. *(Romans 12:15 Rejoice with those who rejoice, mourn for those who mourn.)***

6. **Clean out your closet of life. Throw out the trash and fill it up with good thoughts and deeds. (*Philippians 4:8 Finally, brothers, whatever is true, whatever is noble, whatever is right, whatever is pure, whatever is lovely, whatever is admirable ... if anything is excellent or praiseworthy, think about such things.*)**

This is only a few of the lessons given to you in the Bible by God Himself. The message is free. All we have to do is read it ... pray about it ... believe it ... and receive it! Everything you ever wanted to know about life, is written in this book! READ IT!

****

SALVATION

When we seek Jesus, we receive Salvation. Have you ever thought much about what Salvation means in your every day life? Oh, we know that with Salvation, you can enter Heaven's door, but Salvation in your soul makes life here on earth so much more meaningful. The reward is the greatest! Let's take a look at what Salvation should mean in our lives.

S ... Standing firm for Jesus... even when you know you may lose your life for this cause.

A ... Always listen to Jesus. He will be your Leader, your Comforter, your guide, and your friend, your Counselor, your Father.

L ... Love your neighbor but love Jesus most of all, for Jesus is Love!

V ... Victories are won when you testify to what Jesus has done in your life.

A ... Answer when He calls your name. Say, "Lord, yes, I will go!"

T ... Trust in His word. Read His word. Obey His word!

I ... Invest in your treasures in Heaven. There is no need for earthly treasures.

O ... Obey your Father in Heaven. Whatever He asks you to do, do it with a happy heart, and the rewards will be greater than your mind can imagine!

N ... Never think that you don't need Jesus in your life. That is the biggest mistake you can make!

Acts 4:12
Salvation is found in no one else, for there is no other name under heaven given to men by which we must be saved."

****

OLD CHAMPION

When we ran the dairy, we usually had some of the kids or grandkids over most every weekend. We always found little chores for them to do. Feeding the calves was one of the more popular ones. The children would play with the calves, feed them the bottle, and then to pacify the calves while the others were finishing eating, they would let the calf suck on their fingers. Sometimes, from the look of the "slobber" on their arms, the calf must have almost swallowed the whole arm! Calves would even lick their face and hair if they got close enough.

They would help tote buckets of feed to the older calves and put hay and water out for the little ones. When we got a 4-wheeler, we would load them up in the bed of it, (it had a little bed on it like a dump bed,) and we would ride all over the pasture. But, before we got the 4-wheeler, we had to walk to the creek to get the cows. They would usually have to run through the cold water of the creek, barefoot in the summertime. In the wintertime, they wore rubber boots, but would usually have to wade out into the creek, just to see how deep they could go before the water came into the boots... Then you'd hear, "Oops, Maw Maw, the water went in my boots!" I'd empty them out, slip them back on the child and we would "slosh" home. The cows we had were very gentle, but sometimes we would have a bull there in the pasture, too. We usually had nice gentle bulls, but every now and then we would get one that wouldn't be very friendly.

We had one named Champion. He was a large Holstein bull. To those who don't know, a Holstein is the black and white spotted cattle....The cows make excellent dairy cows. Anyhow, Champion weighed close to a ton. Most of the time he was OK, but he could show his mean streak on his bad days. He once got mad at my father-in-law and butted him into the truck. Luckily, he wasn't hurt. But, my husband thought Champion was just having a bad day. He never seemed to bother my husband or me. One day, two of the small children were helping me to get the cows up to the barn. They were walking beside me and we were talking and laughing. The old bull turned around and saw them and started snorting and pawing dirt. I told them to get behind me and walk behind me....and not to let the bull see them. I also gave them the quick lesson in survival.... If he turns around and starts for us... RUN to the closest fence and get under it ... and fast!

As long as old Champion couldn't see the kids, he was OK. But, if one peeped their head out to look around me, the bull would sense it and get an attitude again.

Finally, we made it to the safety of the barn. My husband just could not believe that old Champion acted up....he thought the kids might be teasing him

or something. Then the very next day Champion made a big mistake! He charged my husband...the next day he took a ride to the sale barn and was sold.

We can compare old Champion to Satan. He sees our weaknesses and he attacks. He does everything in his power to destroy us...(to cause us to sin.) Then we step behind Jesus and there isn't anything he can do but snort and paw. The ability to fight our weaknesses grows stronger when we walk in the footprints of Jesus!

Isaiah 41:13
For I am the Lord, your God,
who takes hold of your right hand
and says to you, Do not fear;
I will help you.

****

MOMMA'S APRON

Back when I was a kid, the most important piece of clothing for a country woman was her apron. She usually didn't have many dresses, and these aprons protected them from dirt and stains. An apron was easier to wash and iron than a dress, too. I can't remember seeing Momma or my Grandma without their apron on when they were home. They were made from scraps, so Momma, like most other women, had a lot of them. She sometimes had to change them quite often during the day.

The aprons were sometimes plain, sometimes trimmed with "rick-rack", and sometimes embellished with a ruffle. There were kids that liked nothing better than pulling the apron strings that were tied around Momma's waist, while she had her hands full, and then watch and giggle as the apron fell to the floor. But, besides protecting Momma's dress, it had a hundred other purposes!

I remember how Momma would wipe her hands on it while cooking dinner. It was also used as a handy potholder to get the hot pans off the stove. Sometimes, she would spit on the corner and wipe a smudge off a child's face, or clean ears. Sometimes it wiped away a tear of a broken heart or a scraped knee.

The apron could be used to cover chilled arms as one stood outside talking to the neighbor. It was used a many a time to wipe the sweat off her brow as she stood over the hot stove on a summer day.

The apron served as a basket for bringing in the vegetables from the garden, then served as a container to put pea hulls in to take back out and throw away. That old apron could surely hold a lot of produce! When she went to gather eggs from the chickens, it was the perfect soft container. The apron held baby chickens, newly hatched, as she carried them to the warm little pen that would become their new home.

I have seen Momma use the apron tail as a fan on those muggy and hot days of summer. The children could sit in Momma's lap, with no fear of ruining her dress with the dirt or the mud. This same apron held splinters for the fire in the fireplace or the stove. When company arrived unexpectedly, she would quickly remove it and use it for a dust cloth on the way to the door. It has been used to flag down the mail carrier to pick up a letter. The perfect gift for a country woman back then was an apron. The only place you see aprons now is in restaurants. Even thought they would still work just as good, for just as many reasons, (maybe more) people just don't wear them anymore.

Nothing has replaced this unique item. It would be hard for something so common to be invented to do so much! Just as the apron protected Momma's clothing, Jesus protects us from Satan's snares. He even carries us like Momma

gently carried the baby chicks in her apron. I guess we could refer to Him as our "Apron In Life!" He is always there for us. As long as we hold on to His hand… Satan cannot "soil" our soul. God bless you.

Matthew 28:20
And teaching them to obey everything I have commanded you.
And surely I am with you always, to the very end of the age.

JOE, THE BARNYARD MOUSE

Have you ever listened to a friend tell you of their problems and wondered or verbally asked, "What does that have to do with me?" Sometimes we coldly think that if we are not directly involved in a friend's problem, we have nothing to worry about. Well, I think that one person's problem could affect a lot of people at times. Here is a little farm story that you might enjoy!

There was a little barn mouse named Joe, who had lived at the old farmstead for many years. One night while waiting for the kitchen to be vacated, he peeped through a small crack and watched as the farmer's wife, Mrs. McDonald, excitedly opened a package. She smiled. Joe thought, "What was this gadget?" He read the paper...."Mouse Trap". This thing was deadly. Joe ran to the farmyard telling each one of his friends of the fate that seemed to await him. How was he going to get food from the kitchen now?

He ran into the pig, Porky, who was playfully wallowing in the soft mud, and told him. There were tears in Joe's eyes as the told Porky about the trap. Porky kinda chuckled under his breath and asked Joe how that concerned him? "There is nothing I can do," said Porky, "but pray for you. I will keep you in my prayers!"

Then he came upon his friend Clucky, the chicken, who was busy pulling a fresh worm out of the ground. Joe told Clucky of the awful device he had seen. Clucky only responded by saying, "Joe, I can see that this bothers you a lot, but it doesn't concern me. I am busy and don't have time to be bothered with this."

As Joe's head hung even lower, he came upon Bossie the cow, as she munched on a mound of green grass. He told her of his dilemma, but she only took a moment to reply, "Like wow, Joe. What am I supposed to do? How does that concern me? Duh! Am I in grave danger?" And she licked her lips and took another bite of the sweet grass.

Well, on and on around the barnyard Joe traveled. No one would lend a sympathic ear. So, Joe figured he would just have to go get his supper and try to avoid the deadly fate. Joe's head hung low, and his heart was broken thinking about the answers of all of his friends. He would have to face this alone and just hope he would not come upon the deadly trap.

That very night while Mrs. McDonald slept, there was a loud snap. Mrs. McDonald awoke with a start, got out of bed, and rushed to see what she had caught in the trap. In the dark room she did not know that she had caught the tail of a venomous snake. When she neared the trap, the snake bit her. Mr. McDonald took her to the hospital. Finally, Mrs. McDonald came home but started running

fever. Now, anyone knows that chicken soup is best for fever. So, Mr. McDonald took his hatchet to the farmyard for the soup's main ingredient, Miss Clucky!

Mrs. McDonald got so sick that friends and neighbors would come and sit with her, and take care of her around the clock. Times were very hard, so to feed them, Mr. McDonald barbecued Porky.

The farmer's wife didn't get well. She continued to get worse. As a matter of fact, she died. She was well loved and respected in the community, and so many people came for the funeral, he had Bossie butchered just to feed them.

The next time someone you know is facing a problem and you think that this is just their problem and it doesn't concern you, then you had better think again. We are all God's children and we need to share each other's problems. Laugh with those who laugh and cry with those who cry.

2 Corinthians 1:4

Who comforts us in all our troubles, so that we can comfort those in any trouble with the comfort we ourselves have received from God.

****

CHURCH SIGNS

Every place we go there are signs. We receive 90% of all of our information on signs. One sign tells us that a town is just a mile away. Some tell us that there is a fast food place on the next exit. Another sign tells us to buckle up, or the speed limit is 70 mph. There are all kinds of sizes and shapes of signs. Signs are found everywhere.... On barns, flagpoles, billboards, flashing lights, marquees, neon lights, on buildings, and the list goes on and on. As I have talked to some of my friends and rode around different places, I am amazed and amused with messages on church signs.

"FREE TRIP TO HEAVEN- DETAILS INSIDE".

"SEARCHING FOR A NEW LOOK? HAVE YOUR FAITH LIFTED!"

"IF YOU KEEP KNEELING, YOU WILL BE IN GOOD STANDING"

"EXERCISE DAILY! WALK WITH THE LORD"

(On a pair of hands holding stone tablets printed with the Ten Commandments, complete with a sign reading:
"FOR FAST RELIEF-TAKE TWO TABLETS"

"SIGN BROKEN...MESSAGE INSIDE THIS SUNDAY"

"DO YOU NEED HOME IMPROVEMENT?
TAKE YOUR FAMILY TO CHURCH."

"THIS IS A SOUL FILLING STATION"

"GIVE GOD WHAT IS RIGHT, NOT WHAT IS LEFT"

"THE BEST VITAMIN FOR A CHRISTIAN IS B-1"

"THIS WORLD HAS MANY CHOICES ... ETERNITY HAS TWO"

"THE BEST THING TO SAVE FOR YOUR FUTURE IS YOUR SOUL"

"UNDER THE SAME MANAGEMENT FOR OVER 2000 YEARS"

"SOUL FOOD SERVED HERE"

"YOU CAN GIVE WITHOUT LOVING, BUT YOU CAN'T LOVE WITHOUT GIVING"

"DON'T GIVE UP...MOSES WAS ONCE A BASKET CASE"

"COME EARLY FOR A GOOD SEAT IN THE BACK"

"DEAR GOD, I HAVE A PROBLEM. IT'S ME"

"NEWS FLASH....THERE IS AN EMPTY TOMB IN JERUSALEM"

"SPRING INTO LIFE WITH JESUS"

"SEVEN DAYS WITHOUT PRAYER MAKES ONE WEAK"

"K-MART ISN'T THE ONLY SAVING PLACE"

"IT'S HARD TO STUMBLE WHEN YOU'RE ON YOUR KNEES"

"WHAT PART OF <u>THOU SHALT NOT</u> DON'T YOU UNDERSTAND"

"MOST FOLKS WANT WHAT THEY DON'T NEED AND NEED WHAT THEY DON'T WANT"

"THE WAGES OF SIN IS DEATH...REPENT BEFORE PAYDAY"

"NEVER GIVE THE DEVIL A RIDE...HE'LL ALWAYS WANT TO DRIVE"

"LIFE HAS MANY CHOICES...ETERNITY HAS 2 ...WHAT'S YOURS?"

"WORRY IS INTEREST PAID ON TROUBLE BEFORE IT IS DUE"

"THOSE WHO ARE FAITHFUL WITH LITTLE, ENJOY MUCH"

"DON'T PUT A PERIOD WHERE GOD HAS PLACED A COMMA"

"DON'T WAIT FOR A HEARSE TO TAKE YOU TO CHURCH"

"WE SHOULD BE MORE CONCERNED WITH THE ROCK OF AGES RATHER THAN THE AGE OF ROCKS"

"PREACH THE GOSPEL AT ALL TIMES... USE WORDS ONLY IF NECESSARY"

"A CLEAR CONSCIENCE MAKES A SOFT PILLOW"

"BEAT THE RUSH, COME TO CHURCH THIS SUNDAY"

"GOD ANSWERS KNEE-MAIL"

"TRY JESUS...IF YOU DON'T LIKE HIM THE DEVIL WILL ALWAYS TAKE YOU BACK"

"CAN'T SLEEP, COUNT YOUR BLESSINGS"

CAN'T SLEEP....DON'T COUNT SHEEP, TALK TO THE SHEPHERD"

"TO BELITTLE IS TO BE LITTLE"

"FIGHT TRUTH DECAY...STUDY THE BIBLE DAILY"

"THE BEST WAY TO STAND UP TO THE WORLD IS TO KNEEL BEFORE GOD"

"JESUS IS COMING ... GET RIGHT OR GET LEFT"

"HOW WILL YOU SPEND ETERNITY... SMOKING OR NON SMOKING?"

"FREE MASTER'S CARD ... APPLY INSIDE"

"COME WORK FOR THE LORD. THE WORK IS HARD, THE HOURS ARE LONG AND THE PAY IS LOW, BUT THE RETIREMENT IS OUT OF THIS WORLD."

"THIS IS A C H _ _ C H. WHAT IS MISSING→ (U R)"

"CARVE YOUR STUMBLING BLOCKS INTO STEPPING STONES.....INSTRUCTIONS INSIDE"

"1 CROSS + 3 NAILS = 4 GIVEN"

"IT'S NOT WHAT YOU GATHER BUT WHAT YOU SCATTER THAT TELLS OTHERS WHAT YOUR LIFE IS ALL ABOUT"

"JESUS IS BOSS BECAUSE OF THE CROSS"

"LET GO OF EVRYTHING BUT JESUS"

"IF YOU DON'T LIKE THE WAY YOU WERE BORN, TRY BEING BORN AGAIN"

"I LOOKED FOR A POT OF GOLD AT THE END OF THE RAINBOW, BUT I FOUND IT AT THE FOOT OF THE CROSS"

" YOU MAY NOT BE WHO YOU THINK YOU ARE, BUT WHAT YOU THINK ... YOU ARE"

"DUSTY BIBLES LEAD TO DIRTY LIVES"

"ITS NOT WHAT YOU GATHER, IT'S WHAT YOU SOW THAT DETERMINES THE QUALITY OF YOUR LIFE"

"IN THE END, IT'S NOT THE YEARS IN YOUR LIFE THAT IS IMPORTANT, IT'S THE LIFE IN YOUR YEARS"

"RUNNING LOW ON FAITH? STOP IN FOR A REFILL"

**"THE SON WENT DOWN
THE SON ROSE"**

"BE A FOUNTAIN, NOT A DRAIN"

I thought these were some good examples. People look at a lot of signs...they don't even read most of them. Signs are so commonplace that only the unique ones really stand out. If you are ever out and just riding around up and down the highway, look at the signs.

When you read your Bible, look at the signs. God has given us the signs of the end of the times. He has written it down in the scriptures. Have you read it? Do you take heed to it? Are you listening? God is coming again soon. The signs in my Bible show that it may not be long. Friend, get your heart and soul ready for this big event! Know that when He comes and you lift your hand up to Him, He will lift you out of this old world and plant your feet on the golden streets of Heaven!

Psalm 95:6
Come, let us bow down in worship,
let us kneel before the Lord our Maker;

****

TODAY

Have you ever thought about how to make today a real good day? If you try just a little, your day could be great! You will probably have to pray a lot in order to make this work, but God loves for you to talk to Him. When you run into someone who is having a bad day, and for some reason they think you caused the problem, do not strike back. If someone is rude or impatient with you, smile and be nice to them. Who knows, this may even make their day better too.

If someone in your midst becomes your enemy today, and treats you badly or harshly, ask God to bless them. We must understand that sometimes the "enemy" may be a family member, co-worker, or even a stranger.

No matter what we hear, we will not gossip. Ask God to help you be careful what you say. You could change the subject or just walk away, or say, "God doesn't like for us to gossip!"

Suppose you come upon someone whose burden is heavy. It could be a stranger or a friend. They are sad or trying hard to do something. Could you stop a minute and talk to them? Or, maybe if the burden is physical, lend a hand...tote a package, open a door, smile. This may lift the spirits of this person. Maybe their day will go better after seeing your smile and hearing a kind word.

If someone says something or does something, either intentionally or unintentionally, to hurt your feelings, forgive them. We don't understand the circumstances behind the words. Maybe this person was extra tired, sick or just down. This could be the driver that cuts a little close, or the sharp word from someone in your midst. Maybe it is the words that someone doesn't speak that hurt. Forgive them as Jesus forgives us.

There are so many opportunities out there for you to do something nice for others. The little old lady at the checkout counter, just a little short of money. Give her a dollar or two. You will never miss it! Open a door, let someone in the line ahead of you, say a kind word, help the old man at the fast food place tote his tray to his table, buy a stranger dinner, or a cola, or a cup of coffee and the list goes on and on. God will surely bless you. The most important blessings are received from doing things anonymously. Treat others the way you would like to be treated. Don't pick and choose who you will practice this with, treat everyone you meet like this. You will lift your spirits just as you will lift the spirit of the other person.

Today, if you see someone who seems to need a little cheering up, take a minute and help. They may be having a bad day and really need a friend. Your smile, your words, your expression of support could make a lot of difference with someone wrestling with life.

Pamper your body today. Eat a little less and try to eat only healthy foods. Exercise just a little more, walk up the steps instead of using the elevator if you can. Thank God for your body. After all, this is His temple!

Spend a little more time in prayer today. Begin the day by reading the Bible or something spiritual. Pray before you start your day. At some time during the day, find a quiet place and listen to God's voice. Thank Him for your blessings and ask for His guidance.

If you live your day by these simple rules, you will find you are walking closer to Jesus and you are a much happier person. The troubles that usually get you down don't seem to bother you anymore. Your friends and loved ones will notice the difference, and that will make them happier.

Jeremiah 29:11-13

For I know the plans I have for you," declares the Lord, "plans to prosper you and not to harm you, plans to give you hope and a future. Then you will call upon me and come and pray to me, and I will listen to you. You will seek me and find me when you seek me with all your heart.

****

THE FLOWER GARDEN

Each day as we go about our way, do we even think of how much our life affects others? Think of life as a flower garden and the ground is rough and hard. No plant would ever grow here. But as we live our life for Jesus, others see our works and our faith, and this tends to make the ground soft and rich, ready to grow flowers.

We then witness to others about Jesus. This plants the seed in that soft, fertile ground. The potential flower (or person) starts to think about what you've said. Then along comes another child of God and witnesses to this potential flower, and this waters the seed.

The seed starts to sprout, putting out roots in their faith in God... reading the Bible, or going to church, sincerely hoping to change their life and grow in Christ. At church one Sunday, this potential flower walks the aisle and asks Jesus into their heart and their whole life starts to change. This makes the seed sprout and reach out in all directions, hungry for the word of God. God reaches down and touches it and it grows into a beautiful plant...(a Christian). With God's touch, it starts to produce beautiful blooms and someone someplace else watches the way this Christian lives their life. Others start asking the beautiful flower how it grew to be so beautiful and bountiful..... and it witnesses to them about Jesus, and the cycle goes on and on, and another flower garden is planted.

God permits this cycle to go round and round and blesses us each time we prepare the soil or plant the seed or water the ground. But only God can make it grow and bear fruit!

Keep on planting flower beds my friend. Your blessings will be many!

Psalm 63:1-3
My body longs for you, in a dry and weary land
where there is no water. I have seen you in the sanctuary
and beheld your power and your glory. Because your
love is better than life, my lips will glorify you.

****

VETERAN'S DAY TRIBUTE

It is almost Veteran's day...a day to honor our armed forces... for the ones who are serving, the ones who served and lived and the ones who served and died. Each is a hero in his or her own way. They put their life on the line someplace at sometimes, just so America could remain free!

Most of the ones who have served in the armed services, no matter which branch, were very proud to put on their uniform and represent our country. They often fought for causes they couldn't understand, or some they didn't really believe in, but they served with their hearts.

Some served in wars where the very people they were protecting, protested their efforts and treated them as criminals when they returned. Some are still fighting battles in their minds. It just won't go away... but, you can sleep at night peacefully and safe. Their nights are filled with nightmares and sights and sounds beyond human imagination. You should be forever grateful to them and tell them how much you appreciate them.

If you have served in the armed forces, I appreciate you. If someone you know has served... tell them thanks! Pray for the families of those who didn't return.

We Christians are serving in the army of God, and we must march with our heads held high, for our goal is Heaven. Some people protest this and want God separated from schools, pledge of allegiance, families, sports and morals. One day God will separate them from the gates of Heaven.

Psalm 3:3
But you are a shield around me, O Lord;
you bestow glory on me and lift up my head.

JESUS IN YOUR LIFE

What does it mean to have Jesus in your life? Well, it means that you have Salvation and you have a reservation in Heaven at the Marriage Supper of the Lamb! It means you are never alone, and you always have someone to tell your troubles to!

He protects you with an army of Angels when you need help. He provides for your every need. He can hear you anytime you call, whether you are in a nursing home, a prison, your home, a church or anyplace else...whether you shout or you whisper. When you are truly sorry you have sinned, He answers your every prayer, in His own way and in His own time. He may not answer them exactly like you thought you may have wanted, but He knows best and He answers each one with love and care! Each prayer that goes up, comes back abundantly blessed!

He forgives you when you ask, no matter what you do, if you only ask from your heart. He gives you strength to do what is right and resist evil. He has the power over the devil and the demons cannot take your soul. The war is won and he gives you the power and fortitude to fight the battles, confident of victory.

Jesus rewards you with blessings too numerous to count when you work for Him. He and the Angles rejoice with each victory you win. Jesus holds you in his arms when your heart is broken and with His own nail-scarred hands, He will wipe away your tears. He will give healing, when earthly doctors say there is no hope, for He is the "Great Physician." He takes your burdens and carries them for you.

He sends you Angels to guide you; friends to love you and prayers from loved ones to keep you on the right path. He gives you the promise of a better tomorrow in Heaven with Him and your very own mansion is being prepared for you!

Jesus loves you, leads you, guides you, protects you, and will give you your heart's desires. Why, He would even move a mountain for you, if you only asked. With Jesus in your heart, feel assured you are loved beyond measure. He is your Father and you are His Child.

Psalm 34:17-18
The righteous cry out, and the Lord hears them;
He delivers them from all their troubles.
The Lord is close to the brokenhearted
and saves those who are crushed in spirit.

****

THANKSGIVING

Here it is Thanksgiving again. We have so much to be thankful for! Do we really think of this day as a day to give thanks, or do we just think of it as a day to enjoy a big turkey dinner and a football game and a big parade? Do we often forget all the things God has given us that we should be thankful for? Why don't we just sit for a moment and try to think of just a few of the wonderful things that God has blessed us with!

T ..... Time for being with families, Trials in life that have made us wiser and brought us closer to God....

H .... Heaven for our home, Hearts full of love for our Brothers and Sisters, Hands that fold to pray ...

A .... Angels to watch over us, Answers to our prayers ...

N .... Natural wonders, Nature's beauty ...

K .... Kisses from loved ones, Kindness from Friends ...

S .... Salvation, free just for the asking, Sunrises, Sunsets, Smiles ....

G .... Good news from the Bible, Grace and Glory from our Savior ...

I .... Inspirational music to worship with ...

V .... Victories over Satan, Valleys to grow in ...

I ..... Idols forsaken in order to worship Jesus ....

N .... Neighbors to fellowship with ...

G .... God's great Love and Forgiveness ...

This is only a list of a few of the things to be thankful for. You could make a list of your own! We should be thankful for the roof over our head, a warm bed to sleep in, and food on the table. There are so many that don't even have that. Pray for them my friend! This makes you rich in their eyes. Oh, what some would give to have just one day to be inside a warm house, sit at a table with abundant food to eat, or lie down in a clean, warm bed to sleep. Remember these souls, pray for them! If it weren't for the grace of God, this may be you instead of them ...

Psalm 100:4
Enter his gates with thanksgiving
and his courts with praise;
give thanks to him and praise his name.

****

WINTER MEMORIES

The weather is finally getting cooler. Today, it actually felt like late November. I don't know where you are from, but down here in southern Mississippi, the winters are usually very mild. In my lifetime, I have seen very little snow and only one or two ice storms that I can remember. Here we usually experience maybe a frost before Christmas, possibly a freezing night or two. Winter brings all kinds of memories to our mind. What does winter bring to your mind?

Do you hear sleigh bells and look to see a horse drawn sleigh emerging from a street? Can you picture people in the sleigh covered with a warm blanket and maybe singing Christmas Carols? Is your memory one of Christmas decorations that are so extensive they boggle the mind? Can you see Carolers standing in front of your house in the snow and the cold, singing Christmas Carols?

Do you think about snow falling and wind blowing and feeling chilled to the bone? Does your memory take place on top of a ski slope and you get ready to descend? Or is it a picture a frozen pond and ice-skating? Can you remember visiting Grandma and Grandpa, and the snow on the roads and the car moving so very slow? Does it cross your mind that some people have no home to live in and they are out there facing the rain, sleet, snow and the cold day and night, with thin, worn clothing and hunger in their stomach?

You can see the children so bundled up they can hardly walk, playing in the snow, making snowmen, throwing snowballs, or riding some makeshift sled down the hills. Can you picture riding down a country road, watching the smoke curl out of chimneys and think of the nice, cozy warmth inside? Some think of the time they gathered in the middle of the snow, by a half frozen water hole, and going for a swim...and then hope they didn't die of pneumonia. Sometimes couples sit on the porch and watch the snow fall. Cold weather brings to mind football games, a hot bowl of soup, a cup of hot chocolate or a hot cup of coffee.

Does your memory consist of shoveling snow off the sidewalk, going inside to warm up, then looking out to see the snow had covered the sidewalk again? Think of the puppy who has never seen snow and tries to walk on the soft stuff. You watch as it rains, sleets and the streets freeze over. People slip and slide, trying to walk and cars seem to have a mind of their own. Does your winter memory include water pipes freezing and bursting, and you are out in the cold and the wind trying to fix them, while your hands have lost all feeling and your whole body is growing numb?

Do you think of that cold Christmas day when Jesus was born in Bethlehem? He was a King and yet He was born in the cold and laid in a feed trough. He humbled himself to man, so that we would humble ourselves to the Father. We

need to get our hearts ready so that when Jesus calls, we can go to Heaven with Him. Sometimes, people think that the winter of our lives is when we grow old, but, not necessarily so. I think the winter of our lives is nearing the time to end our time on earth, and hopefully we will be ready to go on to our Heavenly home. Some are in the winter of their life and don't even know it. They have not asked for forgiveness from their sins, so their soul will not be ready for Heaven. Be ready my friend, you don't know when your name will be called!

Romans 4:7
Blessed are they
whose transgressions are forgiven,
whose sins are covered.

****

CHRISTMAS IN HEAVEN

As we near the Christmas season, and we put up our trees, plug in the lights, send the Christmas cards, do we ever think what Christmas in Heaven might be like? Let's just close our eyes and dream of Heaven... and the date is December 25.

There is a party going on! It is the birthday of Jesus! All around us we hear beautiful Christmas music sang from the Angelic Choir. Songs of praise and worship and thankfulness for the baby that was born long ago in Bethlehem can be heard from all those in Heaven. Melodies from harps and other instruments fill Heaven. There are no Christmas trees with lights twinkling and blinking, but there is the light of Christ, reflecting off the jeweled walls of the mansions and the streets of gold, and it sparkles in an iridescent array of light. Angels and Saints gather around the feet of Jesus to praise and worship Him. They proclaim their love for Him. Think of the rejoicing and the happiness in Heaven each time a soul is saved.

Gifts may not be wrapped in beautiful paper and tied with ribbons, but I think that the gifts will still be there. Can't you just imagine God asking people in Heaven, "Who would you like to give a special gift or blessing to this Christmas Day?"

One said, "Please cure my Grandma Anna of her cancer!"

Or, "God save my son, Johnny."

"Help my sister Susan to find financial help to pay the bills."

"Find my brother Sam a warm place to spend the night."

"Tell Grandpa Jack that I am in the arms of Jesus now."

"Give my Mother, Jane, the strength to get over my death."

"Lord help my Daughter, Emily, to find happiness!"

"Help Uncle Joe to stop drinking and get back in church."

"Lord Jesus, bless Preacher Jim who led me to your grace and salvation!"

"Be with my Grand-Daughter Kathy. Give her the strength to live a good life for you. It is so hard to be a Christian in the world today."

"Jesus, please give my Grandson Tim a Christian wife."

And, "Jesus, be with my friend Janie. Keep her from harm and the abuse of an evil husband. Give her a way out."

The list goes on and on.... Maybe later we can hear Jesus say, "You're wishes have been granted, my children. Thank you for celebrating My birthday with me this year!"

Wouldn't it be wonderful, our very first Christmas in Heaven, wrapped in the arms of Jesus, and maybe asking for gifts to be sent down here to our loved ones, wishing them a Merry Christmas, too? Down here, we look forward to the gifts of material things, but up there we won't need even one of these material goods. God will give us all we need and more. Just the thought of life eternal with Jesus in Heaven, would be more than enough, but, just think of all of the blessings that He has in store for His children, not just on His birthday, but for each and every day for all eternity.... Our minds cannot even start to imagine the wonder and glory of Heaven, and to be in the presence of Jesus, forever and ever and ever!

So my friend if you have a friend or a relative who is lost, give them the best Christmas gift you can give... give them Jesus. Tell them about His love and His mercy and His grace. Tell them about His Salvation! Witness to them, share your faith and your hope. Merry Christmas, my friend.

Zephaniah 3:17
The Lord your God is with you,
he is mighty to save.
He will take great delight in you,
He will quiet you with His love,
He will rejoice over you with singing."

****

CHRISTMAS SHOPPING

I have often become very depressed as Christmas neared, because there were no presents under the tree for family or friends. Then I think about Christmas... It's not about us... it is about Him...Jesus! What if this Christmas we could give our family and friends, gifts from the heart that might not fit under the tree, or couldn't be wrapped in shinny paper or tied with pretty ribbons. Here are a few suggestions... (and you don't have to be rich to do your Christmas shopping!

1. **Tell someone about Jesus. Tell them how His wonderful Grace and Mercy will save them, and they can spend eternity in Heaven with him!**
2. **Hug someone who is lonely or depressed!**
3. **Adopt a family who is hurting financially, get them a small gift and invite them to Christmas Dinner at your home.**
4. **Smile and tell someone they look beautiful!**
5. **Bake something for someone!**
6. **Pray for someone!**
7. **Invite someone to Church!**
8. **Fix up and give your children's used toys to neighborhood children whose parents can't afford Christmas!**
9. **Do chores or run errands for shut-ins or the elderly!**
10. **Unknowingly to others, pay for someone's order at the check-out counter or put a few dollars in their hand. Smile and say "God bless you!"**

    Christmas is not about how much you receive... it's based on how much you give ... from your heart! Because Jesus loves you ... it makes it possible for you to love one another!

John 17:10
All I have is yours, and all you have is mine. And My glory is shown through them.

****

CONTENTMENT

As the daily pace of our lives speed up, we often have so much on our mind, or so many tasks or errands to run, that we can't seem to find the time or place to have peace and contentment. Sometimes we are able to find this by just sitting back in our chair, closing our eyes to the hustle and bustle, the deadlines, and the confusion of the moment, and in our mind see and feel contentment and peace!

In our heart we can hear Jesus telling us, "Come unto me all who are tired and heavy laden, and I will give you rest." Contentment is listening as someone lifts your name to Jesus in prayer ... curled up on the sofa snuggled in your favorite throw reading your Bible ... finishing a meal at Grandma's house ... sitting by the fireside, noticing your favorite dog lying at your feet, ears twitching to pick up any noise so he can protect you ... finding a lost child, safe and sound ... listening to the words of your favorite hymn ... or feeling God's touch in your heart and knowing contentment!

We can see a baby asleep on his Mother's breast feeling so safe and content! Then there's the feeling of snuggling under a nice warm electric blanket on a cold winter night, a hug from Daddy, watching the sparkle and flame of a fire in the fireplace, the purring of a cat, the humming of a hymn by Mother, a mockingbird singing high in a tree, Church, the reading of God's word, or even sitting on the bank of your favorite fishing hole, brings peace and contentment!

For each of us the picture of peace and contentment changes in each mind, each having a special picture of "peacefulness". Where is your Oasis of Peace? Have you found it yet? Well, if not, just close your eyes and think of a spot you'd love to be... and let your troubles and anxieties drift away. Think about being in the arms of Jesus, protected from all harm, all harsh words, all worry....just peace and contentment.

James 5:13
Is any one of you in trouble? He should pray. Is anyone
happy? Let him sing songs of praise.

****

I AM THANKFUL

As the year comes to an end, I want to take time to thank God for His love and grace through this year. Without Jesus my life would really be in a mess. Thank you Jesus!

I thank Jesus for my Mother who is 95 years old, June 25, 2007. She is healthy for the most part. She keeps active by planting and growing beautiful flowers, summer and winter. Sometimes I think God blesses her touch on each and every plant, because they all seem to grow and flourish with beauty. She is able to do her own housework, loves to cook and is continually trying out new recipes. She can't do as much but she still cooks for her for her family and no family gathering is complete without her delicious dumplings and dressing. She is a blessing and an inspiration to me. She fought a bout with breast cancer in 1996 .... Had a mastectomy and never took a pain pill. Arthritis has taken a lot of her freedom, but she goes on. Thank you Jesus for Momma!

I thank Jesus for my two children. My daughter is an RN, has put herself through school, received many degrees, and now has a good position in the heart unit in a hospital in Arizona. She is a wonderful nurse. Visits together don't happen often, but we have a special bond of the heart.

Then there is my son, whom I am very proud of, too! He is an artist with metal, a welder, and very talented with what he does. He takes a piece of metal and gives it a whole new meaning.... shaping and welding it into a work of art. He lives close to home.

Four wonderful Grandchildren make our family aware of how blessed we are. One is still in school and three are out on their own.... One is married with four children of his own, which makes me a proud Great-Grandmother!

I am thankful for being saved, for good health, good friends, a loving Church family, a caring Pastor family, and life itself.

I am thankful for all of my family and friends who enjoy sitting on my front porch with me, and for all of the strangers that God sends my way to brighten my days ... and oh, how they enjoy the porch, too!

I am grateful for sunrises, sunsets, laughter, music, holiday get-to-gethers, phone calls from loved ones, for Treasured Friends, a roof over my head, warm bed to sleep in, food on the table, freedom to read the Bible and pray, and memories, for Spring flowers, Fall trees, Summer sunshine, Winter snow, hugs, good compliments, even honest criticism.

I thank Jesus for raindrops, for dewdrops, rainbows, my front porch, and a cup of coffee with Momma. I am grateful for a pat on the back from a friend, for a

smile of a Grandchild or a squeeze from a Great-Grandchild, for an "I love you", or "I miss you", or "hello Momma"!

I am thankful for eyes that can watch the eagle soar, the clouds move in, or watch my wonderful family growing up or growing older, or seeing the love in the eyes of my faithful dog. I thank God for ears that hear the whispers of my Great-Grandchildren, the statements of my Grandchildren, the gratitude of my children.

I thank God for the talents he has given me, and for enough sense to use most of them, for bits and pieces of wisdom and lots of love to pass on to generations beyond, hoping that there'll always be laughter from something that happened now, cherished memories, and always some fond remembrance of me, my Christianity, my laughter, even my tears, to keep motivating each generation to live life, love family, but most of all, serve Jesus!

Psalm 23:1
The Lord is my shepherd, I shall not want.

****

PRAYER IN YOUR LIFE

How important is prayer in your life? Why is it necessary for us to communicate with God? Our answers go back to a time so long ago. All through Psalms, David prays for strength, wisdom, power, protection and forgiveness. John prayed when he was imprisoned on the island of Patmos, ... and God put him in the Spirit and let him see the New Jerusalem coming down. Sampson prayed for his strength to be renewed just one more time so he could bring the pagan temple down. While the Ark was still afloat on the waters of the flood, Noah prayed for dry land. Moses prayed to God for the children of Israel during the forty years in the wilderness. Daniel prayed and the lion's mouth was closed. Shadrack, Meshack and Abendigo prayed and when they didn't bend, they didn't bow, they were thrown into the fire and they didn't burn. The fourth man was in there with them, and that was God.

Saul prayed for forgiveness and strength and guidance when God called him into the ministry, and God changed his name to Paul. Elijah prayed for fire from Heaven to prove to the pagan worshipers that his God was real. Job prayed when the Devil tested him. He didn't know why he was being tested, but he prayed, "The Lord giveth and the Lord taketh away. Blessed be the name of the Lord!"

I'm sure Mary and Joseph prayed many times while Jesus was in their care. John the Baptist prayed for the people to turn their back on their sins and be baptized now in water, later with the Holy Spirit.

Throughout the Bible, people prayed for healing, for removal of demons, an end to famine, for the well being of family members, and for understanding. They've prayed for rain, or sun, for protection, for safety, and for answers. What more could you want? Jesus even prayed to His Father in our behalf as well as His own, when He asked, "Father, if it be thy will, please take this cup from me." But He went on to say, "Not my will but thine," and he prayed for strength.

This is only a short list of examples. If you have a need or a problem, prayer is the way to ask for help from God our Father. There is nothing that we ask of God, if we ask from the heart, that God will turn his head and not listen to!

We need prayer in our lives each day. We need to pray for forgiveness, for our loved ones who don't know Jesus, for strangers, for friends who are lost, for strength for yet another day, for health, for love of one another, peace, happiness, understanding, resistance from the devil, for boldness to spread the Gospel, for deeper faith, a stronger relationship with Jesus, and even to appreciate and learn from our stays in the valley.

God is always there, no further away than a prayer. He loves you and only wants what is best for you. Sometimes when we are being tested, we don't

understand why God doesn't answer our prayers immediately, or just like we had prayed. Well, my friend, God not only sees where we were, and where we are now, but he knows exactly where we are going, and he knows just when and how to answer those prayers….. in His own time and in His way. The prayers you pray are heard and answered. They are sent back down abundantly blessed. We just need to have the faith that He will answer….on time every time!

1 Tim. 2: 1
I urge, then, first of all, that requests, prayers, intercession and thanksgiving be made for everyone—

****

LEARN TO LET GO

Learn to let go of the fact that a friend hurt your feelings and until they officially apologize, you will keep your distance. If you love them, let it go! Let go of family feuds, sibling rivalries, heartaches, heartbreaks and losses. Just turn to Jesus for strength and faith anew!

Take a walk in the woods, listen to the rustle of leaves beneath your feet, the wind in the pines or the birds singing in the tree. Watch the butterflies dart from flower to flower, or the busy ant going to and fro... gathering food for the colony. Let go of your problems.

Go to the ocean, listen to the waves splash against the shoreline...smell the freshness, watch the sea gulls dip and dive for fish. Look out the window on a stormy night and watch the bolts of lightning light up the world around us. Watch as snow gently falls all around, reshaping and giving a brilliance to everything.... Just let go of your problems and your troubles. Take your worries to Jesus, lay them at His feet and let them go!

You know, no matter how we'd like to change things on our own, for the most part, we have no control over the big things. Things happen whether we want them to or not! The sun comes up in the east each morning and sets in the west! Storms form, rain falls, wind blows, snow accumulates, lightning strikes, thunder rolls, or it turns hot, or turns cold ... skies are blue or they are gray. The tide comes in and the tide goes out. No matter if we like it or not, we can't do anything about it! We need to learn to let go!

The one thing we can do something about is getting our life in order, giving our hearts to Jesus and living for Him! You know, he could make us believe one way or the other, but He is a Gentleman God. He gives us a choice. We can talk to Him in prayer and He'll help us to let go of unimportant things and hold firm to our faith and His hand, which are two things we <u>never</u> want to let go of!

Matthew 18: 21-22

Then Peter came to Jesus and asked, "Lord, how many times shall I forgive my brother when he sins against me? Up to seven times?" Jesus answered, "I tell you, not seven times, but seventy times seven times.

****

MESSAGE IN SONG

When you listen to Hymns, do you often feel Jesus is talking to you through them? It's like mini Sermons at times! Sometimes there are problems or questions in your heart, and when that song starts, you feel like God is giving you the answer. Some of the Hymns offer encouragement or hope. Others share with us the simple peace that God cares! A lot of people have been saved by just words to a song that God permitted to be sung and heard at just the right time, the right place. Tears of joy have flowed along with a new commitment to Jesus. I think that the singing in Heaven by the Angel Choir, is probably the most beautiful sound a human could hear.... Second only to the voice of Jesus!

The old song, "Amazing Grace", has been around for such a long time and it still touches hearts and souls! "Amazing Grace, how sweet the sound.......When we've been there ten thousand years, bright shining as the sun...We've no less years to sing His praise, than when we first begun." Salvation is given to us by the grace of God. By knowing Jesus, Heaven is ours for eternity. We will forever be able to sing praises to God!

"He is here, listen closely, hear Him calling out your name..." Can't you just hear Him calling for you...knocking on your heart's door? He wants so much for you to invite Him into your heart and for Him to be your Lord and Savior!

"For we are standing on Holy ground, and I know that there are Angels all around." This makes me so conscious of the ground beneath my feet, and how unworthy I am to be in His presence! It seems that sometimes I can almost feel the touch of the Angel's wing on my face!

"I'm sailing toward home on that Old Ship of Zion." In your heart, can't you just imagine the shores of Heaven? Can't you see Jesus welcoming you home?

"Because He lives, I can face tomorrow." What hope and inspiration this offers for someone who has almost given up on life itself! Or, you may hear the old song, "I've got a mansion just over the hilltop." This tends to assure me that Jesus has gone to prepare a place for me, and He will come back to get me one day!

The next time you find yourself listening to the music of Hymns, listen carefully to the words. Hear the message the writer is giving you. Feel the presence of Jesus!

Psalm 46:10
"Be still, and know that I am God;
I will be exalted among the nations,
I will be exalted in the earth."

SHADOWS

How many times have you walked in the sunlight and watched your shadow? It never leaves you? The shadow is always close. At times, when it is dark, or the sun isn't shining, you may think your shadow has gone....but the instant you turn on a light or the sun comes out, your shadow appears. Why, it never left! When you walk, it walks, and when you run it runs, and when you stop, it stops! You see, you are never really by yourself. Your shadow is always there, whether you want it to be or not. Sometimes it goes before you; sometimes it follows behind you, and yet at times it is by your side, but it is a constant companion.

At times we have cast large shadows while at other times the shadow is small. When the day is hot outside, and maybe we are waiting in line or looking or watching for something, we tend to slip in the shadow of someone else and instantly it feels better.

Now....have you ever walked in the SON's light and felt Him always near, always there, just like your shadow, even though you can't always feel His presence? He never leaves you! Sometimes we turn away from Jesus and go our own way, thinking we don't need Him. After a while, we have stumbled and fell so many times and now we are sorry. In our hearts sometimes, we think He has forsaken us, but He never does! Just a whisper of a prayer from our heart, and we know He is still there with us. He never left us....we walked away from Him!

When we walk slowly in our faith, He walks slow with us. When we run in our faith, He runs with us. If you should become dormant in your faith...He gives you a nudge.

Sometimes Jesus leads the way for us. Sometimes He follows behind us, and sometimes He walks along beside us...talking to us, puts a song in our heart, and joy in our soul. But, He is always there!

When the devil is continually beating us down, and we find ourselves in the valley, we think surely God has forsaken us. He then brushes a tear from our eye and lets us know He still loves us. When Satan tries to trip us up on our path, we are tempted, but Jesus stands in front of us and we rest in His shadow until Satan retreats.

My friend, Jesus is there for you. He is there with you. Don't walk away from Him! Just hold to His hand and walk in faith that He always knows what is best for you. Just stop and listen!

Job 10:12
You gave me life and showed me kindness,
and in your providence watched over my spirit.

****

SLEEP IN PEACE

As we grow older, a lot of us lose our spouses, and we live in a world of loneliness and fear. We shutter through the storms in the night...and fears start to take over. Things go bump in the night and we tend to let our imagination run wild. Friend, fear is a stumbling block from the devil himself. I think God has a special place in His heart for Widows, just as he does for Orphaned Children. He seems to always be watching out for us, regardless of whether we have asked Him to or even if we want Him there or not.

When the burdens of life weigh us down and we are tired, and we feel like no one cares and no one is there for us... He gently puts His arms around us and holds us close to His bosom. He loves us so much...and He wants us to lean on Him, and depend on Him to be there for us...And He is!

There are nights when sleep won't come, because memories crowd our mind... and we worry about things that we have no control over. One thing that has always seemed to have calmed me, especially when nights seem to have no end, and has brought to me peaceful sleep is repeating the Bible verse:

Psalm 4: 8
"I will both lay me down and sleep, for you Lord, will keep me safe."

If only we would let Jesus calm our fears and give us peace and rest, how blessed we would feel!

Maybe you could find your peace in:

Psalm 16: 7-9
"I will praise the Lord, who counsels me;
Even at night my heart instructs me.
I have set the Lord always before me,
Because He is at my right hand,
I will not be shaken.
Therefore, my heart is glad and
My tongue rejoices;
My body also will rest secure."

Or, maybe you could find your peace in:

Psalm 34: 4-6
"I sought the Lord, and He answered me;
He delivered me from all my fears.
Those who look to Him are radiant;
Their faces are never covered with shame.
This poor man called, and the Lord heard him;
He saved him out of his troubles."

Maybe you will memorize one of these scriptures, and each time your faith is shaken and fear starts to overwhelm you, pray your prayer with a Scripture. God is listening, God is waiting....He loves you so much my friend. He wants to calm your fears and bring you a sweet, peaceful rest....free from any stumbling block that the devil wants to throw your way. He is there friend, watching over you, yes, even while you sleep!

****

SPECIAL VALENTINE

Here we are approaching Valentine's Day once again. The stores are full of cards and heart shaped boxes full of candy. Everything that is advertised for it indicates love. Well, we could have Valentine's Day each day of the year. The most important Valentine in our life should be the love of Jesus Christ! He is our Valentine! He wants us to give Him our heart and to love him. He surely loves us. Our Valentine to Him each day is our prayers. Each time He hears us call His name, His heart probably swells with pride and He smiles. If we invite Him into our heart, we will have a permanent Valentine. He will be with us through good times and through the bad times. He will walk with us along a crowded street, or when we are alone. He will be aware of our needs and will answer our prayers.

Over two thousand years ago, God sent this world the biggest and the best Valentine ever....He sent His son to die on the cross for our sins and then He gave us the Mercy to be set free from our sins, and the Grace to live for Eternity in Heaven with Him! Oh, He didn't have to send us this "Beautiful Valentine". He wanted to! It was stained with blood as it hung there on that old rugged tree for everyone to see. He was made fun of ..... mocked.... spit on....and still He said, "Father, forgive them for they know not what they do!" This Valentine cost more than any other Valentine in history, and it will never be forgotten... It cost Jesus His life!

Don't you remember reading the little messages on the heart shaped candies that appear each year around Valentine's Day? Think of them as messages from Jesus! "Be Mine" "I Love You" "Perfect" "Be My Valentine" "Call Me" "True Love" and the list goes on and on. Jesus loves His Valentines...each and every one of us. I would think we each have an Angel assigned to us, to watch over us, just because Jesus loves us so. I imagine that this Angel loves us almost as much as Jesus does, and they always want to make sure we are safe. They have probably even taken us by the hand and put us back on the right path at times.

Oh, I can hardly wait to get to Heaven, and look upon Jesus' face... to worship Him for eternity and to receive all of the beautiful gifts He has reserved for us who are faithful. I am on my way friend...I have a special Valentine in Heaven, and I long to go! Don't you? I hope I can also see all of my Treasured Valentine Friends in Heaven too. God bless you all!

Song of Solomon 8: 7

Many waters cannot quench love; rivers cannot wash it away. If one were to give all the wealth of his house for love, it would be utterly scorned.

John 3:16
For God so loved the world that He gave His one and only Son, that whoever believes in Him shall not perish but have eternal life.

****

IRAQ

As you know, every time we open the newspaper or listen to the news, we hear Iraq mentioned. I have been gathering some facts from the Bible and I have come up with some rather interesting facts. Did you know that no other nation besides Israel has more prophecy associated with it than Iraq? Is Iraq mentioned in the Bible? Yes! Other names used for Iraq is Babylon, Land of Shinar, and Mesopotamia. Mesopotamia means "between two rivers"...the Tigris and Euphrates Rivers. The name Iraq means "country with deep roots". The only nation mentioned more in the Bible than Iraq is Israel. The Bible says Iraq will rebuild Babylon before the end of time. Historians are seeing this happening now.

It was interesting to find out things that happened in Iraq. Maybe you would be interested in these facts, too.

The Garden of Eden was in Iraq....
Mesopotamia, which is now Iraq, was the
center of civilization....
Noah built the ark in Iraq...
The Tower of Babel was in Iraq...
Abraham was from Ur, which is in Southern
Iraq...
Isaac's wife Rebekah is from Nahor, which
in Iraq...
Jonah preached in Nineveh...which is in
Iraq...
Assyria, which is in Iraq, conquered the ten
Tribes of Israel...
Amos cried out in Iraq...
Babylon, which is in Iraq, destroyed Jerusalem...
Daniel was in the lion's den in Iraq...
The three Hebrew children were in the fire
in Iraq..(Jesus had been in Iraq also as the fourth person in the fiery furnace!)

Belshazzar, the King of Babylon saw the
"writing on the wall" in Iraq...
Nebuhadnezzar, King of Babylon, carried
the Jews captive into Iraq...
Ezekiel preached in Iraq...

The wise men were from Iraq...
Peter preached in Iraq...
The "Empire of Man" described in Revelation
is called Babylon, which was a
city in Iraq...

And here is really something to think about.....Since America is typically represented by an Eagle, Saddam should have read up on his Muslin passages.... (The following is from Koran, (The Islamic Bible)...

Koran (9:11)

For it is written that a son of Arabia would awaken a fearsome Eagle. The wrath of the Eagle would be felt throughout the lands of Allah and lo, while some of the people trembled in despair, still more rejoiced; for the wrath of the Eagle cleansed the lands of Allah; and there was peace.

(Notice the numbers of the passage!)

Revelation 18: 1-3

After this I saw another Angel coming down from Heaven. He had great authority, and the earth was illuminated by his splendor. With a mighty voice he shouted: "Fallen! Fallen is Babylon the Great! She has become a home for demons and a haunt for every evil spirit, a haunt for every unclean and detestable bird. For all the nations have drunk the maddening wine of her adulteries.

****

ONLY IN AMERICA

America is supposed to be an educated country, but it seems like we still have a few things that need to be worked out. This is a list of things to ponder....things that could only happen in America, it seems. Only in America.........

...a pizza can get to your home faster than an ambulance!

...we put handicap parking places in front of a skating rink!

...we leave both doors of the bank open and chain the pen to the counter!

...drugstores make the sick walk all the way to the back of the store to get their prescriptions filled, and healthy people can buy cigarettes in the front!

...we leave our car that is worth thousands parked on the street and junk in the garage!

...we buy hot dogs in a package of 10 and buns in a package of 8!

...people order double cheeseburgers, large fries and a diet cola!

...we use the word "politics" to describe the process so well: In Latin, "poli" means "many" and "tics" mean "bloodsucking creatures"!

Did you ever wonder why......

...sun lightens our hair, but darkens the skin?

...women can't put on mascara with their mouth closed?

...you never see the headline, "Psychic Wins Lottery"?

...lemon juice is made with artificial flavor and dishwashing soap is made with real lemons?

...if con is the opposite of pro, is Congress the opposite of progress?

...why doctors call what they do "practice"?

...the time of day with the slowest traffic is called the rush hour?

Just thought you needed a little chuckle for today. This is just food for thought! God bless you!

Proverbs 30: 7-9
Two things have I required of thee, deny me them not before I die. Remove far from me vanity and lies; give me neither poverty nor riches; feed me with food convenient for me; Lest I be full, and deny thee, and say, Who is the Lord? Or lest I be poor and steal, and take the name of my God in vain.

****

FIVE FINGER PRAYER

Sometimes when we are praying, the devil distracts us in some way, reminds us of something that is not even connected to our prayers. He is good at that! When we are distracted, we often forget to pray for one thing or another. I have found a way to pray, and I seem to be distracted a lot less often. If I feel the devil trying to mess me up, I ask God to put him behind me. I then pray that God will give me a clear, focused mind and I pray that Angels will surround me keeping Satan from interrupting me. After all, nothing is more important than talking to Jesus!

I then hold one hand up. The thumb is closest to me, and this reminds me to pray for those who are closest to my heart. With this you pray for your Father, Mother, Sisters, Brothers, Sons, Daughters, Grandparents, Grandchildren, Aunts, Uncles, Nieces, Nephews and anyone else who is close to your heart. This is when I pray for all of my Treasured Friends, who are my Sisters and Brothers.

Then there is the pointer finger. This finger reminds me to pray for those who point our way to Heaven....for my church, my church family, the Pastor and his wife, for Sunday School teachers, for Missionaries in foreign and hostile lands. I pray for their safety and to let their messages of Jesus be heard and heeded. I pray for Spiritual ears to listen to those who are teaching, and the strength and faith to obey God, no matter what He may ask me to do!

The next finger is the middle finger. It towers over the rest, so it reminds me to pray for those in authority. Pray for the officials of the County, of the City, the State and the Country. Pray for the Military. We need to also remember to pray for America.

The next finger is the ring finger. Believe it or not, this is your weakest finger.... so we are reminded to pray for those who are sick , grieving, depressed, the ones with heavy burdens, and the ones just going through tough times in their life. We pray for those who have financial problems and can't pay their bills. If we know the names of these people, we need to call their name in our prayer....Jesus already knows their name, but this will make us more aware of them and our prayers will be more personal and from the heart.

This now leaves the pinkie finger.... The smallest and most insignificant finger on the hand. This reminds me to pray for myself. This finger is last and should remind us that our needs should come last. We should think of other and their needs before asking for our own needs. During this time we can ask for forgiveness of our sins and thank Him for all of the answered prayers. You talk to Him about your problems and your needs, and for strength to reach your goals.

You pray for mountains to be removed, or at least the strength to go over them. Give Him praise for the things He has done for you!

Now I place my hands together, and I tell Jesus how much I love Him. I sometimes close with a hymn in my heart, and sometimes I drift off to sleep with this hymn still ringing in my soul, and sweet peace and joy engulf my dreams and my sleep.

Remember my friend, prayer is the key to Heaven, but faith unlocks the door!

1 Tim. 2:1
I urge, then, first of all, that requests, prayers, intercession and thanksgiving be made for everyone—

****

PRICELESS

As we go through life, we usually have to work. We need money for food, rent, electricity, gas, insurance, car payments, house payments, education, and so many other things. Yes, we usually enjoy what this expense brings but what about all the things that are priceless that we can enjoy? These are gifts that God Himself has so generously given us. Do you find the time to really enjoy then?

God gave us the blue skies and spring days, cloudy skies and rain. He causes flowers to bloom and for each petal of a rose to unfold perfectly., He has blessed us with trees, oceans, rivers, land with hills, mountains, valleys and flat lands. He gives us the sun to bask in, moonlight, the stars and wind.

There are birds in trees singing, squirrels scampering to and fro, a little rabbit hustling about the yard. The hillsides in the country awaken to the births of calves, goats, sheep and horses. Eggs hatch for the birth of chickens, ducks, turkeys and such. Then there is the smile on a baby's lips, the twinkle in Grandpa's eye, Grandma's lap, Momma's love and Daddy's protection. It is priceless when someone lifts your name in prayer, lush grass to walk on, bees gathering pollen for honey, sunsets and sunrises. The list has no end....it goes on and on!

But the greatest gift He gave us was not free! He gave us a baby, born in a stable and laid in a manger named Jesus. But just a little more than thirty years later, He suffered and He died on a cross on Calvary to save our souls from sin, and with His Grace and Mercy, will make us a home in Heaven for eternity with Him!

He paid the ultimate price....all you have to do in return is give your heart and soul to Him and follow His teachings. Of all of the things He has given us....this is the greatest! Money cannot buy this special gift....it is priceless!

Jeremiah 29:11-13

"For I know the plans I have for you," declares the Lord, "plans to prosper you and not to harm you, plans to give you hope and a future. Then you will call upon me and come and pray to me, and I will listen to you. You will seek me and find me when you seek me with all your heart."

****

EASTER "SON" RISE

Churches all over the nation are now planning Easter Sunrise Service. They will all gather on the Church grounds before daybreak and pray and chat and face the east. As the sun peeks above the horizon there are oohs and aahs and comments about it's beauty. There is a prayer and the crowd breaks up and goes home. This scene is placed behind other memories and life goes on.

But one day we will all look to the east and the sky will roll back like a scroll. There will be a light in the east so bright that the human eye can hardly stand it. But we will look and we will wait....and there on clouds of glory, Jesus comes ....riding His white horse. A host of Angels hover around singing and praising Jesus. This is our "Ultimate Son Rise". It will not be forgotten. No matter if you are a Christian or not, every knee will bow and every tongue will confess that Jesus Christ is Lord.

Can't you just see the millions of people here on earth, each and every one of them facing the east. They will all fall to their knees before Him. Some will even be prostrate, praising Him. Non-Christians will confess that He is Lord, but it will be too late to accept Him as their personal Savior. The saved will then rise with Him on those clouds of Glory.... And will be with Him for eternity, praising Him and enjoying peace and love! They'll instantly change into their glorified bodies and be robed in shimmering white. The unsaved will cry and moan and gnash their teeth. They'll look around to the remaining ones....and everyone seems to take on the shape of demons. They will know that their eternity will be spent with Satan himself. It will be everlasting too late to redeem their soul. Oh, the tears, the weeping and the wailing... all the regrets, the broken hearts for these lost souls.

Friends, I want you to be ready to meet Jesus on that day! Is your soul safe with Jesus? If not, please talk to Jesus and get it right! Jesus is waiting for you!

Rev. 19:11-13

I saw heaven standing open and there before me was a white horse, whose rider is called Faithful and True. With justice he judges and makes war. His eyes are like blazing fire, and on his head are many crowns. He has a name written on him that no one knows but he himself. He is dressed in a robe dipped in blood, and his name is the Word of God. The armies of Heaven were following Him riding white horses and dressed in fine linen, white and clean.

****

WHAT EASTER MEANS

Besides Christmas, Easter is one of the most celebrated occasions in History. Over two thousand years ago, Jesus died on that rugged old cross on Calvary. In three days He arose from that dark lonely tomb jut like He said He would. He defeated Satan and death, and through this gave us victory and hope for an eternity with Him. Easter has a great meaning.....

E.....is for the Eastern sky that Christ promised every eye shall see Him return.... Every tongue will confess and every knee will bow, and everyone will know that Jesus Christ is Lord!

A.....is for His Ascension on clouds of glory right on up to Heaven, to sit at the right hand of His Father!

S.....is for our Savior who died between two thieves on Golgotha, but in three days He arose on a cloud, dressed in white, with a host of Angels singing praises to Him!

T.....is for the shock of Satan when Jesus reached out and Took the keys of Death and Hell out of his hands. From that moment on, Satan knew he was defeated, but he will not give up. He is still trying to win souls for his army, and the sad thing is, people let him!

E.....is for Eternity we can share with Jesus if we believe in Him and follow His teachings!

R.....is for the Rejoicing of ten thousand Angels when the stone was rolled away from the tomb, and Jesus was alive!

During this event there had to be so many mixed feelings....the disciples were confused, scared and mourning. Mary thought someone had moved His body and her heart was broken because she had come to anoint the body with perfume. There was probably real fear when the Angels glowing in white there in the dark tomb spoke to her. Then there was the fear of the friends of Jesus thinking His life was over and wondering why He didn't do anything to save Himself! They were confused.

But then there were the Pharisees thinking that finally they had gotten rid of Jesus. Jesus's mother and family was mourning, even though she knew this

would have to be.....but the nightmares crept into her mind at night of the awful death on the cross.

Just think of the rejoicing in Hell as the devil and his demons thought there would never again be a threat from this man called Jesus, only to look around in horror to see Jesus standing there, and to have the keys to death and hell snatched out of his hand... He knew before a word was spoken, that in that moment of time...he was defeated. But he would never accept it. Until the end of the world he will keep tripping Christians and baiting others to his lies. Hell's fire is waiting for him and his followers.

John 5:28-29
"Do not be amazed at this, for a time is coming when all who are in their graves will hear his voice and come out—those who have done good will rise to live, and those who have done evil will rise to be condemned.

****

THE DREAM

One night after praying, I dozed off to sleep and even though my burdens were heavy, I slept peacefully. I dreamed I was floating up to Heaven. I looked down and I was robed in white. It was soft and flowing. A gold cord was tied around my waist. Upward, still upward I floated.

I came to the Gates of Pearl. They were so beautiful and fragile looking that it seemed just a touch would break them in two. St. Gabriel blew on his trumpet, as an announcement that I was there. St. Peter opened the gates and I walked in. There was such beauty I could hardly catch my breath. Everything was bright and shimmering and clean.

There on the throne by His Father, sat Jesus, with a smile on His face. (The place where God sat was so bright I couldn't even look upon it.) Jesus held out His arms and I could see the nail scars in His hands. .... These were the scars that I put there! A tear fell from my eye, but Jesus reached out and wiped the tear away. He gave me a big hug that seemed to sweep all of my burdens away.

Then He stood and asked me to walk with Him. We strolled around the streets of Heaven. The first thing I saw there was Heaven itself, shimmering and sparkling in light...every color reflecting off of the jeweled walls in the bright pure light of Jesus. We walked by the Crystal River. When you looked down it looked like an enormous fireworks display, and that too, picked up the colors of the city and was accented by the light of Jesus. It was so pure and serene. I asked if I could put my hands in it, and He said, "Yes." It felt so smooth and cool. I thirsted for just a drink of this pure water, but Jesus said, "Not yet!"

Moses and Elijah came up to greet me and they even knew my name! I could hear Angels all over Heaven singing praises to God and playing on instruments for His glory. The streets here were made of pure gold. They were such a rich quality of gold, they looked like spun taffy, and almost transparent. They sparkled of Gold and they looked so thin, but I know they were sculptured thick and bold. In my human mind I noticed there was no scratches or wear on the streets of Heaven and I asked how He kept them all so beautiful. Jesus told me to look down at my feet! I was wearing beautiful white slippers, but I also noticed that my feet didn't touch the ground. I was floating just above the streets.

We walked passed mansions made of Jasper, Emerald, Diamonds, Rubies, Sapphires and all other precious gems. Again, the beauty seemed to take my breath away.

After a while, Jesus told me it was time to go. I asked to stay but He only smiled and said, "In my time, Child, in my time!"

When I woke up the next morning, the dream was so real that I looked to see if I was still wearing the robe of white, but I wasn't....It was only a dream. But, it surely magnified the closeness to my Savior. God bless you.

Luke 15:10
In the same way, I tell you, there is rejoicing in the presence of the angels of God over one sinner who repents."

****

PROMISES OF A RAINBOW

As we look upon a rainbow, we are reminded of a promise from God that He would never again destroy the world with water. Maybe the colors of the rainbow have a promise, too!

When we see the color "RED" it reminds us of the blood He shed there on the cross. He shed it as a promise that we could be forgiven of our sins and we could live life eternal in Heaven with Him and His Father!

"YELLOW" is for the light that shines brighter than the sun... the light of Jesus, promising us if we obey His word we can live where there is no darkness of the deeds of the devil!

"PURPLE" is a color of royalty. This is a promise to all Christians that they are royalty. They are sons and daughters of the King!

"BLUE" is a promise of peace, contentment, love, hope and joy. Don't you always feel better when there are blue skies instead of gray ones?

"GREEN" symbolizes our growth as a Christian, reaching out our roots in every direction. This way we feed and nourish our own spiritual growth. With this growth, there is a promise of producing good fruit for Jesus!

Any shade of these colors should deepen or lighten the intensity of the situations when we see the rainbow. When you look upon a double rainbow, you are receiving an extra blessing form God Himself... a promise to you of His love and faithfulness. (Each time I have seen a double rainbow, since I have been going to my present church, it has been over the church, almost perfectly centered! Just about everyone who comes to the church tells us they can feel God's presence as soon as they enter the door! This church is blessed and filled with the Spirit of Jesus!)

The rainbow is bent, a symbol of humbleness! If we humble ourselves to Jesus, then Jesus promises He will humble Himself to the Father for us!

Think about this theory the next time you see a rainbow! Look at it with a different point of view! Think of all of the promises it holds!

Deuteronomy 7:9
Know therefore that the Lord your God is God; he is the faithful
God, keeping his covenant of love to a thousand generations
of those who love him and keep his commands.

****

DO YOU REMEMBER THIS

As we age, we can look back in time and remember a different time and era. Things seemed a lot more peaceful back then. Here are a few things you may remember from your childhood……

Momma was always at home when the kids came home from school

Supper was always eaten at the table and the whole family ate together

A quarter was a good allowance, and another quarter was a great bonus

If you saw a penny in a muddy gutter you would reach in and get it

All of your male teachers wore neckties, and all the female teachers had their hair fixed nice and wore high heels

When you stopped at a service station, you got your windshield cleaned, oil checked, tire air checked free, and gas was pumped by the attendant

It was a big privilege to be taken out to dinner with your parents, and this did not happen at a fast food place, it happened at a real restaurant

The worst thing that happened at school was to smoke in the bathroom, flunk a test or chew gum

A Chevy was everyone's dream car

People went steady and girls wore a class
ring with an inch of wrapped yarn
so it would fit her finger

No one ever asked where the car keys were..
they were in the ignition

House doors were never locked, and you got
in big trouble if you accidentally
locked the doors at home since no one
ever had a key

Baseball was not a psychological group
learning experience... it was a game

Stuff came from the store without safety
caps and hermetic seals because no
one had yet tried to poison a perfect
stranger

Remember when being in the principal's
office was nothing compared to the
fate that awaited a misbehaving
student when he got home

We were in fear for our lives but it wasn't
because of drive by shootings, drugs,
or gangs, etc., our parents and grandparents were a much bigger threat. We
all survived because their love was
bigger than their threats

Remember...catchin' lightning bugs in a jar, Christmas morning, your first day of school, bedtime stories and goodnight kisses, getting ice cream off the ice cream truck, a million mosquito bites and sticky fingers, (and no one worried about "West Nile" disease or germs), being tired from PLAYING.., and Kool-aid was the drink of summer.

Remember when decisions were made by going, "eeny-meeny-miney-mo", spinning around and getting dizzy and falling down was cause for giggles, and older siblings were the worst tormentors, but also the fiercest protectors.

I hope this brought back a lot of memories for you.... It did for me! God bless you.

Matthew 11:28
"Come to me, all you who are weary and burdened, and I will give you rest.

****

LESSONS IN YOUR LIFE

I have put together a few "Lessons in Life" for you. Hope you enjoy them!

When just one person says to me, "You have made my day!" ... it makes my day!

When a child falls asleep in your arms, it is one of the most peaceful feelings in the world.

You should never say no to a gift from a child.

No matter how serious your life requires you to be, everyone needs a friend to act goofy with!

Sometimes all a person needs is a hand to hold and a heart to understand.

We should be thankful that God doesn't give us everything we ask for!

Money doesn't buy class.

Under everyone's hard shell is someone who wants to be appreciated and loved.

To ignore facts doesn't change the facts!

The easiest way for me to grow as a person is to surround myself with people who are smarter than me.

Everyone deserves to be greeted with a smile.

Opportunities are never lost.... Someone will take the ones you miss!

One should keep his words both soft and tender, because tomorrow he may have to eat them!

When your newly born grandchild holds your little finger in his little fist, you are hooked for life!

You need enough happiness to make you sweet, enough trials to make you strong, enough sorrow to keep you human, enough hope to make you happy!

The happiest people don't necessarily have the best of everything, they just make the most of everything that comes their way.

When you were born, you were crying and everyone around you was smiling...live your life so at the end, you are the one who is smiling and everyone around you is crying....

I hope these little facts help you along life's way. Remember to always smile. Jesus loves you! The best thing you can do in life is talk to Jesus. He will give you an answer to any of your problems....just ask!

Psalm 145:18
The Lord is near to all who call on him,
to all who call on him in truth.

****

PEACE IN YOUR LIFE

Do you long for peace in your life? Do you find yourself worrying needlessly, knowing it isn't doing the problem any good? Well, the first thing to the solution is prayer. Pray for God to give you directions in your life. I found ten ways you can avoid the stress… and be much happier. God will take care of the rest.

1. **Don't worry! It seems that worry is the most unproductive of all human activities. If you worry about something happening and it doesn't happen, then you have needlessly worried twice as much as needed. Take your worries to Jesus and leave them there!**

2. **Don't fear things. Know that God is always with us and there is nothing to be fearful for. Just trust that His will be done.**

3. **Face each problem as it comes. Don't try to tackle life all at once. You can only handle one problem at a time, so just take them one day at a time. Jesus will help us to face all of our problems, and will help us find the solution to them.**

4. **Don't try to cross bridges before you come to them. No one has successfully accomplished this yet. Don't worry about the "What if" factor…just trust in Jesus.**

5. **Don't go to bed angry. Settle the argument before you go to bed. If you have to be the one to say you are sorry, say it. When you go to bed with the problem on your mind, it just festers and gives the devil something to work with. Talk to Jesus!**

6. **Don't try to solve everyone else's problems. You have enough to do with your own. The best thing you can do for them is pray for them. Jesus will work it all out in His own way and in His own time.**

7. **Don't worry about yesterday! It is gone. Don't worry about tomorrow, because we aren't even promised a tomorrow. Just take care of today. Jesus gave you a brand new day to talk to Him, to forgive your friends as well as your enemies, to ask for forgiveness for yourself, and promised to be there for you, no matter what comes up.**

8. **Listen to those who have different ideas from your own. Maybe you can learn something from what they have to say. Listen…maybe Jesus has something to say to you today!**

9. **Don't get depressed with frustration. Talk to Jesus. He will give you a way out of the situation.**

10. **Count your blessings. Don't overlook even the smallest one. Don't dwell on things that have gone wrong or friends who have disappointed you. Thank Jesus for ALL of your blessings.**

When you just can't think of anything else to do, just pray! God is always listening for your prayer, and He will always answer them! He is Lord of Lords and King of Kings, and He is your best friend.

Psalm 40:8
I desire to do your will, O my God; your law is within my heart."

****

THINKING OF MOTHER

Mother's day has just passed. I know that a lot of you have lost your Mother. Some of you are fortunate enough to still have your Mother living. Savor this time with your Mother, for one day she won't be with you anymore. But for all of you, I want you to close your eyes and think of your Mother! Think of how she smelled when she held you close.... OK!

We all have come from different kinds of bringing up, but most Mothers are basically the same! She is the one who sat up with you all night when you were sick, and cleaned you up when you threw up your supper. She changed your diaper, wiped your fevered brow, and somehow, without seeing you, knew exactly what you were doing!

She is the one who held you close to her bosom and rocked you for hours when you couldn't sleep. Mothers were there to calm the nightmares or the panic attacks. Some Mothers gave birth to babies they will never see, and then there are other Mothers who took these children, gave them homes and gave them their heart.

Do you remember when she made your favorite dessert and you wanted more, and how she suddenly decided she didn't want hers? Mothers save the artwork of the child and hangs it on the refrigerator for all to see.

Mothers go to ball games, in sickness or in health, to make sure they see their child hit the home run, or make the basket, or catch the football. This is important to her.

Sometimes in despair, a Mother would swat their child for throwing a tantrum in a grocery store, because they wanted something not on the list! They knew the difference in correction and abuse.

Mothers have read books to their children, twice over in one night for a solid week and never complained. She cleaned your home, washed the dishes, washed the clothes, cooked the meals and still always had time to spend with you.

Remember when Mother taught you to tie your shoelaces, button your shirt, zip your pants, potty trained you, and taught you to dress yourself. Mother was smart enough to teach the son to cook, and the daughter to change a tire. She would often say, "Someone might not be there to do it for you!"

Mothers felt their heart break when they sent their child off to school for the first day, or packed their bags for college. A special alarm goes off in a Mother's head when a baby makes a sound through the night or when a teenager hasn't come home at curfew time. She can't sleep until she hears the key in the door letting her know that all is well.

Weren't you amazed that Momma could help you with your homework, sew on a button, talk to someone on the phone and cook supper all at the same time? Do you remember Momma always being up already when you got up and no matter what time you went to bed, Momma was still up and working.

If you brought your friends home, she always had enough cooked to feed them. There always seemed to be a snack in the house, and Momma's magic kiss always made a bo-bo feel better. No matter how old you got, you were always her baby, and her Mothering instinct was always there.

If you listen closely in your mind, you can probably hear her calling you in to supper. Momma's advice was always the best, and no matter how big you were, a hug from Momma was just what you needed. Did Momma take you to the Matinee on Saturday? Did she take you to Church on Sunday? Did you hear your Momma praying for you? Momma is surely special!

If a tear fell while thinking of Momma, it is OK, for surely she will take the corner of her apron, wherever she may be, and wipe the tear away! God bless you!

James 1:17
Every good and perfect gift is from above, coming down from the Father of the heavenly lights, who does not change like shifting shadows.

(Surely a Mother is a gift from God!)

****

BEFORE AND AFTER

A youngster came up to me the other day and asked me what I thought about all of the violence in the schools and homes, the computer age, immoral acts and lives of famous people and just things in general. I had to think a minute on this one!

You see, I was born way before television, polio shots, fax machines, copy machines, ball point pens, credit cards, laser beams, clothes dryers, electric blankets, panty hose, contact lenses, the pill, air conditioners, radar, Frisbees, and no one had walked on the moon!

Men and women got married first and then lived together. Almost every family had a mother and a father, unless one had died. No one referred to Johnny's two fathers, or Suzie's two mothers.

Every boy over fourteen had a rifle or a shotgun and was taught to use it with respect. People were spoken to with respect, and Policemen and Firemen, Preachers and other important people were always answered with "yes sir" or "no sir" or "yes ma'am" or "no ma'am". We used our closets for clothes and not to "come out of"!

Sundays were special! The whole family would go to church together. Sunday evenings we would visit the neighbors or help a needy family. Maybe we would just sit around and enjoy our family together, go on a picnic or make home-made ice cream.

I was here before gay-rights, computer dating, careers for Mom and Dad, or daycare centers. We had enough sense and charisma to find our own dates, and if Mom had to be away from home for a while, grandma kept the children. Our lives were governed by the Ten Commandments, good judgment, by common sense and Daddy's belt. We were taught the difference between right and wrong and we knew to use this knowledge. We were also taught to take responsibility for our actions.

We served our country with pride. Serving was considered a privilege and living here was an even greater one. We knew all of the words to the "Star Spangled Banner" and we stood with pride when we heard it played.

We thought fast food was food we ate in a hurry when we were late for something. When we referred to time-sharing, it meant making time to share with our family and friends, not condominiums. We had never heard of FM radio, CD's, tape decks, VCR's, DVD's, computers, electric typewriters, artificial hearts, heart transplants, word processors, yogurt or guys wearing earrings.

We listened to big bands, the Grand Ole Opry, Jack Benny and the president's speeches on the radio. I don't ever remember a kid blowing his brains out after listening to Tommy Dorsey.

If you saw something that was "made in Japan" it was junk. The term "making out" referred to how you came out on your final exam in school. Pizza, instant coffee, cappuccino, and McDonalds were unheard of. We had 5 and 10 stores that you could actually buy items for five cents and ten cents. Ice cream cones, phone calls, a ride on a streetcar, and a Pepsi was all a nickel, or you could spend your nickel on enough stamps to mail a letter and two postcards.

A Chevy Coupe was $600, and you still couldn't afford one. Gas was eleven cents a gallon.

Children could play outside and Momma didn't have to keep an eye on them every minute. They were usually safe. You could walk home from the movie and didn't have to worry about a drive by shooting.

In my day grass was mowed, coke was a cold drink, rock music was your grandmother's lullaby, aids were helpers in the office or the hospital. We were not here before the difference between the sexes was discovered, but we were surely here before the sex changes, pornography in a family home and on news stands, and we were probably the last generation that truly believed that you needed a husband to have a baby, and bedroom scenes were a private matter. No wonder people call us old and confused and there is such a big generation gap.

Things have surely changed. Not that everyone or everything was good back then, but as I look around at things today.....the attitudes of the children, the parents who just don't care, the music, the lifestyles, the drugs, and even the laws and the law makers....I wonder just where this old world is heading!

Isaiah 3:10-11

Tell the righteous it will be well with them,
for they will enjoy the fruit of their deeds.
Woe to the wicked! Disaster is upon them!
They will be paid back for what their hands have done

****

HEAL OUR LAND

2 Chronicles 7:14
If my people, who are called by my name, will humble themselves and pray and seek my face and turn from their wicked ways, then will I hear from heaven and will forgive their sin and will heal their land.

America is falling! People are turning away from God! Morals have fallen so low that it has become illegal to speak His name...Yes here in America! People are banning God from schools, from meeting places, from sports arenas, from the courtrooms and from the homes! There are horrors happening around us... Mothers drowning babies, Fathers stabbing, raping or beating babies, sons and daughters killing Mothers and Fathers. So many babies are being aborted each day. Abuse is everywhere. Rape is rampant.

People had just as soon shoot you as to look at you, maybe because they don't like the color of your skin or even your hairstyle. Politicians go with the anti-believers because there seem to be more voters here than on the believers side. You are not safe here in America.

The family is not a prominent item in today's lifestyle. Having a baby out of wedlock is something no one seems to think anything of. Abnormal lifestyles are OK. They even let these perverted couples marry and adopt children, when the Bible clearly states that this is a sin! I have often thought that it seemed easier for these couples to adopt children than for Christian families to adopt. Children have no respect for the parents, and parents have no respect for children. Marriage has no true and lasting meaning, and the Holy Bible is not read.

And this is supposed to be the "Land of the Free and the Home of the Brave"! America is becoming a den for Satan's demons. People are making it so easy for him to move in. Pioneer people dreamed of "One Nation Under God". People now just want "One Nation....". We need to change our ideals, our attitudes, our morals, and start to love God once again!

As God looks down from the throne on high, a tear falls down His cheek and it breaks His heart. He is calling for us to come back to Him, but for the most part, America spits on Him, ridicules Him, looks away from Him, abandons His meeting places, aborts babies, and most of them are so lost they don't even have a conscience to bring them to their knees!

How long will America stand at this rate? Are we the modern day Sodom and Gomorrah? It was destroyed! The people of this great country need to fall on their knees and seek God's face and He will heal this great land... but the sad part is that so many just don't care!

Pray for America, pray for your neighbor, for your enemy, for your government. Pray for the sick and demon following souls that are living here in the United States of America, wanting it to fall. God bless you!

****

OLD SAYINGS

Did you ever wonder how a lot of the "old sayings" or "customs" originated? Well, I discovered a few of the origins and I thought it would be nice to share them with you. For some reason, it seemed like most of them started in the 1500's.

Did you ever wonder why June was the most popular wedding month? Well, back then people took their yearly bath the end of May after the spring thaws, and the body odors weren't too bad in June. However they had started to smell, so the bride would hold a bouquet of fragrant flowers to mask the body odor. Therefore the custom of a bride carrying a bouquet in her wedding started.

Baths had a special order. They would fill a large tub with water. The first to bathe was the man of the house. Then all of the other men in the house and the sons would bathe. The women went next and then all of the children, oldest first. Now remember, this was a once a year bath, so the water toward the end of the bath session was so dirty, you could actually lose someone in it! This is where the saying "Don't throw the baby out with the water" originated.

Houses had thatched roofs. This was thick straw piled high. It had no real wood structure underneath. This was a good place for animals and small bugs to keep warm. When it rained, it sometimes became slippery and the small animals would fall off the roof....thus starting the saying, "raining cats and dogs".

This really posed a problem in the bedroom as there was nothing to stop things from falling into the house. Bugs and other droppings could really make a mess of your nice clean bed. For this reason, you needed a bed with tall post on each corner and then you would hang a sheet over the post. This would offer a little protection from the falling "missiles". That was the start of "Canopy Beds".

Most of the dwellings had dirt floors. However, the rich could afford floors of something other than dirt...this started the saying, "dirt poor".

In the good old days, the rich had slate floors which would get slippery when wet. The homeowners would spread thresh straw on the floor in order to keep them from slipping. As the winter wore on and on, they didn't clean out the old thresh straw, they just added more. Each time you opened the door, the straw would start falling outside. A piece of wood was put in the entranceway, starting the idea of a "thresh hold".

In these days, people cooked their meals over the fire in a big kettle. They didn't throw the contents out of the pot, instead, each day they added things to the pot and cooked it some more. They ate mostly vegetables and not much meat, so they would leave the leftovers in the pot to cool overnight and start anew the next day, adding to the pot. Sometimes stew had food in it that had been there for

quite a while...hence the rhyme...."Peas porridge hot, peas porridge cold, peas porridge in the pot nine days old!"

Bread was divided according to status. The guest got the upper crust of the bread, the family the middle and the workers got the burnt bottom crust of the loaf. This started the idea of "upper crust people".

Lead cups were used for their drinking glasses, especially ale or whiskey. The combination of the metal and the liquor would sometimes knock the drinkers out for a couple of days. If someone found a man passed out, he would take them for dead and start preparing them for burial. The victim was then laid out on the kitchen table for a couple of days and the family would gather around and eat and drink, and party .... And wait to see if the victim would wake up. This is "holding a wake".

England at this time was small and when local folks started running out of room to bury people, they dug up the other graves and removed the bones and took them to a bone box, then reused the grave. When reopening the caskets they found that a great percent of them had scratch marks on the lid....indicating that a lot of the people were being buried alive. So they took a string and tied it to the wrist of the corpse and ran it up through the coffin and attached it to a bell on top of the ground. Someone was hired to sit out in the graveyard all night, (the "graveyard shift") and listen for the bell, thus inspiring the phrase, "saved by the bell", or was considered a "dead ringer".

Caring for the poor is lending to the Lord and you will be repaid.
Proverbs 19:17

The right word at the right time is like precious gold set in silver.
Proverbs 25:11

****

STRENGTH

For so many things in this life we need extra strength. We need the strength to raise and nurture children, to let them go out into a life of their own. We need strength when we work hard on a job and then come home to work for the family. We need strength to get over sickness, for both ourselves and our loved ones...(1 Chronicles 16:11..Look to the Lord and His strength; seek His face always)... We need strength to forgive, strength to pray for our enemies. We sometimes see our whole world come crashing down at our feet, and we need strength to carry on!

There are prisoners who are being punished for wrongs they have done, and they find the prison cells and environment almost unbearable. Someone here tells them about Jesus, and they repent, but the time must still be served. They cry out in agony to Jesus for strength to carry on.

We seek strength after a surgery or a sickness, just to take that first step. There are people in nursing homes who are lonely and seemingly forgotten by family and friends and each day they need the strength to just find a reason to get up in the morning.

Families are falling apart because they don't invite Jesus to live with them, and when things get almost unbearable, they turn to Jesus and pray for strength to carry on. (Psalm 59:16 ... But I will sing of your strength in the morning, I will sing of your love. For you are my fortress, my refuge in times of trouble.)

We lose a loved one, a friend turns against us....We need strength. A lot of us battle finances each day, and one day gets harder than the day before just to meet the bills. God will give us strength to find a way out. We need God's holy strength to get free of addictions, of alcohol, tobacco, drugs, pornography, lying, stealing, gossiping, hatred..... and the list never seems to end. (Psalm 46:1...God is our refuge and strength, an ever present help in trouble.)

Sometimes we feel so tired and so weak. We don't have energy to do our jobs, or talk to our spouses or children. We are drained. We don't care if friends are sick...we are just tired. We don't work for Jesus and we are void of energy. Some of us get to the point where we are spiritually tired, almost spiritually dead. Jesus has the life giving strength to give us...all we have to do is ask!

He will strengthen our will, our home life, our spiritual life, give us strength to overcome loneliness, frustration, age, addictions and anything else that is holding us back.

I think the verse in Isaiah 40 is one of the most beautiful verses in the Bible ... and one of the greatest promises of God!

Isaiah 40:29-31

He gives strength to the weary and increases the power of the weak. Even youths grow tired and weary, and young men stumble and fall; But those who trust the Lord will find new strength. They will soar on wings like eagles, they will run and not grow weary. They will walk and not be faint.

****

THE BULLS EYE

Recently in Church I heard this story and I'd like to pass it on to you! There was this Professor in College, (we will call him Mr. James), who was known for his unusual classes. To keep his students interested, each day he tried to do something different. One day, he announced to the class that he wanted them to draw a picture of someone they were angry with, and bring the picture to school the next day.

When they got to class, there was a huge "bulls eye" in front of the room. Professor James told each student to line up. When their turn came, he wanted them to thumbtack their picture on the "bulls eye", and then take a handful of darts and throw at the picture, releasing their anger. While throwing the darts, they were asked to explain who the picture was representing, and why they were angry at that person.

The first one had a picture of her brother. "He makes me so mad! He always picks on me!" She voiced as she threw the darts. The next one grabbed the darts, explaining that he was mad at his Father because he was grounded for not keeping the curfew. He threw the darts and threw them hard! One was angry with her best friend for repeating a secret. One was angry with his teacher for a bad grade. One had a picture of the President, because his brother had been sent to Iraq. One threw darts angrily at her Mother because she would not let her use the car. An on and on, the Students took their turns. There was so much anger!

Then came the girl with a picture of her Father, who had yelled at her at the supper table last night. She walked to the front of the class and reached for the "bulls eye", but then pulled the picture back and held it close to her breast. She fell to her knees and prayed for her Father who had lost his job and was frustrated. She knew he didn't mean to hurt her feelings. When she got up, the classroom was in total silence.

The next person slowly started up the isle to display their picture on the "bulls eye", but the Professor said, "Please sit down. We will throw no more darts today!" He then walked over to the "bulls eye" and removed it. Behind the target was a picture of Jesus ... His face gored and torn, almost unrecognizable. The class gasped, some cried. Professor James said, "I tell you the truth, whatever you did for one of the least of these brothers of mine, you did for me.....I tell you the truth, whatever you did not do for one of the least of these, you did not do for me." (Matthew 25: 40, 45)

Remember this the next time you feel you must vent anger by throwing darts of angry words or actions at someone you are angry with, whether it be your enemy, your friend or your family....you are doing it to Jesus!

****

IN THE COOL OF THE DAY

Did you ever wonder what a thrill it must have been for Adam... to walk and talk with God in the cool of the day? Each day Adam could walk through the Garden of Eden and talk to God, just like we do with our best friend. Oh, how God must have loved Adam. But this made Satan mad! For listening to Satan, Adam messed that up.

Adam had a life of leisure. He didn't have to work and he had no worries. But, when Eve picked the fruit off the tree, after listening to Satan, and offered it to Adam to take a bite, Adam broke the Father's heart with that one bite. They were driven out of the beautiful Garden of Eden, and from then on, they would have to work for their food and shelter. He could no longer walk with God in the cool of the day.

After a while, God sent His Son, Jesus, to earth. He was born in a stable, a humble beginning. This baby would grow into a man, who would be perfect in every way. He would walk and talk with God's Children. Jesus would tell the world about His Father and tell them about Heaven. He walked on many of a dusty road, healed the lame, the blind, the mute, the deaf, the sick, threw out demons, raised people from the dead and showed the world what love was. Then one day, fulfilling the prophesy, He was crucified on that old cross on Calvary. He died and was buried, but He arose and went home to Heaven to be with his Father on the third day!

He didn't really leave us though. He left the Holy Spirit with each of us. This way, we can, as Adam did, walk and talk with our Savior. We can feel His presence and we know He is there. He hears our prayers whether we pray a formal prayer or just talk to Him. He lifts us up when we fall, mends our broken heart, heals our sickness, raises the dead to life, cast out demons, and wipes away or tears. He loves us too ... just like He loved Adam. After all, for us God sent His only son to die for our sins. If we will only believe and accept Him as our Savior, we will have a home in Heaven with Him. He gives us mercy and grace, so that when we pray, we can reach the throne room itself, and talk to Jesus in the Holiest of Holies.

Even though God has given us all of this, how often do we break God's heart by listening to the plans and schemes of the devil. My friend, my name is in the Lamb's Book of Life. Is yours? One day, I'm going to take my last breath here on earth, but the next breath will be in Heaven. I can almost see Jesus standing there with arms outstretched, saying, "Welcome home, my Child."

Are you ready to meet Jesus in Heaven? If not, call on God in prayer ... and pray until you know you are saved. We don't know when our life will end. Just live each day and be ready. Love Jesus, live your life for Him!

Deut. 7:9
Know therefore that the Lord your God is God; he is the faithful God, keeping his covenant of love to a thousand generations of those who love him and keep his commands.

****

STAGES OF FRIENDSHIP

Have you ever thought of the different stages of friendship? Well, I want to share this with you!

In Kindergarten, you didn't need much. Just a friend who would give you that beautiful red color they were using when the only one left was the ugly black one.

In the First Grade, you needed a friend who would hold your hand as you walked through the scary halls of school, or go with you to the bathroom. This was important.

In the Second Grade, you needed that friend who would stand up for you when the class bully started pushing, or demanded your lunch money.

In the Third Grade, was that special person who would share their lunch with you when you forgot yours at home, and no matter what was in the lunch, it seemed to be your favorite.

In the Fourth Grade, you started forming your own opinions and dislikes. A friend now was the one that volunteered to be your lunch partner, so you wouldn't be paired with the town clown or even the little girl that smelled funny!

In the Fifth Grade, it was your best friend who saved you a seat on the bus so you could share the secrets of the day!

In the Sixth Grade, it was your best friend who went to the party with you, and walked up to your new "crush" and asked them to dance with you, so if they said no, you wouldn't be so embarrassed!

In the Seventh Grade, your best friend was the one who let you copy the Social Studies homework, because you missed school.

In the Eighth Grade, you start growing up. Your friend now helps you pack up your Barbie dolls or Baseball cards so you could make your room look like a teenager's room, and turned their back pretending not to see you wipe your tears as you say goodbye to childhood.

In the Ninth Grade, your friend would go to every cool party with you so you would always have a good friend with you.

In the Tenth Grade, your best friend was the one who would change their schedule so they could have lunch with you, because the tenth grade is a confusing place to be!

In the Eleventh Grade, your best friend is the one who gives you the first ride in their new car, convinces your parents that you shouldn't be grounded, or consoled you when your prom date turned out to be a loser.

In the Twelfth Grade, you needed a friend to help you pick out that perfect College to go to, and they helped you deal with leaving your home and your parents for the first time. It was very hard to deal with!

At Graduation, you needed a good friend who would be crying on the inside, but managed to smile as they congratulated you.

The Summer after Graduation, your idea of a good friend was one who helped you clean up the bottles from the big party, taught you to deal with your parents' frustration of losing you to College. Then, helped you pack and sweetly hugged you as the tears crowded your eyes, leaving 18 years of memories behind. But, most importantly, sent you off to College knowing you were loved!

Now, a good friend is still the person who gives you the better of the two choices, holds your hand when you're scared, helps you fight off those who try to take advantage of you, thinks of you at times when you are not there, reminds you of what you have forgotten, helps you put the past behind you, but understands when you need to hold on to it a little longer, stays with you so that you have confidence, goes out of their way to make time for you, helps you clear up your mistakes, helps you deal with pressure from others, smiles for you when they are sad, helps you become a better person, and most importantly loves you.

God can be that best friend for you!

Psalm 16:2
I said to the Lord, "You are my Lord;
apart from you I have no good thing."

****

FAMILY REUNION

Recently, I attended a family reunion. I was amazed to see the changes in relatives that I had not seen in a few years! Some looked much older ... some much heavier... a lot of them had a lot less hair...quite a few wrinkles and some were even feeble. It seemed like everyone I knew was now wearing glasses or hearing aids, and probably most of them were sporting dentures. Oh, I seem to recognize all of the adults, but where on earth did all of these children come from? Who do they belong to?

I sit here in my easy chair outside, looking at the faces. Where have the years gone? You realize you are getting old when the children you remember changing diapers for, are now parents changing diapers of their own children.

You sit here, not joining in with any of the laughter or the pranks, because you can't seem to put a face and a name together. And, when someone comes and sits beside you, you cheerfully carry on a conversation with them, and all the while they are talking, you are wondering, "Now who did they say they were?"

Do you remember get-to-gethers and how the noise and the chatter was loud and endless ... but I don't hear much of that this time...(Oh, maybe I should turn my hearing aid on....!) I would sure like to gnaw on that corn on the cob, but I am afraid that my dentures would still be out there gnawing when I closed my mouth! I keep hoping some of the folks will come a bit closer, because I just can't see them well enough to figure out just who they are. It's a bit slower getting up, because it usually takes at least three tries to clear the chair. This cane is a handy object for walking, but I think it is necessary to ward off all of these running younguns.

I just can't seem to figure out why all of my friends are looking so old... Why, I bet I don't look like I have aged a day ... ! I really would like to thank someone for having me here, but for the life of me, I just can't remember who this gathering is for!

Thank Goodness! When I get to heaven and sit at the table for the Marriage Supper of the Lamb, I won't have these problems. I won't be feeble, hard of hearing, partly blind and deaf, and my memory will be outstanding. When I talk to someone I will instantly know who I am talking to, even though they may have lived thousands of years before me ... but most of all, I can fall at the feet of Jesus and worship Him, (and my arthritis knees won't hurt)! Will I see you there?

2 Corinthians 4:17
For our light and momentary troubles are achieving for us an eternal glory that far outweighs them all.

****

OUR FLAG

As Independence Day comes around, I guess we all tend to become a bit patriotic. We see the flag in a whole new light right now. Can't you just picture a little old lady named Betsy Ross, sitting in a rocking chair, needle and thread in hand, stitching up this beautiful red and white stripe flag. There were only thirteen stars on the blue background at that time.... Now there are fifty! This was only the first flag. How many hours were spent making more flags in honor of the United States of America? How much respect do you have for the flag?

The red stripes represent the blood that has been shed just to keep America free! The white stands for peace and hope.

The American flag flies high at all of the government buildings, proud and free. It flies in yards, in parks, in parades, and it stands tall and proud! It stands for freedom, honor, peace, truth and justice. The flag makes the statement ..."I am proud, I am free! I am an American!" It is recognized all over the world as a symbol of the good old USA!

This same flag has been carried through every battle, through every war, since Betsy Ross stitched the first one. The Soldiers carried this flag through Gettysburg, Shiloh, Appomattox and Valley Forge. This flag, even though at times it was tattered and torn, proclaimed freedom in the trenches of France, San Juan Hill, the Beaches of Normandy, Okinawa, Korea, Guam, Vietnam, and Iraq.

Every ship, plane or vehicle of the United States Armed Forces carry this flag in some shape or form. Sometimes this great flag is torn, spit on, trampled, or burned on the same streets that we have fought to set free!

As those brave Astronauts walked on the surface of the moon, they erected an American Flag, in honor of their country. When a Soldier or a governmental person passes away, the flag is flown in half mast, in respect.

At the time of the bombing of the Federal Building or the Twin Towers horror, the flag flew in memory of the fallen. This is the same flag that is placed over a coffin of a fallen Soldier, and then gently folded and placed in the arms of a grieving loved one, marking the final battle for the Soldier.

When you hear the Star Spangled Banner, does your heart swell with pride, and you stop what you are doing and honor this dear old flag? Does your heart break when you see the flag being abused? Do you pray for America, and what this flag stands for? Pray for America my friend, and keep America free!

Psalm 116:7-9
Be at rest once more, O my soul,
for the Lord has been good to you.

For you, O Lord, have delivered my soul from death,
my eyes from tears,
my feet from stumbling,
that I may walk before the Lord
in the land of the living.

THE PICNIC

A few years ago I took some of you through the country fields on an imaginary stroll and I had a lot of response saying how much it was enjoyed... so again, put away your walkers, your wheel chairs, your canes, and the bars on your wall. Today you will walk and run and be free.

I would like to take you on your last picnic for the summer. The weather has cooled off a little and the leaves are turning, and the day is just right.... Are you ready? If someone is reading you this letter, just sit back and close your eyes and put yourself in a time, a long time ago. Picture yourself as a child, and you can run and play. Enjoy it!

The car is parked on a hill overlooking a lush, green, shady valley. There's a pond with four ducks swimming peacefully. Your family walks through the grass, carrying the picnic basket and a quilt. Momma and Daddy pick out a perfect place to spread the old quilt.

Momma opens the picnic basket with care. There is a platter of fresh fried chicken, a bowl of potato salad, corn on the cob, a plate of tomato sandwiches, apples and a jar of iced tea, topped off with homemade cookies! It sure looks and smells good! M-m-m-m-m-m-m. Momma spreads the food on the quilt. A couple of ants crawl around hoping someone will drop a crumb...BINGO! They found a piece of chicken crust. One ant loads it on his shoulder and off they go carrying their trophy home.

You all sit down and enjoy this wonderful meal prepared by Momma's hands. After lunch you run and play in the meadow grass, and then pick a bouquet of wildflowers for Momma. Being exhausted, you lay on the quilt and look up at the clouds. Oh, the magic in the hand of the artist, Jesus Himself! He shapes things to amuse you. Some shapes make you think hard, but it's all beautiful...then with just a breath, He wipes the slate and starts a new picture.

In the distance you can hear the mournful cry of a whippoorwill... the mating calls of the Bob White quails, a mocking bird high in a tree singing and chirping, and a half grown squirrel in a tree, on a limb just over you, chattering and scolding you because you spread the quilt on his playground.

In your heart you feel perfect peace. Oh what a beautiful day, and all too soon it is time to pack up and hike up the hill and head home. I hope you enjoyed your picnic with me. And if you think this sounded good, think of this.....

Psalm 23: 1-3
The Lord is my Shepherd, I shall not be in want. He makes me lie down in green pastures, He leads me beside quiet waters, He restores my soul. He guides me in paths of righteousness for His namesake.

****

DON'T WORRY

Did you ever wonder why we often tend to think about the bad times more than the good times? Even the news media accents the bad things, and a lot of the good things are never shared! Here is a list of some of the good things we need to think of instead of the bad ones.

Do not fret and worry about what you're not...just remember that God may not be through with you yet.

Don't dwell on things that you failed to do... just remember the things you did do, and think of the happiness that it brought someone.

Don't worry about the pain you might have caused someone, just keep thinking of ways to make them feel better. Ask for their forgiveness.

Don't cry over what may have been....it can never be. Just focus on the good things that may happen from now on!

Don't try to attain greater happiness... just be happy with all of the little things that bring a smile to your heart.

If you have a venture and it has failed, just keep trying. Maybe you need to change the venture.

If being old grieves you, just think instead of all of the fun you have had getting here.

Don't blame others for things that happen to you in life, just accept them as part of your life and go on! On the other hand, don't laugh at or taunt others for their misfortunes, because that too is just part of their life.

Don't worry and fret about what others say or think about you. Just work at being a better you, and let God mold you into what He wants you to be. Don't be discouraged about days past...you can't change that. Just look ahead with joy and determination to walk closer to God and make your future bright.

Don't despair over lost friends, lost personal property, or other things you can't bring back... just search for new friends, a new look on life, and things that will point you toward Heaven.

Give more than you really can, because that makes it a sacrifice. Giving is dearer to your heart this way.

Don't grieve over things you have lost, just anticipate new things you will find. Quit dwelling on things that you don't have...look for the things you can have, and your life will be more meaningful.

Don't drown in your tears of your own little pity-party. Share your smile and the hope of Jesus in your heart.

Don't ponder on all of your mistakes.... Think of all of the good things that you have done right! You need to hope a lot more and worry a lot less.

If you are going through a time of sickness, think of all the times in your life that you felt good, and you have to have the hope that there will be a lot more days that you will feel good and healthy and blessed.

You can worry a little, but you must accept it all as somehow fitting into God's plan. No matter what happens in your life, somehow, somewhere, someone is touched by that event. If nothing ever went wrong, we would forget how much we need the strength in the hand of Jesus.

Philip. 4:11-13

I am not saying this because I am in need, for I have learned to be content whatever the circumstances. I know what it is to be in need, and I know what it is to have plenty. I have learned the secret of being content in any and every situation, whether well fed or hungry, whether living in plenty or in want. I can do everything through him who gives me strength.

****

A FULL LIFE

I have heard a full life described in a lot of different ways, but, I found one that was better than all of the rest, and I would like to share it with you.

A Professor stood in front of a classroom and in front of him was an empty mayonnaise jar. There were whispers from the class as to what the Professor was going to do. As the class was called to order, he took golf balls and filled the jar. Then he asked the class, "Is this jar full?" Of course all of the class said "Yes!"

He told them it was not yet full. Then he reached under his desk and got a little box full of small pebbles. He poured it in the jar and shook it gently. The little pebbles filled in the spaces between the golf balls. Again he asked the question..."Is this jar full?" Again the class replied, "Yes!"

He shrugged his shoulders and again reached into his desk and pulled out a small box of sand. He gently poured it into the jar, and gain gently shook the jar. The sand shifted to fill all of the empty spaces between the pebbles and the golf balls. Once again, the Professor asked the question and once again he got the same answer.

From under the desk, he gently reached and pulled out two cups of coffee, and poured it slowly into the mayonnaise jar. It soaked into the sand and the Professor said, "Now the jar is full!"

The class then asked the professor what the purpose of the experiment was. He said, "Well, the jar represents your life. The golf balls represent what you need to take care of first in your life...your love for your God, your family, your friends and others important to you in your life.

The pebbles represent smaller things in your life like your job, school, marriage, and other important happenings that have occurred.

The sand represents all of the fun things you can do just to fill your life, like parties, picnics, visits to friends, family, nursing homes, prisons, school reunions, family reunions, shopping sprees, Christmas gifts, and other things that makes your life better and happier.

One student said, "Professor, I can understand the meaning of that, but where does the coffee come in?"

The Professor said, "This just goes to show, that no matter how full your life is, you can always find time to have a cup of coffee with a friend!"

I hope your life is filled with the love of Jesus, good family, good friends, pebbles of good memories and enough of the smaller grains of sand to make your life complete. And....I hope you can always find a friend to share a cup of coffee or a cup of hot chocolate, or a cup of tea with. God bless you!

Matthew 22:37
Jesus replied: " 'Love the Lord your God with all your heart and with all your soul and with all your mind.'

****

HE IS OUR FATHER

We have probably never had much of a problem relating to God as our Lord, or that He is the Supreme Being in the Universe. But, have we ever put much thought into why we would call Him our Father? What does a good earthly father do for his children? He loves the child...he provides for the child and he protects the child, no matter what it cost him. He makes sure the child has basic needs and he shares his name with the child.

God provides for your needs.

Matthew 6:25-34

"Therefore I tell you, do not worry about your life, what you will eat or drink; or about your body, what you will wear. Is not life more important than food, and the body more important than clothes? Look at the birds of the air; they do not sow or reap or store away in barns, and yet your heavenly Father feeds them. Are you not much more valuable than they? Who of you by worrying can add a single hour to his life? "And why do you worry about clothes? See how the lilies of the field grow. They do not labor or spin. Yet I tell you that not even Solomon in all his splendor was dressed like one of these. If that is how God clothes the grass of the field, which is here today and tomorrow is thrown into the fire, will he not much more clothe you, O you of little faith? So do not worry, saying, 'What shall we eat?' or 'What shall we drink?' or 'What shall we wear?' For the pagans run after all these things, and your heavenly Father knows that you need them. But seek first his kingdom and his righteousness, and all these things will be given to you as well. Therefore do not worry about tomorrow, for tomorrow will worry about itself. Each day has enough trouble of its own."

God protects us and keeps us safe.

Psalm 91:14-16

"Because he loves me," says the Lord, "I will rescue him;
I will protect him, for he acknowledges my name.
He will call upon me, and I will answer him;
I will be with him in trouble,
I will deliver him and honor him.
With long life will I satisfy him
and show him my salvation."

God comforts us.

Psalm 94:19
When anxiety was great within me,
your consolation brought joy to my soul.

God loves his children.

Psalm 103:11
For as high as the heavens are above the earth, so
great is his love for those who fear him;

God has adopted you.

Ephesians 1:5
He predestined us to be adopted as his sons through Jesus
Christ, in accordance with his pleasure and will—

God has given you His name.

1 John 3:1
How great is the love the Father has lavished on us, that we should
be called children of God! And that is what we are! The reason
the world does not know us is that it did not know him.

Isn't this proof enough that He is our Father? If we believe in Him, and honor Him, we will have eternity to spend with Him. Claiming Him as Father here on earth is just preparing us for the glorious relationship with Him in Heaven! We need to work even harder at being good and obedient Children so we can one day live with our Heavenly Father.

A LESSON TO BE LEARNED

I sit here and wonder what God is trying to show us or to tell us! People in all of the world are living like there is no living God, and there will be no punishment on judgment day. Some areas seem to be worse than others, but all of us are falling short of worshiping God and telling others the good news.

Just think about Noah's time. Everyone.... absolutely everyone, except Noah, his wife, their three sons and their wives, and the animals he took aboard, were killed.

When God looked down at Sodom and Gomorrah, seeing the sins of every kind, seeing people worship other gods, He rained fire and brimstone down on the whole city.

There are so many other places in the Bible where God just gets tired of waiting for people to turn back to him. He made us all and He can destroy us all, if He wants to. I know it must break His heart to destroy so much of His creation, but He is the Judge. But He wants us to turn from the sins and worship Him and be His children.

I look back in recent history and recall the big earthquake in the east, over around China. It killed thousands of people...men, women and children. I am sure there were good people among these, but God chose this their time to die. For the most part, people in this area do not believe in or worship the living God. They definitely don't like Christians coming over there promoting their God and their way of life. Many are killed when they preach the word to these people. Was this a wake up call?

Then there was the bombing of the Federal Building in Oklahoma City. It too killed many men, women and children....a lot of them being very good people. But this points at the Federal Government. The Government is full of demon controlled politicians who are leading this country straight to hell and are laughing all the way.

Then we saw the bombing of the twin towers in New York. This took the lives of thousands of men, women and children as well. Even though New York is known for its violence, drugs, gangs, theft, and murders, the whole city immediately fell to its knees. They prayed together, they helped clean up the rubble together, they comforted one another, and for a short time, the churches were filled and the crime rate went to almost non-existent but only for a short time. But this didn't last for long. The true lesson was obviously not learned.

When the great tsunami hit, it killed thousands of people. These people worshiped the water as their god... and the living God let their god, the water, devastate their land. Do you think that the ones left learned the lesson that God was trying to teach them?

Wild fires, earthquakes, and mud-slides are getting worse in California. Is God trying to tell us something? California is the "movie capital" of the world. They make movies portraying every evil known to man. They make it graphic and nothing is forbidden to be put on the "big screen". The movies promote sex, murder, rape, homosexuals, law disruption, drugs and of course pornography, and they use it to "entertain" America. California, among a few other states, promote homosexuals as normal lifestyles. Marriages between the sexes are not only legal, but they are supposed to be respected. Children can be adopted by these living this perverted lifestyles. Is there a lesson to be learned here?

Every hurricane that comes into the Gulf of Mexico or anywhere near, seems to hit the southern half of Florida. Florida has become a den for drug dealers from Cuba, Haiti, and South America as well as other nations. They even call it "Little Cuba". Two hurricanes have hit hard, devastating the shores of the Gulf of Mexico within one month.

The first was Katrina, hitting the New Orleans area, spreading out along the Biloxi area. Some cities were almost wiped off of the map. New Orleans was flooded as well as damaged by the wind. This area of the coastline is noted worldwide for crime, drugs, gangs, pornography, rape, homosexuals, murder, gambling, robbery and any other sins you can think of. Even while some were in shelters, there was rape and murder, right there in the shelters where people were sent to be "safe".

Most of the refugees evacuating the New Orleans area headed for Houston. Ironically, the next hurricane, Rita, headed directly for the Houston area, turning at the last minute to miss the direct hit there. Was there a lesson to be learned here.

During the hurricane, for days, there was no lights anywhere, no food stores open, no gas stations. Is God preparing us for the end times, when there will be no luxuries like electricity, plenty of food, gas for cars, or jobs, and we will wonder around in the dark, hungry and lost.

Then come the floods in the New England states. They have never had such floods in all of its history. This area still practices witchcraft openly. Is this a lesson for them maybe?

Friends, we had better wake up and listen to Jesus. This is serious! I feel the end of time here on earth is getting near, and hardships are just beginning. Have you prayed for forgiveness from the Master? Are you going to be swept up to Heaven, or will you be standing here looking up, and you'll be left behind. I want to have my victory with Jesus...If you don't live your life for Jesus, you will have your victory with the devil.

2 Peter 3:9

The Lord is not slow in keeping his promise, as some understand slowness. He is patient with you, not wanting anyone to perish, but everyone to come to repentance.

****

LUMP OF CLAY

An old Grandma was standing close to a mantel looking at a beautiful vase. Sometimes there would be tears in her eyes as she reached out so gently and touched it. Her Granddaughter came to her and asked her about the vase. She put her arm around her Granddaughter and lifted the vase and then motioned for her to come over to the old rocking chair with her.

She lifted the child up on her lap and for a moment she just sat and looked at the vase. She said, "Child, this reminds me of how God is always demonstrating His wonderful love for us. You see, this beautiful vase was once just a big old lump of clay. It had no purpose, and no one ever saw the beauty in it. This was just a lump on the earth.

Then, one day, Jesus came along and picked up the lump of clay. He started molding it. The little lump cried in fear because he didn't know what to expect, but God said, 'It's OK little lump! I have plans for you!' Then Jesus placed it on the wheel and it spun round and round. It was beginning to take a shape but the lump of clay couldn't figure out what he was becoming. The little lump fought to get loose and asked Jesus to put him down. But, Jesus in His gentle voice said, 'Little lump, I'm not through with you yet!'

Then Jesus picked up the clay and placed it in an oven with flames all around. Just as the little lump thought he couldn't take any more, the oven door opened, and the gentle hands of Jesus reached in the oven and took the clay from the fire oven.

For a moment Jesus held the little lump in His loving hands and smiled. 'You're turning out just fine!'

The lump flexed and stretched and somehow felt stronger than ever. He thought the ordeal was over when he noticed that Jesus was holding some special paint brushes and a very special paint. The brushes tickled the lump as they brushed against it softly, but the awful fumes of the paint almost took its breath away. Again he cried and asked what had he done to be treated so. But Jesus just smiled and continued to paint. After a bit, Jesus sat the lump on a shelf in front of a mirror.

Still not knowing what to expect, he shyly looked in the mirror expecting to see the ugly old piece of clay. Instead he saw a beautiful vase, gracefully painted to be one of a kind."

'And now you have a purpose,' Jesus said as He placed a red rose in the vase. 'This represents my love for you and it will always be with you!"

"Honey," Grandma said, "that vase is like me and you. He took us when we were all sinful and ugly, and He gradually shaped us into something beautiful.

Oh, sometimes we fought it all the way, and we thought we would like to live without Jesus and His love. He tested us with the fire of the Holy Spirit so we would be stronger. He gave each of us a personality of our own so we would be one of a kind. He gave us each a gift so we would have a purpose in this world. He put His love in our heart so we would always know right from wrong, and we could always know that He loved us and that He was always with us. Each of God's children is beautiful because we were molded and made by the Master's own hands!"

Romans 9:21

Does not the potter have the right to make out of the same lump of clay some pottery for noble purposes and some for common use?

****

WHO AM I

Who am I that God would deem me so special? I'm just a sinner saved by His blood! Yet, He finds so many ways to make me useful in His work! Maybe there is a Grandchild who needs someone to pattern their life after... someone to teach them the beauty of sewing, or cooking, or praying...or teach them to fish or hunt, or tie a knot or make a kite.

Maybe it's the lonely one who has no friends, and you can share a hug. If you are a mother, you are the nurse, the housekeeper, the referee, the cook, the comforter, the peacekeeper, the one who rocks the fevered baby until it is better, and can kiss away the child's hurt or pain.

If you are a father you teach your child discipline, camping techniques, the best fishing holes, to ride their first bike, to drive a car, and stays under the hood of his first car until it is "purring like a kitten". You may have to talk to the town bully so the child can put fear behind him. Maybe you can play ball with the kid down the street that has no daddy.

Maybe God is using you to be a friend to the one who lives next door, in the next room or the next cell. Maybe He's given you a beautiful voice to sing the message to those who won't listen to the preacher's sermon, or fingers that touch others as they seem to bring the different instruments to life.

Maybe He gave you the ability to be a prayer warrior, a teacher, a preacher, a mentor to someone. Perhaps you take food to the needy, visit the lonely, or give monetary help to the poor without blowing your own whistle. Your call may be to be a missionary, a helper in Bible School, or just to help an old lady across the street or across the hall, or help someone get something off of the top shelf in the grocery store. Maybe He has given you a smile that is contagious to everyone you meet. He may have given you a personality to entertain the ones in your midst with laughter and stories.

Who we are always reflects in what we do. If you love Jesus, and have Jesus in your heart, your activities will speak louder than words. When we work for Jesus, no matter what talent He has blessed us with, no matter the age, the color or the social standing, He smiles and His heart swells with pride and love, and the Angels sing! But, when He gives us talents or He enables us to do something we could not do otherwise, and we use it to glorify "self" it literally breaks His heart.

The Bible tells us that He gave each of His children a gift, and he didn't say anything about when we got old He would take the gift back. But, if as we age, our voice fails or arthritis gets into our hands, or maybe we don't speak as well as

we used to, then He just gives us a hug, and replaces this gift with another, and gives us the ability and pleasure to do another work for Him.

Psalm 92:12-15
The righteous will flourish like a palm tree, they
will grow like a cedar of Lebanon;
planted in the house of the Lord, they will flourish in the courts of our God.
They will still bear fruit in old age, they will stay fresh and green, proclaiming,
"The Lord is upright; he is my Rock, and there is no wickedness in him."

****

I DID IT JUST FOR YOU

When you were small, did your parents ever do anything special for you, and they would say, "I did it just for you!"? Did someone make your favorite meal and say, "I did it just for you!"? Even at times, people say things to help you, and they say, "I did it just for you!" If we would stand still long enough, we would hear Jesus say, "I did it just for you!"

As you stand and look at an awesome sunset, a brilliant sunrise, a beautiful flower opening, you may hear Him say, "I did it just for you!" He's given you babies, husbands or wives and then say, "I did it just for you!"

Some have wonderful, natural, God given talents. Some to sing, or play musical instruments, to preach, to teach, to smile through strife, to give a hug when it is needed most, to pray and reach the Throne Room of God, to love, to be a missionary, and the list goes on and on. As we use these talents for God, and we wonder how we acquired these special gifts, Jesus says to us, "I did it just for you!"

We see healings and miracles and dreams come true...and we feel His arms around us when trouble and sadness seems to be all around. We question why He chose someone like us to bless so greatly, and in the quiet of the moment we hear Him say, "Because of you child, I did this just for you!"

You see the smile of an Angel on the face of a friend, you hear a message from God on the lips of a stranger, or encouragement from a friend at just the right time, when you needed it the most. Then you seem to hear Jesus whisper, "I did it just for you!"

One day, over two thousand years ago, a King was nailed to a cross. Rusty nails were driven through His hands and His feet. As He was dying in agony and pain on that old cross, He thought of me! He looked down through the years and He saw my sins and my life, both the good and the bad, and through His tears He said, "My Child, I'm doing this just for you!"

Isaiah 53:5-6

But he was pierced for our transgressions,
he was crushed for our iniquities;
the punishment that brought us peace was upon him,
and by his wounds we are healed.
We all, like sheep, have gone astray,
each of us has turned to his own way;
and the Lord has laid on him
the iniquity of us all.

****

GOD'S COLORING BOOK

One day a long, long time ago, God got out His great big canvas and His huge box of colors. On the canvas was a ball, a huge black ball...void of color. God, being a God of light, decided to add color to this "world". First of all, He separated lightness from darkness so the colors could be enjoyed more.

He colored water in shades of blue or green, and even the color of muddy water. Some water was crystal clear.

He then colored the dry ground in shades of blacks, browns, tans, clay red and even the white sandy beaches.

He colored the mountain sides in layers of blacks, reds, browns, tans, oranges, yellows and purples.

It was beginning to take shape now, but it still lacked something. So, He pulled out all of His shades of green. (There must have been hundreds of green colors.) He then painted trees, and bushes, plants, and grass on the ground. Boy! It sure looked good...so cool and refreshing!

But, still, it seemed void of something. So again, He reached into His huge box of colors and painted white Magnolia blossoms, pink Azaleas, purple Iris, red Roses, yellow Goldenrods, purple Wisteria, orange Trumpet vines, blue Cornflowers, golden Sunflowers, purple violets, golden wheat, tossing in the wind. Everything looked so beautiful that He started experimenting with different colored flowers, more species... and the "world" grew more beautiful and plush.

As he looked over His work, He sensed that something was still missing. He made the sun to shine in the daytime against a blue sky, painted the clouds red, purple, orange and gold at sunsets. The moon lit up the night with a pale, but beautiful light.

Even with all of this, it seemed to need something else. So, He thought He'd fill the ocean and the other bodies of water with fish...and He made the gigantic whale, the shark, the rainbow trout, the wide mouth bass, the whiskered catfish, the salmon that swims upstream, starfish, octopus, tropical fish, crawfish that walked sideways, lobsters and again, the colors changed and the species grew.

He stood looking at the beauty of His canvas...but it was so quiet. He looked up at the sky and colored an Eagle of black and gray and white, a Red Headed Woodpecker, Red Cardinals, Blue Jays, sparrows, red breasted Robins, colorful Hummingbirds, Parakeets of blues and greens, yellow Canaries, Toucans, Parrots with bright colored feathers, Peacocks with turquoise plumage, and even the clumsy Emu. But, He kept on coloring in birds until there were thousands of different kinds of birds and their colors were outstanding. Their colors would even let them camouflage themselves in the flowers.

Needing even more to make the picture complete, He colored in some yellow cats, white cats, black cats, tabby cats, stripe cats, and even some black cats with a white stripe down their back. (PHEW) He colored black dogs, white dogs, spotted dogs, brown dogs, long haired dogs, short haired dogs, and even wolves. He colored the long neck Giraffe, the Rhino with one horn, the wide mouth Hippo, beautiful, graceful deer, bears of brown, and black and white, striped Zebras, graceful Horses, proud lions, awesome tigers, gigantic Elephants with strange trunks, cows, pigs, goats, monkeys, and then He colored more! Soon the land was full of all kinds of animals. He even painted in some gators and Crocks as well as Reptiles.

With all of the chirping, purring, growling, lowing, snorting and other animal sounds, the "world" still seemed to be a lonely place. So, He made Adam and Eve and then other humans, coloring their skin red, yellow, black and white and all shades in between.

Ah-h-h-h-h, at last His canvas was complete… and God rested.

Genesis 1:1
In the beginning God created the heavens and the earth.

****

HURRICANE KATRINA

"God is watching O'er all, and He hears us when we call.....
I'm so glad I now can say, Love will roll the clouds away!"

On Monday, August 29, 2005, Katrina, a category 5 hurricane, headed angrily for the New Orleans coastline. Before hitting land it dropped to a category 4. Devastation then began. Then it started dancing and prancing up to Magnolia, Mississippi. (We are only about fifty or sixty miles straight shot to New Orleans.) We had experienced the edge of hurricanes before, but never really felt the brunt of one.

We had kinda buckled down and prepared for a bit of bumpy weather. We figured we would maybe be out of power for a day or two, and maybe a few trees down, but we weren't prepared for what happened.

Well, the wind picked up about 6:30 in the morning and the power was lost about 7:00. It wasn't long before I knew this area was in trouble, so I started praying ... praying hard! My porch was full of potted plants so the night before I had pushed them back off the edge to prevent some of the damage.

As the storm progressed to 100 plus mph winds and sheets of rain, I went out on my front porch. It has a roof over it but three sides are open, south, east and west. There was almost a continuous roar as of a jet engine, as the wind screamed through the trees, taking almost all of the leaves off and branches and much to often the tree itself fell victim to the storm.

It was about then that I noticed that something was different. I looked at the highway which runs about the distance of a half of a football field in front of the house, and I watched from the left and saw the wind and rain rage from east to west....sheeting down the highway. Then I looked to the right and saw the rain raging from west to east. Big trees were bending low and snapping. Then the big oak tree right out front of my house caught my attention. It was barely moving, only like in a spring breeze. I was standing here on the open porch and felt no rain, so no movement from wind on the flowers. Such peace I found here on my porch. I felt like God Himself had us hovered under His wings like a momma chicken would cover her biddies and protect them. The whole family sat on the porch in the swings and in chairs, but none of us got wet or felt the brunt of the wind. I could have left all of the flowers on the edge of the porch and they wouldn't have even gotten watered much less, windblown. I spent most of the day on the porch, watching this storm lash out like someone very angry.

My home is surrounded by large oak trees and with the wind as it was, I feared the worst for my house and the house trailer that my mom lived in right next to

me....so I prayed harder. Even though the storm controlled the next seven and one half hours, I didn't get any house damage or even pot plant damage. I did lose a treetop from a Magnolia tree and a china-berry tree, lots of limbs both large and small, and twigs, but not one touched my house or my Mom's trailer. The hardest wind was from the east and west, and the trees and large limbs fell north and south.

The yard is a disaster, but our family and homes are fine. We stayed without power for sixteen days, and we had about gotten used to it when the lights came on. Gas for cars and generators was non-existent for a few days, bread and ice was a luxury, but we survived and grew closer as a family and a lot closer to God. We still see the battle scars of Katrina, but we are going to be fine because.....

"God is watching o'er all, and He hears us when we call....
I'm so glad I now can say, Love will roll the clouds away!"

God is watching over me and you!

Psalm 121:3-4
He will not let your foot slip—he who watches over you will not slumber; indeed, he who watches over Israel will neither slumber nor sleep.

****

THE 23RD PSALM

All of us have read the 23rd Psalm. It is such a beautiful passage, but are we getting all of the meaning from it that God intended? Let's read it together.

"The Lord is my Shepherd...."
(That is RELATIONSHIP)
Jesus wants us to have a good relationship with Him. We need to be able to turn to Him for all of our needs, and for our peace of mind and for our Salvation.

"I shall not want...."
(That is SUPPLY)
Jesus will take care of all of our needs, if we only ask. He loves us and He wants to do this for us.

"He maketh me to lie down in green pastures..."
(That is REST)
He doesn't just pick any old place for us to rest, He picks the green lush pastures...the very best.

"He leadeth me beside the still waters..."
(That is REFRESHMENT)
What a peaceful, refreshing scene... looking out beyond the still waters. This is where the soul can be refreshed and find peace.

"He restoreth my soul..."
(That is HEALING)
God is our Great Physician....He can heal our body, our soul, our relationship, our financial needs, and our mind.

"He leadeth me in the paths of righteousness..."
(That is GUIDANCE)
He leads us to life eternal. He wrote His laws upon our heart so we would always know right from wrong, and He gave us the Holy Spirit to live within us, continually guiding us on the right path.

"For His name sake..."
(That is a PURPOSE)
He adopted us into His royal family. He is our Father and He loves us so much. We should continually strive to live right and be like Him.

"Yea, though I walk through the valley of the shadow of death..."
(That is TESTING)
The devil is always placing snares in our path, trying to trip us up. God gave us the sense to do what is right, but the thing is, we often take the wrong path. He tells us that no matter what the devil throws at us, He is there for us. All we have to do is love Him and believe in Him. Sometimes, I think he lets us be tested by the snares, but this only makes our faith stronger.

"I will fear no evil...."
(That is PROTECTION)
We will all probably face death here on earth unless we get to rise up with the Rapture. But no matter what happens, if we have Salvation, we can die to live again, with Jesus. The devil cannot take our soul, my friend, but we can give it to him!

"For Thou art with me..."
(That is FAITHFULNESS)
Jesus tells us that he will never leave or forsake us. He is there even during the darkest storms in our life. He is there when we are happy. He is faithful. He is the same yesterday, today and tomorrow. He is the Great I Am and not the Great I Was!

"Thy rod and Thy staff they comfort me..."
(That is DISCIPLINE)
Just like a parent disciplines a child when they disobey, God disciplines His children. If there were no discipline, we would run wild, never fearing the consequences of doing wrong, and our Salvation would be forever lost.

"Thou preparest a table before me in the presence of mine enemies..."
(That is HOPE)
He rains downs blessings on us, even when our enemies are looking. He wants them to see that He is a good God and a forgiving God, so they will turn their wicked souls around and worship Him.

"Thou annointest my head with oil..."
(That is CONSECRATION)
He is preparing us to be a priest in Heaven... to be Holy and pure.

"My cup runneth over..."
(That is ABUNDANCE)
When we live our lives for Him and do His work, He gives us blessings. Surely, more than we deserve, and even more than we could ever imagine....only because He loves us so!

"Surely goodness and mercy shall follow me all the days of my life..."
(That is BLESSING))
When He died on that old cross, He gave us mercy and grace to have our sins forgiven, forgotten and covered with blood. The devil can try, but he can not win the war.... Jesus defeated the devil and death... so that even when our eyes close in death, and we take the last breath here on earth and our body is laid in the cold dark grave, we will waken with our next breath in Heaven.

"And I will dwell in the house of the Lord..."
(That is SECURITY)
If we live a good life, fight a good fight, and live our life for Jesus, we are promised a home in Heaven.... A mansion, no less. A home that will never rot down, or termites will never bother it. A home that will never need repair, or insurance, and we will never have to leave our heavenly home!

"Forever..."
(That is ETERNITY)
Eternity has no time span. Time doesn't move. As the song says, "When we've been there ten thousand years .... We've no less days to sing His praise, than when we first begun."

Maybe now, the next time you read the 23rd Psalm, you with realize the promises that go with it.

OUR LAST VACATION

Have you ever gotten ready to go on a great trip, and you were so excited that you could hardly wait? You grabbed your fifteen suitcases and started packing. There were so many things to remember...and you were sure in the back of your mind that you would forget something! You probably had a calendar with the days marked down to the day of departure. You could hardly think about anything else. You anxiously told all of your friends about the trip you would be taking. You had to remember to stop the mail and the newspaper and the milk delivery. Someone would have to come in and feed the cat, the dog and water the plants. It was so exhausting just to get everything in order.

Then comes the day of departure...your cab is late...the suitcase won't shut... you forgot to call and confirm the reservations...the phone is ringing...and the list goes on and on. Will you ever get started on your journey?

As you arrive at your destination, the weather is hot and all you packed is cold weather clothes. The hotel room that you "reserved" has been given to someone else. Finally, the clerk offers you a little small room with one twin bed, for the same price as the huge room and two king beds. The dress code is very dressy and all you brought is jeans...nothing is going right! There is panic in the hotel because there is a bomb threat. You immediately decide that this is not a vacation after all, and you just can't wait to get back home!

But, you know, your final vacation will be much different from this. If your soul is saved, Jesus Himself will take care of all of the details. You won't need the fifteen suitcases. Everything that you need can be packed into your heart and soul. As long as you live your life for Jesus, you won't forget a thing. Before you depart on your trip, you will tell all of your friends and family about your plans. There will be no need to contact the mail or the paper or the milk delivery to stop their services. You will no longer worry about feeding the dog or the cat, nor watering the plants. You have no need to countdown the days for departure, because God makes it like a surprise. One day you're here and the next day you are gone.

The weather will have no bearing on your final vacation. The weather is always perfect. Reservations are not to be bothered with...because God has reserved a mansion of your very own for you in Heaven. Clothes will never be a problem because we will have a snow-white robe and a crown of gold when we reach Heaven! Once we get through the pearly gates and see Jesus on the throne, we wouldn't want to come back. There is a song that sticks in my mind. It tells us that when Jesus heard that Lazarus was dead, He wept. Well, I don't think He cried because Lazarus was dead, but because He had to bring him back.... And

Lazarus would have to leave Heaven...a place of beauty and rest and peace, and to be in the presence of Jesus Himself.

Who would want to leave? Some of us are nearing the time for our departure, and we know it. Some have a long time to wait. Some are a lot closer to the departure than we know. All we can do is to always be ready and faithful to the Master, and live our life in anticipation of life eternal in Heaven with Jesus. What a vacation that will be! I guess the best thing is, this vacation will never end!

Luke 10:20
However, do not rejoice that the spirits submit to you, but rejoice that your names are written in heaven."

****

BIBLE STORIES

Why don't we just sit and close our eyes and picture things that are talked about in the Bible! Even though it happened long ago, in our mind we can view it as if it were happening in our own community and in our own time!

As we look into the distance, entering Egypt, I see Moses and Aaron walking. They are gathering up God's children to get them out of Egypt. I see old Pharaoh on his throne, scheming to keep them there. I see a cloud of fire leading them and I can see the Red Sea part and dry land appear. They joyously dance across to the other side. I hear the moans and screams of Pharaoh's army as they drown. I can even see them walking through the desert for forty years, and their clothes and their shoes neither wearing out or being out-grown. I see Moses taking his shoes off as he stands on the Holy ground by the burning bush, and I see Moses on the mountain as he writes the commandments God gives to him on slate.

I hear Noah is building a huge boat...he calls it an ark. He said it is going to rain...RAIN... down from Heaven. Is he crazy? Water has never fell from the skies. He tells us that he and his wife, and his three sons and their wives would be on the boat. The people here are so wicked and evil that they don't want to be saved.

The boat is finally finished and old Noah is gathering up the animals...a pair of everything. Look how gentle all the animals are...the bears, the lions, the leopards, and all of the other huge and wild creatures. They just line up and go into the big boat!

Then it starts "raining" and people panic and want in, but Jesus Himself closes the door and no one can open it but Him. For forty days and nights it rained. Everything on earth is destroyed, except the ark and the people and the animals on it. When it stops raining, God puts the rainbow in the sky and promised that He will never destroy the world with water again.

Joshua and his army are marching around and around the city of Jericho. They are not saying a word. Do they think they will win a battle like that? They've marched around the city for six times now and this is the seventh time. As they end the circle all of the men in the army shout as loud as they can .... And would you believe.. the walls of the city just collapsed, and he took the city.

Look over that ledge! They just threw a man in the lion's den. They said they told him to stop praying to God and he wouldn't. Poor man! Wait!...He is walking around down there in the midst of the lions. They are not even trying to hurt him. They are just like large kittens. He even laid his head on one of the lions in order to rest. That is amazing!

There is a meeting. I hear a king tell his guards to build the fire seven times hotter than it ought to be. He has three Hebrew men to throw in. He told them to worship the pagan idols and they refused. They said they wouldn't bow and they wouldn't bend to the gods. When they were thrown into the furnace, they wouldn't burn either. And there is a fourth man in there with them... He is dressed in white and they are just walking around and laughing and talking and singing. Wow! The fourth man is Jesus!

And here we are in a courtyard. People cry "Crucify Him, Crucify Him!" Who are they talking about? Then they throw out a man... beaten and bleeding. Was He that bad? Someone standing near me said that was Jesus! They say he had never done any wrong, but evil people wanted Him gone. He carried a heavy wooden cross to a hill called Golgotha and there they put nails in His hands and His feet...and hung Him on a cross between two thieves. My heart feels heavy and sad, and in my heart I know He is the King of Kings and the Lord of Lords... and my Savior died!

Friends, Jesus died on that cross for your sins, and He did it because He loved you so much. Don't you love Him? Will you live your life for Him? Will you pray and read your Bible, and tell others that you love Him? If you don't know Jesus, you need to get on your knees and ask for forgiveness of your sins, and take Him as your Savior. Don't let Him have died in vain!

Hebrews 10:10
And by that will, we have been made holy through the sacrifice of the body of Jesus Christ once for all.

****

GOD'S LOVE

In this life we sometimes get into trouble by doing something too many times. If we try alcohol too many times, we become an alcoholic...enjoying the stupor of the liquor. If you smoke a cigarette too many times, you crave the cigarette, and you soon know you are addicted to it. Eating too much food can put you in an obese situation that can ruin your whole health. It only takes once with some of the drugs and you are in its power. Other things can have bad aftermaths...like too many parties, lying, cheating, pornography, gossiping, stealing, killing, drug dealing, and putting "I" above everything else.

But there are certainly things we can't do too much! Like, we can never love Jesus too much or live for Him too much. We can't go to church too much or help our fellow man too much, pray too much or give too much.

We can't overdose on love. Having love for our families doesn't break up homes or families. Love doesn't cause our body to shut down with diseases. Just think of how much Jesus loves us! He gave His life for us! He was beaten so that we might be healed....died so we could live. He died in agony and pain for our sins that we might have the mercy and the grace to join Him in Heaven. He was spit on, made fun of... just for us.

Could we do this for our children, our family, or a stranger on the street? How much love does it take to lay down your life for another? Because Jesus loves us so much, He could do that. He died for each and every sinner in the world, not just the sinners then, but he died for me and for you, and we weren't even a twinkle in our Mom and Dad's eye...but He knew us and He loved us. After all He has done for us, don't let Him down. There will never be another who will love you this much!

Romans 11:6
And if by grace, then it is no longer by works; if it
were, grace would no longer be grace.

****

THE PURPOSE DRIVEN CHRISTMAS

(How often have we went through a Christmas Season, focusing on ourselves, rather than the real reason for this season, Jesus. How often do we worry about friends and loved ones appreciating the present we bought for them, not focusing on the things we should do for Jesus...after all...Christmas is His birthday! The following is a list of things to put our focus back on Jesus, not only during this special time but all throughout the year!)

1. **It's all about God...His gift of Jesus His Son and for us to live a life that pleases Him. (WORSHIP)**

2. **It's all about loving others, even the ones who are unlovable. (FELLOWSHIP)**

3. **It's all about trying to become more like Christ! (DICIPLESHIP)**

4. **It's all about serving others above self! (MINISTRY)**

5. **It's all about telling the Good News that Jesus was born to save a lost world, one person at a time! (EVANGELISM)**

(Jesus came to become one of us so we could become one of His! May your Christmas Season have a purpose.)

Zephaniah 3:17

The Lord your God is with you, he is mighty to save. He will take great delight in you, he will quiet you with his love, he will rejoice over you with singing."

****

NEW YEAR'S RESOLUTIONS

As the New Year approaches, some people tend to make "New Year Resolutions", or promises to keep during the new year. Some promise to lose weight and to eat better, some say they will be more thrifty with their spending.... some will work on their temper, some will try to stop smoking or drinking or other bad habits...some will vow to be a better Mom or a better Dad, or even a better child or student! Whatever the intention, we cannot succeed completely without the help of God!

Let's be realistic this year! Let our first New Year's resolution be to have a closer walk with Jesus. Let's focus our lives around Him and what He wants for us. Here are a few "New Year's Resolutions" you might try!

1. Let God be first in your life. No matter what you try, if you put God first and follow His will, you will succeed.

2. Read your Bible daily, and ask yourself, "Now how does this apply to my life?"

3. Pray faithfully and earnestly. Pray for family, for friends, for your enemies, for government, for America, and for the lost. Pray from your heart and not just from your lips!

4. Love one another...help one another, and remember not to gossip...for as you gossip about another, someone may just be gossiping about you. Think of how that would hurt. If you hear someone gossiping, just say, "I don't want to go there." Friends and co-workers will soon get the message that you are not a gossip.

5. Share the Gospel with everyone you meet in some shape or form. Even if you don't speak a word at times, people should be able to hear you loud and clear by the way you live your life!

6. Smile....smile at strangers, at family members, even at enemies. A smile for the most part will make anyone feel better, no matter what their situation!

7. Be more helpful to the elderly, the widows, the children without both parents, for the ones who are less fortunate than you, both health-wise and financially.

8. **Make special times to be with your family. Don't just go about your way, cooking, cleaning, working, taking care of the kids, and miss out on the special time with your mate and your children, and your parents. This will be some of the most precious memories in your life. All too soon, they are gone.**

9. **Visit more with shut-ins and the sick. Five minutes of quality time with them is worth much more than you'll ever know.**

10. **Attend Church regularly. Take your family. Don't just go and sit on the pew...listen to the message and listen to what God may be telling you through the message. Listen to the songs....they are messages, too. Go to Church with an open heart and Jesus will fill it, and your cup will overflow.**

Well, I sure hope this new year will be a blessed year, and may Jesus always walk with you. May your troubles be few and your joys be many.

2 Corinthians 9: 15
Thanks be to God for His gift that is too wonderful for words.

WHERE ARE WE GOING

Before Jesus arrived on that cold night in Bethlehem, his coming was predicted. Prophets had told the people to live right and to do right. In Isaiah, His birth and His crucifixion was prophesized. It was told that He would be the King of Kings and Lord of Lords.

At His birth, King Herod tried to find Him and kill Him, because of Herod's evil heart. But God protected Jesus... it wasn't time. Then John the Baptist told of the one who would follow him. He said, "I come to baptize you with water, but the one who is coming will baptize you with the Holy Spirit. Of Him, I am not worthy to even tie His sandals." His followers and Apostles spread the Gospel into other parts of the world. Some, however, still listened to their evil hearts, and persecuted the Christians for their belief. The Christians were stoned to death, beaten to death, boiled in oil, beheaded, thrown in lion's dens, skinned alive, burned, and tortured and persecuted in almost every other way imaginable. But still, His chosen ones refused to bow to the idols. Jesus Himself was persecuted, made fun of, and ridiculed, and crucified on a cross.

The evil hearted people finally found a way to crucify Jesus...or they thought it was their idea. If it had not been time for this event, God would not have permitted it to happen. Jesus hung there on the cross, and He died there. He could have called ten thousand Angels to come to His rescue, but he didn't. Satan and his followers rejoiced...but this was not the end. In three days, He arose from that cold, dark tomb, and went into Hell and took the keys of death away from Satan. Never again would the death of a Christian be a victory for Satan. A Christian would have a home in Heaven with Him after death here on earth. We were given the Holy Spirit to lead and guide us along the way.

Well, as time went on, people seemed to become just a little more civilized in dealing with these "Christians". Oh, I am sure that right up until the present time, many Christians are being martyred for the sake of Jesus...but it is mostly kept "hush-hush".

The people in England once was so hungry for freedom of religion, they got on boats and ventured to America, hoping to be able to worship as they pleased... and for a while it seemed to work. Everything they did was done according to the scriptures...the laws of the new land were based on the morals of the Bible. The children in the homes were raised with true Christian morals, and the school promoted the same. The money had "In God We Trust" inscribed on it. The pledge of allegiance was amended to include the words, "One Nation under God"... and no one at the time protested. This as a Christian nation, and it was known worldwide for its Christian values. But that offended some of the non-

Christians, and again the lawmakers agreed, and they voted to have those words removed from the pledge. As far as I know, that line is still included in the pledge, but how long will it stay? Where is America going?

Then Satan started getting real worried about the Christians. He couldn't have America known for Christianity. He must do something.... Well, he did! One atheist woman protested prayer in school. She said we Christians offended her! So, the lawmakers of the nation ruled that prayer was unlawful in the schools. Bible classes are seldom found...and you are put down if you try to talk to others about your Jesus in school. Then they decided that we didn't need prayer at ball games and other sporting events. The lawmakers, again, decided that was a good idea. The devil must really be celebrating!

Freedom of speech has been proved to us that this was for the foul-mouthed people...they could utter whatever, no matter how it offended the Christians, and their job was secure. But, for someone to talk to others about Jesus on the job, or Heaven forbid, pray with them on the job, lost their job. Where is America going?

Remember the courtroom that displayed the Ten Commandments? Lawmakers voted to have them removed and make it unlawful to display them in government buildings. It offended some of the non-Christians! But it didn't make any difference if someone uttered a dirty joke, or if there might be obscene art on the wall. If this offended the Christian...who cared? With the justice in courts today, it seems that the Ten Commandments were thrown out of the hearts of the lawmakers, too!

Now, we have reached a new level. Stores around the nation have taken "Christ" out of the holidays. Greeting cards have turned to "Happy Holidays' not "Merry Christmas". Some stores won't let the Salvation Army ring Christmas bells in front of their stores. It seems that it offends the non-Christians. Some stores have told their employees that if they were heard telling a customer "Merry Christmas" they would lose their job. They could say "Happy Holidays". But, when their cash registers ring up a "Christmas tree", or "Christmas ornament" or Christmas clothing" or "Christmas toys", it was a good thing. Where is America going?

My friend, I can feel in the very near future, Christians will once again become martyrs for Jesus. The process will not be done in secret, but in full view. I think that right here in America, we will have to die to admit we are Christians. This is not a country in some remote corner of the world....this is America.... Land of the free, home of the brave! Satan is working overtime with crime, abuse, and atheist standards. Where is America going?

One day, standing there in front of Jesus Himself on Judgment Day, we will have to account for the times we were ashamed of the name of Jesus Christ. You will have to confess all of the times you caved in to the pressure of someone who didn't love Jesus and wanted to erase his goodness from the face of the earth. You were a Judas, and you betrayed your Lord and Savior. You know, He won't care what your lame excuse was, he will say, "Depart from me, for I never knew you!" Then you can go spend eternity with your "friends' and "employers" and

with Satan and all of the demons in hell. You won't have to worry about people talking to you about Jesus because they wanted you to have Salvation. People won't care if the Ten Commandments are not displayed, or if you can't pray! Why, they won't even get upset if you take the name of Jesus in vain...but you will care. You will beg and plead to get out, but this is eternity!

James 4:7-8
Surrender to God! Resist the devil, and he will run from you. Come near to God and He will come near to you. Clean up your lives, you sinners. Purify your hearts you people who can't make up your mind.

OUR SPECIAL ANGELS

As you go along your way, did you ever feel the brush of an Angel wing on your cheek, or did you ever feel like you had a little push from someone when you hesitated to do something for someone else? Well, maybe you have special Angels all around you. Angels are real! They are God's helpers and God's warriors. Each one of us is surrounded by Angels. Maybe we should give some of them names!

The twelve most important Angels walk with us each day. They each have a special job to do! The first three are Faith, Hope and Charity. They are very overworked, but much needed. We must have Faith to keep us believing in Jesus, Hope reminds us of a better tomorrow, and Charity bestows on us the need to give to others, even if we have to do without something ourselves.

Tolerance is the fourth Angel. This Angel makes us slow to anger, and allows us to overlook the small things that others do that aggravate us. This Angel keeps us aware of the fact that we shouldn't hate just because someone is different from us, whether it is in race, religion, or financial standing.

Forgiveness is the fifth Angel, and is needed by all of us. This Angel shows us the need to forgive one another so that the Father will forgive us. God will forgive us of anything if only we ask and repent. Shouldn't we do the same for our fellow man?

The seventh angel is Beauty. Beauty tugs on our arm, and reminds us that there is beauty in everyone...no matter what they look like on the outside. We all look very different on the outside, and God gave us this to add variety to our lives. But on the inside, there is beauty in each and every soul that God created. Some it takes a little longer to find...but it is there!

One Angel is named Conscience. This angel gives us a sense of right and wrong, and nudges us when we make the wrong decision.

The next two Angels are usually found side by side. Their names are Joy and Happiness. These two Angels keep us finding things to rejoice about...for the Love of God and the joy of salvation. They shuffle us in directions of making others happy, and this way we can find a special joy in our own soul.

Another Angel is named Friend. This Angel is always there for you, through the good times and the bad, our tears and our laughter, and is always trying to make things right.

Strength is the next Angel. This Angel holds your hand when there are troubles and trials and you feel like you just can't go on. Strength is there when you lose a loved one, or when you feel defeated, there is a whisper saying, "You can go on. I will help you."

The last Angel is probably the best. Her name is Love. With a special touch, this Angel plants love in our hearts for our family, our friends, our co-workers, and especially for Jesus, because He first loved us. With this special Angel, we care about others. We want the best for others. We hurt and cry with others when times are hard, and we laugh and rejoice with others in the good times. We do this because we love them. There is so many kinds of love, so many ways to say "I love you!"

Now, look around! You know, Angels may not always look like "Angels". They may look like your best friends, or your family members, or even co-workers. Some Angels may even look like strangers that you meet on the street.

There is a friend who seems to always build your faith up when you are down, one friend gives you hope...and one reminds you to give to the ones in need. There is a friend who reminds you of tolerance, one that talks to you about forgiveness. When putting others down, one friend will remind you that there is something good and beautiful in each one of God's children...all we have to do is quit looking for the flaws in the person, and look for the beauty.

Another friend is there when you are about to make the wrong decision, or do the wrong thing, and they gently nudge you to the right way.

One friend will give us joy unmeasured, another brings happiness to our otherwise lonely day. One is a true friend who is always there for us, no matter what the situation...one friend gives you strength to endure, and one friend has showed you what love is...how to love your neighbor, your family and especially God!

So you see, you don't have to imagine you can feel the Angels surrounding you...all you have to do is to look at your friends...and it seems like God has put Angles in your midst, in the form of your friends, and unbeknown to them, they are really Angels in disguise. How very blessed we are!

Luke 15: 10
There is joy in the presence of the Angels of
God when one sinner changes his
heart and life.

****

LOOKING BACK FROM OLD AGE

As we grow older, most Christians focus on the years we might have left and we definitely want the promise of Christ abiding in our heart and soul with a promise of life eternal. We can look back on our life and see events unfurl, that at the time seemed like a tragedy. We couldn't understand the circumstances, but now we can view each incident from start to finish. Most of them turn out to be a blessing in some way. We've learned to try to live a good life, putting Christ first. We used to focus on raising our families, or starting careers, and regretfully God sometimes took the back burner. With this all behind us, we seem to realize how important God really is in our life.

Worries burden us. We worry about our Grandchildren and our Great-grandchildren being raised right, our health and hope we can stretch our finances so money will last as long as we do! As we grow older, we know our days are getting shorter. While most of us are not actually afraid of "dying", it's the fear of the unknown that troubles us. But Jesus promised He will always be there with us. He'll be standing on the banks of the Jordan waiting for us.

Our old eyes and heart can look back and see the failures we experienced as young folks, and some are still dealing with those consequences. But, that's in the past, let's just build a better tomorrow.

Our old age brings with it a reserved spirit of humbleness and faithfulness. We can rely on God. He'll provide for us and take care of us. Our riches these days may not be counted in materialist things, but in the richness of wisdom we can share with our family, our love, our heritage. We seem to depend more on God to guide us in our everyday lives. We cling to the hope of a better tomorrow, a new body, no pain, no cancer, no heart attacks, no doctors, no nursing homes, no prisons, heartaches or sorrow.

God tells us if we're faithful, mercy and grace are sufficient to get us to heaven. All of these years we have been trying to learn to be patient. Now as we sit and ponder life, we patiently wait for visits from family and friends, or we patiently wait for a ride to go someplace, patiently wait for the nurse to bring the next pill, or even patiently contend with Grandchildren.

So many of us older folks live alone, and we depend on God for protection in the midst of the storms, whether it be a storm of life or in stormy weather. He wraps His loving arms around us and gives us peace, strength and comfort.

So you see, growing old is really a blessed time. Enjoy it with Jesus, for your reward awaits in Heaven.

1 Samuel 16: 7
God does not see the same way people see. People look at the outside of a person, But, the Lord looks at the heart.

****

LIVE MY LIFE OVER

Have you ever thought about things that you would do differently if you could live your life over, knowing then what you know now? I think I would be a better child, more respective of my parents. I would do more for them, tell them I love them more often and relish each day I have with them. I would have been a better wife to my husband, a better mother to my children.. and I would love them more, forgive their mistakes quicker, hold them in my arms more and tell them I love them and let them know how important they are in my life.

I would live my life closer to God...give more...smile more...laugh more... help others more...see my fellowman and always look for the good in that person and never put him down to make myself look good. I would look in the mirror and realize that I am God's creation and that He really loves me...and I would try to be a better person. I would still my tongue when gossip wanted to emerge.

If I could live my life over, I would not wait so long to give my heart to Jesus. You know, my friend, as we approach Valentine's Day...we need to figure out just where our heart really is. Do we love Jesus just when it is convenient, when there were troubles and heartaches, trials and failures, and disappointments, pain and despair. Or, would you love Jesus with every breath you breathe. I would talk to Him all through the day and thank Him for the blessings...tell Him I love Him... ask his advise for my daily life, read His word and live by it...and know in my heart that He is my "Lord and Savior", and that he is my very own "Special Valentine".

He pledges all of his love to each of us that will follow Him and repent of our sins. He speaks to us softly, asking us to "be His Valentine", and give Him our heart.

I hope you will never find yourself ashamed of being "God's Valentine" ... and when our days are over and we step up to Heaven's Gate, he won't be ashamed to announce us to the Father and say, "This is my special Valentine...this one gave their heart to me." His arms are open wide, and a smile is on His face...His heart swells with pride each time we do His work and confess our love for Him. He's making a place for us in Heaven, just so we can spend eternity with Him and His Father, along with all of the Saints and our loved ones who have gone on before us. Love Him my friend, for He loved us, even before we were born!

We can't change the past....but we can alter the future!

1 Peter 1: 24
He Himself bore our sins in His body on the tree, so that
we might die to sins and live for righteousness.

****

IMPRESSIONS

As we journey through this life, I wonder if we ever think of the impressions that we leave on others. It's not usually the big things that we do for others, it is the small things that leave the biggest impression on those whom we come in contact with.

Think of the Sunday School teacher that prayed with you, and taught you about Jesus. Think of the smile of your best friend and the way they would always be there for you, no matter what was happening at the time...the twinkle in the eye of the one you fell in love with, and how your heart would flutter each time you would see them or think about them.

Then there was the tear from your Mother when you left your home for college or your own home...and the warmth of the hug from your Dad. Remember how happy your puppy seemed each time he would see you, no matter if you had just scolded him or not, and the warm lap of his tongue on your cheek to greet you.

There was always the clean smell of Grandma, and the smell of work with Grandpa, the gentle touch of a friend, a kind, gentle word at just the right time...a door opened by a stranger, the laughter of children...or a hand to hold when the night is too dark to walk alone.

You'll never forget the first time you saw your child...the last time you saw your Mother...or the first time you met your mate...or your home, as you drove away for a life on your own. There is the smell of Momma's kitchen that reminded us all that love surrounded you there...the security when Daddy told you that everything would be OK. You won't forget the pat on the back when you thought you had done poorly and a friend told you "good job". You'll never forget the phone call in the middle of the night saying a loved one was gone... or a new baby had arrived.

Along the way, you may wonder what impression you may have left on someone. Well, think of the smile you passed on to the stranger in the Mall, the kind word for someone that is having a bad day...the prayer for someone in need...the tear shed for someone else when their troubles are greater than yours... the pat on the back when someone needs lifting up...a hug, a hand in the dark, or special little favors for your family and friends. Live your life for Jesus and that will be the greatest impression you could leave someone.

What kind of impression did Jesus leave on the world? His kindness, gentleness, purity, love, healing, promises of Heaven, perfection, obedience... and the list goes on and on. To each of us, in His own special way, he has left a special impression...the day we were saved, the day we were healed...the day he spoke to us...the touch of His hand on ours.... But the greatest impression

should be the way He suffered and died on the cross...not for His sins because he was without sin, but he died for us....sinners. He loved us so much, he wanted to make the ultimate impression on us...something we would never forget. We need to make sure everyone knows this. Tell others about Jesus. Tell them how He loves them, and how He wants us to live in Heaven with him, and how His abundant mercy and grace is sufficient for us to go there if we repent of our sins and live our lives for Him. If you don't leave another impression on anyone....let them know you love Jesus.

Hosea 2:19
I will make you my promised bride forever, I will be good and fair, I will show you my love and mercy

****

AADD

Today I figured out the real meaning of AADD....(Adult Attention Deficit Disorder). When I got up this morning I thanked Jesus for today. I felt so energetic, so I proceeded to get my chores done. I thought first of all, I'd load the dishwasher, but as I passed the coffee pot, I noticed there was one more cup of coffee left. I would drink that so I could wash the pot and the cup! I got my cup, but looked at the plant in the window. It needed watering. So, I filled the cup with water, bumped the pot and spilled the water. I grabbed a kitchen towel to clean it up, after setting the cup down. Well, the towel needed to be put in the laundry basket.

On the way to the laundry basket, I spotted a shirt that needed hanging up. I lay the towel down and proceeded to hang the shirt up. As I approached the open closet, I noticed a pair of shoes that I had not worn in a while. Well, I think I will put them on! I went to sit on the bed, but it was not made. Oh dear, I'll set the shoes down and make the bed. As I fluffed the pillow, I noticed a small rip in the pillowcase. I thought I may as well sew it up while I'm thinking about it. I took it and headed for the sewing machine. I lay it down beside the machine and picked up a dress lying there. It was missing a button. I need to find a button for it.

I go over to the button box to hunt a button and found some postage stamps in the box. I really need to go put them on my desk. I'll surely need them.

Gosh, this desk is a mess...maybe I ought to clean it off. I found a magazine and started thumbing through it. I found a great looking recipe. I think I have everything I need to fix it. Let me go check. I find I have everything I need except milk. I'll just run to the store and get some.

I picked up the car keys and my purse and headed for the door. As I step outside I see a large ant mound by the steps. I think I have some ant poison in the shed...so, I set the purse and my keys on the steps and head for the shed.

On the way to the shed, I see the garbage can. It's garbage day and I must set the can out for pickup. About halfway there, I looked at my rose garden. One of my red roses was blooming. I think I will pick it and put it in a vase. So, I put the garbage can down and picked the rose. I pricked my finger badly and needed a band-aid. I think I saw one in the drawer in the kitchen. As I pull out the drawer, I spot two batteries. Well, these two batteries are just what I need for the TV remote. I put them in the remote, just to see if they work...It did... and Oprah is on!

Well, here it is... the end of the day. I am exhausted, but when I look around, nothing seems to have gotten done. The last cup of coffee is still in the pot, the flower never got watered, the dishes never got loaded into the dishwasher, the

towel is not in the laundry basket, the rip in the pillowcase is still there, the button for the dress was never found, I never made it to the store, the ants are still there, the garbage can never got put out, the rose never got put in the vase.....but the TV remote worked. Why am I am so tired? Does your day go like this too? Maybe you also have AADD!

Isaiah 40:29
He gives strength to the weary and increases the power of the weak.

****

THINK OF THEM

As our daily lives go on, and we go about our chores and our jobs.... How often do the ones who are less fortunate than us cross our mind? I was thinking about this just the other day. I complain because it is cold outside and I have to burn more gas for heating the house...or the light bill is too high. Think of those living on the coastal area in tents, no less. They have no central air or heat, no space heaters, and the power still isn't on in places, even if they did have a house.

I have indigestion and I know I ate too much....think of those who don't have enough to eat. I spend too much for Christmas presents and then I think about those who don't have jobs, some don't even have a place to stay. They cannot buy nor do they get, even one gift for Christmas.

Sometimes I complain about the extra bother when family and friends stay here during the holidays, and I think of those who have no one to care about them. I look in my closet for clothes to wear to work and I gripe about the clothes I have....then I think of the ones who are dressed in rags, wrapped in newspapers...huddled in a corner trying to get warm. You complain a lot about having to run errands, you walk out your door, not thinking anything of the ones who are locked in cells, inside the walls of nursing homes and never have the privilege of leaving the premises.

You put down your co-workers and the things they expect you to do on the job....and there are those who don't have a job....can't find a job. Your children get on your nerves and at times they don't mind. You get aggravated, but think of the parents whose children have died, run away from home, or have been taken away from them.

My friend, there is always someone in worse situations than you. Just thank God for the blessings that you do have... and pray for your fellowman. Pray that His blessings will fall on them like a gentle falling rain...and he too will feel so blessed. Oh, but for the grace of God, theses situations could be reversed!

Psalm 40:8
My God, I want to do what you want,
Your teachings are in my heart.

****

THE LONELY HILL

Have you ever envisioned the scene as God put this world together? All He had to do to make the earth separate from the water, or the sun and moon to appear, or the stars to take their place in the Heavens...was just to speak. They were in just the right place and without anything to anchor to, they stay right in place...just because He commanded them to! What power he has! Can't you see the smile on His face as he looks at what he has created? He takes His hand and shapes the mighty mountains and scoops out the valleys....and with His finger he carves out a course for the rivers to run, then commands the trees and grass and plants to grow.

He speaks and animals of all kinds, breeds, colors, shapes and sizes appeared with only a whisper from His lips. Then, he reached down in the dust and formed Man. Not only was the man to be an overseer to the land and the animals, but was made for God's pleasure too. He would delight in watching the man enjoy what God Himself had created. And with a mind of completeness...He put Adam to sleep and took out one of his ribs. With this rib, he formed Woman, to be a companion to Man. The world was now complete and he smiles and says, "This is good!"

With all of the things that God made, he was pleased, except for one small hill. As he looked at the hill, sadness came over Him and a tear fell down His cheek.... because he looked in the future and he saw his Son, hanging on the cruel cross, on Golgotha hill....crucified for the sins of this world.

As He busied Himself with making mountains, valleys, rivers, and anything else of beauty in this world...His eyes always went back and looked toward that lonely little hill. Even though the world was new and there was not any sin yet... He knew that shortly, sin would be introduced. He knew the humans that He had so gently made, would not appreciate Him nor His beauty. But His love was so great that he continued to make the world beautiful, just for us!

I guess He might have hoped against hope that we would turn out different.... but instead of being better, I think we turned out worse. I am sure it breaks His heart each time we turn away...and He often wonders if it was worth it all. Was it worth letting Jesus hang on that cross on that lonely little hill called Golgotha, dying in agony and pain, for our sins? Do we even care? How often do we thank God that if we live our life for Him and repent of our sins, we too can go to Heaven with him? We can walk with Adam and Moses and David and all the others. Our families are waiting there for us. Will we throw all of this away just to follow the stupid plans of the devil?

Which road will you take my friend? Will you take the straight and narrow road to heaven, or the broad road with the devil contin- ually lying to you, convincing you of how much fun you are having?

Think about it friend....search your heart! Don't ever take your eyes off that lonely little hill called Golgotha...and the price that Jesus paid to save your soul from Hell.

1 John 4:4
God's Spirit, who is in you, is greater than the devil who is in the world.

****

ADVERTISEMENT FOR GOD

How many times have you watched the advertisements and marvel at how clever they were? Well, let's advertise for God! Are you ready?

GOD is like SCOTCH TAPE.....
You can't see Him, but you know He's there!

GOD is like AMERICAN EXPRESS CARD....
You don't want to leave home without Him!

GOD is like FORD.....
He's got a better idea!

GOD is like DELTA AIRLINES.....
He's ready when you are!

GOD is like ALLSTATE.....
You're in good hands with Him!

GOD is like VO-5 HAIR SPRAY.....
He holds through all kinds of weather!

GOD is like DIAL SOAP.....
Aren't you glad you have Him? Don't you wish everybody did?

GOD is like COKE.....
He's the real thing!

GOD is like BAYER ASPIRIN.....
He works miracles!

GOD is like PEPSI.....
He's number one!

GOD is like HALLMARK CARDS.....
He cares enough to send His very best!

GOD is like TIDE.....
He gets the stains out that others leave behind!

GOD is like GENERAL ELECTRIC.....
He brings good things to life!

GOD is like SEARS.....
He has everything!

GOD is like ALKA-SELTZER.....
Try Him, you'll like Him!

GOD is like K-MART.....
He's the savings place!

I sure hope you enjoyed this commercial.....
(Brought to you by GOD!)

Psalm 42: 1
As a deer thirsts for streams of water, I thirst for you God.

****

SPECIAL FOR OLD FOLKS

I came across this the other day and thought you might get a chuckle out of it!

Old folks are worth a fortune: with silver in their hair, gold in their teeth, stones in their kidneys, lead in their feet and gas in their stomachs. I have become more social with the passing of the years; some might even call me a frivolous old gal. I am seeing five gentlemen every day!

As soon as I wake, Will Power helps me get out of bed. Then I go to see John! Charley Horse comes along and when he is here, he takes a lot of my time and attention. When he leaves, Arthur Ritis shows up and stays the rest of the day. (He does not like to stay in one place very long, so he takes me from joint to joint!) After such a busy day, I'm really tired and glad to go to bed...with Ben Gay! What a life!

The Preacher came to call the other day. He said at my age I should be thinking of the hereafter. I told him..."Oh, I do it all the time. No matter where I am... in the parlor...upstairs...in the kitchen...or down in the basement, I ask myself, "Now what am I here after?"

GOD'S PROMISE

When you are sad, I will dry your tears.....
When you are scared, I will comfort your fears.....
When you are worried, I will give you hope.....
When you are confused, I will help you cope.....
When you are lost and cannot see the light...
I will be your beacon shinning ever so bright.

Isaiah 43:1-2
But now, this is what the Lord says...
He who created you, O Jacob,
He who formed you, O Israel;
Fear not, for I have redeemed you;
I have summoned you by name; you are mine.
When you pass through the waters,
I will be with you;
And when you pass through the rivers,
They will not sweep over you.

When you walk through the fire,
You will not be burned.

****

SPIRITUAL GARDEN

It is getting about time for folks to be thinking about planting a garden. It is usually planned out, just how many rows of this vegetable or the other is planted. What if you were planting a "Spiritual Garden"? What would you need to plant?

First, you would prepare the soil with prayer and Bible readings. You would make the ground rich with devotion and kindness, and serving Jesus. When the ground seems to dry out, you could water it with your tears. Are you ready to plant it?

You will need six rows of Peas.....

Presence of the Holy Spirit.....

Promptness in obeying God.....

Preparation for Christian Services to your family and com- munity.....

Perseverance to succeed for Jesus and to push Satan aside...

Putting God first in your life.....

Preaching the Gospel.....

You will need four rows of Squash.....

Squash Gossip before it starts.....

Squash Indifference regarding social status, race, creed, color or religion.....

Squash Criticism of others just because you don't know their situation.....

Squash Sinful habits before they control you.....

You will need five rows of lettuce.....

Let us obey the Ten Commandments.....

Let us live up to our obligations to our fellow man.....

Let us be faithful in our Christian living.....

Let us be loyal to Christ in all that we do.....

Let us laugh more often and share more happiness.....

Let us put "self" last and God first.....

And you can finish up your garden with three rows of turnips.....

Turn up with a positive attitude.....

Turn up with new ways to work for Jesus.....

Turn up with prayer in your heart and joy in your soul.....

If you faithfully tend this Spiritual Garden, your faith and Christianity will surely grow. You will find that the harder you work in your garden, the more God will help you. You will find that He will pull out all of the weeds for you and as the "Son" shines down on it, the roots will spread and it will bring forth good fruit. A good "Spiritual Garden" will make it much easier to be invited to the "Marriage Supper of the Lamb".

Revelation 22:12
Then I was told: I am coming soon! And when I come I will reward everyone for what they have done. I am Alpha and Omega, the first and the last, the beginning and the end.

****

TALK TO ME CHILD

Suppose you woke up one morning and found this letter on your pillow. Would it change your life?

Dear Child,

This morning I woke you up....You stretched and mumbled something about not wanting to get up this early. I waited for you to tell me Good Morning, but you didn't.

You got up and looked into the mirror and commented on the new gray hair you saw and the new wrinkle. But you never thanked me for the pleasure of your long life.

You rummaged through your closet filled with clothes of any kind, and I thought that surely you would thank me for them....but you didn't. You grumbled when you went out the door to your job, but your never thought about the time you needed this job so bad. I gave you this job because you once asked. When you got to the job, you never asked for my advice, never prayed for guidance or strength or a clear mind! You just went on your way. I thought my heart would break because you didn't even think of me!

You sat down for your lunch and I thought that you would indeed stop for a moment and thank me for the food....but again, you just couldn't take the time.

On the ride home from work, the traffic was snarling and everyone seemed to be getting in everyone else's way and you were so tired and edgy. Why didn't you take just a minute to talk to me? As you arrive home, there is still work to be done, and your family gets on your nerves and you snap at them, and you blame your day's troubles on them. If only you would talk to me, I will give you strength to make it through the day....I will give you peace of mind to deal with the world.....if only you would talk to me.....!

As you lay in the bed at night, you think of all of the challenges that face you tomorrow, and you worry and you wonder how you will handle them! You anger at words someone said and your mind festers on the little snips and gripes. Oh, my Child, if you would only talk to me! I would take your burdens and give your rest. I died on the cross for you....That's how much I love you. I have sent my best Angels to keep you safe, and you turn them away!

Isn't it funny that as long as things are going OK, you don't need me, but when a loved one is sick, or bad things happen, or you think you are at the end of your rope and there is no other options....you finally talk to me. Oh, I will listen, my Child, but how sweet it would be to hear from you when there is no trouble.... when you wake in the morning, when you get to work, thank me when you eat

your meal, ask for my protection in the traffic, or to give you peaceful sleep when you lay down at night.

I am always there, and I can ease your burdens. Do you know how much more I could bless you if only you would let me? I am waiting my Child....waiting to hear from you. I have given you Mercy and Grace and all of my love....Talk to me my Child.

God

Matthew 11:28
If you are tired from carrying heavy burdens,
come to me and I will give you rest.

****

PROMISES

How important is promises? A promise is a vow....something that you really mean. But, often we think of a promise as just a bunch of words.

A man promises his wife he will not cheat on her again...but soon he breaks that promise. A woman promises that she will go on a diet and lose weight, but, her favorite food is served and the promise is broken. A child promises that they will be better behaved, but when the promise is tested, it is broken. An old Grandma in the Nursing Home promises her children she will not fuss at them for not visiting her more often, but when they come to visit, without even a thought, loneliness provokes the accusing finger at her children.

A prisoner promises his family and friends that he will never do anything else to get him thrown behind these lonely, cold, prison bars....then he gets with his old friends and to prove he is tough....the same old trouble arises and the same old lonely bars are holding him in.

A bride and a groom take the solemn vow, "Do you promise to love, honor and obey, til death do you part?"..... and a little while into the marriage, words are said and neither wants to say "I'm sorry", so divorce papers are signed.

A politician so loosely promises things to enhance his campaign and strengthen his votes, but as soon as the election is won, he seems to forget most of the promises.

A car salesman promises the customer that the car is in good condition, but as the car drives off, he chuckles under his breath..."Such a fool....he is surely stuck with a lemon!"

Promises are broken every day, and the excuse is...."Well, that's life!" Others say, "Promises are made to be broken!" or "I forgot!" and other lame excuses. So often we make promises just to appease another, and as soon as they leave so does the value of the promise!

But, you know what? I know someone who never breaks His promise. His name is Jesus. He promised us that if we believe and call upon His name and repent of our sins, Heaven will be our home! He promises that He will always be with us! He promised us as He was lifted up on a cloud of glory that He was going to prepare for us a mansion and He would be back to take His children home!

He promised us that Satan and all of his followers will be cast into the lake of fire, and He promised us that if our name is not in the Lamb's Book of Life, that we will not enter into the gates of Heaven! He promised us that He is the Alpha and the Omega....the Beginning and the End. He promised us that He is the same yesterday, today and forever!

When we give our hearts to Jesus, we promise to him to live our life the best as we can for him. How many times do we break our promise to Jesus? How many times do we ask for forgiveness or how many times do we just walk away thinking, "Oh, He'll let that pass. I'm really a good person!" ... and you never ask for forgiveness nor repent of your ways. Well, you will not spend eternity in Heaven. God is a forgiving and a just God...but we truly have to repent and ask for forgiveness from our heart in order to be a child of the King!

John 14:3
After I go and prepare a place for you, I will come back and take you to be with me so that you may be where I am.

****

SPRING

I went to bed the other night and the world still seemed to be in the clutches of winter....and when I woke up this morning, I found spring was in full bloom. The trees have budded out and Robins are singing, announcing the proclamation that spring is here! Flowers are smiling and warm winds are blowing. It's almost like God took His magic wand and waved it over the countryside.

You can see kites dipping and diving in the wind, clothes airing out on clotheslines...windows wide open to air out houses during the spring cleaning... leaves burning and yards being manicured and mowed. Gardeners are breaking up the ground to plant their produce, green grasses flourish to feed the livestock. There's house sprucing...a new coat of paint, an old shutter being repaired, new screens being put on the windows, garage sales, yard sales, white sales and clearance sales.

Easter is drawing near and we start thinking of the day Christ arose from the tomb. We think of Easter bunnies, Easter Sunrise Service, Easter bonnets, Easter outfits, Easter parades, Easter eggs and Easter Dinner with the family. Our minds prepare for the endless jokes on April Fool's Day and the pinches if you're not wearing green on St. Patrick's Day. We prepare for April 15th and taxes...April showers and May flowers.

It's all so beautiful, so fresh and nice. But, one day you will see something even more beautiful. The eastern sky will roll back like a scroll and there on a cloud of glory, all dressed in glowing white, Jesus will return and gather His children home. Sinners will even bow and confess he is Lord, but they cannot be saved...it will be too late! They will cry and beg, but their cries won't be heard by the Savior. They will fall on deaf ears. They will be left behind with no hope of tomorrow!

My friend, don't wait until it is too late. Accept Christ as your Savior today! Be ready when He comes back and you will rise to Heaven with Him on that snowy white cloud with a choir of Angels singing praises to Him. You will hear Jesus welcome you home.

John 9:31
God does not listen to sinners, but he listens to
anyone who worships and obeys Him.

****

PERFECTION

It's a mystery to me as to how much perfection God has put into each and everything He made. Have you ever stopped long enough to notice? Look at the sunsets and the sunrises...Have you ever seen an ugly sunset? The sky is painted with delicate strokes....each color and each stroke...perfectly done. Look at the tree in the back yard. Would you ever attempt to count the leaves or the pine needles on it? Well, God knows just how many leaves are on that tree...and the next tree, and the tree down the road.

As you look at the flowers you see perfection. If the blossom is supposed to have five petals, that is just what it has. Look at the Dogwood tree. There are four petals....two long and two short ones...(representing a cross). Each petal has a "blood stain" on the edge and in the center is a crown. Each Dogwood blossom has this.....a work of wonder and beauty. Have you ever watched as a rose unfolded? Look how delicate and perfect each petal is as it unfolds. If you would try to unfold it, the petals would tear and it wouldn't open right. But when God with His majestic hand touches them, they open up perfectly! How amazing!

As we go to the zoo, we notice that all of God's creatures are unique in their own way...they are made by the Master! The stripes on a Zebra...they're never the same on two animals. Each is striped a little different....the same for the tiger. This is like human fingerprints, never will two be the same. Look at the other animals. There is the massive trunk of the Elephant...it is even used for a hose pipe sometimes to wash down the backside of this huge animal, to cool it down in the steaming summer sun. A giraffe has an extremely long neck so he is able to eat from the taller bushes. A leopard has his beautiful spots, bears have claws for feeding purposes and protection, the skunk has its protective odor, there are hooves on cows, horses and deer, and then there are the owls who can see perfectly in the dark. Porcupines have their quills, ducks have the webbed feet, and penguins are dressed in the beautiful tuxedo look. There are no two humans just alike. They sometimes may seem to look alike, but God made them different in some way. Why, he even knows the number of hairs on our head.

When I look over a body of water with the sun shinning, it looks like a field of diamonds, sparkling and glittering. The world rotates like He told it to, with perfection. Each thing, each animal, each person, each wonder in this world was made to take care of a certain thing in the Universe. Humans were made to enjoy the beauty and awe, and to spread the Gospel through the world. Do you do your share? Do you tell your friends and your neighbors and your family how much

Jesus means to you? Do you tell them what he wants to do for them? The word is written on your heart...you must share the message with all that you can.

Think of how boring the world would be if everyone looked and acted just alike, if there was only one type of flower, one type of tree and one type of animal, foul and fish. Sounds real dull, doesn't it? Well we serve a God who loves variety. He made the world so varied and interesting and so PERFECT!

John 7:10
All I have is yours and all you have is mine. And my glory is shown through them.

****

EASTER STORY

Let's go back to an Easter Morning a little over two thousand years ago. You see, three days ago, Jesus had been hung on a rugged, old, wooden cross on Calvary. He was beaten and spit on, and then between two thieves, He hung there on the cross by three old rusty nails, to die. One thief said he knew he had done bad things and he deserved to die, but he said Jesus had done no wrong, and He should not die. He asked Jesus to remember him when He entered His kingdom. Jesus responded, "Today, you shall join me in Paradise." The other never repented. He only laughed and made fun of my Savior.

Jesus died a cruel and painful death, and He died for all of our sins.... All we have to do is repent of our sins and ask for forgiveness. But, sometimes it seems that that is just too hard for us to do.

Imagine His Mother as she watched Him suffer and die...imagine the pain that must have filled her heart....even though she knew this was to be in order to fulfill God's prophecy. This was her child hanging there.....a perfect man.... one who had never sinned! This has got to be one of the hardest things a Mother could go through, but I think God must have wrapped His arm around her as the tears fell from the eyes of Mary, as well as from the Father.

When Jesus died, they took Him off of the cross and placed Him in a cold and lonely grave....a sort of a cave. A flat sheet of rock made His bed. The Roman Soldiers, as well as Satan, thought this was the end of this man called Jesus. They rejoiced...the followers and family of Jesus cried.

Then on the third day I can imagine a bright light filling the tomb and the Father holding out His hand, saying, "Son, your sleep is over. Arise and come with me!" And Jesus arose and went to take the keys of death away from the devil and then on to Glory to sit on the right hand of His Father and rule.

Can't you vision the Roman Soldiers as they came out of their trance and found the stone rolled away and Jesus gone? I can imagine the fear they felt because they would be held responsible. Some even committed suicide rather than to face the rulers.

Can't you see Mary Magdalene and the other Mary as they came to the tomb in the early morning light, bringing perfume for His body. They saw the stone rolled away and thought someone had came during the night and took the body away. Then two angels in brightest white spoke to them and said, "Why seek ye the living amongst the dead?" this had to scare them tremendously, so she ran to tell Peter and Andrew. They ran to find the tomb empty just as the women had said.

It was probably really hard to understand this, even though Jesus had tried to explain this to all of them before He died, but it seemed to be beyond their understanding. It is still hard to comprehend how God is so powerful, yet so gentle....so just in his judgments, so understanding in His love. He knows where we have been, where we are now and where we are going to be tomorrow. He even knew us before we were born.

He could make us do His will if He wanted to, but He is a gentleman God. He gives us the option of trusting in Him or following the lies of Satan, and so many times we give our lives to Satan rather than to live for Jesus. Have you ever thought about the eternal life you will live after death? Will you be in Heaven with Jesus for eternity or will you be cast in the fires of hell with Satan to burn eternally?

Think about it my friend.....Heaven is real and so is Hell! Why don't you celebrate Easter this year by giving your heart to Jesus. He will make it worth your while if you just repent and ask for forgiveness!

Matthew 28: 5-6

Then the Angel spoke to the women. "Don't be frightened!" He said. "I know you are looking for Jesus who was crucified, but He isn't here. For He has come back to life again, just as He said He would. Come and see where His body was lying.

****

JESUS LOVES ME
(Old Age Version)

Have you ever sat in the pew in Church and listened to those around you singing the old songs....especially the Children's Hymns? Did you ever notice that it is mostly the older ones singing the loudest to certain songs....songs like "Jesus Loves Me"? Well, since they love to sing so much, someone came up with different words to it. Someone sent this to me the other day. I don't know who penned the new words, but it is a special version for folks over forty.... For those with white hair, gray hair, or no hair at all. Sing it if you like!

JESUS LOVES ME

Jesus loves me, this I know, though my hair is white as snow,
Though my sight is growing dim, Still He bids me trust in Him.

(Chorus)
Yes, Jesus loves me, yes, Jesus loves me...
Yes, Jesus loves me, for the Bible tells me so.

Though my steps are oh so slow, with my hand in His I'll go,
On through life, let come what may, He'll be there to lead the way.

(Chorus)

Though I am no longer young, I have much which He's begun,
Let me serve Christ with a smile, go with others the extra mile.

(Chorus)

When the nights are dark and long, in my heart he puts a song,
Telling me in words so clear, "Have no fear, for I am near!"

(Chorus)

When my work on earth is done, and life's victories have been won,
He will take me home above, then I'll understand His love.

(Chorus)

I love Jesus, does he know? Have I ever told Him so?
Jesus loves to hear me say, that I love Him every day!

(Chorus)

Well, the next time you hear that blessed old song, it will have a whole new meaning for us old folks, and maybe some of the younger folks, too!

Ephesians 6: 8
The Lord will reward everyone for whatever good
he does, whether he is slave or free.

****

THINGS YOU WON'T FIND IN HEAVEN

Many times in our talk of Heaven, we often refer to the things we will find there....Jesus on the throne, the tree of life, living water, streets of gold, the crystal river, mansions made of jewels, Angels, music, praises, loved ones who have passed on before us, the Saints mentioned in the Bible, beauty, peace, and love. But have you ever thought of some of the things that we would not find there?

There will never be any temptations from the devil, no prisons, no nursing homes, no lies, no thieves, no hospitals and no tears. We won't have need of Doctors, Nurses or Lawyers in Heaven. (Doctors, Nurses and Lawyers will enter Heaven, but their work will be done!) Any other job skills we have acquired on earth won't be needed in Heaven!

There will never be any arthritis pains crippling our joints, no headaches, no backaches, no heart attacks, no strokes, no cancer, no diabetes, and no sickness of any kind, nor any pain of any kind.

There will be no worries of having enough money to pay the bills, gas prices rising, insurance cost, cost of funerals, job security, destruction from storms of one kind or another or accidents or even traffic jams. There will never be a wreath of death on the mansion door or any need for an obituary column.

No child will be abused or neglected....no elderly person lonely and forgotten, and no worry of spouse abuse. Heaven will not have fussing or fighting, or hurt feelings or gossip. There will be no wars or rumors of wars and people will only know love.

In Heaven there will be no eyeglasses, contact lens, hearing aids, walkers, wheel chairs, hospital beds, walking canes, artificial limbs or even missing limbs. We will have a brand new body and all of these things will be passed away.

You will see no blind people, no deaf, no dumb, no deformed or maimed. I don't think there will even be anyone who can't sing a beautiful song unto Him. We will have a perfect body!

There will be no beggars on the street corners....no one living on the streets, no one lurking around the corner to cause harm. There will be no house in disrepair, no yards that need mowing, no slums, no potholes in the streets of gold, no air conditioner failure....no heat waves, cold snaps, no storms, no floods, no droughts. The weather there will be perfect. Heaven will have no need for Police cars, sirens, guns or weapons of any sort!

Jesus has gone to prepare a perfect place for us. Why, we'll even have a mansion of our own. We can play instruments in the Angel Band, sing songs of worship to Him. We can praise Him forever and ever and maybe we won't even remember the awful things that prevailed while we were on the earth.

The whole Heaven will be filled with love and peace and joy! Will you be there? .....Or, will you be on the outside looking in as the great Judge pronounces your sentence of eternity in Hell? Oh, the heartbreak, the horror, the hopeless future.... And then you turn to see your escorts... the demons of hell, smirking.... rejoicing.

If only you had given your life to Jesus.....you could be escorted by the Angels along the golden streets of Heaven....right up to the throne of Jesus. If there is a breath of life in you yet, it may not be too late to ask Jesus for forgiveness of your sins and turn your life to over to Him. Heaven is waiting, and God is still on the throne!

John 6: 25
Whoever comes to me will never be hungry, and whoever believes in me will never be thirsty!

****

MOTHER VIEWED THROUGH THE EYES OF A CHILD

As Mother's Day nears, I thought it might be interesting to get a child's view of Mother. A lot of time we figure that a small child doesn't know too much about being a Mother, but I think some of the answers will surprise you, and maybe even give you a chuckle.

Maybe you are not a Mother, but everyone had a Mother at some time or other. These questions were asked to a bunch of small children in preschool.

<u>Why did God make Mothers?</u>

1. She's the only one who knows where the scotch tape is!
2. Mostly to clean the house!
3. To help us out when we were getting born!

<u>How did God make Mothers?</u>

1. He used dirt, just like He did for the rest of us!
2. Magic, plus super powers and a lot of stirring!
3. God made my Mom just the same like He made me. He just used bigger parts!

<u>What ingredients are Mothers made of?</u>

1. God makes Mothers out of clouds and Angel hair and every thing nice in the world and one dab of mean!
2. They had to get their start from Men's bones. Then they mostly used string.... I think!
3. They are made of something soft and it smells good.

<u>Why did God give you your Mother and not some other Mom?</u>

1. We're related!
2. God knew she likes me a lot more than other people's moms would like me!
3. Because Daddy asked God to let her be my Mother!

<u>What kind of little girl was you Mom?</u>

1. My Mom, has always been my Mom, and none of that other stuff!
2. I don't know because I wasn't there, but my guess would be pretty bossy!
3. They say she used to be nice!

What did Mom need to know about Dad before she married him?

1. His last name!
2. She had to know his background, like is he a crook? Does he get drunk on beer?
3. Does he make at least $800 a year? Did he say NO to drugs and YES to chores?

Why did your Mom marry your Dad?

1. My Dad makes the best spaghetti in the world and my Mom eats a lot!
2. She got too old to do anything else with him!
3. My Grandma says that Mom didn't have her thinking cap on!

Who's the boss at your house?

1. Mom doesn't want to be boss, but she has to because Dad's such a goof ball!
2. Mom...You can tell by room inspection. She sees the stuff under the bed!
3. I guess Mom is, but only because she has a lot more to do than Dad!

What's the difference between Moms and Dads?

1. Moms work at work and works at home...and Dads just go to work and work!
2. Moms know how to talk to teachers without scaring them!
3. Dads are taller and stronger, but Moms have all the real power 'cause that's who you got to ask if you want to sleep over at a friend's house! Mom's have magic...they make you feel better without medicine.

What would it take to make your Mom perfect?

1. On the inside, she's already perfect. Outside, I think some kind of plastic surgery.
2. Diet....You know, her hair. I'd diet it maybe blue!
3. She would quit cooking all of the green junk that tastes bad, but she says is good for me!

What does your Mother do in her spare time?

1. Mothers don't do spare time!
2. To hear her tell it, she pays bills all day long?
3. She cleans my room!

If you could change one thing about your Mom, what would it be?

1. She has this weird thing about me keeping my room clean. I'd get rid of that!
2. I'd make my Mom smarter. Then she would know it was my Sister who did it and not me!
3. I would like for her to get rid of those invisible eyes on her back!

Well, I see from these answers we surely have a bunch of intelligent youngsters around. God loved Mothers too! He sent then to take care of the world, I think. They are like special Angels. But, unfortunately, some are fallen Angels and serve the Devil instead of God. These are the ones who abuse or abort their children, leave them all alone, neglect feeding or clothing them, drowns them, burns them, or just doesn't love them! Someday, they will stand before the great Judge and will have a lot to answer for. Jesus will not listen to feeble excuses or lies. The consequences will leave them facing an eternity in Hell!

Daniel 6: 10
May the God you serve all the time, save you!

****

A GOOD MOTHER

Have you ever wondered what someone thinks about Motherhood, if they have never been a Mother? If you are a Mother, haven't you, at one time in your life, been offended by someone's advice on how to be a perfect Mother? These comments probably come from someone who has never been around children, especially children of their own, and they venture to comment!

Somebody once said it takes about six weeks to get back to normal, once you've had a baby. What they don't know is; once you're a Mother, "normal" is history. Comments have been made that you learn to be a Mother by instinct, but I'll bet they never took a three year old shopping!

I have heard that Motherhood must be boring....but the children make sure life is different each and every day. What they do one day is not necessarily what they will do the next day!

It has been said that if you are a good Mother, your children will turn out good....but these children do not come with directions and a guarantee. If you are a good Mother, you don't raise your voice to your children....but when you walk out the door just in time to see a ball heading for the window...you forget how to be a "good Mother".

It is stated that you don't have to have a good education to be a good Mother.... but just try to help a fourth grader do their math! Others are quick to remind us that you can find all of the answers to child rearing problems in Dr. Spock's book....but where does it explain what to do when a child stuffs a bean up his nose or in his ears or gets his foot stuck in a ceramic shoe!

Doctors tell us that the hardest part of being a Mother is labor and delivery..... but have they ever watched as their child got on the school bus for the first time, went to college or got married and moved out of the house, or boarded a plane to serve in the military, or watched as they lowered the casket into the grave.

Mothers are said to be able to do her job with her eyes closed and one hand tied behind their back....then try to organize a group of Brownies...a den of scouts... give a birthday party for a three year old who doesn't want to be dressed up, or the big challenge of cooking supper...checking on a sick friend on the phone... helping the child with homework....listening to her husband's day at work .....all at the same time!

Well, I guess a Mother is supposed to quit worrying about her "baby" when they get married...but it seems like they step on your toes when they are small and they tend to tug on the heartstrings when they are grown. They will always be your "baby".

You will always be concerned for their welfare, and will always worry about them. A child says a Mother knows you love her, so you don't need to tell her so. That is the one thing you need to do....tell her you love her! This blesses her soul! A Mother will always get offended when someone says something bad about her children, and they can always find a way to disappoint you now and then.

This is sort of like the way our Heavenly Father feels about us! We step on his toes when we are younger, and rebel against His laws. We turn aside from Him when we are older, breaking His heart, thinking we know it all! We will always be his child. He will always be concerned for our welfare and for our soul being saved. He will always get offended when the unsaved say bad things about good Christians or they take the life of His dear Saints. But just like a child, sooner or later we will find a way to disappoint Him. Tell Him you love Him and He will bless your soul!

2 Thessalonians 3: 5
May the Lord lead your hearts into God's love and Christ's patience.

****

WHAT WENT WRONG

How many times do we look around at the younger generation and wonder what went wrong? We went wrong...that's what happened! Most of us grew up having to work hard, obey strict rules and moral aspects and we didn't want our children to have it so hard. We look at the way they dress....baggy pants, barely hanging on the hips...but who bought the baggy pants? The girls dress like advertisements on a billboard...skimpy little outfits, plunging necklines, short tops, low cut jeans, mini skirts, tight, short shorts....and they think they look great! Who buys them these skimpy little clothes and stand around as they look into the mirror and tell them how cute they look? You do!

They listen to music that would make you sick, if you would just listen carefully to the lyrics. These musicians are directly from hell, and Satan is so proud you let them listen to the morbid, drug promoting, violent lyrics. But who buys these CD's or cassettes for them? You do!

If they get hooked on alcohol, they took lessons from you....or they saw how cool you thought you were when you puffed the cigarette. They hear you on the phone with your best friend, talking about another best friend, but then you tell them gossip is wrong!

They watch TV shows that would make a sailor blush, and they say, "as long as you watch it with me, it's OK!" I'm sorry! Wrong is wrong! You block the internet from their usage on the adult networks, but they walk in while you are watching....what lesson are they learning?

You curse and swear....what makes you think they won't? You lie about things, and pretend it was necessary or that it was just a little white lie....but you tell them it is wrong for them to lie! What makes you think they will believe you?

If you raise your children with no authority, no rules, what have they learned? They have learned to do what the want and when they want and not care who they hurt in the process! When children are raised with no chores and no responsibilities at home, what do they learn? They learn that the world will take care of them....welfare is good! They learn to be lazy and wait for others to do for them, give to them, to listen to their every whine and whim and always feel that the world owes them something, but always blames Mom and Dad because they have nothing!

You are tired and you send them to Church on Sunday... so you can rest. They grow up thinking "just as soon as I grow up, I won't have to go to Church!" Why not take them to Church and when they grow up they will be grounded in the Church and God's Word, and will want to continue to go and raise their families in Church. If your children don't know Jesus....why not? Do you ever tell them?

If they don't know how to pray....why not? Do they ever hear you pray? If you don't read the Bible in your home, how do you expect them to read the Bible in their home when they are out on their own? If you don't raise your children right, instilling in them values, morals, and a Christian attitude, who will teach your Grandchildren and will your Great-Grandchildren ever know the joys and the beauty of God's Word? The government keeps making laws that prevent discipline of children, and they call it child abuse!

They keep taking God out of schools and other public places and try to discourage worship in other places like jobs....or then there are the stores who try to ban their employees from saying "Merry Christmas"....because it offends some! Where are the Great-grand-children or the next generation going to be if we don't take our families back and raise them according to the Word of God?

It isn't the children's fault that this generation is like they are! It is the fault of the parents! It sometimes makes you wonder who is the parent and who is the child. There is no authority!

God chastises His children, and he tells us that if we are lazy to go watch the ant work. If God chastises His own, don't you think He wants us to raise our own with authority, punishments, morals and salvation?

Isaiah 54: 13
All your children will be taught by the Lord and they will have much peace.

****

THINGS GOD WON'T ASK

I know we have all thought of Judgment Day and the questions that we will be asked by Jesus as we stand there before Him. We know we can only answer the questions with the truth. How many of the questions will bare our heart and soul with embarrassment and even fear the verdict of the Master? Will we even be able to talk during this procedure, or will the facts just be stated? Even though the accusations will all be given, you will probably already know the verdict. But Christians are sometimes deceived by Satan as to what is important in the eyes of God. Here are ten things that God will probably not ask you on Judgment Day!

1. **God won't ask the square footage of your home, but He will ask how many people you welcomed into your home.**

2. **He won't ask about the clothes you had in your closet. He'll Ask how many you helped to clothe.**

3. **God won't ask you what your highest salary was, but he'll ask if you compromised your character to obtain it.**

4. **God won't ask you what your job title was. He will ask if you performed your job to the best of your ability.**

5. **God won't ask how many friends you had....He will ask how many people to whom you were a friend.**

6. **God won't ask you what kind of neighborhood you lived in, but He will ask how you treated your neighbor.**

7. **God won't ask for the color of your skin, but He will ask you about the content of your heart and character.**

8. **God won't ask why it took you so long to seek Salvation. He'll lovingly take you to your mansion in Heaven and not send you to Hell!**

9. **God will not ask if you were ever asked to pray for someone...He will ask if you actually prayed for that person.**

10. **God won't ask you how many times you attended Church, but He will ask**

you how many times you had Church in your heart!

Maybe we ought to change the way we think about some things. Maybe on some of these questions, we are missing the main point. Maybe we need to change our ways to Godly ways, and not worldly ways. God is always waiting for us to talk to Him, and if we ever need His advice on matters, He is the best one to ask. He knows all of the answers. He doesn't have to refer to a dictionary or a reference book, or even the endless information on the internet. He knows all....He sees all....hears all....and He will judge all!

Romans 3: 23-24
All have sinned and are not good enough for God's Glory, and all need to be made right with God by His grace, which is a free gift.

****

REWARDS

Do you remember when you were small, that everything had a reward to it? "If you eat your dinner, you can have dessert!" Or "If you do your chores you will get an allowance!" Or "If you win the race you get a medal" Or "If you behave in the store, I'll buy you some ice cream." Or "If you make an A on your report card, I'll give you a dollar!" Or "If you clean up your room, you can go to your friend's house." Or "If you do your homework, then you can watch TV." Or "If you work hard you will get a promotion!"

Jesus Himself even offers a reward. He said if we would love Him, repent of our sins and live our lives for Him, He would give us treasures in Heaven. These treasures cannot be imagined by the human mind. One thing for sure, the treasures on earth will surely look dim compared to these treasures.

To get these treasures, we must walk with Jesus in our daily life. We must fight to show the world that we are a Christian, and tell the world about Jesus! It is a hard battle though, because Satan or his demons walk every step with us, and he is continually trying to make us slip away form the Grace of God. He is so sly at what he does, sometimes we don't even realize we are following in the devil's footsteps. Jesus has to tap us on the shoulder many times and then at times we won't even listen and confess that we are doing wrong. We don't repent. Listen to Jesus, my friend, He wants you to spend eternity in heaven. The devil wants to recruit you into Satan's army and you'll spend eternity in hell!

Philippians 3: 12-14

Not that I have already obtained all this, or have already been made perfect, but I press on to take hold of that for which Christ Jesus took hold of me. Brothers, I do not consider myself yet to have taken hold of it, but one thing I do; forgetting what is behind in circumstance and straining toward what is ahead. I press on toward the goal to win the prize for which God has called me heavenward in Christ Jesus.

****

WOES OF OLD AGE

As we get older, it seems like more changes occur, rather than just in our outward appearance. The summers now seem to be a lot hotter than before. We just can't seem to find a cool place anywhere. The winters are colder and we can never seem to stay warm enough. We can put on layers of clothing and turn the heat way up, but we just can't find a good comfort zone. I can't remember it being this way just a few years ago!

I have things I need to put on a list....grocery list or just a reminder list, but before I get to the paper to write them on....I seem to forget what it was that I needed to write down. We used to find things to do with our time... but now we just want to sleep. We used to go to a friend's home and chat a while, or play bridge, or bar-b-que, but now we go to the Doctor's office, hospitals, or after-funeral brunches, and thank God it is someone else's funeral and not ours.

We used to go out to fancy restaurants and eat our fill. We would always try out the new dishes, and we didn't care if they were full of sugar or carbohydrates, fats or other things. Now we hardly ever eat out, because we have to have low sugar, low carbohydrates, low fat, no greens, nothing that will cause gas, and nothing with seeds. Even with that, when we eat, we have to turn around and take a pill!

We used to travel....sometimes near and sometimes far. We would always enjoy the time riding or flying or sailing....but now we get a backache just riding in a car....not to mention the times we have to stop and empty the old bladder, or stretch our arthritic knees and back. We travel for thirty minutes and we think we have been on the road all day!

We don't even enjoy going shopping to buy clothes any more! When you are shopping, the dresses are too low cut and too dad-blamed short. My rolled down hose always shows. Then they never fit. If they fit on the top, the rest is too tight, and to get the to fit everywhere else, the shoulders are much too big. My body bulges in the wrong spots, sags in others and still others pooch out. So, the best thing to do is to just wear what you have and let somebody else buy those in the stores.

We used to go to church and enjoy the sermon, the songs and the people around you. Now we go, we look at the preacher because we can't hear him, we watch the choir, hoping they are singing pretty, and the rest of the time, we sit there with our heads bowed....catching up on our nap!

I have some good advice for you younger folks. Enjoy each day and live it up. Eat good and enjoy shopping and traveling, before you grow too old!

Revelation 4: 5
Holy, Holy, Holy is the Lord God almighty. He was, He is and He is coming!

****

THE OLD PATHS

As I sit here and ponder how many people are living today, and how they disregard time and circumstance, to place things to our convenience....not necessarily because they are right. Maybe we should look back at the old paths. (if you are not old enough to remember the old paths, just pay attention and learn!)

I liked the old paths, knowing Mom would always be home when we came home from school and a good snack would be waiting. Dad was the one who always went to work. Brothers chose to go into the Armed forces and sisters got married BEFORE having children!

Crime didn't pay....hard work did, and folks knew the difference and knew they would suffer the consequences for wrongs. Moms could all cook and dads would take care of the yard and things around the home....and children knew how to behave!

Most husbands were loving, most wives were supportive and most children were polite. Women looked like ladies and men looked like gentlemen and children looked decent.

Women worried about hair-dos and the men kept the barbers busy. The whole neighborhood loved the truth and hated lies...and all eyes were watching the children playing. They bought their kids to church, and didn't just send them. Hymns sounded like they came from the throne room of God, Holy and special... sermons were not sidestepped as to not step on the toes, rejoicing sounded normal and crying sounded sincere. Cursing was considered evil, drinking was wicked and for the most part divorce was almost unheard of. Unless there was a death, most children were raised by Mother and Daddy!

The flag was always honored, America was respected and considered beautiful, God was welcome in homes, schools, at sports events, displayed in courtrooms.... without shame. We could read the Bible on the street corners, if one wanted to. We could pray in the schoolrooms, tell friends about Jesus on the job without fear of losing the job, and saying "Merry Christmas" was heard from all!

Sex was a personal word, homosexual was an unheard of word, and abortion was illegal. This was a time when being a Preacher meant you proclaimed the Word of God, being a deacon meant you would serve the Lord and being a Christian meant you would live for Jesus! Being a sinner meant someone was praying for you!

Laws were based on the justice in the Bible. There was a Bible in most every home and it was read! A Church was where you found Christians on Sunday, rather than on the Golf Course, at the old Fishing Hole, in the Garden, or being

"entertained" someplace else. I still like the old paths best and I think it is the only path to Heaven!

Isaiah 59: 1
Surely the arm of the Lord is not too short to save nor His ear to dull to hear!

****

THE EASTERN SKY

What if you woke up one morning and looked to the eastern sky? ... Something is going on! It is bright....brighter than the rising morning sun! As you stand there staring in awe, the sky seems to roll up like a scroll....and there is a cloud coming nearer. It is so bright that the human eye pains to look at it, but you can't seem to take your eyes off it!

As it nears, there is a man on a white horse, and He is clothed in a white robe....and He glows. He is so bright! He comes closer and you know that this is Jesus, coming to take His children home! As the eastern sky breaks open, people all over the world, with no exceptions, look upon Him...and every tongue will confess that He is Lord, and every knee will bow in worship of him. There won't even be one who can look away, or not bow, or not confess that this is the Christ! Millions and millions of people, people of every creed and color and every nation, all facing the east on their knees.... What a blessed sight to behold!

Even those who blasphemed His Holy Name, the ones who took prayer out of schools, the ones who wanted the Ten Commandments taken out of Government Buildings, the ones who wanted to discourage others from even believing in Jesus, even demon possessed individuals here on earth that are working so hard to push people away from God...They will all face the east....they will confess He is Christ and they will bow!

Those in Iraq and Iran and Korea and China, in Africa, South America and any place else where they actively kill Christians, will now fall to their knees and their lips will confess that this is Jesus, Lord of Lords, King of Kings, but they won't be able to change their destiny. They have waited too late!

What a sight to behold! There in the brilliant light of Jesus, and a host of ten-thousand Angels singing, everyone on this earth will be facing the east.... every knee will bow, and some will lie prostrate, praising His name. People will be rejoicing and crying with joy, and praising His name and welcoming the Savior....some will be crying and begging and pleading for forgiveness and for just one more chance....but they will know that this finalized their decision for serving Jesus! They didn't believe in living their life for Him, and they thought this day would never come. Their lips confessed that He was Lord, even though they tried hard to hush them! Their knees bowed before Him, even though they resisted. The power of Christ was more than they could fight against. Even the devil himself, confessed that this is the Messiah, the Lord of Lords, the King of Kings, and even his knees are bent. He surely doesn't want to bow and confess, but he is helpless.

The faithful ones rejoiced to know that they had been faithful to the call and they had worked and prayed and lived their lives according to what Jesus had asked. Now they were ready to get their reward in Heaven and they will travel to Glory with their Lord and Master, Jesus Christ. They will never again have to worry about Satan and his army!

There stand the lost, looking at God's children being taken home and they are left behind. Oh, what a helpless feeling that must be!

Friend, you must live your life for Jesus and be faithful to His calling. You must talk to others about Salvation and live your life so others can see Jesus in you! You surely don't want to be here....left behind....watching Jesus rise to the sky on a cloud of Glory with all of His children...knowing the only one you can now turn to is the devil himself. That doesn't leave you much hope, does it?

Matthew 5: 12
Rejoice and be glad, because you have a reward awaiting you in Heaven.

****

THE U IN JESUS

A friend of mine sent me this the other day....and I would like to share it with you. I do not know who the author is.

THE U IN JESUS
Before U were thought of, or time had begun,
God stuck U in the mane of His Son.
And each time U pray, U'll see it's true,
U can't even spell JesUs and not include U.
U're a pretty big part of His wonderful name,
For U, He was born; that's why He came!
And His great love for U is the reason He died.
It even takes U to spell crucified.
Isn't it thrilling and splendidly grand,
He rose from the dead, with U in His plan?
The stones split away, and for U the gold trUmpet blew,
And even the resUrrection wouldn't be complete without U.
When JesUs left earth at His upward ascension,
He felt there was one thing He just had to mention....
"Go into the world and tell them it's true,
That I love them all....just like I love U!"
There are so many good people just like U....
Don't they have a right to know JesUs too?
It all depends on what U will do....
He'd surely like for U to tell them about JesUs!

I thought you might enjoy this. It brings a brand new meaning to the spelling of JesUs and U. It seems like everything JesUs does, He does it just for U!

John 17: 10
All I have is yours, and all you have is mine, and
My Glory is shown through them.

****

THE OLD FOLKS A B C'S

As you remember from childhood, the alphabet is pretty easy to remember. But now there is an alphabet just for old folks! Here it is!

A is for ARTHRITIS, AGE Spots, and ACHING joints
B is for BAD BACKS, BROKEN BONES and BAD health
C is for CHEST pains, CARDIAC arrest and CRAMPS in our legs
D is for DENTURES, DOCTORS and DEATH planning
E is for EYESIGHT, (declining), EARS (that don't hear) and EVERY- THING falls apart
F is for FALLING, FRAILNESS and FLUID retention
G is for GRACE, GLASSES and GAS
H is for HIGH blood pressure, HISTORY and HEART problems
I is for ILLNESSES, ICE-PACKS and ITCHES
J is for JOINTS that swell and hurt, JARS that won't open, and JUICE for every meal
K is for KNEES that wont bend, KNOWLEDGE dimming, and KNOW-HOW now unused
L is for LAB work, LIMITED walking, and LUCKY day at Bingo
M is for MONEY you don't have, MEMORY you don't remember having, and MEDICARE you can't do without
N is for NURSES, NEEDLES and NOSES that snore
O is for OPERATIONS, OLD folks, and OVERWEIGHT
P is for PRESCRIPTIONS, PREACHERS, and POTTY chairs
Q is for QUEASINESS, QUESTIONS and QUACKS
R is for REFLUX, REMEMBERING, and REPEATING
S is for SCARS to brag on, SLEEPLESS nights and SHOTS
T is for TREATMENTS, TINNITUS, (ringing in the ears) and THREE TRIES to get up
U is for URINARY problems, ULTRASOUNDS and UNDERSTANDING
V is for VERICOSE VEINS, VERTIGO and VALIUM
W is for WORRY, WHEELCHAIRS, and WRINKLES
X is for X-rays
Y is for another YEAR that I've left behind and
Z is for the ZEST that I still have my mind, and have survived all the symptoms my body's deployed, and kept twenty-six doctors gainfully employed.

I hope you enjoyed this...you see, I know where you are because I am an "Old Folk" too! But I feel blessed that God let me hang around this long, and that He gave someone knowledge of how to take care of my A B C's of life. ALWAYS BE CHRISTLIKE!

ROMANS 8: 31
If God is for us, who can be against us?

****

I'VE EARNED IT

I am a widow. I have some friends who often comment on that, saying how hard it must be for me. Don't worry about me! My Father in Heaven takes real good care of me! With the right attitude, living alone puts you in a world of your own!

I have a lot of friends who look into their mirror and gripe and complain about growing old, about wrinkles, gray hair, baggy eyes, pooching stomach, and sagging hiney....But I am proud of that old gal that lives in my mirror.

She carries a lot of memories, a lot of promises, and lot of grace from God, just to get here. I have a lot of friends who never made it this far. They never experienced "Senior Citizen Status" and it often makes me sad. I don't try to cover up the flaws in my face, the gray in my hair...I am who I am! I don't apologize to friends or foe. I only thank God for getting me here.

Through all of these long years, I have made many friends....and I wouldn't trade that experience for anything. I don't have to scold myself for eating that extra cookie, because it might make me "fat." If I don't want to fix my bed, it's OK. I have earned that right. No one has the right to fuss at me if I buy something that you think looks hideous, but I think it is adorable, like a cement frog that just makes my porch complete.

When you get old and live alone....you are entitled to overeat, to be messy, and buy things you just want and don't necessarily need. I wonder if any of my friends who have gone on before me ever had a chance to think about the blessings of growing old!

It is nobody's business if I stay up all night reading, watching TV or playing games on the computer, then sleep until noon the next day! I have earned this privilege when I was younger....with going to bed late, trying to get all of the work done, then up with the dawn fixing lunches, getting children and spouse off to school or work, and probably on to my job too. I come in drained, with supper to fix, clothes to wash, house to clean, and life went on!

If I feel brave enough, I can parade the beaches in a swimsuit stretched over this bulging body, and not worry about if I look good. I just wanna have fun! Let the Bikini set talk if they want....but one day, if they are lucky, they too will grow old.

I know I'm sometimes forgetful, but there again....some of life is just as well forgotten. I seem to remember the more important things. Oh, I laugh now, but surely my heart has been broken many times. Your heart breaks when you lose your spouse, or a child, (even if the child is just moving out on their own). Your heart has been broken when your sweet little pet dies as you cradle it in your

arms. But I have come to the understanding that broken hearts seem to give us strength and more compassion, and it draws us closer to Jesus.

It is a joy sometimes to be imperfect! I am blessed to have lived long enough to have my hair turn gray, and to have my laughter and happiness forever etched in deep grooves on my face. When you grow old you think less about what others think of you, but wake in wonder when God asks something of you....and He still finds work for you to do for His Kingdom! If you handle it right, old age can set you free to be the person you have always wanted to be!

Proverbs 27: 17
Just as iron sharpens iron, friends sharpen the minds of each other.

THE NAVY OF THE LORD

Have you ever thought about being in the Navy of the Lord? Well, when we became a Christian, we enlisted in the Navy of the Lord for a lifetime of service to God. I think that the main purpose of this enlistment was to carry us on a journey, (from birth to death) and reach the other shore safely and with Salvation in our soul.

This is not for a life of fun and games however. This is not a cruise ship....It is a Battleship! Oh there is laughter, and there is fun, but we always need to be ready for the enemy.

Just like the crew on a ship, we each have our job....each of us have a talent and a purpose. Some stand on the deck to watch for someone drowning, (lost spiritually) and their job is to witness to them about Salvation bring them in out of the dark, unknown waters and bring them to Jesus. Some are manned at battle stations...stations of prayer warriors and worshipers, singers, instrument players.....each with a special station. Others, (like Preachers and Teachers) feed the crew and train the members to live their life for Jesus. Each of us have a special mission on this ship, and God Himself has given us the ability and talent to do just what He has called us to do!

Each one on this Battleship of life can personally talk to the Captain anytime they want to. They can talk to Him without fear of being eloquent, of fear of stuttering.

There is no rest because the enemy is all around. The enemy is the devil and he is always sneaking up on us, firing missiles of lies, murder, adultery, idolatry, thievery, envy, gossip and anything else he can think of! Sometimes these missiles land right at our feet, sometimes they land in our heart, and it is up to us to destroy them before they destroy us.

The Captain, (God) has armed us with the power of His name and with the power of the Holy Spirit, and He has placed warrior Angels all around us. If we only call on His Holy Name, we can defeat the purpose of each missile the devil launches. The battle is fierce and it is a war for your own soul. We must remember that Jesus has already won the war, but there are a lot of battles that must be fought! Without the help of God, we can do nothing. Remember, the devil can't take your soul.....but you can give it to him!

Out here in this battleship, the waters of life sometimes get rough and there are rocks jutted out of the water just waiting to tear the boat to pieces. Winds of depression, discouragement and anger blow all around us, but then there is the Lighthouse on the hill that reminds us that all is not lost and there is hope....if only we have faith and repent of our sins! We must always remember to let Jesus

pilot our ship, and all we have to do is to love Him and obey Him and He will faithfully bring our ship safely into the harbor on the other shore!

Romans 5: 4-5
Patience produces character and character produces hope, and hope will never disappoint us.

****

DARKNESS

Have you ever found yourself in total darkness? Well, if you have lost your eyesight I know that is how you must spend your entire life...but I have heard that some blind people say they can see light faintly... they say they can tell the difference when they are standing facing the sun rather than the wall. But, they still live in darkness!

During Hurricane Katrina, we were without lights for over two weeks and at night we were in total darkness! During the day, things were OK, but at night things were much different. At times we burned candles, but when we would go outside at night we would just douse the candle and relight when we came back inside.

Our family has sat out in the front yard sometimes until the wee hours of the morning...talking, because it was just too hot to go to bed. We would try to get situated before darkness fell, because moving chairs after dark was a real chore. We tried to conserve the batteries in the flashlights because we had no idea how much longer we would have to do without lights, and there was quite a while that no stores were open because of the power outage, and batteries and candles couldn't be replaced. The traffic on the road was almost non-existent because of the shortage of gas.

I can remember sitting out there and knowing the voices of the ones around you but not being able to see anyone or anything...not even a shadow of a person. For some reason, the moon didn't shine during this time and all of the nights were dark nights. The only thing that made us feel halfway safe from people walking up on us was the amount of debris that was covering the yard. It was covered with twigs, limbs and other loose objects. No one could walk to the house in the daylight without falling, much less attempt it in the dark.

We would be talking and hear a strange sound...fear would grip even the strongest...because even if you knew where the sound was coming from, you were helpless in the total darkness. Babies would cry and Momma or Daddy, or Grandma or Grandpa would hold them and try to comfort them. They wouldn't put them down while they slept at night because of the severe darkness.

One night, someone stopped on the roadside just out front of the house. Soon they got into a heated argument. You could hear them, but the darkness played tricks on you, and at times they seemed closer than they were. We wondered if they had flashlights and if they were going to seek us out....or if they were up to harm. God surely listened to us that night and an air of peace floated all around us. We would try to keep talking so that we would know the others were still there.

When we would go into the house, furniture that had been in the same place for years, seemed now in another place. You thought you were in familiar territory, but you couldn't find your way. You'd run into things, stumble over things and feel completely lost in your own home. Darkness moved in and it seemed so thick you could cut it with a knife. You never remembered it being this dark! We would pray for night to move swiftly to bring in the dawning light, but all too quickly, night would be upon us again!

I got to thinking...maybe God is trying to tell us something! Maybe he is trying to get us to seek Him and His Kingdom, and repent of our sins....maybe this is a small preview of things to come. I don't know about you, but I don't want to live in a world of darkness...listening to screaming, crying and falling.... and realize it is me!

In the Bible it tells us that in the end times the stars will fall out of the sky, and the sun and moon will not shine. They say it will be darkness all around, and when we put our hand on the walls to guide us, we'll put our hands on a snake. They will moan and gnash their teeth and some will take their own life. Seemingly, there will be no way to get food, to eat or get any other of the things we take for granted. It will be a horrible time! I don't know about all of you, but I would really like to be taken up in the Rapture and not one of those "left behind."

Revelation 16: 10-11

The fifth Angel poured out his bowl on the throne of the beast and his kingdom was plunged into darkness. Men gnawed their tongues in agony and cursed the God of Heaven because of their pains and their sores, but they refused to repent of what they had done.

****

MY PORCH

My porch has become like a sanctuary in my home. I sit on my porch a lot and enjoy the breeze that is almost always stirring there. I take my morning cup of coffee out there and thank God for the day. I sit in the swing and sway back and forth as I ponder what I must do today. I sit out there during a soft summer shower and watch as the raindrops gently water the lawn. I go and sit on the porch when I am worried or have burdens on my heart. This is my prayer room and this is where God has answered so many of my prayers.

When I have company, they usually want to sit on the porch, even though the air conditioner is running inside. They say there is something special about this porch. They tell me they sense a presence of peace and comfort there. (I think God sits here on my porch with me a lot!) I have had family or friends over and the temperature would be nearing 100…but here we are sitting out on the porch…. not even feeling the brunt of the heat! Then there are times in the winter that we have to wrap in blankets in almost freezing temperature, while the inside of the house is comfy and cozy….yet, we don't feel chilled. It is just something special about my porch!

My Bible is read out here and my daily meditation is done here….and there is no place in my house that I feel any closer to God than on my porch! My Mom came and visited me the other day and didn't even let me know she was there. When I opened the door, it startled me to see her there and I asked why she didn't let me know she was out here….and her reply was, "I just wanted to enjoy your porch for a while!"

I have a lot of flowers on my porch. It is in the shade a lot so I have a lot of vines, ferns and green plants. Five or six years ago, I had fallen away from my walk with God. I had a friend who reminded me of those days just the other day. She said back then, my porch was a pitiful mess… just like my life. I couldn't grow many live plants…my green thumb had turned black! I got so aggravated with plants dying on the porch, I stuck some silk, artificial flowers in pots. My friend said they looked so pathetic….and they too looked like they were dying. The porch was not a good place to be. I did not feel peace there.

Then I got my life back on the right track….I prayed and I read my Bible and I have cried and talked to Jesus a lot….right out here on my porch. God has blessed my porch ever since!

I plant flowers in the spring and each year they get more and more plush. This year, I have not even fertilized them much as they are growing so fast….I don't know where I would put them if they get much bigger. My friend said she had

never seen anything like it. It was like God was making the porch special, even more beautiful, for me and my family and friends.

Raising flowers has always been a chore for me because I couldn't get them to look good and healthy. Now, it would almost make a florist envious. Each day I sit out there and I thank the Master for the beautiful plants, and for the peaceful feeling. I thank Him for listening to all of the prayers, the complaints, for wiping my tears from my eyes, and for sometimes just holding me while I cried....right here on my porch. I thank Him for loving me enough to bless my porch and for making it beautiful....and to let my friends and my family feel his special presence here!

Matthew 6:29-30
And why do you worry about clothes? See how the lilies of the field grow. They do not labor or spin, yet I tell you that not even Solomon in all his splendor was dressed like one of these.

****

PROVERBS

I was reading through Proverbs the other day and I thought, "This surely has a lot of good advice." I know you have read them time and time again, but I would like to share a few with you that really seemed to stand out. I think if folks would use them in their daily life, things would be so much simpler and more peaceful.

"Wisdom is worth more than silver. It makes you
much richer than gold." Proverbs 3:14

"Share your plans with the Lord and you will succeed." Proverbs 16: 3

"With all your heart you must love the Lord and not your own judgments.
Always let Him lead you and he will clear the road." Proverbs 3: 5-6

"Broken promises are worse than rain clouds that
don't bring rain." Proverbs 25: 14

"Young people take pride in their strength, but the gray hairs
of wisdom are even more beautiful." Proverbs 20: 29

"Just as iron sharpens iron, friends sharpen the
minds of each other." Proverbs 4: 28

"There are two things, Lord, I want you to do for me before I die. Make
me absolutely honest and don't let me be too poor or rich. Give me what
I need. If I have too much to eat, I might forget about you, and if I don't
have enough, I might steal and disgrace your name." Proverbs 30: 7-9

"The right word at the right time is like precious
gold set in silver." Proverbs 25: 11

"Caring for the poor is lending to the Lord. You
will be well repaid." Proverbs 19: 17

"The lifestyle of good people is like sunlight at dawn...that keeps
getting brighter until broad daylight." Proverbs 4: 18

"The start of an argument is like a water leak, so stop it before real trouble breaks out." Proverbs 17: 14

If you are curious about any other question that life brings, just read proverbs and I am sure you will find the answer. Obviously, Solomon was a very wise man, and it would make us very wise if we would put Proverbs to use in our own daily life.

****

OCCUPATIONAL HYMNS

As we sing the good old Gospel Hymns, we never probably think of them as occupational Hymns. Everyone needs a little chuckle every now and then, so let's put a few of the songs to an occupation!

Dentist Hymn............ "Crown Him With Many Crowns"
Contractor Hymn......... "I'm Working On A Building"
A Politician Hymn......... "Standing On The Promises"
Optometrist Hymn......... "I Saw The Light"
A Florist Hymn............ "Flowers For The Master's Bouquet"
A Realtor Hymn............ "I've Got a Mansion Just Over The Hilltop"
"A Cabin In The Corner Of Gloryland"
Weatherman Hymn....... "There Shall Be Showers Of Blessings"
"On The Next Cloud Passing By"
"The Uncloudy Day"
The Golfer Hymn........ "There's A Green Hill Far Away"
The Tailor Hymn......... "Holy, Holy, Holy"
The IRS Agent Hymn.... "I Surrender All"
The Gossip Hymn......... "Pass It On"
The Electrician Hymn..... "Send The Light"
The Shopper Hymn........ "The Sweet Bye And Bye"
The Massage Therapist Hymn.. "He Touched Me"
The Doctor Hymn.......... "The Great Physician"
The Plumber Hymn...... "Step Into The Water"
The Potter Hymn.......... "The Potter's Hands"
And for those who speed down the Highway, there are several Hymns.......
45 mph ...."God Will Take Care Of You"
65 mph....................."Nearer My God To Thee"
85 mph....................."This World Is Not My Home"
95 mph..................... "Lord, I'm Coming Home"
100 mph...................."Precious Memories"

I hope you enjoyed these hymns. A little laughter always makes the day better.

Ecclesiastes 2: 26
For God giveth to a man that is good in His sight,
wisdom and knowledge and joy.

****

RULES TO LIVE BY

The other day I ran across a list of some things that would be good rules to live by. I would like to share them with you, and hope you would share them with your friends and loved ones.

Say "Bless you" when you hear someone sneeze. Maybe it has nothing to do with the sneeze, but it is a way to remind you to say "bless you."

When you lose, don't lose the lesson!

Remember the three R's, respect for self, respect for others, and responsibility for all of your actions.

Talk slowly but think quickly.

Remember that great love and great achievements involve great risks!

In disagreements, fight fairly....no name calling....no bringing up actions from the past.

Don't judge people by their relatives. We all have a relative that we don't want to be compared with.

Don't believe all you hear, spend all you have or sleep all you want.

When you say "I love you", mean it!

When you say, "I'm sorry" look the person in the eye!

Never laugh at anyone's dream. People who don't have dreams, don't have much!

Give people more than they expect and do it cheerfully!

Don't let a little dispute injure a great friendship!

Smile when picking up the phone. The caller will hear it in your voice!

Try these little rules of a good life and see if they help to improve your personality as well as your quality of life. I think they are all some good points that each of us could improve on, but the best one of all is:

Always live your life for the glory of God, and the Kingdom of Heaven will be yours!

Colossians 1: 9
For this cause we also, since the day we heard it, do not cease to pray for you, and to desire that ye might be filled with the knowledge of His will in all wisdom and spiritual understanding.

****

CELL PHONES

I watch the world go by in different aspects of life, and I see children, young children, holding on to a cell phone, talking ninety miles an hour to a friend. What are they talking about? Well, it is probably very trivial, but the expression on their face says it's very important. You go to the Mall and it seems like no one can shop without the little phone glued to their ear. They don't have time to talk to anyone....no one but the one on the other end of that little cell phone. No wonder they spend too much money in the store or they don't buy the right item, or the right size! They can't think or do anything it seems, without first consulting that little ole phone.

You watch as the car in front of you swerves and the driver looks away, waving the hands as if he is in a heated argument. Yep! You're right. That little ole cell phone has taken over yet one more life.

Have you ever asked a co-worker why they were late and they replied, "Oh, I had to go back and get my cell phone!" The greatest gift a child thinks he can get is his own cell phone. People can't travel without it, and what would they do in an emergency without it? Then there is the continual beep, beep, beep, beep of the text messaging. The phone never seems to rest. Folks find it impossible to function without these little phones! Most women always have one in their purse and men have them hanging from a pocket. How did one ever function without these little critters clinging to them?

Wouldn't it be wonderful to see a child open their Bible with as much excitement? They would turn to John 3:16 and tell their friend, "For God so loved the world He gave His one and only Son, that whoever believes in him shall not perish but have everlasting life!"

Have you ever had a person at the Mall pull out a well worn Bible and say, "Friend, have you heard?" (And they open their Bible to Psalm 91: 11-12) "God will command His Angels to protect you wherever you go. They will carry you in their arms so you won't hurt your feet on the stones." Now, wouldn't you really feel loved?

What if the driver who looked away for a moment was talking to the Lord.... holding the Bible tightly in one hand.

Maybe the co-worker who was late would respond, "I just had to take a minute to pray. Then I turned in my Bible and read Psalm 119: 114 and read...'You are my plan of safety and my shield. Your word is my only hope!' It sure made me feel like I was ready for whatever the day might throw at me!"

But what about the text messaging? Well, in the silence of your heart you can talk to Jesus. You can respond to the Lord as Isaiah did in Isaiah 6:8, "After this

I heard the Lord ask, is there anyone I can send? Will someone go for us? I'll go, I answered. Send me!" .... (And no one hears the annoying beep, beep, beep, beep of sending the message.) God is there and He answers every time!

Wouldn't it be great for someone to get as excited over a gift of a Bible as they do when they get their own cell phone? Couldn't you just see God smile if everyone carried a Bible in their purse or in their pocket or His words in their heart? How precious it would be if the Bible was the first thing packed when going on a trip, because you couldn't leave home without it!

And what about an emergency? Well, that would be as simple as a prayer. It would get to its destination faster and clearer than any phone message could. You would never have to worry about dialing the right number in haste, never worry about a busy signal, and God is always home. Then you could open your Bible to Isaiah 41:10 and read, "Don't be afraid, I am with you. Don't tremble with fear. I am your God. I will make you strong as I protect you with my arm and give you victories." Or, maybe you would open the Bible to Psalm 32: 8...."You said to me, I will point the road that you should follow. I will be your teacher and watch over you."

Personally, I don't see where a cell phone can hold a light to the blessings of God's word. Try using the phone less and the Bible more and see how God will bless you!

****

STORMS

Tonight I sit here watching a storm. Lightening is striking, thunder is rolling and it is raining hard! I sense fear when it is storming, but I pray for strength to endure and for safety from the storm. God gives me peace and I feel safe. Then the brunt of the storm moves on.

Each day we face storms in our life. Each storm is different with different consequences, but God is always there. He'll hold you in the hollow of His hand until the storm passes by, or He'll just raise his mighty arm and tell the storm, "Peace be still!" And the storm obeys!

As the storms rage with the loss of a loved one, we cry and we try to put the blame on someone and then ask "Why?" But death is a natural part of life itself. It does hurt, but God is there to comfort us. He'll put his arms around us and put beautiful memories in place of the pain...if we will just let Him!

Finances are sometimes the storm. We try to figure out how we can stretch the money to pay the bills and there just doesn't seem to be a way. But, if we pray, God will help us to see a way to pay the bills.

Storms of sickness, fear, loneliness and problems in the home are a few of the storms that blow through our lives. Pray! God is the great Physician, your Knight in shining armor, your Friend, your Counselor and your Savior. He can calm any storm that arises. There is no storm too big or too violent that He can't handle. If He chooses not to actually calm the storm, He will give you peace and strength to endure it.

The next time you find yourself in the midst of a storm, just pray and believe and let God carry you through. He loves us and He is there for us! He is never too busy to listen to us....God is still on the throne! But, one of the greatest pleasures is just to talk to God when sunshine streaks through your heart and soul. Thank Him for the sunshine and thank Him for getting you through all of the storms in your life.... Whether He held you close to His bosom during the storm or if he stilled the storm. He loves you so very much!

Matthew 8: 26

But Jesus replied, "Why are you so afraid? You surely don't have much faith." Then He got up and ordered the wind and the waves to calm down and everything was calm.

Psalm 91: 14-15

The Lord says, "If you love me and truly know who I am, I will rescue you and keep you safe. When you are in trouble call out to me. I will answer and be there to protect and honor you."

****

DANIEL

I was sitting here the other night just thinking of how God always prepares the way for us when we do His will. The first thing that came to my mind was the story of Daniel. Think of the lion's den. It must have been fifteen or twenty feet deep, because one certainly didn't want the lions to be able to jump out. They were probably kept hungry so they would be sure to take care of the food tossed in quickly to be a sport. I am sure if you listen, you can hear them roar. The roar could probably be heard through out the city, striking fear into all who heard.... all but Daniel.

You see, they had made a law against praying to God. They said all petitions should be taken to the king to be solved, not God. But Daniel loved the Lord and he wanted to be obedient to God. Old Daniel would get right in front of his window, open the curtain and face Jerusalem and pray unashamed three times a day. He wasn't going to hide his love of his God even though he knew that he would be thrown into the lion's den. But, because he was faithful, God took care of him!

One day the king sent men to arrest him, ordering them to throw him into the lion's den. I know God closed their mouth and made them tame as a house cat, but I think He done a couple of other things, too. It would have probably killed a person to be thrown into the pit, even if the lions didn't get to him first. But, I can imagine a few of the biggest lions grouping together making a soft landing for Daniel. Instead of trying to kill him, I can see them nudging against him, wanting to be petted just like an old tabby barn cat. Their purring was probably like a soothing lullaby throughout the night. One lay down to be used as a pillow while others snuggled close to keep him warm. God filled Daniel with peace and joy, knowing this was a safe place to be, because God was watching over him.

As the king came inching over to the edge of the pit the next morning, and there was Daniel, asleep in the midst of these wild, hungry creatures, I am sure that in an instant he knew that Daniel worshiped the true and living God.

You know, He does the same for us when we are doing His will. When He tells us to do something, he opens doors, prepares the way. He provides us the opportunity, the place, and He puts a band of Angels around us to keep us safe. When the devil pushes us around and throws us into the pit, He is always there to soften the landing and comfort us through the hard times. He gives us peace and joy in the midst of our enemies. He lets us find comfort in situations that would sometimes terrify us, all because we are doing His will. He is our God! He never sleeps! He never takes His eyes off of us! He is a precious, wonderful Savior!

Daniel 6: 23
The king was overjoyed and gave orders to lift Daniel out of the den. And when Daniel was lifted from the den, no wound was found on him because he had trusted in God.

****

REFINED SILVER

The other night I was reading psalm 12: 6..."And the words of the Lord are flawless, like silver refined in a furnace of clay, purified seven times."

I didn't know exactly what was meant by this, except to accept the fact that the words of the Lord were without error, without imperfection. I knew a friend who worked with silver at times, and I asked him to show me what it meant to refine silver. Well, he built a hot fire, just the right temperature, and held the silver over the fire to heat it up. He said he held it in the middle of the fire. That is where the fire is the hottest, in order to burn away the impurities in the metal.

There is a verse in Zechariah 13: 8-9..."In the whole land", declares the Lord, "two thirds will be struck down and perish, yet one third will be left in it. This third I will bring into the fire. I will refine them like silver and test them like gold. They will call on my name and I will answer them. I will say, 'They are my people,' and they will say, 'The Lord is our God!"

The silversmith explained to me that he had to sit there the whole time. He said if the silver was left in the furnace oven a moment too long, it would be destroyed from the heat. I then asked, "How do you know the exact time it is ready to take out of the fire?" He smiled and said, "Oh, that is easy....when I can see my image in it!"

Think about the fire that the Lord lets us go through. This only takes away the impurities in our lives....our sins and short comings. God holds us over the fire right in the right spot, but He never leaves us. He is holding on to our hand the whole time, and He never takes His eyes off of us. How does He know when we are completely purified? That is easy ....when He can see His image in us!

****

PRECIOUS MEMORIES

I think that for the most part, we never take the proper time to just sit and reminisce about our past. Some of us have a lot of memories because of our age and some have only a few....but we need to go back and think of them every now and then and just see how they helped get us where we are right now. They help to keep one alive in the hearts of the generations beyond. Some of the memories are just "memories" and really had nothing to do with shaping us now, but they are usually fun to remember!

Think back to your childhood...the games you loved to play, the pets you had, and talks you had with your Mom and Dad...the first time you stayed away from home and how you sure wished your Momma was there. Think about the first day of school, the strangers, the ones you made friends with, the teachers...some bad and some good. There was probably always the town bully who was sure to shove you around sooner or later. How about the first time you found yourself with a crush on the opposite sex...do you even remember their name? Can you recall what kind of impression that they left on your life? Do you remember when you gave your life to Jesus?

Do you remember the hard times you spent working a farm or maybe in a factory for little or nothing in pay? If there were more than one child in your family, and you were younger, can you remember the hand-me-down clothes and shoes, and remember wondering why you never got anything new? Can you picture what your Momma or Dad looked like when they were younger? Can you recall how Momma and Daddy most influenced your life so that you are who you are now? Can you remember your first love, your wedding day, having your first child, or even the first death of someone dear to you? Can you remember a friend who has always seemed to be there for you, and even though you don't see them very often, you know they still care?

Now as life is taking a toll on all of us, that doesn't mean that memories are not being made. Each day we live we are surrounded by memories. Each time someone does something for us or against us, or we do something for someone or against someone, this turns into a memory. All memories are not good, but when they happen in your lifetime, they are your memories. Every time you recall them, you probably remember something else that happened along that line. Keep telling your children, your grandchildren, your great-grandchildren these stories of your memories, because what impressed you or formed your life or thinking, will eventually affect them. By hearing these stories, they will have precious memories of your lifetime to live by in their lifetime, and will pass them on to ages of generations for many years. These stories could be told over and

over to generations, and in some special way we will always be remembered.... our laughter, our journeys, our hard times, our good times, our sad times, our personality, our occupations, but especially our love for Jesus.

When you seem to have run out of memories, remember that over two thousand years ago, Jesus died on a cross so that we could be forgiven of our sins. He loved us then and He loves us now! Each time we need someone, He is there for us. Each time the road gets rough, He takes our hand. When our burdens get too heavy for us to bear, he lifts the cross from our shoulder and He takes it Himself. When you remember what Jesus has done for you, and what He is still doing for you ...it is one of the best memories you can bring into your life and the best one to pass on to your family. This could influence many family members to turn to Jesus and live their life as you lived yours.

Psalm 143: 10
You are my God. Show me what you want me to do,
And let your gentle Spirit lead me in the right path.

****

YOU HAVE WON THE RACE

Along a crooked, narrow road,
I was bent and weary from my heavy load.
I passed a man walking fast and free,
His head held high and never looked at me.
I stumbled on the stones so sharp, and my feet they bled.
I was hungry and couldn't remember when I'd last been fed.
A group of boys stood in my path,
They taunted and teased and begin to laugh...
"The funny old man, so humped, so forlorn,
His face is dirty and his clothes are torn!"
On down the road I walked so slow,
With food for the widow for a month or more.
No one to help me, no one to care...
And at times it seemed like more than I could bear.
On down the road with miles to go,
I trudged along, each step a chore.
I smiled as I thought of how she'd feel
When she pulled out the groceries and made a meal.
I had just about gone my limit, you see,
When a light shone around me as bright as could be.
It was Jesus standing there with a smile on His face.
He took my hand and said, "You have won the race!
I'll take your burden and carry it for you,
For you have been faithful with what I told you to do.
The widow will live a long, long life,
Without the burdens of fears and strife.
And for you, my dear friend,
I'll walk with you and bless your life 'til the very end!"

As I read this poem over, I wondered why God had given me it to me. God answered and said this was a parable. The road we travel is rough, full of distractions from Satan. Some want to have nothing to do with a Christian. They sometimes push and shove until it just breaks our heart, but we go on, not worrying about what they think or even food for our body....God will provide that. They make fun of us and they laugh at us, but we go on...and we help those who are in need. (The widow represents someone in need) When our burdens seem more than we can bear, we must think of the good things we are

doing for the glory of God. Just about the time we seem so weary that we are ready to give up, Jesus takes us by the hand and takes our burden. He fills the lives of those we help with abundant blessings, just as He blesses our own lives.

Isaiah 30:20
The Lord is waiting to show how kind He is and to have pity on you.
The Lord always does right; He blesses those who trust in Him.

****

THE PENCIL

Have you ever heard the parable of the pencil? Well, it seems as though the maker of the pencil thought it to be such an important invention, he thought it needed instructions so it could be the best it could be!

As he held the finished product in his hand, he said to it...."Pencil, there are five things you need to learn before going out into the world. If you go by these rules, you will be the best pencil one could hope to be!

First....You will be able to do a lot of different things, but only if you allow yourself to be held in the hand of someone. Alone you are worthless!

Second....You must experience a painful sharpening every now and then in order to do your best, but this is needed if you want to become a better pencil!

Third....I have given you the ability to correct any mistake you may make.

Fourth....The most important part of you is what is inside you. Don't dwell on the outside.

Fifth....No matter how tired you are, or what the condition is, you must continue to write and leave a clear legible mark. This mark may even be used to change history or a person's life."

The little pencil understood the instructions and crawled into the box to start its journey into the world.

Now, suppose you put yourself in place of that little pencil, to be the best you can be. Suppose your maker held you in His hand after you had found Salvation, and He gave you instructions for being the best Christian you could be!

He might would say..."You can do many great things, but only if you let me lead you. Without me you can do nothing. You will have to experience a good sharpening every now and then, by going through troubles and trials. But this will only make you stronger and better. I am giving you the ability to correct any mistake you make by asking me for forgiveness and mercy. You will be able to learn from them and find you will need to use the eraser fewer times in the future. The most important thing about you is on the inside....your heart and soul. Don't dwell on what is on the outside. On every surface you walk, you must leave your mark. You must continue to serve God no matter what the circumstances or how tired you might be. You must continue to glorify your Maker in everything you do. After all, this might just change a person's life or even history."

Everyone is like a pencil....created by the Maker for a unique and special purpose, by understanding and remembering to live our life for Jesus. Let us live our life on this earth, having a meaningful purpose in our heart and a close relationship with God, our Maker, daily.

You were made to do great things....but we can do nothing without God.

Exodus 33:14
My presence will go with you,
And I will give you rest!

****

MY PRAYER

A friend sent me this prayer on the computer the other day, and I would like to share it with you. I don't know who originally wrote it, or where it started, but it really touched my heart. I hope it touches yours!

Heavenly Father, we come before you today and ask your forgiveness
And to seek your direction and guidance. We know Your Word says...
"Woe to those who call evil good"...but....that is exactly what we have
done. We have lost our spiritual equilibrium and reversed our values.
We confess that!
We have ridiculed the absolute truth of Your Word and called
it Pluralism.
We have rewarded laziness and called it welfare!
We have killed our unborn and called it choice!
We have shot abortionists and called it justifiable!
We have neglected to discipline our children and called it
building their self-esteem!
We have coveted our neighbor's possessions and called
it ambition!
We have polluted the air with profanity and
pornography and called it freedom of statement!
We have ridiculed the time-honored values of our forefathers
and called it enlightenment!
Search us, Oh, God, and know our hearts today...
cleanse us from every sin and set us free.
Guide and bless the men and women who have been
Sent to direct and teach us,
To be in the center of Your will and to openly ask these things in
the name of Your Son, our Saviour, Jesus Christ our Lord.
Amen

Titus 2: 11-12
For the grace of God that brings Salvation has appeared to all men. It
teaches us to say "No" to ungodliness and worldly passions, and to live
self-controlled, upright and godly lives in this present age.

****

CHRISTMAS SEASON

As we approach the Christmas Season, do we lose touch with the real meaning of Christmas? As we decorate the trees and hang the lights, do we forget who is the light of the world? As we spend endless hours and too much money on presents for friends and family, worry about them being the perfect gift, do we remember the gift that God sent down to this world? This was the perfect gift. He sent His Son to us on that cold December night, in a little town called Bethlehem. This was the Christ-child, and he is the reason for Christmas. By giving us this gift, God enabled us to seek and find Salvation.

This Christ-child would be able to heal the sick, raise the dead, cast out demons and He would be the perfect man! He preached and He taught the Gospel to everyone. But then it came time to hang on that cruel cross at Calvary and he shed his blood for you and for me. Dying in agony and pain, with His arms stretched out, he bridged the span for us to become forgiven of our sins if we would only ask, and we could spend our eternity in Heaven.

Christmastime has become so commercial, and the people we give gifts to are probably the less needy of all. They have someone to care! They have someone who loves them! How about concentrating this Christmas on helping someone less fortunate. Remember to always keep Jesus Christ first, and remember why we have a Christmas Season....but help those who have no one to care.

Help the child whose parents are too busy with booze and drugs to care! Help the neighbor down the street who is down on their luck, and there won't be any Christmas for the children....no Christmas dinner for the family. Could you do without buying a couple of those expensive presents and buy food for them and gifts for the children?

How about the old person who doesn't have anyone to care, no one to invite them to dinner on Christmas? Could you find it in your heart to invite them to your home?

In the stores while you are shopping, look around! There are mothers shuffling through the toys, trying to find just one they can afford for the child at home. Would it hurt you to buy it for her?

There are the homeless who are cold and hungry. Could you maybe find the compassion to help them in someway? There is the old coat hanging in the closet. You never use it. It would sure help to keep them warm.

Then there are the ones who spend the holidays in hospitals, nursing homes, prisons or just home alone. Could you do something special for them?

There are so many ways we can celebrate Christmas. Give of ourselves. Give unselfishly! These gifts will be blessed more than any beautifully wrapped

package that is draped in bright curly ribbons. It will never be the wrong size or the wrong color or forgotten tomorrow. It will be remembered by the person receiving it, for a lifetime!

God's gift to us will be remembered for a lifetime. He gave us His only Son. This is the gift that keeps on giving, and His grace and mercy and love never ends!

Mark 10: 45

He came to serve others and to give His life as a ransom for many people.

****

FILE CABINET OF MEMORIES

As we go through life, we love people and then they die. When something sparks their memory, we often have thoughts of bitterness from things they have done, or the harsh words that were spoken. This way the memories of our friends and loved ones continue to hurt and just thinking about the memories depresses us. They may even bring tears of sadness to our eyes and regret to our heart.

I believe that for each one who comes into our life...and we love them... I think there is a special place in our heart for their memories. Think of it as sort of a file cabinet. Well, I think we should live our lives thinking of this file cabinet that will someday be opened. We should take each golden treasured memory, or treasured word, or grateful deed, wrap it up in pretty paper and pretty ribbons, and store it in this file cabinet. This way, when the loved one's memory comes to mind, we can reach into this old file cabinet, take out one of the finely wrapped packages and relive a happy memory. Some would make us smile, and some might even make us cry, but it would be happy tears.

We could remember how someone held us in their arms and kissed us goodnight, or the flower that one gave us. There are the sounds of children, laughing and playing, or the Momma or Daddy, always there for us. There could be the kindness from the friend down the road, the prayer from the preacher, the touch of a hand in sympathy, the special gift, kind words, smiles, jokes, or even special characteristics that you always enjoyed.

Wouldn't it be great to remember loved ones and friends in this way? Well, one thing for sure, we must clean out the file cabinet. We must throw away things that make us hurt.....harsh words, something someone forgot to do, habits of the one we love that irritates us. We must replace them all with happy thoughts. This will make happy memories for you later, and it will fill your heart with peace each time you remember them.

You see, it's like God does for us. When we are saved, He cleans out his file cabinet, starting with all of our sins, all of our words that hurt someone, things we didn't do and should have done, things we have done but should not have done, and He remembers them no more. Our space in the file cabinet starts anew. He always remembers the good things....the times we talked to friends and loved ones about salvation, when we help someone, the prayers we pray for others, the smile for the stranger....but most of all, He remembers that we asked for forgiveness, and that we love Him.

Now that it is Christmastime....let's start wrapping up those good memories, storing them in the file cabinet of our heart and getting rid of the things that have hurt our feelings, or just plain made us mad....even things that we just don't

understand...but it bothers us. If you are a Christian, you must be Christ-like. There is no better time to start than now!

2 Corinthians 12: 9
My grace is enough for you. When you are weak,
my power is made perfect in you.

****

THE REAL CHRISTMAS TREE

Each year most of us trim a Christmas tree! We adorn it with lights and ornaments of every kind, even sometimes ropes of tinsel. We sing carols and laugh, and just have a really good time. We don't even wonder where this tradition started. I don't really know either.

But, I do know that a little over 2000 years ago, on a tree shaped like a cross, God decorated it with his Son, Jesus Christ. It was not a happy and joyful time for God, the Father, and definitely not for Jesus Christ.

As Jesus hung there, a crown with large, sharp thorns was on His head. Oh how God must have cried to see His Son in such agony and pain. Ribbons of red flowed down the tree and arms of understanding and love spread across the tree, and was held in place by some old rusty nails! Each tear that fell on that old tree left a shimmering image of an icicle....representing the coldness of the world. His eyes of love and wisdom beheld each soul that had lived or would ever touch the soil of the earth. Even though He could foresee our sins, He whispered, "Father, forgive them for they know not what they do!

The tree was decorated with promises of salvation for anyone who repents and asks of Him. And the lights....well, that was the grandest display of all. For there on that old tree was the greatest light of all, the Light of the World!

The next time you decorate a tree for Christmas, remember that tree on Calvary's Hill that God adorned with His Son, Jesus....giving us all a chance to be set free from all of our sins and the clutches of Satan.

Praise God! He loves us that much! Merry Christmas, Jesus!

Romans 5:28
God shows His great love for us in this way.
Christ died for us while we were still sinners.

****

COMMON SENSE

The other day a friend sent me this over the computer. I do not know who wrote it originally, but it really carries a good lesson, so I would like to share it with you. It is written in the form of an obituary.

"Today we mourn the passing of a beloved old friend, Common Sense, who has been with us for many years. No one knows for sure how old he was since his birth records were long ago lost in bureaucratic red tape. He will be remembered as having cultivated such valuable lessons as knowing when to come in out of the rain, why the early bird gets the worm, life isn't always fair, and maybe it was my fault.

Common sense lived by simple, sound financial policies, (don't spend more than you earn) and reliable parenting strategies, (adults, not children, are in charge). His health began to deteriorate rapidly when well intentioned but overbearing regulations were set in place....Reports of a six-year-old boy charged with sexual harassment for kissing a classmate; Teen suspended from school for using mouthwash after lunch; and a teacher fired for reprimanding an unruly student, only worsened Common Sense's condition.

Common Sense lost ground when parents attacked teachers for doing the job they failed to do in disciplining their unruly children. It declined even further when schools were required to get parental consent to administer Tylenol, sun lotion, or a sticky plaster to a student; but, could not inform the parents when a student became pregnant and wanted to have an abortion, or to pass out condoms.

Common Sense lost the will to live as the Ten Commandments became contraband; churches became businesses, and criminals received better treatment than their victims. Common Sense took a beating when you couldn't defend yourself from a burglar in your own home and the burglar can sue you for assault. Common Sense finally gave up the will to live, after a woman failed to realize that a steaming cup of coffee was hot. She spilled a little in her lap, and was promptly awarded a huge settlement.

Common Sense was predeceased by his parents, Truth and Trust; his wife, Discretion; his daughter, Responsibility; and his son, Reason. He is survived by three stepbrothers; I Know My Rights, Someone Else Is To Blame, and I'm A Victim. Not many attended his funeral because so few realized he was gone."

Think about this, my friend. Who killed Common Sense? We all did! Common Sense should keep us on our knees, repenting for our sins, but we are losing that, too!

Ecclesiastes 7: 11-12
Wisdom, like an inheritance, is a good thing and benefits those who see the sun. Wisdom is a shelter as money is a shelter, but the advantage of knowledge is this; that wisdom preserves the life of its possessor.

****

WHEN LIFE GETS HARD

There comes a time in everyone's life when trouble and difficulties seem to gang up. We no longer get one problem settled and another one comes along. When this happens...when life gets hard to bear....here is a creative way to handle it!

FIRST: Don't try to do it all yourself. Do not struggle and fret. Do not strain and complain. Do all you can about these things and then put everything into God's hands. Let go and let God help!

SECOND: Pray for guidance and believe that God speaks to you. Believe that God will guide you in the right direction. Believe that God will not fail you!

THIRD: Pray for a calm attitude. Disturbing things will only get worse when you have a disturbing attitude. When you become peaceful, things will start to smooth out. You can not think positive when your mind is upset!

FOURTH: Learn to lean on your faith. When you feel troubled, repeat this out loud, "Thou shalt keep him in perfect peace, whose mind is stayed on thee." (Isaiah 26:3) "In the quietness and confidence shall be your strength." (Isaiah 30:15) "Peace I give unto you; not as the world giveth, give I unto you. Let not your heart be troubled; neither let it be afraid." (John 14:27)

FIFTH: Remind yourself of one great truth; hard experiences WILL pass away. They WILL yield to peace. They CAN be changed. So just hold on and trust in Jesus!

SIXTH: There is always a light in the darkness. Believe that. Jesus is the light. Look for that light. The light is the love of God. "Thy word is a lamp unto my feet and a light unto my path." (Psalm 119:5)

SEVENTH: Ask the Lord to release your own strength and wisdom, which together with Jesus can solve any problem.

EIGHTH: Never forget that God loves you. He cares for you. He wants to help you and He is waiting for you to ask!

<u>NINTH:</u> Remember that all human beings experience troubles and trials, but God will help each of us, if only we ask and believe.

<u>TENTH:</u> Finally, hold on to this great promise; "God is our refuge and strength, a very present help in trouble." God will see you through and a brighter day will dawn for you!

LET THESE PROBLEMS GO! "God must rule our hearts if our feet are to walk His way." (Hebrews 3:15)

****

FREE NEW YEAR'S ADVICE

As we enter the New Year, most of us are making resolutions. I would like to give you a bit of free New Year's advice!

1. Never look down on someone unless you're helping him up.
2. Experience is what you get when you don't get what you want.
3. No matter how we are dressed, we are all wearing our feelings.
4. Try to follow your own advice before you offer it to others.
5. Speak what you feel, not what you ought to say.
6. Small opportunities often lead to great enterprises.
7. If you never try to do what you know you can't do, you will never know what you can do!
8. Desiring to appear clever often prevents our becoming clever.
9. A true gentleman never claims superiority in anything.
10. Suspicion on our part encourages deceit in others.
11. Zeal will do more than knowledge.
12. Your deep mind knows all the needed answers in life.
13. Our critics are our best guides.
14. It is better to learn late than never.
15. Life is short and we never have enough time for gladdening the hearts of those who are on this journey with us.
16. To finish the moment, to find the journey's end, to live the greatest number of good hours, is wisdom.

17. Whatever you do, do it with all of your might.

18. Live your life according to the Bible.

19. Love Jesus with all of your heart, your soul, your mind and your strength.

20. When you see others in need, always try to help them.

Even with all of this free advice, I have read one that to means so much to me. As I go along life's road, getting older and my strength playing out at times, there is a promise that makes me feel renewed.

1 Timothy 6:6-7
For Godliness with contentment is great gain. For we brought nothing into the world and we can take nothing out of it.

****

MY SAVIOR, MY REDEEMER, MY FRIEND

Have you ever thought of how many roles God plays in your life? Well, here are a few of the very important roles He plays in my life!

He is my Savior...He saved me from a life of sin. He is my Redeemer...He took this old sinful piece of clay and made it into something precious in His sight.

He is my Friend...and when I need someone to talk to, when days seem lonely and nights seem long...He is there anytime I need Him. He is my Judge...and when this life is over, He will judge my life, and if I live my life for Him, He will judge me to an eternity with Him.

He is my Great Physician...for there is no disease that He cannot heal. Sometimes He speaks healing into my body, sometimes He just works through the doctors. Sometimes, for reasons I don't understand, they are left as a thorn in my side.

He is my Advisor...because for any question I can turn to His word, and with prayer He will lead me to the answer. He is my Father...and he takes care of me as a father would, including chastise- ment when I am wrong.

He is my Strength...in the midst of my storms, whether they be storms of nature or storms of life. He is my Promise of a better tomorrow. He is the Arms to hold me when burdens seem to be so heavy and life gets me down.

He is the Ray of Light when my world seems to be bound in darkness and problems are all around. He is my Guide...why, He left me a roadmap in the form of the Bible.

He is my Protector...when Satan puts snares all around me to make me stumble. He is a Listener to each prayer I pray. He never turns away or is never too busy to listen.

He is my Provider ...for when the bills are due and there is no money, He provides. He is my Joy...for with Him I know I have eternity in Heaven.

He is my Peace...and when the world is in turmoil, He whispers sweet peace to me, or when the storms are raging, He reaches out His mighty hand and says, "Peace, be still!"

He is my Comforter...for when my heart breaks, or I have lost a loved one, or my world just simply falls apart, He puts His arms around me, holds me close to His bosom and He comforts me.

There are so many more ways he is there for me...but, I think the most important thing He is to me is He is the one who died on the cross for me. Even though my life was sinful, He loved me enough to stretch out His arms and die. I know I will never be worthy of that, but without that promise of Salvation in

my soul, I could not enjoy the love and the fellowship of my Jesus, my Savior, my Redeemer, my Friend.

Colossians 2: 13-14
God made you alive with Christ and He forgave all your sins. He canceled the debt, which listed all the rules we failed to follow.

****

FAULTS AND SHORTCOMINGS

How many times has the opportunity came along that would allow us to do a service for God, but we would always find an excuse with ourselves, our ability, or our past and say, "Well, God just couldn't use me!"

But God is a forgiving God, and He will forgive us of our sins, our faults, and over look our shortcomings, if we only ask from our heart and believe and trust in Him as we live our life for Him.

A lot of the famous people in the Bible had "faults" or "shortcomings," but God used them for His Glory and they will be remembered forever.

Some of them are:

Noah had a drinking problem;
Abraham was too old;
Isaac was a daydreamer;
Jacob was a liar;
Leah was ugly;
Joseph was abused;
Moses had a stuttering problem;
Gideon was afraid;
Samson had long hair and was a womanizer;
Rahab was a prostitute;
Jeremiah and Timothy were too young;
David had an affair and was a murderer;
Elijah was suicidal;
Jonah ran from God;
Job went bankrupt;
Naomi was a widow;
Peter denied Christ;
The Disciples fell asleep while praying;
Martha worried about everything;'
Zaccheus was too small;
Paul was too religious;
And Lazarus was dead!

Now, no more excuses! God can use you to your full potential, and besides, you aren't the message, you are just the messenger. In the circle of God's love, God is waiting for you to use your full potential.

A few things to remember are;

"God wants spiritual fruit, not spiritual nuts!"
"Dear God, I have a problem, It's me!"
"Growing old is inevitable....growing up is optional!"
"There is no key to happiness... the door is always open!"
"Silence is often misinterpreted but never misquoted!"
"Do the math.....count your blessings!"
"Faith is the ability to not panic!"
"Laugh every day. It's like inner jogging."
"If you worry, you didn't pray. If you pray, don't worry!"
"As a child of God, prayer is kind of like calling home everyday!"
"Blessed are the flexible, for they shall not be bent out of shape!""
"The most important things in your home are your people!'
"When we get tangled up in our problems, be still. God wants us to be still so He can untangle the knot!"
"A grudge is a heavy thing to carry!"
"He who dies with the most toys is still dead!"

John 14: 8
Lord, show us the Father. That is all we need.

****

PSALM 138 - 139

Did you ever wonder just how involved God is in each earthly life? Is there any truth in the theory of evolution? Did we really evolve from apes? In the abortion issue....Is there life immediately after con- ception? Well, in Psalm 138 and 139, I think the Bible answers all of these questions. The Scripture is taken from the Living Bible, which makes it a bit easier to understand.

Psalm 138 - 139

Lord, with all my heart I thank you. I will sing your praises before the armies of Angels in Heaven. I face your Temple as I worship, giving thanks to you for all your loving-kindness and your faithfulness, for your promises are backed by all the honor of your name. When I pray you answer me, and encourage me by giving me the strength I need. Every king in all the earth shall give you thanks, O Lord, for all of them shall hear your voice. Yes, they shall sing about Jehovah's glorious ways, for His glory is very great. Yet though He is so great, He respects the humble, but proud men must keep their distance. Though I am surrounded by troubles, you will bring me safely through them. You will clench your fist against my enemies. Your power will save me. The Lord will work out His plans for my life - for your loving-kindness, Lord, continues forever. Don't abandon me...for you made me! O Lord, You have examined my heart and know everything about me. You know when I sit or stand. When far away, you know my every thought. You chart the path ahead of me, and tell me where to stop and rest. Every moment, you know where I am. You know what I am going to say before I even say it. You both precede and follow me, and place your hand of blessings on my head. This is too glorious, too wonderful to believe. I can never be lost to your Spirit. I can never get away from my God. If I go up to the Heaven, you are there; if I go down to the place of the dead, you are there. If I ride the morning winds to the fartherest oceans, even there your hand will guide me, your strength will support me. If I try to hide in the darkness, the night becomes light around me. For even darkness can not hide from God. To you the night shines as bright as the day. Darkness and light are both alike to you. You made all the delicate inner parts of my body, and knit them together in my Mother's womb. Thank you for making me so wonderfully complex. It is amazing to think about. Your workmanship is marvelous and how well I know it.

You were there while I was being formed in utter seclusion. You saw me before I was born and scheduled each day of my life before I began to breathe. Every day was recorded in your book. How precious it is Lord, to realize that you are thinking about me constantly. I can't even count how many times a day your thoughts turn towards me. And when I waken in the morning, you are still thinking of me. Surely you will slay the wicked, Lord. Away, blood thirsty men. Begone! They blaspheme your name and stand in arrogance against you. How silly can they be? O Lord, shouldn't I hate those who hate you? I be grieved with them. Yes, I hate them, for your enemies are my enemies, too. Search me, O God, and know my heart; test my thoughts. Point out anything you find in me that makes you sad and lead me along the path of everlasting life!

This is a beautiful part of the Scripture. To me, it covers a lot of questions that others may ask. It gives me comfort, hope, peace and joy. Each time I think I am unloved, and no one cares, I read this scripture and hope abounds....God is always there. Sometimes I stray from Him, but He never strays from me. Sometimes I feel like no one cares, or even knows what is going on in my life, but this passage assures me that God always knows where I am and He guides my ways, if only I stop to listen to Him!

****

LOVE

As Valentine's Day approaches, the key word becomes "LOVE." There are so many kinds of love...love for your parents love for your children, love for your family, love for the spouse. Then there is the home you love, the church you love, the sport you love, the book you love, the movie you love, the country you love, the car you would just love to have, and the list goes on and on.

But there is one special kind of love. It is the ultimate love. This is the love that God has for us. He loved us so much He made an entire universe, complete with stars, moon, sunrises, sunsets, and everything else here on earth. He made the sun and the rain, because He wanted things to be beautiful for us. He made a wife for Adam, just because He loved Adam so. But the greatest love one could show, was when He sent His only begotten son to die on the cross for our sins.

The Bible tells us that God is Love. He commands us to "love the Lord thy God with all thy heart, all thy mind and all thy strength, and to love thy neighbor as thyself."

If we had this much love in our hearts, we wouldn't have to worry about abuse, abortion, wars, disrespect for others, hurtful words or deeds. The divorce courts would be empty. The jails would be vacant, because if you love someone you won't kill them, or rob them, or abuse them. There wouldn't be anyone living on the streets just because no one cared. No children would be left to fend on their own, just because the parents didn't care enough to take care of them. There wouldn't be hunger or poverty, because the ones with a little to spare, would love their neighbor enough to help them. If there was enough love, there would be no suicides, because people would love themselves, too.

The three words, "I love you" would be heard all of the time by everyone, not just a few. (Some probably never hear another person say "I love you.") If we all had this great love, we would worry more about our fellow man who is lost and we would love him enough to teach him about the love of God and salvation.

I think one of the greatest aspects of Heaven is the presence of absolute love! God is there, so that tells me that there is enough love for everyone. I am so glad that I am saved and I can spend eternity in this "LOVE." We need to practice love while we are down here on earth.... Not just lip service, but real love from the bottom of our heart.

Romans 12: 9 –12

Don't just pretend that you love others; really love them. Hate what is wrong. Stand on the side of the good. Love each other with brotherly affection and delight in honoring each other. Never be lazy in your

work, but serve the Lord enthusiastically. Be glad for all God is planning for you. Be patient in trouble and prayerful always.

****

HIS HANDS

Have you ever imagined God's hands? These hands were large enough to hold the planets of the universe in their palm. His hands were strong enough to lift the sun and place it where he wanted it to stay, and He spoke to the sun and it remains! When He made the earth, He formed the mountains, the rivers, the valleys ... with His own hands. He proceeded to make each and every thing found on this earth; the birds, the animals, the fish, the trees, flowers, grass, dirt, water, and every other thing! Then, He reached down into the dust and with His hands, formed man, then formed a mate for man. He led the children of Israel out of Egypt, leading them with His mighty hand. With His strong hand, he closed the door on Noah's ark as the rains started, and no one could open the door but God. God had His hand on the small little stone that David used to slay the Giant. God's hands closed the mouth of the lions when Daniel was thrown into the lion's den, and this same hand saved Jonah from the belly of the whale. God's hand was on Job, even though the devil was trying so hard to get him to deny the Lord. God's hands were on the chains in the prison cell with Paul and Silas.

Then He sent His Son to earth, in His own image, but as a baby. As He grew into a young man, God kept his hands on Jesus, giving Him the will to be sinless, and to tell the world about His Father. Jesus called Lazarus out of the grave, and he had been dead four days! What about the field of bones that God brought back, and breathed life into them? Then, the hands of Jesus were nailed upon a cross for our sins. He suffered and died, but after three days, God came to the tomb, laid His hand on His Son, and beckoned Him home with the Father! God writes our name in the "Book Of Life" with his own hand, and He tells us that our names are written in the palm of His mighty hand!

But, then, here I am. I was sinful ... I was lost, and I was without God. I repented of my sins, and I asked God to forgive me, and God laid those same hands on me. A God that is big enough to create and take care of a whole Universe, can hear each whisper of a prayer to Him! He knows when each of us is hurting, and he even knows the number of tears that fall. He knows the number of hairs on each of our heads and the number of leaves on each of the trees. What an awesome and great God we serve. He will reach down and place His mighty hands on us ... if we will just ask!

Ephesians 3: 16-20
God is wonderful and glorious. I pray that His Spirit will make you become strong followers and that Christ will live in your hearts because of your faith! Stand firm and be deeply rooted in His love. I pray that you and all

of God's people will understand what is called wide or long or high or deep. I want you to know all about Christ's love, although it is too wonderful to be measured. Then your lives will be filled with all that God is!

****

SPRING GARDEN

Here it is spring again. Almost everywhere, there are flower gardens springing up. The flowers are warmed by the sun and kissed by the dew. Storms come and shake them from the top to the tip of the roots, and only the ones deeply rooted survive. Winds blow and sway them. The gardeners are busy pruning the dead limbs and the withered flowers. Pestilence of all kinds makes themselves known; aphids, worms, snails, ants, fungus, bugs, mites, grasshoppers and other things, are bent on destroying the plant. Pesticide must be used. A generous helping of fertilizer insures good growth and health.

This is very similar to the garden of our heart. Our heart is warmed to glowing with the love of Jesus. Each time we feel we are no longer able to go on, His special touch refreshes us. Storms of life threaten our very soul ... storms of sickness, pain, distrust, finances, and threats from enemies, are just a few.

When the storms of life threaten us, we need to turn to God, and no matter what the storm is, He can reach out His mighty hand and say; "Peace, be still." He may just give us the strength and wisdom to walk through the storm! There is no storm that can hit us that He cannot take care of, but we must ask for help, and believe, and repent! If we are strong in our faith, our roots will not be damaged, just strengthened. But, if we are weak, the storm can destroy us, and Satan will be the winner. We must keep strength for the storms ... and God is our source of strength.

Evil winds of unbelievers try to sway our Christian beliefs. Some succeed, but if we are deeply rooted in our faith, we are still grounded in God's love and grace. If we don't bear Spiritual fruit, God prunes us! For, unless we are connected to the vine, (God), we cannot bear fruit.

Pestilence attacks from every side; gossip, low self esteem, fear, greed, grief, health, peer pressure, lust, envy, are just a few. These are easy to handle. Just turn them over to Jesus, pray, and listen to what he tells you to do! He will give you the wisdom and the strength to overcome them.

To insure sound Spiritual growth we need to feed on the "Word" each and every day. We need to study the word, not just read it. If you are a Christian, the Bible will open up so many answers to questions you have asked. There is a solution to every problem on earth, printed in this "Book"! A healthy prayer life is also needed to insure good growth and fruit from our lives.

God knows each of us by name, and we don't even have to identify ourselves when we speak to Him. He tells us that He knows each of His sheep by name, and His sheep know His voice! It is amazing that thousands may be speaking to him at one time, but He is able to hear and see each individual, and work with

their problem. This is surely an awesome God! Isn't it time you took better care of your "Spiritual Garden"?

Psalm 62: 11-12
I heard God say two things: "I am powerful, and I am very kind."
The Lord rewards each of us according to what we do!

****

GOD'S JUDGMENT

Suppose you have just entered the gates of heaven. Here you stand in front of God. Suppose Jesus speaks to you and says: "Thanks for those beautiful songs you sung for me!" or "I am so glad you were obedient to preach the sermons I gave you!" or "Thanks for teaching the children and adults about salvation!" Maybe He would say, "Thanks for all of your prayers for others!" or "Living a Christian life surely made a difference!" Maybe He would tell you, "It was great to know you were raising your children in a Christian home!" or "I remember the time you prayed with a friend, until they accepted Me as their Savior!" or "Thanks for the beautiful hymn you wrote!" or "I'm so glad you took your pen and wrote down the beautiful poems about Me that filled your heart!" or "I filled your soul with music. Thanks for using it to sing praises to me!" or "Thanks for all of the strangers you took into your home, and for feeding them, for clothing some, giving some money, and sharing My word with them all!" or maybe He will tell me, "Thanks for putting those stories I gave you on paper and sharing them with others!"

There are so many more things that He could tell us "thank you" for. He has given each of us a talent, and we need to use it for His honor and His glory. Sometimes we have talents that stand out to the world, and sometimes we have only a beautiful smile, but, if we use it for Him, we are blessed beyond measure.

What if ... that day in Heaven, God would ask us ... "Do you know how many souls you touched for the Kingdom, by using your God given talent for My glory? Would you like to meet them all? And there for miles, a line of people were waiting to tell you "thank you" for getting the message to them, so they could repent of their sins and they could spend eternity in Heaven!

Oh the horror to enter Heaven for the Judgment, and God tell you, "It broke my heart that I gave you a song in your heart, and you used it to promote Satan!" or "I called you as a preacher, and you only preached what made you comfortable, not the messages I gave you!" or "You were the Sunday school teacher. They watched the way you lived your life, and you only had time for me on Sunday!" or "Why didn't your talk to me? Why didn't you pray for your salvation and for your friends?" or "The stories or poems you passed on to others were not for My glory, but for the glory of the devil!" or "I gave you your children, and you aborted them, abused them, taught them to curse, to drink, to lie, to steal, to commit adultery, and to grow up never hearing my name!"

Then, with a tear on His cheek, He turns you toward Hell, and asks, "Do you want to see all of those you influenced in this manner?" And there are miles of people, heads bowed, pleading eyes, cursing and accusing you of being responsible

for them being here ... and God gently shuts the gate with you on the outside, and you join the miles of people, heading for the fires of Hell!

Luke 1: 50
God will show His mercy forever and ever to those who worship and serve Him!

****

THE ALTAR

In front of a lot of churches is an altar. This is used for special prayers and special closeness to God. In the police department, there is a powder, that when dusted on objects, disclose fingerprints ... a light that picks up any traces of blood. But, what if there was some special instrument to use on the altar. What would it see? What would it hear?

Would it see the tears cried from those who were seeking salvation, the lonely, the wife whose husband was abusive, the child in trouble, the husband with an unfaithful wife, the one who desperately needs a job, the confused, the one who is losing the battle with their health, the dying, and the lost. Some go to the altar with tears of praise for answered prayers.

This is a place to pour out your troubles to God, in the privacy of your own heart and soul. This is a place to beg for forgiveness, for understanding, for comfort, for questions unanswered in your life, for guidance, and to reassure yourself that God does listen to your prayers and He does answer them! This is a place we can simply say, "Praise God!" We can pray aloud or pray silently, and God hears each and every word ... He even hears what we don't say. He knows our heart inside and out, and He knows what we need. He knows what we are asking for, even if we can't find the words to ask.

The altars have been visited by the brokenhearted, the drug addicts, the drunkards, the troubled, the lost, the misunderstood and all, (at the same time), are reaching the heart of God. The altar stands as a symbol of laying down our old life, and starting a new one ... with letting go of our problems and letting God handle them. The battles with the demons sometime try to destroy our lives, but God can rescue us.

We sometimes kneel there and feel like we are all alone, then God sends someone to kneel there beside you, not knowing your problem, but there is another prayer sent up. Sometimes, we find ourselves at our altar in the chair at work, the bed at night, (when troubles of the day surround us), the hospital bed, the cell of a jail. Our altar may be in the car as we go to work, or maybe it is just out in the back yard on our knees! God doesn't have a special place that you have to go just to talk to Him. If you ask with a sincere heart, He hears you, no matter where your altar is! He just loves for you to talk to Him.

So, the next time you need someone to listen to you, wipe your tears, or help you with your problems, find your altar of prayer and talk to the Master! He is there! He is never too busy, or never out of range, or "on the other line" or any of the other lame excuses we use all of the time when we don't want to talk to

someone! God loves you and He wants to help you, but He is waiting for you to ask. Talk to Him, my friend. That is one thing that is still free in America!

Romans 8:14
The true children of God are those who let God's Spirit lead them!

****

ADVICE TO BE HAPPY

A friend sent me this over the internet the other day. I do not know who wrote it, but I thought it was worth passing along to my friends.

Remember the five simple rules to be happy.....Free your heart from hatred..... Free your mind from worries.....Live simply.....Give more .....and Expect less.

No one can go back and make a brand new start. Anyone can start from now and make a brand new ending.

God didn't promise days without pain, laughter without sorrow, sun without rain, but He did promise strength for the day, comfort for the tears, and light for the way.

Disappointments are like road bumps, they slow you down a bit, but you enjoy the smooth road afterward. (Don't stay on the bumps too long!)

When you feel down because you didn't get what you wanted, just sit tight and be happy, because God is thinking of something better to give you!

When something happens to you, good or bad, consider what it means. There's a purpose to life's events...to teach you how to laugh more and not to cry too hard.

You can't make someone love you, all you can do is to be someone who can be loved..... the rest is up to the person to realize your worth!

When you truly care for someone, you don't look for answers, you don't look for faults, you don't look for mistakes. Instead, you fight the mistakes, you accept the faults and you overlook the excuses.

Never abandon an old friend. You will never find one who can take his place. Friendship is like wine, it gets better as it grows older.

A day spent without God is a wasted day!

This is some well thought of advice. My advice to you is to stay close to Jesus.....never let go of His hand, and you will never fall short of His blessings. Sometimes it is a struggle to walk each

day, each hour, with Jesus, but believe me my friend, God will surely make it worth your while, with blessings and a heart full of love!

Psalm 20: 1
I pray that the Lord will listen when you are in trouble,
and that the God of Jacob will keep you safe.

****

FARMER'S ADVICE

A long time ago, most of the population was farmers. People weren't as educated as they are now, and they were not book learned, but they sure had a lot of advice that could not be argued with. This is what is called "Farmer's Advice." You have probably heard some of them as you grew up.....I have!

"Your fences need to be horse-high, pig-tight and bull-strong!"

"Keep skunks, bankers and lawyers at a distance!"

"Words that sink into your ears are whispered...not yelled!"

"Meanness don't jes' happen overnight!"

"Forgive your enemies. It messes up their heads!"

"Do not corner something that you know is meaner than you!"

"It don't take a very big person to carry a grudge!"

You cannot unsay a cruel word!"

"The best sermons are lived, not preached!"

"When you wallow with pigs, expect to get dirty!"

"Every path has a few puddles!"

"Most of the stuff people worry about ain't never gonna happen anyhow!"

"Don't judge people by their relatives!"

"Remember that silence is sometimes the best answer!"

"Live a good, honorable life. Then when you get older
and think back, you'll enjoy it a second time!"

"Don't interfere with anythin' that ain't botherin' you none!"

"If you find yourself in a hole, the first thing to do is stop digging!"

"The biggest troublemaker you'll probably ever have to deal with, watches you from the mirror every morning!"

"Always drink upstream from the herd!"

"Good judgment comes from experience, and a lotta that comes from bad judgment!"

"Lettin' the cat outta the bag is a whole lot easier than puttin' it back in!"

"If you get to thinking you're a person of some influence, try ordering somebody else's dog around!"

"Live simply. Love generously. Care deeply. Speak kindly. Leave the rest to God!"

If we were to follow this old Farmer's Advice now days, we would probably find it to be a lot better world. This advice is quite simple, but it covers a lot of territory. Think about it!

John 15: 7
Stay joined to me and let my teachings become part of you. Then you can pray for whatever you want and your prayer will be answered.

****

I BELIEVE IN GOD

There are a lot of things that a human believes in. The main thing one believes in should be God! With that belief, other things just naturally come to life. The sun comes up in the east, sets in the west, like so many other things that God has done, and commanded it be done just that way until the end of the world. A lot of things like this, we just take for granted, but God meant for things to be this way. I believe that God must have loved the color green. Just think, he could have made the grass in shades of blues or reds. I believe He has an answer for every problem that we may face. Here are a few beliefs that I have found very useful throughout the times:

I believe... that you can do something in an instant that will give you a heartache forever!

I believe... that you can keep going long after you think you can't!

I believe...that either you control your attitude or it controls you!

I believe...that money is a lousy way to keep score!

I believe...that sometimes when I'm angry, I have the right to be angry, but that doesn't give me the right to be cruel!

I believe...that we are responsible for what we do, no matter how we feel!

I believe...that heroes are the people who do what has to be done when it needs to be done, regardless of the consequences.

I believe...that it isn't always enough to be forgiven by others, sometimes you have to learn to forgive yourself!

I believe...that our background and circumstances may have influenced who we are, but we are responsible for who we become!

I believe...that sometimes the people you expect to kick you when you're down, will be the ones to help you get back up!

I believe…that two people can look at the exact same thing and see something totally different!

I believe…that when you think you have no more to give, when a friend cries out to you, you will find the strength to help!

I believe…that your life can be changed in a matter of minutes by people who don't even know you!

I believe…that credentials on the wall does not make you a decent human being!

I believe…that just because two people argue, it doesn't mean they don't love each other. And just because they don't argue, it doesn't mean they do!

I believe…that my best friend and I can do anything or nothing and have the best time!

I believe…that maturity has more to do with what types of experiences you've had and what you've learned from them and less to do with how many birthdays you've celebrated.

I believe…that no matter how bad your heart is broken, the world doesn't stop for your grief!

I believe…that we don't have to change friends to understand that friends change!

I believe…that no matter how good a friend is, they're going to hurt you every once in a while and you must forgive them for that!

I believe…that true friendship continues to grow, even over the longest distance. The same goes for true love.

I believe…that you should always leave loved ones with loving words. It may be the last time you will ever see them!

I believe…that people you care about most are taken away from you too soon!

I believe…that God loves you, and that He died for you. I believe that He will forgive you of all of your sins, if only you repent and ask for forgiveness!

Malachi 3: 17

Then the Lord All-Powerful said: "You people are precious to me, and when I come to bring justice, I will protect you, just as parents protect an obedient child.

****

AN AWESOME GOD

Have you ever just sat and visualized what God was really like? Well, I have. It may not be the way it really is, but I can picture Him in my mind!

When God sent Jesus to this earth, He sent an image of Himself.... Not necessarily His size and statue, but an image of Him. He came to earth as a baby, in the size of earth's ordinary babies. But, I think the picture will look a lot different when He comes the next time!

Picture just His hands! It is said that He could hold the stars of the universe in His hands...He took the Sun and placed in it in the heavens with His hands... or that He would write each of His children's name in the palm of His hand. His hands shaped and molded mountains, valleys, plains, and with one finger He carved the way for a river. That is some large hands!

In Revelation, it is said that all the souls that had been killed for speaking His message were under the altar in Heaven....hundreds and thousands of souls. It is said that He could stand with one foot on the water and one foot on the land.

When God breaks open the eastern sky, it is not going to be a wimp of a human that we will have to strain our eyes to see what it is....It will be a giant, riding a huge white horse, and surrounded by Angels praising His Holy name.

No one will have to wonder who this awesome rider is! We will know that this is Jesus! With a voice like thunder and lightening flashing across the sky, every knee will bow and every tongue will confess, that this is Christ the Lord. We will all know in an instant who it is and we will also know that it will be too late to set our life in order. The name written on His thigh, King of Kings and Lord of Lords, will be visible for every eye to read.

His mind is so vast He knows everything...He can speak all languages. He can heal all sicknesses, the blind, the deaf, the lame, the deformed. He knows how many tears we have shed, the number of hairs on our head, the leaves on the trees, and each blade of grass. There is no question He can't answer, no problem He can't solve. He can hear the prayers of millions of people at the same time, in all kinds of languages and circumstances and He knows which of His children is talking to Him! He never forgets one of His own! No matter how far we may stray away from Him, He is always there for us to call on when we need to find the way!

What will Jesus look like as He returns for His Children? Read Revelation 1: 12-16.... "When I turned to see who was speaking to me, I saw seven gold lamp stands. There with the lamp stands was someone who seemed to be the Son of Man. He was wearing a robe that reached down to His feet, and a gold cloth was wrapped around His chest. His head and His hair was white as wool or snow,

and His eyes looked like flames of fire. His feet were glowing like bronze being heated in a furnace and His voice sounded like the roar of a waterfall. He held seven stars in His right hand, and a sharp double-edged sword was coming from His mouth. His face was shining as bright as the sun at noon!"

This is surely going to be an awesome sight to behold... especially for the Christians. It will be a very fearful time for the non-believers though. They will instantly know they have followed the wrong path. They did not put their trust in God!

Friend, if you have not already turned to Jesus, you need to fall to your knees and pray. Pray for forgiveness and Salvation.

This time, Jesus will come to earth in all of His Glory! He will not be made fun of, blasphemed, mistreated, spit on, sold out, crucified or wear a crown of thorns. He will wear a crown of pure gold, and he will judge the people. Your fate will be in His hands. His word will be the law! Where will your soul stand?

****

WHY GOD

On the news we see shootings at schools all around the country, and we ask God, "God, why did this happen? Why didn't you protect our children? Why did you let them die? And God answers.......

"One woman, Madeline Murray O'Hare, complained that as an atheist, she didn't want prayer in schools...and without much of a fight at all, you said OK.

Someone then said that we must not let our children read the Bible in school because it says 'Thou shalt not have any other Gods before me...Thou shalt not kill....Thou shalt not steal....And love your neighbors as yourself!' ....And you said OK. Isn't it strange that the children in schools are not allowed to pray or read the Bible and prisoners are?

Dr. Benjamin Spock said we shouldn't spank our children when they misbehaved because this would warp their little personalities...and without further proof, you just thought he must be an expert and you said OK.

Then someone complained and said teachers and principals couldn't discipline our children when they misbehave, so the school administrators ruled that teachers could not touch children to correct them because they didn't want any bad publicity...or even be sued!

Then Satan whispered in someone's ear, 'Let's let your daughters have abortions if they want, and they won't even have to tell their parents.' And you said that was a grand idea!

Then Satan conferred with a wise school board member and said, 'Since boys will be boys, let's give your sons all of the condoms they want, and we don't even have to ask permission from their parents.' And the school administrators said that was another good idea.

Then some of our top elected officials remarked that it doesn't matter what we do in private as long as we have jobs and the economy is good! What kind of an example do they set?

Then Satan stepped up to the entertainment business...He filled the songs with filth and drug promotion, made games that teach children how to kill, filled the Internet with porn and other satanic information that children can easily access, filled the TV shows with nudity, profanity, crime and alternate life styles and makes the people think it is OK. And you nodded and said, 'Well, everyone is entitled to freedom of speech...' and you purchased them for your children.

Then you ask why your children have no conscience, no morals...why they don't know right from wrong, and why it doesn't bother them to kill someone, whether it be family, strangers, classmates or even themselves.

Well, you took me out of the schools, remember! You took me out of the home, and the Bibles are not read to them! You took me out of sports, out of public places, and my Gideons cannot even pass out the Bible on campus anymore.

How long do you think I will protect you when you treat me worse than anyone else? Wake up America! Turn back to me or I will rain wrath upon your great land!"

Proverbs 29: 1-2
If you keep being stubborn after many warnings, you will suddenly discover you have gone too far. When justice rules a nation, everyone is glad; when injustice rules, everyone groans.

****

THE NAPKIN

We read in the bible that when Jesus was buried in the borrowed tomb, a napkin was placed over His face, but when the tomb was found empty, the napkin was neatly folded and placed at the head of the stone where He lay. It was not just tossed aside as a motion of getting up off of the slab. Did you ever wonder why an entire verse in the Bible was used to describe the folded napkin? Did you ever think that a folded napkin had any significance at all?

John 20: 6-7 ... "Then Simon Peter, who was behind him, arrived and went into the tomb. He saw strips of linen lying there, as well as the burial cloth that had been around Jesus' head. The cloth was folded up by itself, separate from the linen!"

What did this mean? Well, in order to understand the significance of the folded napkin, you need to know a little about Hebrew tradition at this time. The napkin was a message between the master and the servant. It was taught to every Jewish boy so that he would always know.

When a servant set the table for the master, he knew to set it exactly like the master wanted it to be. Everything would be set in place, and the master would sit at the table. The servant would stand back just out of sight and wait for the master to finish eating. Then, and only then, could the servant go over and clear the table. The servant would not dare touch the table until the master was done!

Now, how did he know the master was through eating? Well, if the master was through eating, he would rise from the table, wipe his fingers, his mouth, and clean his beard. Then he would wad the napkin up and toss it on the table. The wadded napkin in those days meant, "I am done!"

But, if the master got up from the table and folded his napkin and laid it beside the plate, the servant knew that this meant, "I am not finished yet." The folded napkin meant, "I am coming back!"

This is exactly the message that Jesus left in that cold and dark tomb...He told us, "I am coming back." He is coming back. No one knows the day or the hour, but we know the promise...He is coming back! Are you ready for Him to come back and gather His children and take them home?

Mark 14: 32-33
No one knows the day or the time. The Angels in Heaven don't know and the Son Himself doesn't know. Only the Father knows. So watch out and be ready. You don't know when this time will come.

****

THE TOMB OF THE UNKNOWN SOLDIER

I know all of you have heard of the "Tomb of the Unknown Soldier." Well, have you ever heard the ritual of the Guard of the Tomb?

(1) <u>How many steps does the Guard take during his walk across the Tomb of the Unknowns and why?</u>
21 steps. It alludes to the twenty-one gun salute, which is the highest honor given any military or foreign dignitary.

(2) <u>How long does he hesitate after his about face to begin his return walk and why?</u>
21 seconds for the same reason as #1.

(3) <u>Why are his gloves wet?</u>
His gloves are moistened to prevent his losing his grip on the gun.

(4) <u>Does he carry his rifle on the same shoulder all the time and if not, why not?</u>
He carries the rifle on the shoulder away from the tomb. After his march across the path, he executes an about face and moves the rifle to the outside shoulder.

(5) <u>How often are the guards changed?</u>
Guards are changed every thirty minutes, twenty four hours a day, 365 days a year.

(6) <u>What are the physical traits of the Guard limited to?</u>
For a person to apply for guard, he must be between 5′ 10″ and 6′ 2″ tall, and his waist size cannot exceed 30″. Other requirements of the guard: They must commit 2 years of life to guard the tomb, live in a barracks under the tomb, and cannot drink any alcohol on or off duty for the rest of their lives. They cannot swear in public for the rest of their lives and cannot disgrace the uniform, (fighting) or the tomb in any way. After two years, the Guard is given a wreath pin that is worn on their lapel signifying they served as guard of the tomb. There are only 400 such pins worn today. The Guard must obey these rules for the rest of his life or give up the pin. The shoes are specially made with very thick soles to keep the heat and the cold from their feet. There are metal heel plates that

extend to the top of the shoe in order to make a loud click as they come to a halt. There are no wrinkles, folds or lint on the uniform. Guards dress for duty in front of a full-length mirror. The first six months of duty, a guard cannot talk to anyone, nor watch TV. All off duty time is spent studying the 175 notable people laid to rest in Arlington Cemetery. A guard must memorize who they are and where they are interred. Every guard spends five hours a day getting his uniforms ready for guard duty.

On the stone is written: "ETERNAL REST GRANT THEM O LORD, AND LET PERPETUAL LIGHT SHINE UPON THEM."

In 2003 as Hurricane Isabelle was approaching Washington, D.C., our U.S. Senate / House took 2 days off with anticipation of the storm. On the ABC evening news, it was reported that because of the dangers from the hurricane, the military members assigned the duty of guarding the Tomb of the Unknown Soldier were given permission to suspend the assignment. They respectfully declined the offer, "No way, Sir! Soaked to the skin, marching in the pelting rain of a tropical storm, they said that guarding the Tomb was not just an assignment; it was the highest honor that can be afforded to a service person. The tomb has been patrolled continuously 24 / 7 since 1930.

We should feel just that honored, because I think God has placed Angels as our guards, 24 / 7. I can just imagine one on either side, with swords drawn to protect us.

Psalm 91: 11-12
God will command His Angels to protect you wherever you go. They will carry you in their arms and you won't hurt your feet on the stones.

****

COMMENTS TO SHARE

I love my family, my friends, strangers and even my enemies ... well, most of them, anyhow! Do you? If not, what's wrong with you? Are you allergic to love? God came into this world, took on a body of flesh, was ridiculed, scorned, spit on, beaten and crucified. He died for you! He rose again to give you a new life in Heaven. God is love!

You may make fun of this old house I live in. It's not really much, but it is all I need now. You see, I have a mansion in Heaven. There are no mansions in Hell, you know!

Satanist don't scare me! Do you expect me to run? Me? Listen, I am told that greater is He who is within me than he that is in this world. You know that Satan is a big fat liar, don't you? He's headed for the lake of fire and guess what ... he would love to have you for company.

Let me think now...If Satan was an Angel, and God made the Angels, then how could Satan think he is stronger than God? I think Satan got stuck on the wrong track with his thinking!

God made you, Satan didn't. God loves you and He wants you to love Him back. But it's your choice...Heaven or Hell ...Joy or Misery!

Do you think you're too dirty for God? Then take a bath in the blood of Jesus and He'll wash you clean...just as white as snow!

So what's the holdup? Are you willing to take Jesus as your Savior now? Do you wanna be left behind? Jesus is coming one day, and this old world will be destroyed, and the good will be separated from the bad! Are you ready?

Romans 10: 9-10

So you will be saved, if you honestly say, "Jesus is Lord." And if you believe with all your heart that God raised Him from death, God will accept you and save you, if you truly believe this and tell it to others.

****

MOUNTAINS

In the Bible, God tells us that if we truly believe we could tell a mountain to moved and it would move. Nothing is impossible. Well, personally I don't think all mountains were meant to be moved. I think sometimes a mountain is there to teach us to climb...to teach us obedience and to give us strength for the next one. If each problem we faced were to be gently removed from our pathway, don't you think we would forget to depend on the Lord? We would have the impression that we could just tell the mountain to move and it would go, and we would trod on a path of soft grass, no potholes or even any hills. We would forget to humble ourselves and prayer would not be as intense.

Mountains are made of a lot of things. Sometimes there is a serious illness and we may even ask why we were chosen to be sick. But if we keep leaning on Jesus, we will acquire strength beyond our wildest dreams, to fight for life, to withstand pain, and we learn to walk closer to Jesus. Sometimes this inspiration reaches out to a family member who does not walk as close to Jesus as they should, and they watch or climb, and soon repent of their sins and make their life different.

Sometimes we have mountains that don't move because we don't want to listen to God any other way. We tend to be hard-headed at times and think we can do it all...all by ourselves. But God didn't intend it to be this way. He wants us to love Him and live our lives for His glory and honor.

Other times the mountain may be hardships. This is like a Mother and a Father who have nothing but love to give their children. Sometimes we give the child everything they desire...the child tends not to really appreciate these things. The eventually seem to have a tendency to demand what they want, not ask for what they need. A Christian sometimes does the same. God blesses us so much, we tend to become selfish, and when we talk to him, we demand that He does something for us. We should humble ourselves and ask for what we need. God loves us so much more when we ask for the mountains to be moved...when they don't we reject Him just because things are not right in our lives. Look at His life. It was filled with misery, with ridicule, with pain and rejection. His greatest mountain was when He was hung on the cross, and instead of blaming us for this cruelness, He begged His Father to forgive us for we knew not what we had done. He does move a lot of mountains for us. He knows just which mountain to move and just which one to give us strength to climb.

Ephesians 3: 16
I ask the Father in His great glory to give you the power to be strong inwardly through His Spirit.

****

FLUFFY WHITE ROBE

Picture this...When we are born, God gives us a beautiful, soft, fluffy white robe and a pure gold crown. But, each time we sin, there is a spot on the robe or a scratch or dent on the crown. The bigger the sin, the bigger the spots. Just imagine the time you were saved! Did you even know your robe was white... or, if you had a bright, shinny crown? Think of the all of the spots we placed on them with all of our sins!

In this time in your life, you want to give your heart to Jesus and you will try to serve Him for the rest of your life span. You must truly repent of all of your sins. You avoid places that would tempt you to do these sins again...bar rooms, porn spots on TV or the internet, violent TV shows that promote killing, drugs or other crimes, casinos, friends that refuse to turn from their sins, adultery, stop lying, stealing gossiping, coveting your neighbor's properties, hate. You would honor your Mother and Dad and serve the Lord with all of your heart and your soul!

When you do this, God will restore your white robe and your bright gold crown. With one drop of his red blood, He will wash our black sins and make your soul as white as snow. Your robe and crown will now be as new. It will be as though He dips your robe and crown in something protective like Scotchguard, that prevents stain from soiling the robes, and prevents scratches and dents on the crown. Each time you sin, you can ask for forgiveness from your heart and try not to sin again...the spots will just disappear. God will toss all of the sin and dirt in the Sea of Forgetfulness and remember them no more.

Some folks think that if you intentionally sin, then you simply utter, "I'm sorry," that God will forgive you. But, it just don't work that way. If you don't truly repent of those sins and really try to live a Holy life, God won't hear you when you say, "I'm sorry."

When we get to the Heavenly Gate, only the pure will be able to enter...the ones with the fluffy white robe and the shinning golden crown. Sin will not be permitted inside the gates. Dirty garments represent dirty lives, and God does not like dirty lives. He loves each of us, and it probably breaks His heart to turn some away, but after all, He made a way for us all....with the red blood from the cross at Calvary to cleanse the black sins in our lives and make our soul white as snow. Are you ready to enter the Heavenly Gates? Or, do you need to repent of your sins and have your soul be washed in His blood. The choice is yours, my friend.

2 Corinthians 5: 17
Anyone who belongs to Christ is a new person. The past is forgotten and everything is now new!

****

ARE YOU TIRED

In this old earthly body, we live in a very fast pace. We crawl into bed at night, dead tired. We sleep and too many times the night is much too short. The morning brings the same tiredness. We often wonder where we will find this much needed rest.

But, there is a different kind of labor...working for Jesus and this too surely gets tiring. We talk to family and friends, even strangers, about Jesus. Some listen, some just slam the door in our face. But, no matter how hard it becomes to witness, we know we can't give up. We must press onward. If we serve Jesus, He will give us a new strength and we will be strong.

God promises his children rest from our earthly burdens. He holds His arms outstretched, just waiting for us to ask for this strength and peace. Oh, how lovely the time will be when we do find this rest, when we find this strength.

God has a home of rest in Heaven, but we can have this peace and strength here on earth through our storms, and ample strength to get through them. Satan confuses us and makes us think that we just need to give up and stop working. It is too hard and we must be so-o-o-o tired. He puts potholes in front of us to make us trip up and to frustrate us. Jesus will listen to our prayers and the pleas of our heart, holds out His hand to us, and Satan has to flee!

Personally, I don't know how anyone here on earth can get through their storms without the incredible strength and rest from the Master.

Isaiah 40:31

But those who trust the Lord will find new strength. They will be strong like eagles, soaring upward on wings. They will walk and run without getting tired.

****

PAUL IN PRISON

Let's look at a bit of Paul's life. Well, picture him in prison. I imagine that the jail cells back then were horrible ... small, damp, dark dirty and very smelly. The prisoner was treated badly and even beaten. All Paul was guilty of is preaching the gospel. This prison cell is enough to depress anyone, but Paul took advantage of this time to write letters. They were all uplifting and informative messages to his friends in neighboring towns. Let me write you a bit of the letter that he wrote to the Ephesians while he was in this prison. (This comes from Ephesians 1. It is not the whole verse, only highlighted. You may want to read the whole verse.)

"Praise the God and Father of our Lord Jesus Christ for the spiritual blessings that Christ has brought us from Heaven! Before the world was created, God had Christ choose us to live with Him and to be His Holy and innocent loving people. Christ sacrificed His life's blood to set us free, which means that our sins are now forgiven. When the time is right, God will do all that He has planned, and Christ will bring together everything in Heaven and on earth.

So, I never stop being grateful for you, as I mention you in my prayers. I ask the glorious Father and God of our Lord Jesus Christ to give you His Spirit. The Spirit will make you wise and let you understand what it means to know God! My prayer is that light will flood your hearts and that you will understand the hope that was given to you when God chose you.

I want you to know about the great and mighty power that God has for us followers. It is the same wonderful power He used when He raised Christ from death and let Him sit at His right side in Heaven. There, Christ rules over all forces, authorities, powers and rulers. He rules over all beings in this world and will rule in the future world as well. God has put all things under the power of Christ and for the good in the church, He has made Him the head of everything. The church is Christ's body and is filled with Christ who completely fills everything."

Now, if you were in a prison, whether it be in the small prison cell that Paul was in, or in a cell in one of the modern prisons, or if you were in a prison all your own of poverty, financial, mental, spiritual, or physical, could you speak so uplifted to friends? Or, would you gripe and complain about the wrongs done to you, and focus everything on your own troubles. Paul never seemed to complain about his situation, only tried to pass God's gospel on to his friends. God wants you to serve Him at all times, in the good times as well as the bad, and we must be more concerned with problems of others rather than our own problems. He will always give you the strength to do His will!

Psalm 4: 3
The Lord has chosen everyone who is faithful to be His very own, and He answers my prayers.

****

I SAW CALLIE

As I look back on my life, I see the many times that I held the hammer and pounded the nails into my Savior's hands and feet. I see the times I helped push the thorns deeper into His brow. I know He has shed tears for me and I've made Him very sad, but then he comes back and does something special just for me, and I feel so sorry that I've broken his heart so many times!

On October 28, Callie, my faithful Australian Shepherd died. I had her as a companion for a little over eighteen years and she was always there it seems. She had lost her hearing, most of her eyesight and her teeth. Arthritis had set in her spine and was hurting her back legs. But, I learned a good lesson from her ... she never whined and complained unless it really hurt bad.

When she died, I was in a battle with a lot of health problems. With this pain and grief, I stopped eating, sleep eluded me and I cried all of the time and could not think of anything but how I missed Callie. After almost a week of this, I could feel my health failing more, so I prayed for God to just put His arms around me and give me comfort through this storm, peace with the loss of Callie and for strength to get me through this and my health problems. I immediately stopped crying and felt comfort in knowing God was there.

I was wide awake in my bed, but I was sorta transformed somehow to my front porch. It was pitch dark out there. I looked out across the front yard and in the blink of an eye, I saw Callie. At first she was in a ghost like form, but I knew it was her, but she was much younger! She was running and jumping and barking ... enjoying her new body. In another blink of the eye, I saw this beautiful green field with big shade trees, lots of green, lush grass, rolling hills and a running stream. I could see for miles it seemed ... but all I saw was dogs! Then I saw Callie, (now looking completely alive) entering the field, but still running, jumping and looking at everything around her. Her ears perked up at each little sound. She looked like she was ten years younger.

At this point I saw a few dogs running toward her. She got so excited, like she knew each one of them. The first one to get to her was a red-mearle Australian Shepherd ... her mother ... Cow-li-co. She died about eighteen years ago when Callie was only six weeks old. Cow-li-co was about five years old when she died.

A deep red Australian Shepherd named Ginger, walked beside Callie. Ginger was almost four years old when she died. Others gathered around Callie to welcome her. I recognized Poo-Chee, a lovely, blue mearle Australian Shepherd who lived to be about seventeen years. Then there was the beautiful blue mearle Australian Shepherd with a pair of the prettiest blue eyes you have ever seen.

Her name was Misty. She died when she was only a year old. Almost lost among the Australian Shepherds was Tippy. She was a dainty little black Chihuahua with a white tip on her tail and two white feet. She was with me for sixteen years. They all looked very young and in the prime of their lives. They ran and played and barked like they all knew each other and even though they all seemed to be barking, I thought I heard one of them say to another, "Aren't you glad you got to spend some time with her?"

From this time on, I am at peace ... no more grieving. I have been completely comforted and each time I think of Callie, I see her running on that hillside with all of my other faithful friends. I have the strength to get past this and concentrate on my health. I asked God, "How could you love me so much?" and He answered, "Because you are my child!"

I don't know if there is really a place like that for dogs. God painted a picture and real or not, it gave me peace and comfort I need each time Callie comes to my memories. I know she's OK.

I sometimes wonder if Heaven will be something like that, but even more beautiful. I wonder if us old folks with our aching bones and other health problems will be able to run and play in Heaven ... and we won't be old anymore. I can't wait to get my new body and be able to walk without hurting, or hear good and see good. One day I am gonna get my new body and live in Heaven! Are you?

James 5:16
When a believing person prays, great things happen.

****

RAINBOW BRIDGE

A few weeks after Callie died, the local vet found out about it. The office sent me a sympathy card to comfort me in my loss of my best friend. Inside the card was a little card with a comfort all in itself. It was called "Rainbow Bridge", author unknown. Up until this time, I had never heard of this story. I was amazed how it went along with the story God had given me about Callie! This is what it said.....

"Just this side of Heaven is a place called Rainbow Bridge. When an animal dies that has been especially close to someone here, that pet goes to Rainbow Bridge. There are meadows and hills for all of our special friends so that they can run and play together. There is plenty of food, water and sunshine, and our friends are warm and comfortable.

All the animals who had been ill are restored to health and vigor, those who were hurt or maimed are made whole and strong again, just as we remember them in our dreams of days and times gone by. The animals are happy and content, except for one small thing ... they each miss someone very special to them, who had to be left behind.

They all run and play together, but the day comes when one suddenly stops and looks into the distance. His bright eyes are intent; his eager body quivers. Suddenly, he begins to run from the group, flying over the green grass, his legs carrying him faster and faster.

You have been spotted, and when you and your special friend finally meet, you cling together in joyous reunion, never to be parted again. The happy kisses rain upon your face; your hands again caress the beloved head; and you look once more into the trusting eyes of your pet, so long gone from your life, but never absent from your heart.

Then you cross Rainbow Bridge together .... "

****

TAKEN FOR GRANTED

Americans take so much for granted. We worry about the number one and tend not to think of the soldiers who are always there protecting our country. Let's compare lifestyles ....!

You stay up for sixteen hours ... he stays up for days on end! You take a warm shower to help you wake up or relax you, or just wash away the day of dirt and grime ... he goes days or weeks without running water and washes up with a wet one, or maybe in a mud hole. You complain with a headache and call in sick ... he has blisters on his feet from walking miles in full gear and keeps on going!

You put on your "anti-war" / "don't support the troops" shirt and go meet up with your friends ... he still fights for you to be able to wear that shirt. You make sure your cell phone is in your pocket ... he clutches to the cross hanging on his chain next to his dog tags. You talk trash about your "buddies" that aren't with you ... his buddies are closer than a brother and he would lay down his life for anyone of them!

You walk down the beach staring at all the pretty girls or cute guys ... he patrols the streets and mountains, searching for insurgents and terrorists. You complain about how hot it is ... he wears his heavy gear, not daring to take off his helmet to even wipe his brow. You go out to lunch and complain because the restaurant got your order wrong ... he gets to eat a cold MRE or beef jerky. Your maid makes your bed and washes your clothes ... he wears the same things for weeks, but makes sure his weapons are clean!

You go to the mall and get your hair redone ... he doesn't have time to brush his teeth today! You're angry because your class ran five minutes over ... he's told he will be held over an extra two months. You call your girl-friend and set a date for tonight ... he waits for the mail to see if there is a letter from home! You hug and kiss your spouse like you do everyday ... he holds his letter close and smells his love's perfume.

You roll your eyes as your baby cries ... he gets a letter with pictures of his new child and misses hearing the sound of its cry or the mirth in its laughter.

You criticize your government and say that war never solves anything ... he sees the innocent, tortured and killed by their own people and remembers why he is fighting. You hear the jokes about the war and make fun of men like him ... he hears the gunfire, bombs and screams of the innocent that he is trying to protect. You see only what the media wants you to see ... he sees people experiencing freedom and democracy for the first time. You are asked to do something for someone ... he does exactly what he is ordered to do. You stay at home and watch TV ... he takes whatever time he is given to call, write home, sleep or eat.

You crawl into a soft, clean bed, with warm blankets and soft pillows, and sleep comfortably all night ... he tries to sleep but is awakened by nightmares, mortars and helicopters all night long. You sit there and judge him saying the world is probably a worse place because of soldiers like them ... if only there were more brave men like him!

SUPPORT YOUR TROOPS!
THEY SUPPORT YOU!

Psalm 31: 24
All you who put hope in the Lord be strong and brave.

****

YOU CAN'T DESTROY IT

Each day on the news we hear of someone somewhere taking the life of another ... drive by shootings, drug deals prejudice, hatred, confusion, gang related, accidents and even self-defense. But even though you take their life, you can't destroy their soul. Their soul either belongs to God or to the Devil!

You can fill the air with smog and pollution and the beautiful sunrises and the stunning sunsets you cannot find ... but, just because you cannot see them doesn't mean they have been destroyed. Someone in another town or city is watching in breath-taking awe, the colors of the sunset or the bright colors of the sunrise. You cannot destroy them!

When a child dies, you can't destroy the Mother and Father's love and compassion for that child, no matter how old they live to be, they will always love that child!

From the early days of the Bible, people have tried to destroy it. They have burned it, tore it up, hid it, forbid it, killed people for reading it, and tried any other way possible to destroy it ... but somehow, God's word returns even stronger than ever. More copies are printed and it still speaks to God's children. It cannot be destroyed!

You can't destroy love no matter how many people you hate, because God is love. He is the creator of the Universe, of man and anything else in this Universe. God and his love will not be destroyed.

You can't destroy the blood stains of that old rugged cross, because it was shed for all ... for those who lived before, those living now and generations to the end of the world. When you need forgiveness for your sins, you can still hear the cry of the blood that flowed from the body of Jesus. The blood flowed down that old rugged cross and saturated the ground. No matter how hard the Atheist protest and try to prove different, God shed His blood for our sins, and there will always be the blood of forgiveness for the sinner. All we have to do is repent and ask Jesus to wash away our sins with His precious blood. That blood can never be destroyed!

Romans 5:28
God shows his great love for us in this way; Christ
died for us while we were yet sinners!

****

THE HUMAN SIDE OF JESUS

Here I sit and eat my last meal before I am crucified. Gathered around me are my twelve disciples. One sitting here with me is a traitor. I won't call him by name, but he knows that I know about his schemes. The human part of me is scared of what is about to happen, but the Godly part of me knows this is the way it has to be!

I take one last stroll through the Garden of Gethsemane and I kneel and pray to my Father ... "Father, if it be Thy will, take this cup from me." I prayed so hard my sweat became as drops of blood, but I know I must die for the sins of this world. This is the only way!

Well, Judas is heading this way with the Roman soldiers. He stops and greets me and kisses my cheek. The Roman soldiers arrest me and take me to the authorities. (Later Judas regretted turning me over to the soldiers and he hanged himself. He betrayed me for thirty pieces of silver!) The authorities asked the crowd, "Who should we release ... Barabbas the murderer, or Jesus, the man who goes around doing good?" The devil controlled crowd yells, "Set Barabbas free! Crucify this man called Jesus!"

Then, they take me to a courtyard in the back and they beat me until I can hardly stand, I can hardly breathe ... but I did not yell or cry out ... this had to be. The pain is unbearable, beyond anything I could imagine! But, I look up and I see my Father standing there with tears in His eyes. Sadly, he said, "Son, this is the only way!"

They threw my bleeding body out on the street and demanded that I carry a heavy old rugged cross. My Father was there the whole time reminding me He loved me and it would soon be over. All of the way to Calvary's Hill, the Roman soldiers beat me, the crowd cursed me and spat on me. Somewhere along the way a man helped me with the cross. Great is his blessings in Glory.

As we got to the top of Calvary's Hill, a Roman soldier took three big old rusty nails and he nailed my hands and feet to that old cross. They raised the cross and the pain was almost beyond what I could endure, but I looked into the future and I saw you. I knew I had to do this for this world of sin. I know I am dying, but, my Father tells me that He will come to get me in three days and I will sit at His right hand.

Two thieves were hanging beside me. One cursed and taunted me, but the other one asked for forgiveness. I told him, "Today you will be with me in Paradise."

I know I could have called ten-thousand Angels to take me down off of this cross, but if I don't die for your sins, you will be forever lost. As I hang here, you

are on my mind, all sinful and lost. This is for you! Repent and believe and you too will join me in Paradise.

As death nears, I ask if my Father has forsaken me. I ask Him to forgive these people for they know not what they do ... then I died.

Three days later, there in the tomb, my Father holds His hand out and beckons me to join Him. "It's over!" He said. "For I love the world so much, I sent my only Son to die for their sins. My Son was not guilty of any sin. He was a spotless Lamb." As I arose, I whispered your name to Him and now all you have to do is whisper my name! I will always be with you!

Romans 12: 2
Fix your attention on God. You'll be changed from the inside out.

****

A LITTLE GOOD NEWS

Have you read the local newspaper lately? Were you deeply depressed when you finished? I have often wondered why "good news" seems so unimportant and "bad news" travels like wild fire! Do you remember some of the headlines from the front pages these days?

"12 SOLDIERS KILLED IN IRAQ IN BY A ROAD BOMB"

"A SIX YEAR OLD'S BODY WAS FOUND IN DUMPSTER"

"A MOTHER DROWNS HER FIVE CHILDREN IN A BATHTUB"

A DRIVE-BY SHOOTING RESULTS IN THE DEATH OF A ONE YEAR OLD"

"TWO KILED IN A CAR WRECK ... ALCOHOL RELATED"

"A TEENAGER LEAPS FROM THE ROOF OF HER BUILDING TO HER DEATH ... (SUICIDE NOTE SAID SHE WAS SEEKING PEACE)"

"A DRUG DEAL GOES BAD AND THREE ARE KILLED ... ONE OF THE FATALITIES WAS A POLICEMAN"

"LOCAL GANG BEATS AND ROBS WIDOW FOR $2.00 IN HER PURSE"

"DEATH OF A 13 YEAR OLD BOY ... BLAMED ON OVERDOSE"

"A WALK IN THE PARK RESULTED IN A COUPLE OF SENIOR CITIZENS BEING ROBBED AND KILLED"

"CHILD RESCUED ... HAD BEEN LOCKED IN A CLOSET FOR TWO WEEKS ... WAS STARVING WHEN FOUND"

"ANOTHER CHURCH IS VANDALIZED AND BURNED"

Wouldn't it be nice to read the headlines that would focus on "good news" or on testimonies of what Jesus had done in the lives of each of us. Maybe we could read headlines like this:

"12 SOLDIERS RETURN HOME FROM THEIR TOUR IN IRAQ TO BE WITH THEIR FAMILIES"

"A SIX YEAR OLD WAS FOUND SAFE AND ALIVE ... SAID TO HAVE JUST WANDERED OFF."

"A WOMAN SEEKS THE GUIDANCE OF JESUS TO RAISE HER CHILDREN RIGHT"

"GUNS ARE NO LONGER NEEDED: THERE IS COMPLETE PEACE"

"LOCAL POLICEMAN HONORED BY FORMER GANG MEMBERS FOR HELPING THEM GET BACK ON THE RIGHT TRACK"

"YOUNG MAN OFFERS TO DO CHORES FREE OF CHARGE FOR A LOCAL WIDOW"

"AN ELDERLY COUPLE CAN NOW ENJOY A PEACEFUL WALK IN THE PARK ... ANYTIME"

"FAMILIES ARE ON THE RISE AGAIN ... WITH A MOTHER AND A FATHER AND PLENTY OF LOVE FOR THE CHILDREN .. THE BIBLE IS READ IN THE HOME AND CHURCH IS ATTENDED REGULARLY"

"ONE SINNER WALKED THE AISLE AT LOCAL CHURCH AND FOUND JESUS"

One thing I really look forward to in Heaven is there will never be any bad news! I doubt if there will be any newspapers up there, but if there is, it will only be printed with good news. Each time a soul is saved, Angels sing and it is gladly announced. Each time a Saint enters the gates of Heaven, there are harps playing and Angels saying, "Amen" and the smile will shine on the face of Jesus. There will be no more tactics of the devil to harm others, but all that is known there is love! I'm hoping somehow that God will let us forget the evil that prevailed here on this earth so that it will not even be a memory. I pray that we will be able to remember the face of each one we shared the word with and the smile of the sweet old lady down the street who prayed for me when no one else cared! I keep hoping that one day here on earth we will learn that "good news" is better than "bad news"!

James 5:16
When a believing person prays, great things happen.

****

FLOWERS IN THE MASTER'S BOUQUET

An old abandoned home was up for sale. The yard was covered with weeds and briars. It was sold and as the new family moved in, they started pulling up the weeds and the briars. The lady of the house loved gardening. Over in a corner she discovered a beautiful, bright colored flower. They gently pulled the weeds up and put a little dirt on the flower so it would grow. The lady told the little flower how beautiful it was and that one day it would be the most beautiful flower in that garden and would brighten the corner wherever it was!

One day, a stranger walked through the garden and stepped on the beautiful flower. It lay there bent and broken and crying. The flower thought it was dying and that it would never be able to fulfill the promise of the gardener. But, the lady gardener came out into the garden. She poured some cool water on it and packed the dirt closer to it. She took some sticks and propped it up so it could heal and get strong again ... and it did. This flower lived up to the expectations of the gardener.

You know we are so like that little flower. We are hidden under our sins with a great potential to preach the Gospel and tell the world about Jesus. But, we just sit there in the safety of the weeds. No one even knows we are there!

Then God hears our plea for forgiveness and He finds us bent and broken and sinful. But He gently puts His loving arms around us and comforts us ... He anoints us with the cool living water, and he summons His best Angels to stand around us and help us to become strong in the gospel and to make God proud of us by serving Him. After we have gotten our strength back, the Angels walk with us, and some carry us along so we won't gnash our feet on the stones of sin. Oh, what a loving God we serve. We are the flowers in the Master's Bouquet. When we live our life for Him, in His eyes we become the most beautiful flower in the garden!

1 Corinthians 3:9
We are God's workers, working together.

****

WORLDLY WISDOM

I thought I would share just a few bits of worldly wisdom with you today! I find most of them very amusing, but very true.

"Everything that irritates us about others can lead to an understanding of ourselves"

"Nobody ever died of laughter"

"An ounce of don't-say-it is worth a pound of didn't-mean-it"

"Too many of us think it's a hardship to do without things our grandparents never heard of"

'Never have more children than you have car windows"

"Behind every great man is a woman rolling her eyes"

"Initiative is doing the right thing without being told"

"The only way to get the best of an argument is to stay out of it"

"Two things are bad for the heart; running up stairs and running people down"

"Gossip is what no one claims to like but nearly everybody enjoys"

"The first duty of love is to listen"

"If you really want to do something you will find a way. If you don't, then you will find an excuse"

"Any fool can criticize, condemn and complain ... and most fools do"

"Remember, a rumor is about as easy to unspread as butter on bread"

"We could take a lesson from the weather ... it pays no attention to criticism"

"The future belongs to those who believe in their dreams"

"Stop thinking in terms of limitations, think in terms of possibilities"

"Have patience with all things, but first of all with yourself"

"Don't bite the bait of pleasure until you're sure there's no hook beneath it"

I hope some of these little worldly words of wisdom will be remembered, hoping others will just bring you a chuckle!

1 Timothy 1: 19
Continue to have faith and do what you know is right. Some people have rejected this and their faith has been shipwrecked.

****

ABC'S OF LIFE

As a small child, we learned the ABC's. Well, here is a different type of ABC's, which I call the ABC's of life.

Avoid negative sources, places, people, things and habits

Believe in God ... then in yourself

Consider things from all angles

Don't give up ... don't give in to wrong ethics

Enjoy life today ... yesterday is gone and tomorrow may never come

Family and friends are hidden treasures ... seek them and enjoy their riches

Give more than you plan to give

Hang on to your dreams

Ignore those who try to discourage you or try to turn you from God

Just trust in Jesus

Keep on trying ... no matter how hard it seems ... things will get easier

Love God then love your family

Make it happen

Never cheat or steal ... strike a fair deal

Open your eyes and see things as they really are

Practice a good prayer life

Quitters never win ... winners never quit

Read, study, and learn about everything important in your life

Stop procrastinating

Take control of your destiny

Understand yourself in order to understand others

Visualize your dreams

X-cellerate your efforts for doing good

You are unique ... one of God's creations and no one is just like you

Zero in on your target and go for it

John 13: 25
By this all men will know that you are my disciples, if you love one another.

****

THE TRAVEL TRAILER STORY

God has always urged me to invite strangers into my home ... to feed them, fellowship with them and to tell them about Jesus. Well, I feel so very blessed that God sends people here for one reason or the other, and I have made so many new friends this way. For the most of them, I don't remember their name and probably they don't remember mine, but I do hope they remember being here.

God has sent me a variety of folks and I hope I have not let Him down! When I was home all of the time, there were more visitors, but now I work and I miss them. I live close to the highway and during the summer especially, I got a lot of people stopping in who were traveling on foot. I'd keep the fridge stocked with cold water and sandwich stuff.

I had a lady stop here who was having heart problems. She told her husband that she was so sick she didn't even remember pulling in the drive way and she was sure God brought her here. We have entertained people from South America, Central America, people who asked for just a drink of water or something to eat, or just a peaceful place to rest for a while. They'd sit on the porch and it wouldn't be long until the conversation would turn to Jesus. I have come home from work to find travel trailers or strange vehicles parked in the driveway. I've even had a couple of men hauling show horses break down on the inter- state. They unloaded a couple of the horses and came here seeking help. One man who stopped here said he had walked across America in the northern part and was walking across the southern part at that time. Oh, the stories he had to tell us. One day an elderly couple pulled up in the yard and parked under one of my shade trees. I asked if I could help them and they asked if they could use the shade to rest a while. Some came from Texas to wait out hurricane Rita. Of all of the people who came this way, I never felt fear from one. I never hid my purse or anything else. God gave me the peace in my heart of knowing they were OK, and I hope he gave them the same peace.

One of the most remembered visits happened shortly after hurricanes Katrina and Rita. My nephew and his wife from Conroe, Texas, (the Houston area), were visiting. He and my son are very close and both have a heart as big as Texas when it comes to helping folks. These visitors were from Pennsylvania. Both had just retired and they had bought a brand new travel trailer. They were heading home from Houston visiting relatives. A couple of miles up the road on the Interstate, they lost a wheel on their new trailer.

My nephew was on his way to town for something, and he told his wife, "If they are still there when we come back, I'll stop and see if I can help." Sure enough, on the return trip they were still there and he stopped. They said they had been there for about three hours, and no one stopped. They had called a local truck stop and they offered a lame excuse of they didn't have anything to fix the wheel; the insurance company didn't get back in touch with them. Do you think God was just waiting for the right person to stop? They said they were a little scared when my nephew stopped, but then they felt peace and safety.

As they looked the situation over, my nephew suggested that since his truck was higher than the travelers, that he hook the trailer to it to keep it off the ground while being towed. He then called my son to see where to tow it. These weary travelers were OK with that, but it must have made them a bit nervous to see their brand new trailer hooked to a stranger's truck. My son said he would meet them there. Now, my son and my nephew are always joking around, so the first thing out of my son's mouth at the scene was, "Well, I leave you alone for five minutes and you steal another trailer!!!" (Of course he was only joking, but I'm not sure how the travelers felt!) My nephew asked where was the best place to tow it, and my son said, "Take it to Momma's. We'll help them fix it there." (As they drove up in the yard, they could see another travel trailer parked there with a for sale sign. It really belonged to my nephew and he was trying to sell it, but think of the horror that these folks must have felt. They forgave the boys though, and we all laughed about it later.)

The trailer was not road-worthy, so my son suggested they take the backroads to get here. My son was leading the pack, showing the way; my nephew was towing the trailer, and tagging behind was the couple from Pennsylvania. Do you reckon it crossed their mind that they might be in danger, maybe, if they had chosen the wrong person to help?

Meanwhile, I knew nothing of this episode. I was busy cooking supper for my nephew and his wife and my son and his wife. I thought I was cooking enough, but I kept feeling God speak to me "Cook more!" I got another pack of meat out, added some more beans and a couple of other things. I didn't know why, but I knew when God spoke to me, He had a reason.

Just as I finished cooking, turned the last burner out, I headed for the porch to rest. That's when I spotted this little parade coming up the driveway. I knew then why God had urged me to fix more food. The weary travelers got out and we introduced ourselves, and I asked if they had eaten. They said they were OK and didn't want to bother us, but I was quick to inform them that they were expected ... God had already announced their arrival by telling me to cook more food. I assured them I was glad to have them as our guests. As we sat down at the table the man broke down and cried, and I felt so humbled. He said after we had just been through two hurricanes and had to sacrifice through them, we cared enough to set a table of food for them. I told them we were just doing what God expected us to do!

After supper, we all went out to the front porch and talked and laughed and exchanged life stories, until late in the night. I asked them if they wanted to stay in the house but they opted to stay in the trailer. They said they would be fine there. The next day the boys found someone who had the parts to fix the trailer wheel and they were on their way.

We still keep in touch, and I hope if they ever make it down this way again to visit the relatives, I hope they can find time to stop by and visit us. God surely blesses me with these unexpected visitors.

Ephesians 4: 2-3
Be completely humble and gentle; be patient, bearing with one another in love. Make every effort to keep the unity of the Spirit through the bond of peace.

****

1957 PREDICTIONS

Have you ever thought that things were about as bad as they could get, then they have a way of getting worse? Here are a few comments and predictions from the year of 1957. People then thought the economy was getting bad ... compare it to 2008.

"I'll tell you one thing, if things keep going the way they are, it's going to be impossible to buy a week's groceries for $20.00."
($20.00 will hardly buy groceries for one day now!)

"Have you seen the prices on the new cars for this year? It won't be long before $2000.00 will only buy a used car."
(That money will only buy a <u>real</u> used car now!)

"If cigarettes keep going up in price, I'm going to quit. A quarter a pack is ridiculous!"
(Cigarettes cost close to $3.00 a pack now.)

"Did you hear that the post office is thinking about charging a dime just to mail a letter?
(It cost 42 cents to mail a letter today!)

"If they raise the minimum wage to $1.00 an hour, nobody will be able to hire outside help at the store."
(Minimum wage is now $5.25 per hour.)

"When I first started driving, who would have thought gas would someday cost 29 cents a gallon? Guess we'd be better off leaving the car in the garage!"
(Gas now cost $3.55 a gallon and is still going up!)

"Kids today are impossible. Those duck tail hair cuts make impossible to stay groomed. Next thing you know, boys will be wearing their hair as long as girls."
(This day has definitely come.)

"I'm afraid to send my kids to the movies any more. Ever since they let Clark Gable get by with saying 'damn' in Gone With The Wind, it seems every new movie has at least one curse word in it!"

(There are no limits on what goes into movies now days... not with words or with actions, or lifestyle promotions. It is definitely scary now!)

"I heard the other day where some scientist think it's possible to put a man on the moon by the end of the century. They even have some fellows they call astronauts preparing for it down in Texas."
(It happened! Now they are exploring other planets in other ways.)

"Did you see where some baseball player just signed a contract for $75,000 a year, just to play ball? It wouldn't surprise me if one day they would make more than the president!"
(I heard the other day where one team player was offered $7,000, 000.00 for one season of baseball.)

"I never thought I'd see the day all of our kitchen appliances would be electric. They are even making electric typewriters now!"
(Now there are all kinds of electronic computers, games, movie screen TV sets, etc.)

"It's too bad things are so tough now days. I see where a few married women are having to work to make ends meet."
(Most every household now needs the income of both parents to make ends meet.)

"Marriage doesn't mean a thing any more. Those Hollywood stars seem to be getting divorced at the drop of a hat."
(The whole world sees divorce as a quick way out. Some don't even believe in marriage as a starting point!)

"The drive in restaurant is convenient in nice weather, but I seriously doubt it will ever catch on!"
(There are drive in or drive through restaurants all over now, thriving very well!)

"No one can afford to get sick anymore. $35.00 a day in the hospital is too rich for my blood."
(It now cost $250.00 per day and up.)

"If they think I will pay fifty cents for a haircut, forget it!"
(Haircuts now cost $12.00.)

"There is no need going to one of the big cities for a weekend. It cost nearly $15.00 a night for a room."
(Rooms in the smaller towns, in the off brand motels usually start at $40.00, but the ones in the bigger cities cost $150.00 and up. I read where

some of the motels in Las Vegas go for $4000.00 a night. You can even rent a pet motel room for your dog or cat for $400.00 in some places.)

This is about like it is with a Christian. We sometimes think that the devil has just about thrown everything at us that he can, but he always finds something else to trip us up. But the best thing about this situation is that if we ask, and believe, God will put our lives back on the smooth path.

Isaiah 28: 10
A rule here, a rule there, a little lesson here, a little lesson there.

****

THE OBITUARY COLUMN

Someone sent me this over the Internet the other day ... I don't know who wrote it, but I thought you might enjoy it. It is written in the format of an obituary column.

CALVARY

Jesus Christ, 33, of Nazareth, died Friday on Mount Calvary, also known as Golgotha, the place of the skull. He was betrayed by the Apostle Judas, and Jesus was crucified by the Romans by order of the ruler Pontius Pilate. The reason for His death was to save souls from hell. The causes of His death were crucifixion, extreme exhaustion, severe torture and loss of blood. Jesus Christ, a descendant of Abraham, was a member of the House of David. Jesus was born in a stable in the city of Bethlehem. He is the son of God and the stepson of the late Joseph, the carpenter and Mary, His devoted Mother. He is survived by His Mother, Mary, His faithful Apostles, numerous disciples and many adopted brothers and sisters. Jesus was self-educated and spent most of His adult life working as a teacher. Jesus also worked as a medical doctor and it is reported that He healed many patients. He also was known to have cast demons from people. Up until the time of His death, Jesus was teaching and sharing the good news, healing the sick, touching the lonely, feeding the hungry, and helping the poor. Jesus was most noted for telling parables about His Father's kingdom and performing miracles, such as feeding over 5,000 people with only five loaves of bread and four fish, and healing the blind, the deaf, the mute, the lame, even the lepers. On the day before His death, He held the last supper, celebrating the Passover Feast, at which he foretold His death. The body was quickly buried in a borrowed stone grave, which was donated by Joseph of Arimathos, a loyal friend of the family. A boulder was rolled in front of the tomb, and Pontius Pilate ordered Roman soldiers to guard it. (Mysteriously, the next morning the stone was rolled away and the body was gone! Christians say His Father in Heaven came and took Him to Heaven, to sit on the right side of God and rule with Him.)

(In lieu of flowers, the family has requested that everyone try to live as Jesus did. Contributions may be sent to anyone in need!)

2 Peter 3: 9
God is being patient with you. He does not want anyone to be lost, but He wants all people to change their hearts and lives.

****

THE BAR-B-QUE KING

I watch as neighbors and friends enjoy bar-b-que cookouts, now that it is summertime. This seems to be the time for the spotlight to be on the husband, who has deemed himself as the "bar-b-que king." Well, while he is proclaiming his rank, I hear that there are two sides to every story ... and maybe everyone doesn't see it this way!

I went to a bar-b-que the other night and the man of the house de- clared this a day off for his wife. He was going to cook on the grill tonight for her and their friends. She could just take it easy. Well, this party turned out just a bit different than I imagined.

The wife went to the store and bought all of the food, colas, charcoal and snacks. He sits at home relaxing in front of the TV. The wife prepares the vegetables for cooking and makes the salads. He is out on the deck, relaxing with his friends. The wife prepares the meat for cooking, seasoning it and then places it on a tray and takes it outside to the man who is lounging beside the grill, with a cola in his hand. (Here comes the best part ...) THE MAN PLACES THE MEAT ON THE GRILL! The wife goes inside to organize the silverware and the plates and glasses. Then she comes outside to tell the husband that the meat is burning. He thanks her and asks her if she'll bring him another cola while he handles the situation. (Important part again...) THE MAN TAKES THE MEAT OFF THE GRILL AND HANDS IT TO THE WOMAN... who is holding the platter. The wife prepares the plates, salad, bread, utensils, napkins, sauces, etc. and brings them out to the table. After the meal, the woman clears the table and does the dishes. (And most important of all ...) everyone PRAISES THE MAN AND THANKS HIM for his cooking efforts.

The man asks his wife how she enjoyed "her night off." After seeing her annoyed reaction, he comes o the conclusion that there is just no pleasing some women!

Our Christianity is sometimes like that. We want to say we are Christians, but when it comes to working for Christ, someone else is always doing the work, and the "star" of the show is doing nothing much at all to promote God's glory. But ... he is always in church, always saying he is a Christian, but somehow, there is no fruit on his vine!

Romans 8: 6
If people's thinking is controlled by the sinful self, there is death. But if their thinking is controlled by the spirit, there is life and peace.

****

WISE OLD SAYINGS

Recently I ran across some wise old sayings and I would like to share them with you!

"The nicest thing about the future is that it always starts tomorrow"

"Money will buy a fine dog, but only kindness will make him wag his tail"

"If you don't have a sense of humor, you probably don't have any sense at all"

"Seat belts are not as confining as wheelchairs"

"A good time to keep your mouth shut is when you're in deep water"

"How come it takes so little time for a child who is afraid of the dark to become a teenager who wants to stay out all night"

"Why is it that at class reunions you feel younger than everyone else looks"

"There are no new sins, the old ones just get more publicity"

"There are worse things than getting a call from a wrong number at 4 AM, like this could be the right number"

"Think about this... no one ever says it's 'only a game' when their team is winning"

"I've reached the age where the happy hour is a nap"

"The trouble with bucket seats is that not everybody has the same size bucket"
"Do you realize that in about 40 years, the golden oldies will be rap music"

"After 60, if you don't wake up aching in every joint, you're probably dead"

That was a list of earthly, old wise sayings... now for a few spiritual wise sayings.

"Know where you're headed and you will stay on solid ground" (Proverbs 4:26)

"It is better to be poor and live right than to be rich and dishonest" (Proverbs 28:6)"

"Don't be a fool and lose your temper ... be sensible and patient" (Proverbs 29:11)

"A door turns on hinges, but a lazy person just turns over in bed" (Proverbs 26:14)

"Giving an honest answer is a sign of true friendship" (Proverbs 24: 26)

"Watching what you say can save you a lot of trouble" (Proverbs 24: 23)

"A man's greatest treasure is his wife, she is a gift from the Lord" (Proverbs 18: 22)

"Share your plans with the Lord and you will succeed" (Proverbs 15: 3)

"Sometimes you can become rich by being generous, or poor by being greedy" (Proverbs 11: 24)

I hope you enjoyed these ... and for more wise sayings, read the book of Proverbs. It is just full of spiritual wisdom!

****

MY HEAVENLY BODY

I was pondering the other day about this old earthly body. It gets tired, the ears don't work like they used to, the eyes are blurred at times and without glasses, reading is sometimes hopeless, and we all thank the inventor of the dentures. Arthritis sets in every joint, and words don't come as easy as they used to. Memory is something that doesn't linger with us for very long, and we forget where we are at times, or we forget the faces or the names of our loved ones. We forget where we once lived or where we once worked. Either we find we sleep too much or we don't hardly sleep at all. Foods have to be dieted special in order for our digestive system to tolerate them, and then there are so many foods that we just have to do without. Diseases invade the body, age spots form on the skin, and the skin wrinkles. It seems like we have more pity parties, cry more and worry about our body parts just playing out. But, you know, my friend, there is hope for even the frailest of bodies. Our Heavenly Father has taken care of even that.

As I was reading my Bible the other night in 2 Corinthians, I came across a comforting Scripture, and I would like to share it with all of you. (2 Corinthians 4: 6-7) ... "The Scriptures say, God commanded light to shine in the dark. Now God is shinning in our hearts to let you know that His glory is seen in Jesus Christ. We are like clay jars in which this treasure is stored." .... (2 Corinthians 5: 1-4) "Our bodies are like tents that we live in here on earth. But when these tents are destroyed we know that God will give each of us a place to live! These homes will not be buildings that someone has made but they are in Heaven and will last forever. ... These tents we now live in are like a heavy burden and we groan. But we don't do this just because we want to leave these bodies that will die. It is because we want to change them for bodies that will never die."

In one translation of the Bible, Paul explains to us that when we die, we will put on our new bodies like we would put on our robe. I don't know how it will happen, but the promise is there, and God will give us a brand new, perfect body. We will be able to hear perfectly, see perfectly, have beautiful teeth, walk youthfully, and if we have been maimed because of diseases or accidents, we will be restored to be perfect. Our memory will be perfect and we will know everyone, even those who have entered Heaven long before our time. We will instantly know their name. None of us will be hooked up to an IV or sit in a wheel chair, or be bed bound, because we'll have a brand new body and it will be a perfect Heavenly body. I personally believe that we will have a body in His image, not just a soul in a white robe. I may be wrong, but it doesn't really

matter. I just want to be able to bow down at the feet of my Savior and thank Him for saving my soul! As long as He knows this is me....everything is OK!

****

FAITH

Did you ever wonder what real faith could bring you? Our three greatest assets are FAITH, HOPE and LOVE. Did you ever wonder just how important faith is? Well, if you pray and don't actually have the faith that your prayers will be answered, then the prayer probably won't be answered. If we have FAITH the size of a mustard seed, (and that is just very, very small ...) we can move mountains. So, just close your eyes with me and let's think of how important FAITH really is! Maybe you fit in one of the categories and if so, just have FAITH that things will get better!

Think of the Soldiers fighting in a foreign land, their hearts are filled with fear but also with strength. Think of the old man in a nursing home who wakes each day hoping some of his family will visit him ... his children, his grandchildren and even his great-grandchildren. He waits all day and watches each time the door opens, but no one he knows enters. Then at night when he closes the door to his room and turns out the light, he cries. He misses his family so much.

Think of the child who was born deformed or with health issues, physical or mental. They watch other children but they can't play or run or even talk like them.

Then there is the young man that through illness, lost both of his legs. A woman holds her only child close to her breast ... the child is dying. She says a prayer for her, and asked the Father if she would ever see her precious child again. Only the faith of seeing her child will keep her going.

An old man stands by the graveside of his bride of sixty years. He feels lost and brokenhearted. You see, for sixty years, almost every morning she brought him his coffee to the bed and she had his children, kept his house and loved him. How will he ever get through the long days?

There is the prisoner who probably done the crime he is being punished for ... but he's prayed and has been forgiven. He has faith that there is a better place for him. He read in the Bible that even Paul spent some time in prison.

Well, faith eventually takes the soldiers into Heaven where there is no war, no fear and no death. Faith takes the old man home to see his family and friends waiting for him. He doesn't have to sit and watch the door anymore and there are no more tears.

The child born with problems now lives in Heaven. He can run and play, walk and talk like all of the other children there in Heaven. He is as perfect as anyone there.

The young man who lost his legs in a health battle here on earth, now has new legs, a new body and he walks on the golden streets of Heaven.

The Momma enters the gates of Heaven and sees her little child standing with arms outstretched and she knows that faith got her here.

By faith the old man once again sees his bride of sixty years and she looks as young and as beautiful as she did the day they were married.

The prisoner finds that here there are no more bars, because one day he gave his heart to Jesus and had faith that Jesus loved him enough to bring him to Heaven.

There is an old song, and some of the words go, "Prayer is the keys to Heaven, but faith unlocks the door!" If you pray and believe and have faith, nothing is impossible. If we have been forgiven here on earth, and live the life Jesus would be proud of, our faith will lead us straight through the pearly gates of Heaven, and we can bow down at the feet of our Savior. We will all have a brand new body, a long soft robe and a golden crown. There will be no fear or death and no one will look down on another for any reason. No unkindness shall ever enter the Holy Place! I have faith, my friend, that all of this is possible ... and I have faith that I will one day go to Heaven. I sure hope to see you there!

Psalm 106: 1
Praise ye the Lord. O give thanks unto the Lord for He is good; for His mercy endureth forever.

****

THE 4TH OF JULY

As I write this it is July. We have just celebrated the 4th of July. I wonder just what it might have meant to you! Without being prodded by advertisements on the television, did your thoughts turn to what freedom really costs? Do you ever think of the Service men and women fighting in wars just so you could be free? Do you ever shed a tear for the ones who died fighting for you?

America is free ... and we as Americans are free to speak about anything we want to, (and if you don't believe me, just watch TV for about fifteen minutes. It would be shocking ...) There is a commandment from God Himself saying, "Thou shalt not take the name of the Lord thy God in vain." Most movies or rap songs, and other things, think they can't be a success unless the name of the Lord is used in vain, and vulgar messages are repeated over and over!

People use freedom of speech to promote music ... if you can actually call it that. Personally, I think some of this stuff is just messages from the devil himself! We brag about freedom of expression ... so some say that homosexuality is their way of expressing their personal feelings, and they try to convince you they are right. But, the Bible says that is a sin! Some say they are expressing themselves when they wear little or no clothing in public, and expose themselves indecently.

Children know all to well, more about the human body or the adult words and expressions than most of the adults knew at the time of marriage just a few years ago.

America is free ... but do you ever feel chill bumps crawl up your back when you hear the "Star Spangled Banner" being sung, or do you just use this time to catch up on some juicy gossip with your friends. Back when I was a child, we usually all knew the words to the "Star Spangled Banner" and we would stand and place our hand on our heart when it was being played. We respected the flag and we respected our homes and our families and we respected America. Do you feel sadness and loss when you see flag draped coffins coming home from the war? Are you cold and indifferent to the fact that these people lay down their lives so you could live in America?

America is free ... but did that give us the right to abort children? God has created these children in His image, and He gave them to us as gifts, to take care of, to feed and clothe, to teach His word to, and to set good morals in front of them. He told us in His word to love them and to punish them if they need it to keep them on the right path.

Just as men and women have laid down their lives to keep our country free, Jesus died on that old rugged cross to give us the freedom from sin. He gave us a way that we could be saved and promised us a home in Heaven, free from sin.

He promised us that we could spend eternity in Heaven with Him. Are we going to bow down on our knees and accept that gift from Him, or will we do like the typical American, and turn our backs on Him, living our lives just like we want to and not how we need to. Do we embrace His love in our heart or do we spit on Him and turn away. What will He do when we face Him for the great Judgment Day ...? Will He embrace us and say, "Welcome home ..." or will he just turn away and say, "Sorry, I never knew you!"

Revelation 2: 12-14
And behold I come quickly and my reward is with me, to give every man according to his work shall be. I am the Alpha and Omega, the beginning and the end, the first and the last. Blessed are they that do His commandments that they may have right to the tree of life, and may enter in through the gates of that city.

TRYING TO IMPRESS JESUS

Suppose that one evening, in the cool of the day, you get a chance to walk with Jesus. Well, in your human mind, you think maybe you might ought to try to impress Him ... so, as you walk, you talk, and He drops His head but listens quietly.

You say to Him ... "You know, Jesus, I've been a Christian since I was twelve years old!" ... "I go to church most all of the time!" ... "I talk to others about you!" ... "I read my Bible!" ... "When Jenny asked me to pray for her, I assured her I would!" ... "When John asked me to pray with him, I did!" ... "When they had the altar call, I went and knelt at the altar!" ... "If I were to die right now, I hope I'd have a home in Heaven!"

Then with tears in His eyes, He looked at me and said ... "You may have had a profession of faith at twelve, but you never really gave your life to me!" ... "You did go to church a lot, but that's about all it was. You sat there cold and indifferent to the words of the sermon!" ... "You do talk to others about me, but it isn't from the heart and most of your life didn't reflect the truth!" ... "You read my word, but it was only to say that you had read it. It surely wasn't for the knowledge there!" ... "You said you would pray for Jenny, but you never did!" ... "When you prayed with John, it was only words, it was not a prayer from your heart!" ... "When you knelt at the altar, you didn't talk to me, you strained to hear what kind of problems the lady next to you was having, or wondered what the man on the other side of you was crying for!" ... "If I should take you out of this world right now, I'm sorry, but you would not enter the Gates of Heaven."

But, God is a good God and maybe he'll give you another chance to change your eternal fate. Just pray, ask God for forgiveness and then live your life for Jesus. When you pray, pray from your heart, and when you read His word, use it as an instruction Book to live your life by. Then, when your time on earth ends, you'll be in Glory the moment you're gone. What a blessed reward for just a bit of extra effort. God really loves you and He doesn't want to lose you to the devil's plans! But the choice is really yours!

Revelation 6: 2
In the scripture God says, "When the time came I listened to you and when you needed help, I came to save you. The time has come. This is the day for you to be saved."

****

RUNNING THE RACE

Have you ever entered a race of some kind of competition, and a prize was promised to the winner? Probably, with each breath you took, you thought about being the winner. You pictured in your mind what it would feel like to walk up and get your prize ... to hold it in your hands! You'd think about how this would benefit you in the future. I'll bet you would just beam with pride when you were announced the winner. You would probably tell everyone you met that you had won the prize ... and most likely, elaborate on just how you had won it!

But, friend, as we live here on this earth, we are in the greatest race of all, running the race for Jesus. We race to live our lives for Him, setting good examples to others ... and we do His work ... preach His Gospel ... and win others to Jesus.

But, the prize is out of this world! We will get a home in Heaven, and we can spend eternity with Jesus. We'll never again be sick, or sad, or sinful and we'll never die again. Our friends and loved ones who win the prize will be with us and they will never leave us again, and other loved ones will join us as winners of the race when their race on earth has ended. The best thing about winning this big race is that the winner will not be limited to only one person, but to all who run the race with a repented heart, loves Jesus with all their soul and tells others about Jesus.

As we anticipate this great prize, we need to feel the excitement in our heart. We need to think about it with each breath we take. We need to picture in our mind what it will feel like to walk through the Pearly Gates of Heaven to claim our prize, and how this prize will affect your eternity. You need to tell everyone you see just how to get this prize and elaborate on your testimony of how God saved you.

Think about it my friend, and get your running shoes on ... (open your Bible, read and pray), and start this race, and run it to WIN!

Philippians 3: 12-14

I have not yet reached my goal and I am not perfect. But Christ has taken hold of me. So, I keep on running and struggling to take hold of the prize. My friends, I don't feel that I have already arrived, but I forget what is behind me and struggle for what is ahead. I run toward the goal so that I can win the prize for which God has called me Heavenward. This is the prize that God offers, because of what Christ Jesus has done!

****

THERE'LL BE ANOTHER SUNDAY

An old lady named Myrtis was placed in a nursing home. Oh, the children had checked out the nursing home, and only the best care was offered. The staff was great and the children were assured that Myrtis would make friends and they would treat her with love and respect.

The children hurriedly helped unpack her personal belongings and make her room feel comfortable. An old family photograph sat on the dresser, a Bible was placed on the night stand, and a couple of picture albums were put on a shelf. A few little knick-knacks were scattered around and a couple of pictures were hung on the wall. Her clothing was very meager. She wouldn't need many outfits, so soon everything was put in the right place.

The children hugged her neck, kissed her cheek, and told her they loved her. One even brushed a tear from her eye. Then, they promised the dear old lady that they would be back to visit on Sunday ... and out the door they went!

Each Sunday for a year now, Myrtis gets up, puts on her Sunday best, fixes her hair, puts a bit of makeup on her face, and sits in the old rocker by the front door! From here she can see out the window and watch the parking lot. She watches each auto pull up, hoping to see a familiar one. Then she watches the people who get out. Maybe the family had bought a different car. As the visitors come through the door, she would smile in anticipation ... but each one was a stranger. Each one would speak and smile, but would go on by.

As daylight faded to dusk, she'd slowly get up and go to her room. Her heart would be breaking and loneliness would surround her. But, she wasn't angry with the children ... she knew each of them had a job or a career, and their spare time was probably very scarce. She knew they were all very busy, and after all, Sunday will come again!

She sits on her bed with the old photo albums open, and she prays for each one of her family. She asks God to bless them and let them come on Sunday to visit. She turns off the light and goes to bed, and lets this take it's place in the back of her mind, until Sunday comes again!

Well, it's Sunday, and Myrtis is dressed in her Sunday best, and her hair is fixed and her makeup is on, but she's not sitting by the door waiting. She's gone to her home in Heaven. Yes, the children finally come to see her, but she won't hear their good-bys, because she never heard their hellos!

God is always watching over us, and he is there with us a lot of times when we think we are alone and that no one cares. We're on His mind when we may feel that we don't matter to anyone, and He will be there to show us mercy and grace when it comes time to go to our Heavenly home. Millions of people may

be talking to Him at the same time, but He always listen to us, individually. He is always there for us, as well as for the rest of the children who are talking to Him. He knows each of us by name and He knows our voice ... and He knows our needs even before we realize we have needs sometimes!

Psalm 40: 11
Withhold not thy tender mercies from me, O Lord. Let thy loving kindness and thy truth continually preserve me.

****

CAPSULES OF WISDOM

Sometimes we want to make a point, but it needs to be said in a few words. Often we feel that we don't need to elaborate on the problem, but just state the fact! Here are a few "capsules of wisdom" that can be used a lot of ways, and a lot of times, as we walk down the highway of life!

"Success breeds confidence, but confidence also breeds success"

"No one ever learned anything by talking"

"Instead of putting someone in their place, try putting yourself in their place"

"Grief yearns for compassion, not advice"

"The doors of opportunity are marked PUSH and PULL"

"Out of the mouths of babes come things parents never should have said"

"Love is circular ... the more you give the more you get"

"One nice thing you can say about an egotist is they don't talk about others"

"It takes a great sense of humor to appreciate a bad joke"

"If you're looking for a long rest, be on time for an appointment"

"The road to success is always under construction"

"Even the simplest task can be meaningful, if you do it in the right spirit"

"Inaction breeds doubts and fears, action breeds confidence and courage ... if you want to conquer fear, don't sit at home and think ... go out and get busy"

"There are some people so addicted to exaggeration,
they can't tell the truth without lying"

I hope these little capsules of wisdom bring you a few thoughts to ponder on, or maybe even a little chuckle or two! God bless you!

Job 10: 12
You gave me life and showed me kindness and in your providence watched over my spirit

****

YOU'RE BEST FRIEND

In our human minds, we sometimes think we do not need anyone or anything. We sit back in the corner of our world and just think, if we back off long enough, the problems will just go away! But, whether or not we want to admit it, we do have needs, and they do not solve themselves!

You always need a friend! A friend will listen when you have a problem and will not judge you just because of your situation. A friend will be there when you ask him to. They will listen to your most inner thoughts and worries and secrets, and never repeat them to others. If they can't help your situation, they will listen, they will pray with you, and they will put their arms around you and make you feel safe and secure!

God is also like that friend ... but even more faithful. He's never too busy to answer, He's never out of town or on the other line. He doesn't judge you because of your situation, but what is in your heart, (even though he will judge you when this life is over, and if you've been faithful, He will let you call Heaven your home)! With a simple prayer to Him, His attention is on you! He can always help ... He can comfort you, wipe your tears from your eyes, put His arms around you and hold you close to his bosom. He can calm your fiercest storm or give you strength to endure it. He can move your mountains or provide you a way over it or around it! There's no friend on earth that can, or would, do so much for you! He even died on the cross for your sins because He loved you so much!

So, when you need a friend, no matter what for, call on your best friend, Jesus. Put your hand in his and your head on His bosom, and give your worries to Him. Feel the peace ... feel the strength ... feel the love!

Psalm 62: 6-8

He only is my rock and my salvation. He is my defense. I shall not be moved. In God is my salvation and my glory, the rock of my strength, and my refuge is in God. Trust in Him at all times, ye people. Pour out your heart before Him. God is a refuge for us!

****

SILVER ANGELS

There are so many people in nursing homes. For the most part, it is a good place to be. Here, they can have the attention they need for medicine, or just have someone to watch over them. I guess I feel very close to these "Silver Angels" because I am an old folk, too! Some of these friends have lost their hearing, their eyesight and their mobility. Some have just lost their health. But, even through these losses, they can still feel! They can feel happiness, despair, loneliness, forsakenness, fear and confusion.

Happiness happens when family and friends faithfully visit. They feel loneliness when there is no one to visit with them!

Feelings of despair comes into view when they sit and ponder what they might have said or done to loved ones to make them not visit. A million thoughts cross their mind during their long, lonely days.

Some feel forsaken, like maybe no one cares. Fear nudges them, as they think of the end of their life, and they wonder about the unknown.

Some are confused. They try to speak, knowing what words they want to say, but the right ones just won't come out. Age has a way of robbing one of these simple things that we all take for granted, and we sometimes run out of patience when trying to speak to them.

You know, if you have family in a nursing home, wake up! One day you may be there. Will your children see your attitude now and treat you the same? The staff of the nursing home is there to assist these "Silver Angels", but they need to be assured of your love. They are your family ... visit them, read the Bible to them, pray with them, talk to them about things going on in the family, or just take them in your arms and hold them ... tell them you love them! Give them a good reason to wake up in the morning. I know your day goes by fast and there never seems to be enough time to visit these loved ones, but just think of how long their day might be!

I may not be related to most of you, or there are even some I have never met ... but in my heart I love you and I pray for you. I hope these little letters help to brighten your day!

You know, all of you are very important to Jesus. He loves each of you and He watches over you. He listens when you talk to Him, and even though you may not be able to convey your message clearly to Jesus at times, He always knows what you are saying, because He can see your heart! He is always with you, even though you may often feel alone. He said He would never leave or forsake you and He will keep His promise. He loves you so much. He died on that old cross for you and is building you a mansion in Heaven, so you can spend your eternity

there, and you won't have to spend it bed-ridden, or in wheel chairs, or even in prison cells. For prisoners who have repented, God watches over them just like He does these "Silver Angels"! May God's peace surround you and may Heaven be yours!

Romans 6: 22
But now being made free from sin and become servants to God, ye have your fruit unto holiness and the end, everlasting life!

****

REFERENCES OF LIFE

I know that each of us go through trials and tribulations in our life, and sometimes we feel we just don't' have an answer to how we can cope with these things. I have put together a list of situations and a Bible verse that may help you along the way, as the Devil puts snares and traps in front of you. I surely hope they help you!

ANGER: James 1: 19-20 .. "My dear brother, take note of this; everyone should be quick to listen, slow to speak, and slow to anger, for a man's anger does not bring about the righteous life that God deserves."

CHARITY: Luke 6: 38 .. "Give and it will be given you, a good measure pressed down, shaken together and running over, will be poured into your lap, for with the measure you use, it will be measured to you."

FAITH: Hebrews 11: 1 .. "Now faith is being sure of what we hope for and certain of what we do not see."

FEAR: Proverbs 3: 24 .. "When you lie down you will not be afraid, when you lie down, your sleep will be sweet."

FORGIVENESS: Matthew 6:14 .. "For if you forgive men when they sin against you, your Heavenly Father will also forgive you."

GUIDANCE: Isaiah 30: 21 .. "Whether you turn to the right or to the left, your ears will hear a voice behind you saying, "This is the way, walk in it."

JOY: Isaiah 51: 11 .. "The ransomed of the Lord will return. They will enter Zion with singing; everlasting joy will crown their heads. Gladness and joy will overtake them, and sorrow and sighing will flee away."

LAZINESS: Proverbs 28: 19 .. "He who works his land will have abundant food, but the one who chases fantasies will have his fill of poverty."

LONELINESS: Isaiah 58: 9 .. "Then you will call, and the Lord will answer; you will cry for help and He will say, Here am I."

LOVE: John 3: 16 .. "For God so loved the world that He gave

His one and only son, that whosoever believeth in Him shall not perish but have eternal life."

PATIENCE: Romans 5: 3-4 .. "And not only so, but we glory in tribulations also, knowing that tribulation worketh patience, and patience ... experience, and experience ... hope."

REPENTENCE: Luke 15: 10 .. "In the same way, I tell you, there is rejoicing in the presence of the Angels of God over one sinner who repents."

SEEKING GOD: 2 Chronicles 15: 2 .. "The Lord is with you when you are with Him. If you seek Him, He will be found by you, but if you forsake Him, He will forsake you."

SPIRITUAL GROWTH: Philippians 1: 9 .. "And this is my prayer; that your love may abound more and more in knowledge and depth of insight."

TRIALS: Psalm 69: 16-17 .. "Answer me, O Lord, out of the goodness of your love; in your great mercy turn to me. Do not hide your face from your servant; answer me quickly, for I am in trouble."

WISDOM: Psalm 32: 8 .. "I will instruct you and teach you in the way you should go. I will counsel you and watch over you."

I hope these references will be helpful to you as you travel along life's highway. May the works of the Devil be under your feet and the love of God be in your heart!

****

TEACH YOUR CHILDREN

I ran across this the other day. A friend of mine sent this to me over the Internet, and I thought that you might enjoy it. As Christmas- time approaches, it would be a lesson well learned.

This is how it happened ... I just finished the household chores for the night and was preparing to go to bed, when I heard a noise in the front of the house. I opened the door to the front room and to my surprise, Santa himself stepped out from behind the Christmas tree.

He placed his finger over his mouth so I would not cry out. "What are you doing?" I started to ask. The words choked up in my throat, and I saw he had tears in his eyes. His usual jolly manner was gone. Gone was the eager, boisterous soul we all know! He then answered me with a simple statement. "TEACH THE CHILDREN!"

I was puzzled; what did he mean? He anticipated my question and with one quick movement brought forth a miniature toy bag from behind the tree. As I stood there bewildered, Santa said, "Teach the children! Teach them the old meaning of Christmas ... the meaning that now-a-days on Christmas has been forgotten."

Santa reached into his bag and pulled out a FIR TREE and placed it before the mantle. "Teach the children that the pure green color of the stately fir tree remains all year round, depicting the everlasting hope of mankind, all the needles point Heavenward, making a symbol of man's thoughts turning toward Heaven."

He again reached into his bag and pulled out a brilliant STAR. "Teach the children that the star was the Heavenly sign of promises long ago. God promised a Savior for the world and the star was the sign of the fulfillment of His promise."

He then reached into his bag and pulled out a CANDLE. "Teach the children that the candle symbolizes that Christ is the light of the world, and when we see this great light we are reminded of He who displaces the darkness."

Once again he reached into his bag and removed a WREATH and placed it on the tree. "Teach the children that the wreath symbolizes the real nature of love. Real love never ceases. Love is one continuous round of affection."

Then he pulled from the bag an ornament of himself. "Teach the children that I, Santa Clause, symbolize the generosity and good will we feel during the month of December."

He then brought out a HOLLY LEAF. "Teach the children that the holly plant represents immortality. It represents the crown of thorns worn by our Savior. The red holly berry represents the blood shed by him."

Next he pulled from the bag a GIFT and said, "Teach the children that God so loved the world that HE gave HIS begotten SON. Thanks be to God for this unspeakable gift."

"Teach the children that wise men bowed before the Holy BABE and presented HIM with gold, frankincense and myrrh. We should always give gifts in the same spirit as the wise men."

Santa then reached in his bag and pulled out a CANDY CANE and hung it on the tree. "Teach the children that the candy cane represents the shepherds' crook. The crook on the staff helps to bring back strayed sheep to the flock. The candy cane is the symbol that we are our brother's keeper."

He reached in again and pulled out an ANGEL. "Teach the children that it was the Angels that heralded in the glorious news of the Savior's birth. The Angels sang, 'Glory to God in the highest, on earth peace and good will toward men."

Suddenly, I heard a soft twinkling sound, and from his bag he pulled out a BELL. "Teach the children that as the lost sheep are found by the sound of the bell, it should ring mankind to the fold. The bell symbolizes guidance and return."

Santa looked back and was pleased. He looked back at me and I saw that the twinkle was back in his eyes. He said, "Remember, teach the children the true meaning of Christmas and do not put me in the center, for I am but a humble servant of the One that is and I bow down to worship HIM, our LORD, our GOD."

HAVE A SPIRIT FILLED CHRISTMAS!

Luke 2: 13-14
And suddenly there was with the Angel a multitude of the heavenly host praising God, and saying, "Glory to God in the highest, and on earth peace, good will toward men.

****

CHRISTMAS HOMECOMING

You know, my favorite time of the year is Christmas. I love what Christmas stands for, the birth of Jesus, and the plan of salvation that was set into place on that cold winter night in Jerusalem. I love the lights and the trees and the store windows that are decorated to entice you to come in and buy a gift. There is a certain gleefulness in the cold wintery air. People on the street smile and greet you with a "Merry Christmas", and children anxiously await the arrival of Santa. They have their list ready and are hopeful that it will be completely filled!

The homes smell of fresh fruits, holly and gingerbread cookies. Presents are wrapped in bright paper and ribbons and placed under the tree. The children, (as well as the adults), find it hard to wait to open them. The mailbox is filled with Christmas cards from relatives and friends that we haven't heard from all year!

The sounds coming from the radio is Christmas carols and other kinds of Christmas music. The television airs special Christmas movies, mostly with a story around the closeness of families and Christmas miracles. In front of almost every church is the nativity scene, complete with the precious baby Jesus. Every one seems to be in a festive mood.

Family and friends come in from far and wide, and the home is filled with children's laughter, smells of turkey and dressing and fresh apple pie, as well as all of the other traditional foods prepared for the Christmas meal. The family tries to have a homecoming at one of the family homes, and they all gather around the table for the family feast. This is a Christmas homecoming.

My table won't be complete this year. Momma went to be with Jesus in November, and I will really miss her. But, she is sitting at the table with Jesus, celebrating His birthday. There is a big hole in my heart right now, but each time I think of Momma, God gives me another good memory to fill the big ole hole. I have so many good memories, and that is what keeps me healing. "Because He lives I can face tomorrow", is my motto, and I know He and Momma are watching over me!

I think each of us should try to enjoy the time we are with loved ones and try to be with family and friends just as much as we can, for one day you will need those good memories to fill the big ole hole in your heart!

There is one thing for certain, though ... when I get to Heaven, I can sit down with my Momma and my Daddy at the table with Jesus, and I too can celebrate the "greatest homecoming" one could ever imagine. I sure hope all of my "Treasured Friends" can be there, too!

HAPPY BIRTHDAY JESUS
AND
MERRY CHRISTMAS TO YOU

Luke 2: 7

And she brought forth her firstborn son, and wrapped Him in swaddling clothes, and laid Him in a manger, because there was no room for them in the inn.

****

MY CHRISTMAS PRAYER

Dear Jesus,

I would just like to say "Happy Birthday" and to tell you that I love you so very much. Thank you Lord, for the breath you breathed into my body, and for the years you have let me spend with my family and friends.

Thank you Jesus, for always having food on the table, and clothes to wear and to keep warm, a roof over my head, good friends and a good family ... a family who is there for me whenever I need them ... for a family that glues back the pieces when I fall apart, and they help me to mend and go on.

Thank you Jesus for the job I have, or the Social Security income, and helping me to stretch the payday to manage to pay all of the bills.

Thank you Jesus for filling me with these spirit filled letters and letting me share them with all of my "Treasured Friends", and anyone else who wants to listen.

Lord, even though the year has been filled with problems, sicknesses, and even the loss of loved ones, I thank you Lord, for the blessings you have given me ... for the peace in my life and for the strength to carry on, no matter what the devil throws at me. But thank you for that precious baby Jesus that was born in a stable many years ago, and thank you most of all for saving my soul and writing my name in the "Lamb's Book of Life".

Amen

Psalm 27: 4
One thing have I desired of the Lord, that will I seek after, that I may dwell in the house of the Lord all the days of my life, to behold the beauty of the Lord, and to enquire in His temple.

****

NEW YEAR REMINISING

Well, here it is ... New Year's Day. Christmas is over and the shinny wrapping and empty boxes are stuffed in the garbage. Children sit playing with their new toys and Daddy sits there showing his son how to operate the new toy train set. The boy is wondering if Santa brought the train set to his dad or to him! Others gather up gifts that need to be exchanged and head for the long lines and the tenseness of irritated people and tired store clerks.

Leftovers from Christmas dinner are now but a memory, except for the five pound bulge it left on our body. The house that you worked so hard to have spotless before Christmas, now looks like a tornado came through. Some just seem to be glad that Christmas is over.

But, as a Christian, Christmas should never be pushed back into a corner, not to be thought of again until the end of the year. Christmas is every day. God sent His Son as a gift to us so that salvation would be free. He didn't just send us this Christ-child to make December 25 a great day ... He wanted us to celebrate Christmas every day of the year. The Christmas miracle of a new birth happens each time someone gives their heart and life to Jesus. They are re-born to a spiritual birth.

Wouldn't it be awful if God would only save our soul on Christmas day? Or, if good things and miracles would only be given to us on Christmas Day? What if we were only allowed to go to Church, or read the Bible, or pray ... only on Christmas Day. We would really be in trouble the rest of the year, wouldn't we? What about those who die during the year? Would they often miss out on the plan of salvation because it was the wrong time of the year?

We need to remember Jesus each day. We need to think of the Baby, born in a stable, laid in a manger, that was the birth of salvation for all of us. We need to think of Jesus as He walked on this earth, and how He taught us to love one another, even our enemies. He showed us His love when He died on the cross at Calvary' s Hill, making a way for us to rise again after death and join Him and His Father in Heaven, for eternity, and we wouldn't have to be hung on the cross ... because He died for our sins! All He asks of us is to repent of our sins and ask forgiveness and then live our life for Him.

I think the beautiful songs of Christmas like "Silent Night", "Beautiful Star Of Bethlehem", "Away In A Manger", "It Came Upon A Midnight Clear", "Hark The Herald Angels Sing", "Go Tell It On The Mountain", and "O Little Town Of Bethlehem", should be sung all year, just like regular hymns; "The Old Rugged Cross", "Because He Lives", and all the others, not only because they are beautiful,

but it would keep reminding us that He lives, and He loves, and He is there for us, all year! We should never forget the sacrifices that He made, just for us!

Psalm 58: 16-17

But I will sing of Thy power, yea, I will sing aloud of Thy mercy in the morning; for Thou hast been my defense, and refuge in the day of my trouble. Unto Thee, O, my strength, will I sing for God is my defense and the God of my mercy.

****

I THINK

Let's put the old brain to work. Let's think. I put together a few things that I think, and maybe they will help you at one time or the other.

I think ... common sense and a sense of humor are the same thing, moving at different speeds. A sense of humor is just common sense dancing.

I think ... the first step to getting what you want out of life is first figuring out what you want.

I think ... you should never expect good news in an envelope with a window.

I think ... our attitude toward life determines life's attitude toward us.

I think ... life isn't so much about where you've been, but where you're going.

I think ... if you plan to teach today's children the value of today's dollar, you had better hurry.

I think ... bad habits are like a soft chair, easy to get into, but very hard to get out of.

I think ... you can never be hurt by something you haven't said, unless it is something you really should have said.

I think ... the two hardest things to handle in life are success and failure.

I think ... you should never exercise by jumping to conclusions. Do it by digging for the facts.

I think ... there is nothing wrong with having nothing to say, unless you say it.

I think ... the best way to keep your mind clean is to get your hands dirty.

I think ... the view is better from the front porch than from the sofa.

I think ... you should live your life so that no one should have to ask you if you are a Christian, but if they do, you need to witness at every opportunity.

I hope you have enjoyed these.

Psalm 111: 3
Everything the Lord does is glorious and majestic, and
His power to bring justice will never end.

****

SIN WILL TAKE YOU FARTHER

Have you ever just sat and pondered what sin does to you? How long it will keep you in its grip or how much it will cost you? Well, if you have been down that sinful road in your lifetime, you know. I have learned that lesson well from experience, but praise God, I now belong to Jesus and He takes such good care of me. The devil doesn't stand a chance as long as I follow in the footprints of Jesus!

Let me give you an example of what I'm talking about. Suppose you start up with the sin of lying. The truth would have been easy at first, but it might have made you look kinda bad in a certain situation, so you chose to lie ... to put the blame on someone else, or deny the accusation. Anyhow, you have started on that road of sin.

"Sin will take you farther than you want to go!" The next time something comes up concerning the thing you lied about, you have to tell another lie in order to cover your tracks, and on and on you go ... one lie after another, one lie bigger than the other. You can't dare tell the truth, people would lose respect for you, so you lie again.

"Sin will keep you longer than you meant to stay!" Well, after one lie and then another, you live your life, walking the road of lies. You find it easy now to lie about other matters, and you don't feel near as guilty. You always make yourself look good, and lie about others. Oh, you never intended for that one lie to continue so long, but, it is now uncontrollable it seams.

"Sin will cost you far more than you want to pay!" This lying will cost you the respect of your friends, (which, by the way, is why you avoided the truth to start with). Sometimes your job takes the hit, sometimes your family tires of the lies, and you find yourself alone. But, the biggest price you can pay for all of this lying, is you could lose your soul. The devil would be proud of you! But this life is not to make the devil proud ... it is to make Jesus proud of you! So, if this story fits you, or if you could replace lies by some other sin that has taken over your life, wake up! Eternity may be knocking on your door! Get on your knees and repent of your sins and ask God to give you strength to stop and strength to live your life for Him. Spend eternity with Jesus! I can't think of a better reason for living a good life ... with Jesus in control!

Isaiah 43: 18-19
Forget the former things; do not dwell on the past. See, I am doing a new thing! Now it springs up; do you not perceive it? I am making a way in the desert and streams in the wasteland.

****

LOVE

Do you really know how powerful love is? First of all, God is love, and there just isn't anything more powerful than that! God loves us all ... but He doesn't love all of the things that we do!

If we all had just a small portion of the love that Jesus has for us, the world would not be in the mess it is in. Greed, not love, makes one rob another, kill another, and then walk away with no regret. If only we could love more and display greed less!

Hate makes one country make war against another and the people of one country looks on the people of the other country with hate. They don't want to work together on anything, and anything even close to co-operation causes distrust, because one thinks the other one is up to something. If only we could learn to love more and hate less!

Abuse makes one distrustful of another, and love can't find its way, because we don't want to be hurt or abused anymore ... so the true feelings are hid. Many may never know what it means to have someone truly love them because they won't ever give another a chance. They just make sure they don't let anyone get close! If only fewer were abused and more were loved!

What has caused love to disappear from the world? Well, first we lost touch with God in the home, and we let the Holy Bible gather dust. We didn't read it to the children and we didn't pray with them. Then we stood by and let them take prayer out of schools, out of sports arenas, out of public places ... and we ask "Where has love gone?"

Well, look back ... we took God out of the home, out of the family, out of the schools, out of the sports arenas, out of public places, and we still expect God to look down on us and bless us and be proud of us!!! God is love and when we take God out of something, we take love out. I wish we would love God more, and fight harder for Him.

But God didn't give up on us ... He didn't take us out of the picture. He still loves us ... and hopes ... and waits for us to turn back to Him so He can bless us once again. This is Valentine season. Remember your greatest Valentine and give Him the valentine He is waiting for ... your heart and your love and your life.

1 Corinthians 13: 7-8
Love knows no limit to its endurance, no end to its trust, no fading
of its hope. It can outlast anything. Love never fails.

****

THE NEW JERUSALEM

As I was reading my Bible the other day, I became intrigued with the description that John gave when he saw the New Jerusalem coming down from the heavens. He tells us that it flashed and glowed like a great gem, because it was filled with the glory of God! Its walls were broad and high, with twelve gates guarded by Angels! The names of the twelve tribes of Israel were written on the gates. There were three gates on each side ... three on the north, three on the east, three on the south, and three on the west.

Now, in your human mind ... try to picture this! The city was like a cube ... 1,500 miles wide, 1,500 miles long, and 1,500 miles high. The walls were 216 feet across. (That is about 84 feet shorter than a football field! Can you even start to imagine the width of the walls!)

The city itself was pure, transparent gold, like glass. The walls were made of Jasper, and was built on twelve layers of foundation stone inlaid with gems, and on them was written the names of the twelve apostles of the Lamb.

The first layer was Jasper, (highly colored quartz)
The second with Sapphire, (a blue gem)
The third with Chalcedony, (a whitish or bluish quartz)
The fourth with Emerald, (a bright green gem)
The fifth of Sardonyx, (brightly colored was the only description)
The sixth layer was with Sardus, (no description found)
The seventh with Chrysolite, (a yellowish green precious stone)
The eighth with Beryl, (a green or bluish stone)
The ninth with Topaz, (varied colored stone)
The tenth with Chrysoprase, (a yellowish green gem)
The eleventh with Jacinth, (only described as a precious stone)
And the twelfth with Amethyst, (a violet, purple-blue stone)

(Now this gorgeous beauty is not even imaginable to a human!)

The twelve gates were made of pearls ... each gate was a single pearl. The main street was pure, transparent gold, like glass. There is no temple in this city, because the Lord is worshiped everywhere, by everyone. Its gates will never close because in this city it will never be any night there! Nothing evil will be permitted into the city, no one immoral or dishonest ... but only those that have their names written in the Lamb's Book Of Life!

There was a river of pure, Water of Life, clear as crystal, flowing from the throne of God and running down the center of the main street. On each side of the river,

Trees of Life, bearing twelve crops of fruit, with a fresh crop each month, and the leaves were used to heal the nations. The throne of God is here and His servants will worship Him! They will finally see His face and His name shall be written on their foreheads. God will be their light and they shall reign forever.

I can't even imagine what beauty and peace and love is there, but I want to live my life so that I can one day find out! I want to enter the pearly gates, walk the streets of gold, drink from the River of Living Water, and eat from the Trees of Life. I want to be able to bow down and worship my Savior and thank Him for dying on the cross for my sins so that I could spend eternity in the Great New Jerusalem with Him and all of the rest of his children. Don't you want to go?

Revelation 22: 14

Blessed forever are all who are washing their robes to have the right to enter in through the gates of the city and to eat the fruit from the Tree of Life!

****

SNIPPITS TO PONDER ON

Here are some little snippets to ponder on. I hope you enjoy them, and maybe they will come in handy during your journey down this road of life.

"Difficulties are not bad for you if they make you better not bitter"

"For every minute of action, there should be an hour of thought"

"The cure to boredom is curiosity, for which there is no cure"

"What you possess is much less significant than what possesses you"

"Football is a wonderful way to get rid of aggression without going to jail for it"

"To advance in business, help the person ahead of you to get promoted"

"More important than where we stand is where we are going"

"If only we could think twice and still be in the conversation"

"A young person knows the rules, an older person knows the exceptions"

"Those who say, 'work well done never needs redoing' never weeded a garden"

"Itching for what you want isn't good enough, you have to scratch for it"

"He who hesitates is interrupted"

"Learn to laugh at yourself, you will have a lifelong source of amusement"

"When your work speaks for itself, don't interrupt it"

"Nothing is really work unless you'd rather be doing something else"

"Look at life through the windshield, not the rear view mirror"

"Never go to a doctor whose plants have died"

"You cannot control what goes on outside, but you can control what goes on inside"

"Cheerfulness sharpens the edge and removes the rut from your mind"

"Through humor, you can soften some of the worst blows that life delivers"

"Don't judge each day by the harvest you reap, but by the seeds you planted"

I hope you have enjoyed these, and maybe even got a chuckle or two out of them. Live your life the best you can so your reward will be the greatest!

Proverbs 4:11-12
I have taught thee in the way of wisdom, I have led thee in right paths. When thou goest, thou steps shall not be straightened, and when thou runnest, thou shalt not stumble.

****

TROUBLES AND TRIBULATIONS

I was speaking to a friend the other day and Satan had her so confused. She had been through a lot in the past months ... the loss of a loved one ... trouble with the marriage ... money problems ... trouble coping with problems at work ... problems with her self-esteem ... and health issues.

She told me she didn't know why all of this was happening, because she was a good Christian and she was in church and working for God. She was convinced that she was not doing something right for God.

I explained to her that it seemed like she was working hard for Jesus, because the devil was sure upset with her.

A lot of us go through troubles and trials and wonder what we are doing wrong. God didn't die on the cross so that we would not have troubles and tribulations ... He died there for our sins! He himself, had troubles and tribulations and was treated worse than anyone else. He lost loved ones, and faced each temptation that we face each day. If the King of Kings faced trials, then why should we think that someone as lowly as we are, should be spared! But we were promised that He would help us to carry the burdens. He would make a way for us to climb every mountain, or strength to go around it. He told us that it is certain that everyone must die ... but by arising from death after three days, and taking the keys to death and hell away from the devil, it assured us that we would have a home in Heaven, if only we would believe and repent of our sins! He tells us that He will be there through all of the storms in our life, if we would only ask!

The devil doesn't like for a Christian to do good, so he tries every way he can to trip us up. The harder your work for Jesus, the tougher the devil is on us. If the devil is not working against you, then maybe you are not a threat to him!

If our paths were always smooth, would we tend to be as close to Jesus, or would we figure we could live like we wanted to and not need Jesus? Satan would love that! I think that our troubles only tend to strengthen our Christianity, and we learn to walk even closer to Jesus. Into each life ... a little rain must fall. If you feel Satan at work, pray ... and God will be right by your side and the devil won't stand a chance.

1 Peter 1: 6-8
So be truly glad! There is a wonderful joy ahead, even though the going is rough for a while down here. You love Him even though you have never seen Him; though not seeing Him, you trust Him; and even now you are happy with the inexpressible joy that comes from Heaven itself.

****

MY FAVORITE BIBLE VERSES

I thought you might enjoy some Bible verses that are very special to me, and maybe they will become special to you!

Ezekiel 34: 26
I will send down showers in season; there will be showers of blessings!

Psalm 37: 11
But all who humble themse3lves before the Lord shall be given every blessing and shall have wonderful peace!

1 Corinthians 2: 9
No eye has seen, no ear has heard, no mind has conceived, what God has prepared for those who love Him!

1 Corinthians 13: 7
Love knows no limit to its endurance, no end to its trust, no fading of its hope. It can outlast anything. Love never fails!

Isaiah 40: 31
Those who hope in the Lord will renew their strength. They will soar on wings like eagles; they will run and not grow weary. They will walk and not faint!

Genesis 28: 15
I am with you and will protect you wherever you go!

Psalm 128: 5
May the Lord continually bless you with Heaven's blessings as well as with human joys!

Ruth 1: 16
Whither thou goest, I will go; and where thou lodgest, I will lodge; thy people shall be my people and thy God shall be my God!

Romans 8: 26-28
God's Spirit is right along side helping us along. If we don't know how or what to pray, it doesn't matter. He does our praying in and for us, making prayer out of our wordless sighs, our aching groans. He knows us far better than we know

ourselves ... and keeps us present before God. That is why we can be so sure that every detail in our lives of love for God is worked into something good.

Each time I read my Bible, I find verses that I don't remember reading before. I guess that is just God's way of continually teaching us along the way, and how beautiful the message becomes!

****

HOW GREAT IT IS TO SERVE A LIVING GOD

Has it ever occurred to you how great it is to serve a living God? How great is my God who created the whole universe and done it for me! He sent His Son into this world to teach us about Heaven, about love and forgiveness ... and was then crucified on that old cross for your sins and for my sins, and after three days, He arose and took the keys of death away from Satan ... just so we would have a way to spend eternity in Heaven with Him!

He can touch the eyes of the blind and make him see, the lips of the mute and they talk, the ears of the deaf and they hear! He touches the crippled, the sick, the possessed and they are healed! He takes care of a whole world, and yet can take care of just me. He has brought the dead back to life, and He miraculously forms a baby. He knows how many hairs are on the head of each of us, and how many leaves are on each tree.

He can cradle me in His loving arms and comfort me when the world is falling down around me, and I can feel His presence. He speaks to me in the still of a moment, and directs my path, or even gently chastises me for maybe a sin that I was unaware of even committing, or punishes me for sins I know I have committed!

He is there when loved ones are leaving this old world and my heart is breaking. And, He gives me these stories to share with you, and it seems they always touch someone they are sent to! He is always there when I have a problem, and if I will just be still and listen, He gives me the answer!

With my great, living God, I don't need anything else. I don't need a god of love, a god of war, a god of the sun, a god of fertility, or any other kind of idol. My God is not carved out of wood, or stone or jade, or any other material. My Jesus is not in the borrowed tomb ... but in Heaven watching over me. How can anyone think that something carved or made by man can affect their lives in any kind of way? Statues of Budda and Baal are made in factories ...and they think this is a "god"! Other "gods" are made in the same manner.

Let me introduce you to my God, my Jesus! All you have to do to be a child of His is to repent of y or sins, live your life for Him and throw all of the other "gods" away, for worshiping these false "gods" will not get you to Heaven, but will send you to hell! HOW GREAT IT IS TO SERVE A LIVING GOD!

Isaiah 53: 4-5
Surely He hath born our griefs, and carried our sorrows; yet we did esteem Him stricken, smitten of God, and afflicted. But He was wounded for our transgressions, He was bruised for our iniquities; the chastisement of our peace was upon him, and with His stripes we are healed.

****

VIEWS FROM MY PORCH

Here I sit on my porch again. The breeze is blowing, the flowers are blooming and there is a serenity and peace that I never find anywhere else. But today as I am drinking my cup of coffee, I am watching the wonders of my porch. I can always feel God's presence here. So many times I sat here with Momma and drank coffee. Momma is with Jesus now, but sometimes I feel her presence here, too. As much as she loved flowers, I think God lets her give these a special touch!

There is a kiss of water still on the plants from the watering last night. Two or three little lizards are running around the porch ... jumping and playing in the flowers. It is so interesting to watch as they change colors from greens to brown and somehow even blend into a purple jew!

Bumblebees circle the blooms, stopping to check for nectar, I guess. Yes, there are even some honeybees. Unwelcomed guest, such as wasps, are looking for a quiet spot to start a nest ... but they aren't welcome here. Butterflies flitter across the flowers, landing on their favorites to taste the nectar, and dragonflies wait for their meal of mosquitoes.

Hummingbirds feed on the nectar feeders, swoop off and then dart back ... their little wings continually fluttering. I could sit and watch them for hours. They are so graceful and beautiful, and each one different. After feeding on the porch for a while, they don't' worry about me at all. They know they are not in any kind of danger!

Then, there are the little sparrows ... always seemingly so happy. They come on the porch, sit on swing chains or on backs of chairs and they sing and they chirp to their heart's content. Then they parade across the floor, picking up flower petals to fix their nest. From what I've seen them pick up, they must have a beautiful, colorful, soft nest. The grass has just been cut and a family of blue jays are continually swooping down catching grasshoppers and crickets.

A mockingbird sits on the porch rail and fusses because the dog is too close to her nest. Then she goes high in the tree and sings to me.

I came out here early this morning and a family of baby squirrels and baby rabbits were playing in the yard. They ran and chased each other and seemed to be having the best time ... just like children

When I sit on the porch at night, sometimes the family of deer are grazing in my front yard. The dog goes out and sniffs them, and they look up and continue to eat.

Each day I come out on the porch, I can feel the touch of God's hand. I watch as new leaves appear on plants, a new blossom unfolds or can almost see the plant grow. I can watch as a flower has sat in the sun all day and in the evening

it's weary and wilted a bit, but then as I gently water them in the cool of the day in the evening, I can see the stems straighten up and once again I am almost sure they praise God for giving them a caretaker!

I don't think I will ever tire of sitting on my porch. Other duties call, and I reluctantly go in and do them, but my heart is always on my porch! I am so glad that God gave me this sanctuary to find peace and enjoy the wonders that He has made. If I find such peace in a simple place like my porch, I can't even start to imagine the peace and happiness I'll find in Heaven!

Isaiah 26: 3-4

> **The Lord gives perfect peace to those whose faith is firm. So always trust the Lord because He is forever our mighty rock.**

****

A DIFFERENT EASTER STORY

Here it is, the season of Easter, and we are reminded of the cross and the resurrection. We are all reminded of God's great mercy and grace for making a way for us to spend eternity in Heaven with Him. But, what if things had turned out different?

What if Jesus was sent to earth, and He taught us the way we should live, and He showed us love and compassion ... asking us to treat our fellow man in the same way? He wrote the words on our heart so that we might know the right and the wrong way. Then God gently took Him back to heaven on a cloud with ten thousand Angels singing.

Is there something missing? Yes! There was no crucifixion on a cross! What if God said He sent His Son to show us the way, and if we messed up, we would have to pay the price? What if ... in order to receive salvation, we would have to be beaten, tortured, ridiculed, spit on, and crucified on the cross. As humans, could we do it ... would we do it? I'm afraid there wouldn't be many Christians, would it? There wouldn't be many to make it to Heaven.

But, God loved us so much that He let Jesus bear the burden of our sins, even though He was pure and sinless. He was beaten, bruised, tortured, ridiculed, spit on, and crucified for us! This way, by His mercy and His grace, we could receive salvation by just repenting of our sins, and accepting Him as our Savior. He couldn't have made it much easier, could he?

Yet, there are so many that won't turn to Him, they won't repent, and they won't follow Him. They are trodding in sin and they think there will be no punishment ... but hell is waiting. They party and drink and do drugs, as well as the other sins, and they think that one day, maybe, they will turn their life around ... one day! Then their "one day" is taken away from them, and the demons dance with joy!

Jesus made the way for us to live in Heaven for eternity ... why not take Him by the hand and give your life to Him! The devil made a way for you to spend eternity in hell. Don't throw your life away on his lies!

Psalm 103: 203

Bless the Lord, O my soul and forget none of His benefits; who pardons all your iniquities; who heals all your diseases; who redeems your life from the pit; who crowns you with loving-kindness and compassion; who satisfies your years with good things, so that your youth is renewed like the eagle.

****

GOD'S BLESSINGS

We have just passed the St. Patrick Day holiday not long ago. All of you are probably familiar with the Irish blessing. In the Bible there are REAL blessings that God has laid out for us. Here are a few of my favorites.

"May you be given more and more of God's kindness, peace and love!
Jude 1: 2

"May the Lord continually bless you with Heaven's blessings
as well as with human joys!" Psalm 128: 5

"May the God who gives patience, steadiness and encouragement ... help you to live in complete harmony with each other!" Romans 15: 5

"You're blessed when you are content with just who you are, no more, no less. That's the moment you find yourselves proud owners of everything that can't be bought. You're blessed when you've worked up a good appetite for God. He's food and drink in the best meal you'll ever eat!"
Matthew 4: 5-6

"But all who humble themselves before the Lord shall be given every blessing and shall have wonderful peace!" Psalm 37: 11

"May the God of hope fill you with all joy and peace as you trust in Him, so that you may overflow with hope by the power of the Holy Spirit!"
Romans 15: 13

"May the Lord make your love increase and overflow for each other and for every one else, just as it does for you. May He strengthen your heart so that you will be blameless and holy in the presence of our God and Father when the Lord Jesus comes with all His Holy Ones.
1 Thessalonians 3: 12-13

"My child, use common sense and sound judgment. Always keep them in mind. They will help you to live a long and beautiful life and never stumble; you will rest without a worry and sleep soundly."
Proverbs 3: 21-24

"The Lord forgives or sins, heals us when we are sick, and protects us from death. His kindness and love are a crown on our heads. Each day that we live he provides for our needs and gives us the strength of a young eagle."
Psalm 103: 3-5

If you feel you need more blessings, just open your Bible and start to read and feel the Spirit bless you. The more you worship with Jesus, the more He will rain blessings upon you. He loves you so much!

****

I WANT TO BE FREE

July 4, 2009, was the 233rd birthday of the nation. Flags are displayed; there are a few parades; cook-outs are dominant; and fire-works are a traditional end to the day of celebration! But, do you ever stop long enough on the 4th to thank God that we have a free country? Do you thank Him for freedom of attending the church of your choice, or the freedom of not attending a church?

Our forefathers fought for this "freedom", and this "freedom" was not free. Men have died for this cause. Doesn't that mean anything to you? Do you thank God for these people? Men and women are still fighting and dying for the U.S.A., and for the ones that come home, we sometimes treat them like criminals.

You are truly a blessed people to be born in America ... land of the free, home of the brave. But I have noticed through the years that more and more, we are taking God out of America ... out of homes, out of schools, out of sports, out of government, out of relationships, and often, just out of our mind. Do you think God will continue to bless us? Do we deserve to be blessed?

You know, a little over two thousand years ago, one man took the sins of this world upon Himself, and He stretched out his arms on a cross and He died ... just so we could be free. We could be free to worship and live our life for Him, and be free of sin so we could spend eternity in Heaven. But lots of folks through the ages didn't respect Him either. A lot still don't!

But, one day, my friend, He's going to judge this world, and if you have salvation in your soul, you will be set free ... free from your worries and your problems; free from sin and Satan's snares; free from death; and all of Heaven will be laid at your feet! I want to be free! How about you?

Isaiah 45: 5-6

I am the Lord, and there is no other; apart from me there is no God. I will strengthen you, though you have not acknowledged me, so that from the rising of the sun to the place of its setting, men may know there is none besides me.

****

WHAT WAS JESUS LIKE AS A CHILD

As I was thinking today, I realized that we really knew nothing about Jesus from the time He was born until the time He was twelve and was speaking in the Temple. Then we never heard anything else until He was thirty or so, and His life the ended when He was a little over thirty-three years old. I wonder what His life was like through all of these years!

Even though He was sent here as a human being, He was still the "Son of God". So, being He was human, He must have experienced all of the things an ordinary boy would experience, less the sin.

I wonder what Mary thought as He lay there in the manger. Did she think of Him as the "Son of God" who would one day face that cross, or was He just her precious little baby boy? As she changed His diaper, did He seem like Jesus, the King, to her? Did His face and hands drip of mud as He found an old mud hole to play in?

Did He ever want to pull the tail of a cat just to see if it would yell? Did he ever have a crush on a little girl, or did a girl ever have a real crush on him? Did He keep His room clean, or eat all of His vegetables? Did He and Joseph ever go hunting or fishing together? Did He have friends that He went hunting or fishing with? Did He have His own pet dog, or cat, or any other animal?

Did He ever back off when the favorite Aunt wanted to pinch His rosy little cheeks and kiss Him? When His earthly father died, did He feel the same pain and loss we feel when we lose a loved one?

When He was young, did storms scare Him? Did He ever have nightmares, or face the town bully? Was He ever sick, discouraged, confused, or bored?

God had told Mary the purpose of Jesus' birth, but did she fully understand that the baby she held in her arms would one day be taken back to His Father in Heaven, after dying on that cross, being buried three days, and rising to Glory on a cloud? As she watched Him hanging there on the cross, and she knew this had to be ... did she see her son, who had never sinned, or did she see Jesus, the King of Kings and the Lord of Lords?

You know, the Bible tells us a lot of His human qualities while He lived here on the earth. He got tired and needed sleep, because on the boat during the storm, He was sleeping. He ate like ordinary people, He cried, He laughed, He even got angry when the people were making money in the temple and He turned over the tables of the money changers and ran them out of the temple.

He had fears, like before the crucifixion, and He was in the garden praying ... and He begged His Father to take the cup from Him "if it be thy will". He prayed so hard, His sweat became as drops of blood. So, He sweated like an ordinary

man, too. He felt pain during the crucifixion process, from the beating, to the load of the cross, to the nails that were driven into His hands and feet.

He faced the temptations of life, just as we face them, but He never sinned. That is a goal we need to reach for ... and if we pray to Him and serve Him, He will wash us in His blood, so that our sins will be white as snow ... and we can enter Heaven with Him and His Father, along with the Angels and the Saints that have already gone on to Heaven.

Psalm 67: 1

O, God, in mercy bless us; let your face beam with joy as you look down at us.

****

ANATOMY FOR GOD

I think when God made man, He made him with more in mind than just to enjoy the Universe that He had formed. Man's eyes were first used to enjoy the beauty that surrounded him in the Garden of Eden. He could see the animals and the birds, the fish and behold other humans. The eyes are marvelous things. They are used for all of this, but still, we have other obligations. They can be used to read the word, see the evil in the world so we can stay away from it. We can watch as our children grow and we can see in the mirror that we are gently aging.

Ears were for hearing the singing of the birds, the sounds of the animals and to hear each other speak. They are used for all of this, but the ears are for hearing the Gospel. God put one on each side of your head so you could hear it in stereo. Then He put your head in the middle so you would have a place to put your hat and hang your glasses.

He gave you a mouth to communicate with Him, other humans and the animals. He only gave us one mouth. Well, to hear what comes out of some mouths, that is really good! We couldn't deal with those people having two mouths. The mouth is used for songs pouring forth; for sermons preached; for telling someone about salvation, or just telling someone "I love you". It is also used for getting nourishment to our bodies.

The nose is an important sensor. We can smell the scents coming from a kitchen, or a lady's sweet perfume, and a man' s cologne. We can smell the odor of a wet dog, rain, something burning on the stove, or an unwanted animal approaching, like a skunk.

God gave us two hands. These hands have a lot of purposes. We can use them to wipe tears away from the eyes of our loved ones, stroke the fur of our favorite pet, feel heat and cold, pat a friend on the back, to work with, wave at someone or to hold a baby. But best of all, we can fold our hands and pray to our Father.

God was nice enough to give us two knees. This keeps us balanced as we kneel by the altar or by the bed and seek favors from God, or just to thank Him for blessings.

Two feet give us a good foundation. We can stand and praise God, walk, dance, jump, and at the end of the day we can sit in our favorite chair and rest these tired old feet on an old ottoman.

He gave each of us a heart. Our heart is no bigger than our fist. That is sort of small, consider all it has to do. The heart is the lifeline, in more ways than one. It keeps the blood pumping through our body, thus keeping us alive. But, I think that the biggest lifeline is that Jesus lives in my heart. He walks with me and He talks with me, and He guides and directs my steps and my thoughts. I don't want

to go places I shouldn't or say things I shouldn't, or even think things I shouldn't, because I know He is right there with me.

When I am happy He laughs with me, and He sings with me, and when I am sad and broken hearted, He cries with me! He comforts me with peace and understanding and love. Does Jesus live in your heart?

Psalm 51: 12

Create in me a clean heart, O God; and renew a right spirit within me. Cast me not away from thy presence and take not thy holy spirit from me. Restore unto me the joy of thy salvation; and uphold me with thy free spirit.

****

May God bless you and keep you safe in the palm of His hands